On the beach, a small fire flickered in the blackness. Waves crashed and sighed as Calling Crow danced in the flickering light. Mennewah sat before the fire, beating a drum as he stared into the flames. He held his hand up suddenly and called Calling Crow's name. Calling Crow knelt before him, and Mennewah placed a necklace of black feathers about his neck. "Just as the black crow cannot be seen at night," intoned the old man, "so you shall be invisible to the Wolf people."

"I am the anger of my people," sang Calling Crow as a large wave crashed, its weight and force reverberating through the cold, hard sand beneath them, "I shall not let them down."

Calling Crow

First in the brilliant historical trilogy by Paul Clayton, hailed as a powerful and talented new voice in frontier fiction.

CALLING CROW

PAUL CLAYTON

BERKLEY BOOKS, NEW YORK

CALLING CROW

A Berkley Book / published by arrangement with
the author

PRINTING HISTORY
Berkley edition / January 1995

For information address: The Berkley Publishing Group,
200 Madison Avenue, New York, New York 10016.

ISBN: 0-425-14532-8

BERKLEY®
Berkley Books are published by The Berkley Publishing Group,
200 Madison Avenue, New York, New York 10016.
BERKLEY and the "B" design
are trademarks belonging to Berkley Publishing Corporation.

PRINTED IN THE UNITED STATES OF AMERICA

10 9 8 7 6 5 4 3 2 1

"Furthermore we command you in the virtue of holy obedience, to send to the said firm lands and islands, honest, virtuous, and learned men, such as fear God and are able to instruct the native inhabitants in the Catholic faith and good manners, applying all their possible diligence in this."

ALEXANDER BORGIA, *a Spanish pope*
indebted to Ferdinand and Isabella for his election,
after dividing the earth in half,
and granting the undiscovered lands
in the western half to the Spanish,
the eastern to the Portuguese.

1555, along what would someday be called the South Carolina coast . . .

Chapter I

The blue sky stretched over and away from the green bean field, seemingly all the way to the ends of the earth. It was a medicine sky, and as Calling Crow worked with two other men, he knew something bad was coming. A small fire crackled around the already-narrowed base of a tree they were felling as they chopped away the brittle, blackened wood with their stone axes. Calling Crow was the tallest of the three, muscled and slender. He paused in his chopping and glanced back at the sky.

The tree was still as big around as a fat old man, and he knew this job would take them most of the day. He removed the short mantle of woven bark which covered just the upper part of his body. Now, like the other two braves, he wore only a breechclout of deerskin held in place by a leather girdle. His pleasing, oval face was copper-colored like a leaf in autumn, and he had high cheeks and a full, proud nose. He picked up the axe and chopped powerfully at the tree. The largest of the other two braves, Sun Watcher, knelt as he used his axe to heap glowing embers up and against the trunk. Birdfoot, a small thin brave, swung tiredly at the tree, breaking off a piece with a clinking sound. His intense face was blackened here and there with soot.

Calling Crow noticed something moving in the distance and put down his axe. With brown eyes the color of a pool of cedar water, he stared at the far-off tree line. A solitary figure was approaching, running very fast.

Both young men turned to Calling Crow after a while. The runner had momentarily disappeared behind a distant sand dune.

"What is it?" said Sun Watcher.

"A runner is coming," said Calling Crow. A moment later the figure crested the dune moving so fast they all immediately grabbed their clubs, looking to see if he was being chased. He was not, being instead in a great state of excitement. He tried to shout and lost his footing, tumbling and throwing up a spray of sand. He rolled into a heap as the others ran up to him. It was Calling Crow's cousin, Runs Like Deer. He got to his knees, coughing as he fought for breath.

Calling Crow clapped him on the back. "Cousin, what is it? What have you to tell us?"

"Hurry," said Runs Like Deer between gasps, "it is the men from the heavens, come down in their cloudboats!" He got to his feet and staggered back up the dune.

Calling Crow, Sun Watcher, and Birdfoot looked at each other for a moment and then went back to the tree to get their bows. They followed Runs Like Deer up the dune.

Only a handful of villagers had ever seen the men from the heavens in their beautiful cloudboats. It was said that they roamed the big water in search of newly dead souls to take to the land of the dead.

A half hour later Calling Crow, Sun Watcher, and Birdfoot gasped for breath as they reached the top of the bluff. They found a swarm of little ones, boys mostly, looking out to sea. Their shouting pierced the air like gull cries as they jumped and pointed. A somber-faced old man and woman knelt facing the sea as they prayed.

Calling Crow climbed to a higher vantage and looked out. He could not believe what he saw. Out on the sea at a great distance, two white clouds had detached themselves from the blue heavens and now sat on the waters. As the warm rays of the sun burned into his face, a chill went through him. There was no doubt that this was a sign, but what did it mean?

Calling Crow watched a boy put an arrow to his bow. His arm muscles bulged as he pulled the feathered shaft back to his cheek. Calling Crow frowned at the other boys watching expectantly. They should know by now that even if an arrow could reach the distant cloudboats, it would only pass harmlessly through them, for they were from the spirit world.

The boy released his arrow, and it arced out a good distance and fell into the sea beyond the rocks. Undaunted, he lay on his back, and using his legs to hold his bow, launched another arrow. It too fell woefully short. Disappointed, the crowd of boys again fixed their attention on the distant cloudboats. A mild seaward breeze started up behind them as Runs Like Deer came over to stand beside Calling Crow. Together they watched the two white shapes in silence.

"I think they're moving," said Runs Like Deer.

Calling Crow strained his eyes and detected the ships closing the distance to the dark point of land jutting out on the periphery of his vision. What did these things bode for his people? A huge cloud passed overhead, and the sea turned the wintry color of dead leaves. Smoke reached Calling Crow's nostrils. He turned to see two boys on their haunches, blowing a handful of smoking kindling into flame to call the people from heaven. Calling Crow ran over. "No," he said angrily as he kicked the flames out. "We must not call them until the Council of Old Men has been consulted."

The boys glowered at Calling Crow, and he glared back at them.

"Go away!"

The boys walked off, and Calling Crow turned and looked back out to sea. The cloudboats had disappeared, but he could not take his eyes off the sea. What were those things? The sight of them caused a great fear and sadness in his heart. He said nothing to the others, and after a while they wandered off. He sat in the sand and stared out at the waters. Despite the warmness of the day, he shivered. The sea often had that effect on him, ever since it had taken his father. Back when he was a boy, his father had gone out fishing with some other men when a storm suddenly came up. Calling Crow remembered running to the beach, crying as the wind lashed his face and lightning lit the angry sky. The next morning the empty canoe had washed up on the beach and his father and the other man had never been found.

Chapter 2

Under a dizzying array of stars, two caravels, the *Guadalupe* and the *Speeding Hound*, moved slightly at their anchors in the black swells like two great seabirds. The ships were from Spain's island colony of Hispaniola in the Caribbean Sea and were on a—so far—unsuccessful slaving expedition. Carrying sixty-five men, the ships contained two armories filled with dozens of deadly accurate crossbows and, more importantly, thunderous, fire and black smoke–belching arquebuses. The arquebuses were woefully inaccurate, but were known to terrify the natives into mute paralysis. Each ship carried a small boat lashed down on the upper deck. The bigger of the two ships, the *Guadalupe*, also carried two horses and towed a lateen-rigged long boat for landing them.

The commander of the expedition, Francisco Mateo, a Creole, or criollo landowner and merchant, sat in his cabin in the rear of the *Guadalupe*, talking with his friend, an older colonist named Diego Vega. Diego, a sad-faced man in his mid-fifties, had been a friend of Mateo's father, having come over on the *Galician*'s second voyage with him. Now that Mateo's own father had died, he treasured the old man's company, as he was the only living link to his family's past.

Senor Mateo blinked his tea-brown eyes and ran his hand tiredly through his red hair. He did not like what he had been hearing. Before he'd left Santo Domingo, he had hired a contingent of soldiers newly arrived from Spain to help him. Now, under the guidance of their two officers they were complaining and causing trouble, wanting him to turn round and go back to Santo Domingo. Even his crew, loyal criollo and mestizo farmers and ranchers, were beginning to tire of the search and put up resistance.

"You know," said Diego tiredly, "the cook was lying about being out of ship's biscuits."

Senor Mateo's large head came forward. "What?"

Diego nodded. "I found three barrels of them hidden under some canvas."

Mateo said nothing for a moment, and Diego went on. "You know, Francisco, I think that the reason you have found no Indians is that God looks unkindly on this venture."

Mateo remained silent. Diego was married to an Arawak Indian woman. These marriages were now common among the criollos on the island, but to the newly arrived Peninsulars, the idea was repulsive. The Peninsulars considered Indian women only as whores and servants. Finally Mateo sighed tiredly. "Diego, what we are doing is completely within the limits of the law."

"Man's law," said Diego, almost in a whisper. "I should never have agreed to come along on this. It is wrong. I needed the money so bad that I did not . . ."

Both men heard faint footsteps out on deck. As Mateo listened to them fade away he made a mental note to deal with the cook in the morning. A thought came to him. Perhaps they were measuring the latitudes wrong and therefore searching for Indians in the wrong area? That could account for their terrible luck. Perhaps he should take the latitude with the backstaff himself . . .

A loud, dull thud suddenly reverberated through the wood of the cabin. Mateo looked over at Diego. "See what it is."

Diego quickly got to his feet. As he went toward the door, the strong smell of lamp oil reached Mateo's nostrils. Diego opened the door and turned to look upward at the high stern of the ship. A glow spread around him and then golden, liquid fire poured down onto his shoulder. He beat his doublet furiously as his face blossomed in fear.

Mateo ran to him, roughly pulling his hands away. In the light of the fires Mateo saw melted flesh on one hand. He quickly glanced up at the stern. Bright flames half as high as a man moved in the slight breeze. The large oil lamp which hung above had evidently broken loose from its fixture and crashed down. Mateo pushed Diego into his cabin. Taking his own doublet off, he quickly dunked it into a vase of water and extinguished the smoldering fabric of Diego's doublet. "Are you okay?" he shouted at him.

· Diego appeared in a daze, but he nodded.

"Go tell the others. Quickly! And then find the barber to take care of that hand."

Diego ran off with Mateo's wet doublet wrapped in a wad around his hand. Mateo ran to the door of the cabin and shouted, "Fuego! Fuego! Come quickly!"

He ran back into the cabin and returned with a cape. As quickly as he slapped the flames out they reappeared. Like the fires of hell, small flaming rivulets of lamp oil flowed about his feet as the flaming heat scorched him. He beat at the flames and his cape caught fire. He stomped it out and turned to call again for help. He saw the ship's cooper staring incredulously at the sight.

He shouted at him, "Don't just stand there, fool, get the others and some buckets! Get that pump on the port side working!"

"*Sí,*" yelled the man, running back toward the center of the ship. "Fire! Help! Fire! Come quickly!"

Chapter 3

Calling Crow had taken his name four years earlier after praying for, and receiving, his first vision. He had fasted alone for three days on the mountain and seen the Great Spirit move on the other side of the sky, like someone brushing against a skin stretched across an entryway as he passed. Then a large crow had settled in a tree nearby and called to him. That noble bird became his spirit guide.

Now he, Sun Watcher, and Birdfoot emerged from the great forest of slash pine and broad-leafed magnolias, elms, and hickories that bordered on the village of Tumaqua. Each wore his bow over one arm, and a quiver of arrows hung from their backs. They had been sent to scout the forests that bordered the Flathead People's lands and had seen nothing unusual. Heading back toward the village, they walked quickly across a field of clover.

Calling Crow turned round to Sun Watcher as they walked. Although Calling Crow was a handsbreadth taller than Sun Watcher, Sun Watcher was stronger, being very broad and muscled in the chest. "The Flatheads are nowhere in evidence."

Sun Watcher smiled. "They are probably afraid to come around." Sun Watcher's smile turned to a frown. "Tell me, Calling Crow," he said, "did you also see this light Birdfoot speaks of?"

"Yes," said Calling Crow.

Sun Watcher looked straight ahead, his face stony in its seriousness. "Tell me, what was it like?"

Calling Crow remembered the mysterious light. He and others had watched it out in the black sky over the sea last night. He still wasn't sure what it portended. Perhaps he should speak to Mennewah the Shaman about it. "It burned like a star fallen onto the waters."

"*Aieyah*, I told you so," said Birdfoot as he tried to keep up with the two bigger braves. Birdfoot's delicate features and large eyes flashed annoyance at the other, bigger brave for doubting him. "It is a sign."

"No, Grandfather," said Sun Watcher. He turned round and smiled. "It is not."

Birdfoot was actually younger than the other two, but because of his pensive, questioning ways he was often called Grandfather.

Sun Watcher filled his chest as they walked, bulging out his muscles. He looked crossly at Birdfoot. "You are too serious, Birdfoot. If it really was a sign, Caldo would have already called a meeting with the Council of Old Men."

"Perhaps." Birdfoot rubbed a rivulet of sweat from his brow.

The three men fell silent. Calling Crow thought of the dreams he'd been having. In one of them he'd heard his dead father's voice as he watched the strange cloudboats sail by.

Calling Crow and the other two braves reached the dirt path that led to Tumaqua. Worn smooth by the moccasins of over a hundred men and women, it felt good beneath their feet. They could see the village up ahead. Almost on the edge of the sea, it sat between several large dunes. Three dozen roughly rectangular dwellings with semicircular roofs made of bent saplings covered with mats of woven cattails and bark were situated haphazardly around a large circular building with a domed roof, called a *chokafa*. Built on a mound, the chokafa served as the Clan's meetinghouse. Next to the chokafa was a large rectangular field called a *chunkey yard* in which ball games were played against neighboring villages. All was enclosed within a defensive palisade of sturdy upright timbers and sharpened stakes pointing outward.

As the three neared the palisade, they heard the women wailing. Someone had died! They began running. As they entered the village, Calling Crow was saddened and moved by the deep many-toned harmonies of the women. It was like a storm wind moaning late at night. Who had died? he wondered. One of *his* loved ones?

Death was, of course, not an unusual thing, but as the volume of sound swelled with their every step, Calling Crow knew that it must have been someone of great importance. Never had he heard wailing like this. "I think it was Mennewah," Calling Crow shouted to Birdfoot as they ran along.

"Perhaps," said Birdfoot worriedly.

Sun Watcher said nothing.

Mennewah the Shaman was the oldest man in the village, and Calling Crow had dreamed of him twice in the past moon.

They rounded one of the bigger huts and saw that the chunkey yard was full of sitting-women, their heads bowed as they wailed. It was the custom for the women to mourn a death in this way.

In front of the firewell, a body lay on a raised pallet of willow poles and skins. Before Calling Crow and the other two braves could get close enough to see who it was, the maiden, Tiamai, ran up to them. Her large eyes were glazed with held-back tears. "It is our beloved Chief," she said.

Calling Crow felt as if a knife had punctured his heart. The cloudboats had appeared and now the bravest, noblest man in Tumaqua was dead! "What happened?" he said.

Tiamai's were still moist. "Our Chief and Cries At Night had been stalking a big buck deer all day. When our Chief shot his arrow into him, another arrow also struck the buck. It belonged to Many Skins Man, of the Wolf Clan. Both their arrows seemed to strike the buck at the same time. Our Chief suggested that they should share the kill, but Many Skins Man insisted that his arrow had pierced the buck first and the kill should be all his. They fought and Many Skins Man killed our Chief." Tiamai deliberately avoided saying Chief Caldo's name. To speak the name of the dead was taboo.

Sun Watcher looked skyward and howled in rage. Calling Crow took Tiamai's hands in his. "How do you know all this?"

"I talked to Cries At Night after they brought our Chief's body back to Tumaqua." She held Calling Crow's eyes for a moment and then ran back to the nearest group of women and sat down.

Calling Crow gripped his bow tightly. Perhaps he would soon use it for killing men. It would be the first time for him. If a death was due to a killing, accidental or otherwise, reparation was required from the guilty party. Failure to provide reparation meant war. As long as anyone of the five villages could remember, reparation had always been made and war averted. There was no reason to believe that this time would be any different.

Once reparation had been made, the Council of Old Men voted on whether or not to accept it. Always it had been offered in good faith and always it had been accepted. If it were not, the young braves of the tribe would prepare to exact revenge.

After eight days of mourning, Many Skins Man still had not shown up to make reparation, and the village began making preparations for war. The cloudboats now forgotten, the men shaped stones for arrows and lances while the women scraped the fire-hardened tips of stakes and buried them in the dirt around the palisade. Old women cooked all day as old men and boys carried water, arrows, and stones up to the top of the palisade. As the people worked hurriedly, there was an overwhelming quiet as if a summer storm were gathering. No one spoke more than needed because nothing could be as it was and people could not truly have peace until the reparation was made, or war begun. But finally, on the morning of the ninth day, a runner informed the village of Tumaqua that Many Skins Man was to come today.

Calling Crow thought about these things as he sat in the cool interior of his aunt Three Pearls's hut. She brought him a steaming calabash of corn soup. He sipped the hot sweet liquid hurriedly and noisily, not wanting to insult

Three Pearls by leaving it unfinished. Still, he could not take his time with it. He gulped the rest of it down and got to his feet. His throat ached from the burn it gave him but that didn't matter. He must get out and watch the reparation.

"Nephew," Three Pearls called to him angrily, "stay and eat more."

"I am sorry, Aunt," he said. "I must go." He rushed out of the hut.

Calling Crow quickly made his way to the square next to the chunkey yard. This was where the people came to cure hides and grind maize and grains, or just to gossip, and it was here that Many Skins Man would stand before them all to make his reparation.

Today it would be decided—reparation or war! The Council of Old Men sat on the ground in the center of the yard, while most of the villagers milled about behind them, talking and waiting. Calling Crow saw that Caldo's body had been taken away to the beach where it would be raised up on lodge poles to protect it from small animals. Months later, when the flesh was gone from the bones, certain ones of them would be given to the Old Men and the braves as talismans.

Calling Crow pushed through the crowd to where he spotted Tiamai kneeling in the sand, grinding corn. He watched her as she worked. Wearing only a skirt of woven bark, she pounded the blue and yellow kernels of corn into the hollow of a grinding rock with a wooden mortar, the action moving her small breasts. It was understood that the young people of the village would lie with one another, changing partners from time to time as they discovered themselves and their likes and dislikes. But by the time a brave had been on the earth twenty turnings of the seasons, he was expected to have selected one girl for his wife. Calling Crow had already selected Tiamai. He knew it and so did she, and so did any others who happened to see how they looked at each other. Like most girls, Tiamai was an obedient, hard worker for her mother. Although she was but fifteen, Calling Crow was struck with the noble way she carried herself. She was also beautiful. Her long, dark hair fell to her waist and her black eyes shone like the moon on the sea at night. It was this combination of nobility and childlike beauty that had made him love her.

He walked over and stood by her side. She looked up at him and smiled sadly, then went back to her grinding.

From the other side of the dunes, the sea called to Calling Crow as it surged and sighed up and down the wide beach of white sand. As he listened to its voice he watched the troubled look on Tiamai's cinnamon face and thought about the last time he lay with her in the forest.

As if hearing his thought, Tiamai paused in her grinding and looked at him. In the look they shared, he knew that soon he would make their love known to the whole village.

She raised her hand to quickly brush a sweat-dampened strand of hair from her face. "Tell me about the cloudboats. I've never seen them."

"And I pray you never will. They appeared and our great Chief died. I knew they were not a good sign."

Tiamai lowered her head at the mention of the tragedy. "I wonder what Many Skins Man will bring," she said.

"I don't know, but this death will require many fine gifts." He looked down at Tiamai and felt his sadness lighten a little. She always worked this magic on him.

"Soon," said Tiamai, "if the reparation is accepted and the matter of our Chief's death settled, the Council of Old Men will pick a new Chief from among the top braves. Then life in the village will be as it was. Perhaps they will pick you." Tiamai smiled and turned away to her work.

Calling Crow said nothing. He knew that he was a candidate, along with a dozen or so other braves, but, like everyone else in the village, he thought the Old Men would pick Sun Watcher. He was the bravest and strongest in the village. Whenever they gathered in the chunkey yard to play ball against a neighboring village, they would always win because of Sun Watcher. As a boy, Calling Crow had challenged him many times in wrestling, footraces, and shooting arrows, but try as he could, not once had he been able to best him.

A gull glided overhead, crying out sorrowfully to the people below. Calling Crow looked toward the sea. "The other day," he said slowly, "as I watched the cloudboats, in spite of my repulsion, I felt they were calling me."

Tiamai looked up at him and frowned. "I am afraid for all of us." Turning away, she brushed the last bits of moist ground meal that clung to the rock into her basket and began pounding another pile of maize kernels. She looked at Calling Crow. "You could ask Mennewah what it all means." As Shaman, Mennewah was leader of the Council of Old Men.

"Yes. Or I could enter the dreamworld myself and find out."

Tiamai pounded the corn harder as concern darkened her face. She was about to say something when excited voices sounded from the far end of the village. They turned and saw the delegation of Wolf Clan people coming through the village gate. Many Skins Man towered over his people as he walked among them. Forest dwellers, the Wolf Clan people came regularly to Tumaqua to trade. They had much that Calling Crow's tribe desired, such as pemmican, buffalo robes that had been traded from tribe to tribe all the way from the banks of the great river, moccasins from the Flathead People, so called because of that tribe's custom of binding the heads of their infants to boards. They also had small gold ornaments from the Mountain People, and even greenstone jewelry from the People of the Hot Lands. The Turtle Clan paid for these things with the bounty of the sea and the small rivers feeding it. They gathered these things, fish, shells, and river pearls for wampum belts, from their small dugout canoes.

Many Skins Man led his group through the huts toward the square. Despite the recent spell of warm weather, he wore a bearskin mantle. It was open at the front, showing off his wide muscled chest, glistening with sweat and grease beneath a necklace of white bear's teeth. Two of his Flathead slaves flanked him, each carrying a large bundle of his goods, and behind him walked six Wolf Clan braves. One of the Flathead slaves tripped on a root and fell, spilling his bundles. Cursing angrily, Many Skins Man kicked him in the rear, and the man rolled quickly out of range. The assembled Turtle Clan people watched closely, a few laughing nervously, as the frightened slave gathered the bundles up, furtively keeping his eyes on Many Skins Man the whole time.

The group advanced once again and as Calling Crow watched them, he thought that Many Skins Man's bearing was too proud for the occasion. He searched the big man's face for sorrow or contrition but could find none. When the Wolf Clan group drew up before the sitting Council of Old Men, Many Skins Man gave a command in a deep resonant voice and his party began putting down their bundles.

Sun Watcher, Big Nose, Birdfoot, and a half dozen other braves crowded around Calling Crow. The Turtle Clan people were silent as Many Skins Man cut open one of the bundles of skins. Quickly and dramatically, he raised a large bear pelt before the crowd, completely obscuring himself behind it except for his big hands.

"Ah," said several people as they shook their heads in appreciation of the size and quality of the skins. Calling Crow and Sun Watcher moved closer as Many Skins Man held up a number of fine stone calumets in one large hand. Again the crowd showed their amazement at such wealth with sighs and muttered words of wonder. Calling Crow looked over at the Council of Old Men. Unlike the people, they remained still and quiet, their ancient black eyes mere slits under their heavy lids.

"Many Skins Man!" The voice was loud and challenging, silencing the crowd. It was Sun Watcher. "Tell us how our beloved Chief died."

The crowd boiled with murmured conversations as Many Skins Man's dark eyes searched the crowd for his questioner. Settling on Sun Watcher, he said, "I will tell it only one more time. You forget, it was I who was wronged." He waited till the crowd had quieted. "I tracked a powerful buck for most of that day. Finally, my arrow found him and I was following his blood trail. I was very happy because I knew that soon he would be mine. It was then that the deceased put his arrow into him. He mistakenly thought the buck was his. We fought and I killed him."

On this last admission Calling Crow saw a slight smile pass over Many Skins Man's face like the shadow of a cloud moving over a field on a sunny day. Hot anger boiled deep within him. "How was our Chief's death?" Calling Crow called out to the Wolf warrior. "Was it a good death? Did he speak to you?"

Many Skins Man turned in his direction, and Calling Crow's anger flared even higher when the Wolf warrior's eyes paused momentarily to admire Tiamai. Many Skins Man's eyes again sought Calling Crow. "I do not know. He said nothing. He died like a man."

"Not like a Chief?" cried Big Nose in anguished anger.

"I will speak of this no more." Many Skins Man folded his arms and remained sullenly silent and for a while the world stood still. Calling Crow and the other braves watched the Old Men to see what they would do.

"I have more gifts," said Many Skins Man finally, but no one looked his way. All eyes remained on the Old Men. Finally Mennewah raised his hand. "Go on, Many Skins Man. Finish your business. Then we will begin ours."

Many Skins Man held up a bundle of deerskins as thick as a man and again the crowd muttered appreciatively. The pile grew into a mound as the Wolf Clan people finished displaying the gifts. Finally the Council of Old Men got to their feet and walked off. Most of the Turtle Clan people followed them to await their decision.

Only a handful of curious boys remained as Many Skins Man's entourage prepared to leave. Birdfoot wandered over to stand beside Calling Crow. A few feet away, Tiamai knelt as she gathered up her corn into a basket.

"He has brought many fine things," said Tiamai. "I wonder if the Council of Old Men will accept them."

"I think they will," said Birdfoot.

"I don't know," said Calling Crow. He watched the
Wolf Clan group walk past on their way to the gate. Calling Crow was surprised to see Many Skins Man leave the
group and come closer. He stood before Tiamai. "What a
fine-looking girl you are!" he said. "What is your name?"

Tiamai said nothing, keeping her head down. Calling
Crow looked at Many Skins Man in angry incredulity.

Birdfoot said quickly, "She is Calling Crow's woman.
You should not speak to her."

Many Skins Man looked at Calling Crow. "His?" he
said, and laughed. He turned back to Tiamai and draped a
beaver skin cape on the ground before her. "For the beautiful doe girl," he said, "a fine warm covering to keep the
wet chill of winter from her smooth young skin."

Using his bow, Calling Crow flipped the skin away as if
it were a deadly whitemouth snake. Many Skins Man's
face betrayed his shock. One of his slaves quickly rushed
up to recover the skin as Tiamai walked away, her head
down in embarrassment.

Calling Crow stared angrily at Many Skins Man. "Even
if she wanted your flea-infested skin, while we mourn
there can be no courting and gift-giving. That is our custom."

"We have our customs, too, Turtle brave, and one of
them is to honor beauty wherever and whenever we find
it."

His face burning with fury, Calling Crow stared at the
other man. "I think you shall learn more than you care to
about our customs."

Many Skins Man smiled at Calling Crow and turned to
his party. "Let's go." As they disappeared through the
gate, Many Skins Man's loud laughter floated back.

Chapter 4

The chokafa was circular in shape and higher than the tallest man in the village. Its conical roof had an opening in the center to let out smoke, and the walls and ceiling were made of bark smeared with clay. Woven mats of cane carpeted the cold ground, and a single fire burned in the center. Calling Crow sat on the matting with Sun Watcher, Big Nose, Birdfoot, and the other braves, while across from them sat Mennewah and the rest of the Council of Old Men. The Old Men were dressed in their ceremonial raven's feathers. In front of them on a straw mat, the Chief's raven-feather mantle and deerskin-fringed medicine pipe was placed for all to see.

Old Mennewah clasped his withered hands around his round belly as his watery eyes appraised the young men before him. "We have discussed our Chief's death and Many Skins Man's reparation, but we wanted to hear from you young men and find out what is in your hearts."

Calling Crow opened his mouth to speak when Sun Watcher jumped to his feet. "Many Skins Man is like the snake in the grass you don't see. He is an arrogant liar. Many times he and other Wolf Clan braves have crossed the rivers and trails that mark our borders in search of game. They are a menace which must be dealt with. I say burn his gifts and make war on them!"

Big Nose, Laughing Man, and four other braves jumped to their feet beside Sun Watcher and yelled their agreement.

Mennewah's face remained impassive. "I agree that Many Skins Man is an arrogant fool, but is arrogance and foolishness reason enough to go to war? If it were, we

would have to go to war against some of our own, would
we not?"

The other two members of the Council of Old Men, Red
Dog and Flathead Killer, smiled, but Sun Watcher and the
other braves remained on their feet, their anger unabated.

After a moment Birdfoot said, "You speak well, Grandfather. I agree with what you say."

Mennewah motioned Sun Watcher and the others to sit.
"Stand and speak."

In the dimness of the hut, Birdfoot's large eyes gave
him an owllike appearance. "We have lived near the Wolf
Clan for many generations now. There have been problems, but that is natural for different peoples living so
close to one another. I say that if contrition does not come
easily to Many Skins Man, we should demand more reparation."

"No, Grandfather," cried Sun Watcher angrily. "No."

Old Red Dog held up his bony hand for silence. "Is that
enough, Birdfoot?" he said. "Because there has long been
peace, we should choose peace?"

"No, but what of our beloved Chief? He was a man of
peace. I vote as I think he would have voted. For peace."

"Yes," said Slim Boy, rising to stand beside Birdfoot.
"I, too, vote for peace."

Another brave stood beside them. "Peace," he said.

Mennewah looked at Calling Crow. "What have you to
say, Calling Crow?"

"Yes," said Red Dog, his emaciated face wrinkling like
an autumn leaf. "Calling Crow is the only one who hasn't
spoken." Flathead Killer, the other member of the Council
of Old Men, nodded in agreement.

Calling Crow's heart was heavy as he rose to his feet.
He had thought hard about this matter and none of the
possible courses of action were good. He faced the Old
Men. For a moment he said nothing.

Mennewah looked at him sadly. "Well, Calling Crow,
do you vote for peace or war?"

"I vote for neither, Grandfather."

Sun Watcher laughed derisively. "What kind of answer

is that?" The other braves laughed with him as they cast
sidelong glances at Calling Crow.

"Enough," said Mennewah. "What do you mean, Calling Crow?"

"I do not want war because many innocent people from
both villages will die. As Birdfoot said, our beloved Chief
was a strong, gentle man, a man of peace. However, I saw
through Many Skins Man's eyes into his heart, and I know
that his remorse is a sham. Because of that, all his fine
gifts are not worth their weight in excrement."

"So you agree with me that we should have war," said
Sun Watcher in triumph.

Again Mennewah held up his frail arm, casting silence
over the group. "So what do you propose, Calling Crow?"

"We can regain the honor of our clan by killing only
Many Skins Man. Then the Wolf Clan will have to decide
whether or not the matter is settled. I do not think they
want a war, and I think Many Skins Man's death will be
the end of this matter."

"How do you propose we kill Many Skins Man?" said
Mennewah.

"One of us must go alone into the Wolf Clan village
and kill him." Calling Crow looked around at the others
and then back at Mennewah. "Today, after all of you had
left, Many Skins Man insulted me. It was deliberate;
Birdfoot witnessed it. For that reason I would like to go do
it."

Sun Watcher jumped to his feet. "No! It is too risky.
Calling Crow is not *ottsi* enough to do it; he has never
killed a man! What if he, too, is killed? Then we are dou-
bly shamed." He held out his hands pleadingly to
Mennewah. "Let me go and I will surely kill him."

"No," said Mennewah. He struggled to get to his feet,
and Sun Watcher and Birdfoot helped him up. "It is settled. Calling Crow will kill Many Skins Man and avenge
our Chief's death." Mennewah turned to Sun Watcher.
"Go see to the destruction of Many Skins Man's gifts."

Sun Watcher bowed and followed the Old Men outside.
Calling Crow waited till the others had left and then sat

back down, the silence wrapping around him like a warm blanket of woven bark.

On the beach, a small fire flickered in the blackness. Waves crashed and sighed as Calling Crow danced in the flickering light. Mennewah sat before the fire, beating a drum as he stared into the flames. He held his hand up suddenly and called Calling Crow's name. Calling Crow knelt before him, and Mennewah placed a necklace of black feathers about his neck. "Just as the black crow cannot be seen at night," intoned the old man, "so you shall be invisible to the Wolf people."

"I am the anger of my people," sang Calling Crow as a large wave crashed, its weight and force reverberating through the cold, hard sand beneath them, "I shall not let them down."

Mennewah smeared bear fat on Calling Crow's unseeing face. "I give you the strength of the bear. Now, bring back our honor!" Mennewah walked back toward the village. The tongue of flame licked the blackness one more time and blinked out, the embers glowing like the eyes of a panther.

Calling Crow got to his feet and took his flint knife from its sheath hanging at his side. In a stupor, he waved it about as he danced. A moan escaped his lips as he stepped on the coals. Embers burst from his feet and shot away on the breeze like angry hornets. He sang the warrior's chant once again and felt himself growing stronger. He was now invisible in the blackness, like a crow. His breath rasped like a wounded animal's as he moved off, a shadow in the swirling mist. There was only a sliver of moon to guide him, and a coastal fog obscured its light and the light of the stars. The night air was cool and wet; the sky indistinguishable from the ground. His village now behind him, Calling Crow turned and walked toward the sea. He would use its sounds to guide him. With the smooth sand beneath his naked feet, he began running, knowing he'd have to finish and be on his way back before Father Sun rose from the sea. Ahead a filmy white shape raced quickly across the beach and disappeared into the dunes. Not knowing if it was a puff of sea foam or a spirit, Calling Crow's heart raced momentarily and he reached into the medicine bag he wore at his side. Fondling the bones of Tall One and Fish Catcher, two of the bravest warriors in the Turtle Clan, and the beak, feet, and feathers of his guiding spirit, he knew he would be safe. He ran faster now, and after a few minutes the running filled him with sweat and courage and he forgot everything except what he must do.

After a while Calling Crow discerned the black shapes of Big Dunes against the night sky. He turned toward them and came to the edge of the forest. Slowing to a walk, he felt his way cautiously between the trees. Soon afterward the mist disappeared, and there was just enough light to pick out the trail. He began running again. An hour later he stopped when he spotted the outline of the Wolf Clan palisade. Two silhouettes moved about on the catwalk above the sharpened timber uprights.

Calling Crow moved into the shadowed darkness of the trees to hide. This was swampland and he found himself in cool water up to his knees. From the shining black surfaces, a multitude of bullfrogs and crickets filled the cool night air with their music. Calling Crow drank in the sounds. He looked down and noticed a large frog on a half-submerged log. A white-winged moth flitted by, and the big frog spat out its tongue, catching the moth in midflight. It was a good omen. That's what he must do to Many Skins Man. His people were depending on him.

Calling Crow crouched like a panther and watched the movements of the guards. For a long time they remained in the same place talking quietly, and he supplanted his discomfort with the memory of Caldo and the voice of his spirit calling out for revenge. The singing of the frogs and crickets grew louder and intoxicating, and he heard encouragement in their music. One of the sentries laughed loudly at something. Calling Crow felt at his feet and picked up a stone. He threw it at the far end of the wall and the two sentries moved off. When they were no bigger

than his finger, he quickly pulled himself up to the top of
the wall and dropped down noiselessly on the other side.
As he crept silently past the dark huts he heard the sounds
of life all about him, a child crying somewhere, the
phlegmy cough of an old man, the furtive breathing of lovers. Then he saw the dark outline of the big hut at the corner of the compound just as Mennewah and the other Old
Men had described it. He had to restrain himself from running. Soon it would be over and his village would know
peace again.

Calling Crow stepped through the entryway of the hut
and stood still as a panther until his eyes adjusted. He
scanned the hut and saw only Many Skins Man lying on
a pallet next to the fire. A single flame danced alone, casting a wobbly glow. Without a sound Calling Crow glided
across the dirt floor and stood looking down on the man.
His heart was pounding as he withdrew his stone knife and
knelt.

Many Skins Man's lips were parted and pulled away
from his big teeth. For a few moments Calling Crow listened to the sound of Many Skins Man's deep breathing
and watched his bare chest rise and fall. He did not think
it would be this easy and he was grateful to his spirit
guide. Arms trembling slightly, Calling Crow raised the
knife in both hands. He was about to bring it down force-
fully when a spirit voice spoke in his head. Would it not
be more honorable, the voice said, and the Clan's revenge
sweeter, if Calling Crow woke Many Skins Man first and
let him see the face of his killer before he died?

Calling Crow touched the big man on the chest. Many
Skins Man smacked his lips as he stirred dumbly. His eyelids quivered like a bird shaking the wet out of its wings,
but they did not open and he quickly fell back into his
sleep. Calling Crow reached down to touch Many Skins
Man again when the big man rolled off the pallet with the
speed of a hare. Calling Crow brought the knife down
wildly, stabbing at nothing. The fire hissed and went
black. Calling Crow moved backward, but not before he
felt a sudden current of air. A blow from a club whistled

by his ear and crashed into his arm. Intense pain flared in his hand as he dropped his knife.

Calling Crow ducked to the ground and rolled away. For a few frightening moments, his fighting arm hung uselessly from his shoulder like a leather thong. Slowly feeling returned as he edged backward. From somewhere in the darkness Many Skins Man whispered hoarsely, "Turtle brave! You are a fool to come here. I could call out now and many braves would come and kill you, but I want the pleasure for myself."

Calling Crow crouched silently, working the fingers of his hand.

"Were my skins not good enough for your Clan?" The voice seemed to come from everywhere.

Calling Crow moved backward. "You do not possess enough wealth to make reparation for our Chief's death."

"Ah, it is you." Many Skins Man's voice now seemed to come from the bark roof above. "I thought they would have sent their biggest brave."

Calling Crow said nothing. He continued to work his fingers painfully, running them across the ground as he searched for his knife. His ears strained for any sound of the other's movements.

"It is just as well," said the large voice softly, "for I am tired. I will kill you much faster and wear your headskin on my belt."

Calling Crow's heart pounded against his chest. How could a big man like him move so silently? His voice seemed to float about the hut. Then Calling Crow realized that the man knew the layout of his hut well. He searched the thick blackness and thought he could feel the big man approaching. Kneading the medicine bag tied to his side, he said a prayer and slipped sideways. Many Skins Man's breath exploded in a hiss as a flurry of blows whipped the air. Calling Crow jumped backward and moved toward the pallet. He prayed wildly to his spirit guide as he searched the ground with his fingers. He touched the smooth bone handle of his knife and grasped it like the hand of a good friend. Frantically he tried to get a sense of where the other was. Again the voice came from the blackness, this time from near the entryway. "I shall deliver your bashed brains to the doe girl in a calabash, fool."

Calling Crow turned and stumbled slightly, his breath coming too noisily. Squatting, his eyes flitted about nervously as he searched the darkness. Where was he? His ears picked up no sound, his nose no smell. Oh, Great Spirit, he prayed, give me the eyes of an owl, the ears of a deer. Putting all his trust into his prayers, he sensed the other's presence close by. With the speed of a striking rattlesnake, he jabbed his knife in that direction and felt it penetrate flesh, then strike bone as Many Skins Man grunted sharply. Many Skins Man's war club whipped by as Calling Crow threw himself backward. A weak blow grazed his chest, knocking the wind out of him, and he dropped to the ground and rolled away. Forcing breath into his lungs, he got to his feet. As the sickly, sucking sounds of the big man's breathing filled the hut, Calling Crow felt calm return to him. With his knife outstretched, he slowly advanced on the sound. When he could feel the heat of the man and smell his blood, he dodged to the side as a weak club blow fell harmlessly across his back. Then he rushed forward, jabbing his knife. He felt it pierce flesh and go in deep. The fecal smell of Many Skins Man's opened intestines flooded the hut. Many Skins Man groaned loudly, his big arms wrapping around Calling Crow as he pulled the knife out. Calling Crow recoiled in disgust from the big man's hot breath as his great weight threatened to pull him to the ground. He rolled away from him and was ready to launch another attack, but the other lay still. Thinking it a trick, he kicked at the dark shape on the floor, but nothing happened.

Calling Crow knelt in the darkness. Somewhere outside a dog howled and his skin crawled. He wondered if it was Many Skins Man's spirit lamenting his passing. He pulled Many Skins Man's thick hair backward. He was glad for the darkness as he sawed at his scalp with his knife. He did not want to do this thing, but the Council had told him he must. As the scalp came off freely and easily he felt Many Skins Man's courage and strength flowing into him. From a nearby hut someone coughed suddenly and another voice called out. Calling Crow stopped moving and the voices died. He daubed the bloody scalp into the dust of the earth to dry it. Getting to his feet, he tied the scalp to his girdle and wiped the smear of blood from his face and hands. He took the biggest bundle of skins he could carry and went out into the blackness.

Chapter 5

The dawn's light was greenish pale, and fog covered the open field between Tumaqua and the forest. A small, quiet crowd of old men and little boys followed Calling Crow down Tumaqua's main path. Two of the biggest boys carried the large bundle of skins for him. Smeared with dried blood, Calling Crow ran out onto the chunkey yard and tied Many Skins Man's scalp to a trophy pole festooned with a half dozen others. He turned and headed for the chokafa where he would undergo the smoke purification ceremony, or smoke bath. It was the tribe's custom that whenever one of its members killed, he had to be purified in this way before he could rejoin the society of the tribe. The crowd grew as some braves and women followed along. When they reached the entryway of the chokafa, Calling Crow saw Sun Watcher and Big Nose approaching. He paused before going inside. Sun Watcher and Big Nose smiled when they saw the blood that covered Calling Crow.

"Well?" said Sun Watcher.

Calling Crow looked tiredly at him. "He is dead."

Sun Watcher stared at Calling Crow and said nothing.

Big Nose nodded his head in appreciation. "*Aieyah*, Calling Crow, you did it!" He turned to face the small crowd. "Many Skins Man is dead!" he shouted at them.

Calling Crow nodded to the crowd as they cheered. A great joy filled his heart. He touched Big Nose on the arm. "Take these skins to Doe Woman for me. Tell her I wish to make Tiamai my wife. I will wait here for my answer."

Big Nose nodded. "I go."

Sun Watcher continued to stare at Calling Crow as he entered the cool darkness of the chokafa. He made a pallet of some dried bulrushes and covered it with a skin. He lay down and, for what seemed like a long time, his wounds throbbed with a life of their own. Finally, blessed sleep came over him. He came to briefly to hear Mennewah chanting over him, wafting fragrant smoke his way with an eagle's feather. He watched for a few moments before falling back to sleep.

Tiamai knelt down beside him, handing him a gourd of hot corn soup. Calling Crow's body ached, but he was able to sit and drink it. Immediately he felt the soothing, life-giving properties of Mother Corn flowing through his body. He sighed and looked at Tiamai.

"They are fine skins," she said. "And my mother thinks so, too. I will be ready in a moon's time."

Calling Crow nodded. "It is good." He felt complete and happy as they looked into each other's eyes. Tiamai took his root in her hand and fondled it. Still looking into his eyes, she lay beside him and opened her legs. As he entered her hot wetness, she held his head and whispered his name. Almost immediately after his seed spilled into her, he tumbled back into sleep.

For a long time they lay on the pallet, their limbs happily entwined in their warmth. The skin covering of the chokafa entryway flapped open noisily and light flashed briefly against the wall. Tiamai looked up to see who had entered. She quietly got to her feet and left. Realizing she was gone, Calling Crow brought himself to a sitting position as Mennewah, Red Dog, and Flathead Killer stood before him solemnly. Mennewah carried the Chief's raven-feather mantle in his hands, Red Dog, the Chief's calumet. Calling Crow struggled to get to his feet, but Mennewah held up his hand. "A runner from the Wolf Clan came this morning bearing an eagle's feather. They consider the matter settled. There will be no war."

"That is good," said Calling Crow.

Red Dog and Flathead Killer smiled and nodded.

Without a word, and with great respect, Mennewah and Red Dog lay the mantle and calumet at Calling Crow's feet and went away.

Calling Crow was astounded that they had chosen him. Worried about how his friend Sun Watcher would react, he went to see him. Sun Watcher was not in his hut and for the next few days he avoided Calling Crow, and he knew it did not sit well with him. It will pass, though, thought Calling Crow. And when it does, I will counsel with him and we will be close once more.

Three days of feasting followed Calling Crow's appointment as Chief. There were ball games, footraces, and wrestling matches. On the third night the entire village crowded into the chokafa for dancing and singing. Sitting in the position of honor next to Mennewah, Calling Crow was filled with joy and love for his people. He would serve them well by becoming a good Chief. Like Caldo, he would seek counsel and consensus; he would strive for magnanimity and dignity.

After the women had danced, it was the men's turn. What a beautiful thing it was, thought Calling Crow as he watched them. In the flickering firelight the figures moved like birds to the pounding of the drums and the chirping trill of the flutes. The dancing and singing was a powerful prayer to the Great Spirit. It filled the old men with such strength that they moved gracefully again, forgetting their aches and pains. Arms outstretched like bird wings, they wove their way through the people, more graceful even than young girls.

Three braves led two strangers into the chokafa. They were Mountain People from the west. The two spoke to one of the Turtle men and he turned to another. Calling

Crow heard a slight commotion and turned. He saw that a small crowd now surrounded the Mountain People braves.

Sun Watcher shouted at the two and the dancing stopped. Calling Crow went over and placed himself between Sun Watcher and the two men. "I will speak to them," he said to Sun Watcher.

Sun Watcher stormed off.

Calling Crow turned to the two men. "Why do you disrupt our celebration?" he said.

"We have seen the cloudboats."

"Where?" asked Calling Crow.

"Four days walk to the south," said one of the men.

Immediately the men began wondering and arguing aloud, the women wailing worriedly.

Sun Watcher walked over, his eyes full of fire. "We must find them and fight them!"

"Yes!" shouted some other braves. "Let us go and kill them."

"How can you fight them?" said an old man. "They are like the wind!"

"They came and our Chief died!" someone shouted. "They will kill us all!"

Calling Crow spread his arms and shouted angrily, "Enough!"

The people looked at him in shock.

"I will seek a vision to find out more about these cloudboats, and then I will go to find them."

"No," they cried out, "no!"

Someone shouted, "We will lose you, too, our new Chief!"

"No," said Calling Crow in a loud, calm voice. "I will find the secret of the cloudboats and I will come back. That is my promise to you all. Now, go to your huts and speak no more of this."

Calling Crow turned to Mennewah. "I must go to the spirit world and find out what these things are. Then I will know how to deal with them. Can you prepare a potion to send me across?"

Mennewah nodded somberly.

Calling Crow turned back to the crowd. "Now go home."

No one spoke as the people filed out of the chokafa.

Calling Crow sat alone in a dark corner of the chokafa. All night he had taken one strong bowl after another of the black drink purgative and now he was weak and empty. His hunger was like a dog chewing on his entrails. Soon it would go away and his spirit would have quiet to prepare for its journey.

From outside came the muffled cries of children at play and the faint smoke of cook fires. Inside a single large fly happily raced back and forth in the long open space of the chokafa. Calling Crow looked forward to seeing Caldo in the spirit world. He breathed deeply and his hunger began to leave him. His spirit was peaceful now because soon he would know the mystery of the cloudboats and the people from heaven. Mennewah would bring him one more calabash full of black drink, this one containing the dream medicine, and he would drift off like an unattended canoe on the tides, gently rising and falling on the swells.

Someone called his name. He saw an old woman enter the dimness of the chokafa carrying the steaming calabash. She poured black drink into a conch shell cup and handed it to him. It was more bitter than any herb he had ever tasted and burnt his throat as it went down. A moment later it began churning in his stomach, and he had to go outside and vomit. He went in again, and the old woman poured him another conch shell full of the foul-tasting stuff. He could not feel his fingers, and she had to hold it to his lips and pour it down his throat.

Calling Crow felt as if he were falling from a cliff. He heard something and looked up to see a small group of people before him. Old Red Dog's face was withered and dark like a fallen leaf. "We want you to take our messages with you to the spirit world," he said in an ancient voice.

Calling Crow's head lolled uncontrollably, and he fought to keep his eyes open. "Yes, I will take your messages."

Red Dog leaned close to Calling Crow. "Tell my brother-in-law that I know it was he who took my pipe, but I forgive him."

In spite of the black drink–induced nausea, Calling Crow smiled. An old woman with blue, unseeing pools in her eyes was next. She put her lips close to Calling Crow's ear. "If you see Clam Gatherer, tell him that I am coming soon."

Calling Crow nodded.

Young Swan Woman, whose man had drowned the summer before, leaned close to Calling Crow. "If you see Tall Thin Man, tell him he had a son."

A withered hand held another conch full of the black drink in front of Calling Crow's face, and he quickly drained it. He looked at the people to assure them he would do as they wished. Then his eyes closed and his head fell backward.

A great many women and children cried. Their voices rose like a flock of blackbirds. Calling Crow heard an answering chorus of male voices moan in great pain and sorrow. An old woman's wail pierced the general din of voices like the cry of the wolf. Such a sorrowful sound, it pierced his heart like a knife.

He was floating above the earth. He could see his people in the dimness below, huddled around the dying embers of a number of fires. He knew they were waiting for the one who kills, the Destroyer. In the distance the sea called louder and louder as a great storm approached. The wind began blowing very hard, whipping the garments of the people below and sending coals flying in red-blurring lines across the blackness of the beach. Buffeted by the strong wind, Calling Crow kept his place, floating magically just above the heads of the people. Then suddenly a new cry went up and he knew the Destroyer was approaching. He moved away from the people and down toward the beach. White foam rode the waves up to the beach, and the wind lifted the foam and sent it flying like ghosts across the village. Lightning shattered the sky, illuminating the beach in a brief white flash. In that instant he saw a cloudboat out on the sea and a figure on the beach, struggling through the surf. The figure was too far away to see clearly.

Knowing somehow that he was invisible to the Destroyer, immune to his killing power, Calling Crow floated closer in the blackness. He was merely a witness to this terrible thing and his safeness repulsed him. He longed to drive the Destroyer off and save his people, but he knew that he could not. He was merely wind and air, a ghost.

Then the Destroyer was there. Calling Crow tried to see his face. Who was this evil demon who would kill his people? Try as he could, though, he could only see him from the chest down. He watched in helpless horror as the feet and legs of the Destroyer moved closer and closer toward his people.

The Destroyer emerged from the water, his body wrapped in a water-soaked coat of strange white skin. Calling Crow hovered closer in the blackness, screaming at him to be gone, but no sound left his lips. He could only float along behind, as the Destroyer headed toward the people, leaving his horrid footsteps in the sand. The shouting and crying stopped abruptly and the wind died. Calling Crow moved up the beach and over the dune. Everything had changed. Only four stout poles remained upright where the chokafa had stood. The circular depressions of the cook fires were still visible, but there was not a hut or a canoe in sight and everyone was gone.

The next day, Calling Crow sat up straight in the chokafa across from the Council of Old Men. The Old Men were dressed in their ceremonial raven's feathers, and Calling Crow held the Chief's long calumet in his hands. He drew the sweet tobacco smoke into his lungs and passed it to Mennewah.

"Now that I have told you of my vision, Mennewah, tell me what you know of these people from the heavens. Do they live, or are they the spirits of the dead?"

Mennewah smiled. His small, almost womanlike chest rose and fell as his breath whistled out. "They live in the sky and they come down from time to time on their cloudboats. Whether they are spirits or gods I cannot say, but they cannot live on the land. If they come onto the land they die."

Calling Crow remained stock-still as the terrible images of his vision flickered across the back of his eyes. The Old Ones did not think the cloudboats a threat, but after his vision he was not so sure. If they carried the Destroyer of his vision, then the village would never be safe.

Calling Crow took more of the warm smoke into his lungs and blew it in the four directions. "Has anybody ever seen the cloudboats up close?"

Red Dog nodded with great dignity.

"Tell us about them," said Calling Crow.

"When I was a young man, I took Running Child and Cries At Night out on their First Hunt. We heard a great many odd sounds on the sea and went down to the beach to see what they were. Not far from the shore we saw one of the great cloudboats. There were strange-looking spirits on it with seashells on their heads and seaweed growing from their faces. They called to us in loud harsh voices like crows and waved at us to swim out."

"Did you swim out to them?" asked Flathead Killer.

Red Dog frowned and shook his head. "No. Just as I am now in no hurry to go to the spirit world, neither was I in a hurry then."

The others laughed.

Calling Crow knew he must go and see if these things were a threat to his people. He regretted having to leave Tiamai, but he could not send other braves out on such a dangerous journey as his first act as Chief. He himself must go. He got to his feet, and the Old Men looked at him attentively. "I have made up my mind. I will go and find these things. Perhaps they are still where the Mountain People saw them. I must find out if they bring this Destroyer. I shall take two other braves with me."

Mennewah smiled sadly.

Calling Crow knew that if they traveled by foot they might not be able to catch the cloudboats, and so they

would have to take a canoe. Ever since his father's death
he had avoided traveling on the water when he could, but
this time he had no choice. "We will leave tomorrow."

Stepping out into the bright sunshine, Calling Crow saw
Tiamai and another maid across the way preparing a skin
for curing. Even though she wasn't turned his way, he
knew she had been watching and waiting and had seen
him exit the chokafa. His heart was not happy over leaving
her and for a moment he even thought of taking her with
them, but he knew he must not. This was not the time.
There were too many evil spirits about, too many signs.
He walked over and stood before her.

She stopped her scraping, but did not look up at him.

"I go to find these cloudboats tomorrow."

Tiamai put the sharp rock against the skin and continued
her scraping, saying nothing.

"I go because I must," said Calling Crow, "not because
I want to. I will return soon."

Tiamai looked up at him and smiled, warming his heart.
This was why he desired her so.

"I will be waiting," she said.

Chapter 6

The *Guadalupe* lay anchored peacefully in a cove protected by a long sandy spit of land. Sailors pounded and
sawed planks as they replaced the last of her blackened
timbers. The water beneath the ship was crystal clear, and
it was as if the ship sat suspended upon a great sheet of
Venetian crystal. Dozens of bright blue and yellow fish
moved gracefully below. Three fathoms down, large rocks
lay scattered across an expanse of dark sand. Senor

Francisco Mateo was resting in his cabin in the rear of the ship when two of his men pushed in a third. It was Juan Zacuto, a goatherd from Samana. The man was breathing heavily and looked at the other two in fright.

"He saw the one who set the fire," said Paco Nacrillo, one of Mateo's ranchero hands.

Mateo's intense eyes fixed on Zacuto, and the little man shrunk visibly. "Son of a whore," said Mateo, "is this true?"

Zacuto nodded, his eyes blinking rapidly.

"And you didn't say anything."

Zacuto shook his head, his eyes continuing their nervous fluttering.

Mateo thought of the fire. If they hadn't got it under control they would have had to crowd aboard the smaller ship and go home. The expedition would have been over and all the money he had invested wasted. He would have been ruined! He wanted to seize the little man by the throat, but he made no move. He would let the *Cabildo* decide his fate when they returned to the island. Now he would deal with the one who had started the conflagration.

"Who was it?" he said.

Zacuto trembled. "The big fat soldier, Garcia."

Mateo pushed his chair back and quickly got to his feet. He pulled on his sword and went outside, the others following.

"There's Roldan," said Paco, "but I don't see Garcia."

Senor Alonso Roldan was in his forties and of a small build, but he had a soldier's granite-hard strength obvious in his every limb, and unlike most men his age, there wasn't a spare ounce of fat on him.

Mateo angrily watched Roldan and his soldiers standing about idly near the landing boat. He walked up to Roldan. "Where is Senor Garcia?"

"Why do you want to know?"

Mateo heard a clatter and turned. Diego and some of his men ran up. They were wearing their swords. Mateo turned back to Roldan. "I'm going to put him in chains for setting my ship on fire."

Roldan scoffed. "You must be mad. What proof do you have?"

Mateo's face darkened. "One of my men saw him."

"Ah," said Roldan, "he was with me and my men all that night. Your man's a liar." Roldan walked over to the rail and spat over the side, glaring sullenly at Mateo.

Diego came up to Mateo. "Francisco, wait till we return to the island. Then we will deal with this."

Mateo shook his head and looked at his men. "Follow me," he said, starting for the steps to the below decks.

"Advance in line!" shouted Roldan, and his men pulled their swords as one. They quickly ran and blocked Mateo's path. Roldan slowly walked over.

Mateo turned round to his men. Farmers and ranchers, they were nervous confronting the eight soldiers before them. They knew they would get the worst of it in a fight. Mateo looked at Roldan.

"Call off your men and bring me Garcia! I give you one last chance."

Roldan stared coldly at him. "You are a fool if you think we will listen to your orders any longer."

Mateo turned to his men. "Draw your swords! If it's a fight he wants, we shall give him one."

The men nervously pulled their swords as they eyed the cold, unmoving faces of the soldiers arrayed before them.

"This has dragged on too long," said Roldan, ignoring Mateo as he addressed himself directly to the men on both sides. "My men have no fight with you. They simply wish to go back to the island, as you do also. Senor Mateo said we would be gone a month and a half and no longer, and it has been over two months now. . . ." Roldan held up his arms dramatically. "And we have seen no Indian villages, not a one!"

Mateo could feel the resolve of his men fading. His voice boomed out in a controlled roar, "I said we would be out until we located a sizable village, and that that would probably take a month and a half. Now disperse your men and see that they attend to their work."

Gaspar Hojeda, a small mestizo colonist, his dark oily

hair still mussed from his night's sleep, pushed up behind
Mateo. "Senor, please do not push the matter. I fear for
our lives."

Another colonist edged up behind him. *"Sí,"* he said in
hushed tones, "they are too strong for us to fight."

Mateo turned angrily to the two men. "Shut up!"

"I have a proposition," said Roldan. "Since it is my
man Garcia you want, why don't you and he fight a du-
ello? If Senor Garcia wins, then you shall give us the
Speeding Hound and we will go back to Santo Domingo.
If you win, then my men and I shall do your bidding."

Mateo thought quickly. Garcia was a large man with
pendulous breasts and a fat belly, but Mateo knew there
was much muscle under the fat. Back in Santo Domingo
he had seen Garcia win a bet by lifting an ass on his back.
Still, Mateo knew he himself was one of the best swords-
men on the island of Hispaniola. In the tourneys and fairs
they had held he had never been bested. As the sun beat
down on the bleached boards of the deck, radiating heat up
like an oven, Mateo knew he had to agree to it. His men
could never prevail against professional soldiers in a fight.

Diego put his hand on Mateo's shoulder. "Don't do it,
Francisco. I don't trust him."

Mateo turned to Diego. "I must do it. And I shall dis-
patch him quickly, you will see."

Mateo looked into Roldan's cold gray eyes. "I have
your word as a gentleman that if I win there will be no
more trouble?"

Roldan nodded. *"Sí."*

"It is agreed," said Mateo.

Roldan smiled as he walked over to the steps. Some of
his men began laughing conspiratorially. "Send Garcia
up," Roldan shouted down into the ship.

Mateo heard heavy footsteps sound from the below
decks. He watched in astonishment as Garcia came up the
steps wearing a three-quarter suit of armor with long, fully
articulated arm and thigh plates. Someone had polished the
metal to a gleaming silvery shine. Mail leggings encased
Garcia's stout thighs, and reinforcing plates hung on his

shins and knees. His feet were encased in heavy iron boots, and his hands in fully articulated finger gauntlets. The many ridges and scales gave him a gleaming, serpentine appearance. He carried a long, broad, two-handed sword over his shoulder. Garcia took the sword and stabbed the point of it into the deck. It was a head taller than he.

Mateo's blood pounded in his temples. He looked over at Roldan and bellowed, "You think such trickery will give you advantage, do you? Well, you watch. I shall open him up like a clam!"

Alonso Roldan smiled coldly and said nothing.

Taking a deep breath, Mateo turned his angry attention to Garcia. How, in God's name, he wondered, would he ever manage to puncture this fat grape of a fellow? He must find a way.

Mateo pulled his sword. "You shall pay for what you did the other night, Garcia."

Garcia spat at his feet and smoothed his beard down against his metal breastplate. Light, hurried footsteps came from below. Miramor, the fourteen-year-old Moorish ship's boy, emerged carrying a comb morion helmet with a graceful upswept brim. He gave it a few furtive wipes with a polishing cloth and, poised on his toes, pulled it over Garcia's head and secured the leather thongs. A moment later the rest of the soldiers came up on deck, talking in low, excited voices.

Mateo frowned. "I had no idea you were so well equipped," he said to Garcia. "Such extravagance for a poor soldier, I do not understand."

"*Sí*, Senor Mateo, you are right," said Garcia sarcastically. "I am a poor soldier and only the helmet belongs to me. The arm plates are Rivera's, the suit, Nuno's. The rest of these things belong to the other soldiers. You see, they all have a stake in the outcome, and we all know of your expertise with a blade. Therefore they insisted that I wear these things to even the odds." Garcia made this last statement with a loud show of smiling bravado and the soldiers laughed. They moved away from him and into a wide circle, eyeing Mateo and his men.

Garcia raised the sword, testing its weight. "You better hope that God will be more merciful with you than I."

Mateo scoffed. "God? What does a pig know of God?" Some of the men laughed nervously. Mateo shifted his weight from side to side, preparing himself. He would have to use his own lightness and speed to advantage, but was that enough? This walking, metal-encased sausage would cut him in half with that broadsword if he connected. Mateo looked around quickly and saw a possible answer to his problem in the sparkle of the sea.

"Francisco!" came Diego's worried voice. "Here, put this on." He ran up and quickly enclosed Mateo within a rusting breastplate which was hinged like a clamshell. Diego secured the leather ties and quickly backed away.

The sun had climbed halfway to its zenith and now burned down powerfully on the two men. Garcia advanced slowly and cautiously, his heavy sword held high with both hands. Mateo moved in quickly, striking a blow to Garcia's shoulder that glanced off harmlessly. Garcia's sword whistled overhead as Mateo ducked quickly and rolled away.

"I will toss you overboard today and then we shall go home," said Garcia as he quickly recovered his momentum and stalked after Mateo.

Mateo feigned a lunge and, after Garcia half-completed his swing, jumped in to deliver a stinging blow to Garcia's mail-encased legs. Cursing in fury, Garcia ran heavily and slowly at Mateo, swinging the huge two-handed sword powerfully in a wide arc. Mateo backed up nimbly, bringing his sword up to fend off the blow. The shock of it numbed his hand, and before he could recover, Garcia's sword was again arcing across at him. Mateo brought his sword up late, and Garcia's blade clanged loudly against it, breaking it in half.

Garcia's men broke into a cheer and crowded closer. Mateo fell to the deck and rolled clear. Garcia pointed his great sword at Mateo and lumbered forward powerfully.

Mateo tried to get close enough to deliver a blow with the broken sword and found it impossible. Determinedly he parried blow after powerful blow as Garcia, breathing heavily, advanced unrelentingly. A wide swing from Garcia clanged into Mateo's sword, knocking him to his knees. Mateo's sword went flying. His right arm and hand were numb from the shock, and he used his left to push himself up off the deck.

"Son of a monkey-fucking Indian!" cried Garcia in triumph. "Now I shall cut you open and feed your shit to the fishes!" He ran at Mateo in his lumbering gait, his sword held high. Mateo danced backward nimbly as the wide blade sliced right and left. Backed up against the rail, he dove out of the way as Garcia brought his sword down, driving it deeply into the oaken rail. As Garcia struggled to free it, Mateo got to his feet and jumped at him. Garcia yanked the blade free just as Mateo's hands closed around the hilt. They struggled and fell to the deck. Cursing furiously, they got to their feet, each not relinquishing his death grip on the sword. Mateo slammed Garcia back hard against the rail, and the crowd roared as he struck hard at Garcia's unprotected face. Garcia returned the blows, his metal gauntlet–encased fists bloodying Mateo's face as they fought for possession of the sword. With one hand on Garcia's fat neck, Mateo pushed him out over the rail. Fear blossomed on Garcia's face as he suddenly realized what Mateo was attempting. Mateo felt a mild swell heel the boat over slightly and at that moment dug his feet into the wooden deck and pushed with all his strength. Garcia fell backward, his one hand tearing at Mateo's hair. Still clutching the great sword, Garcia splashed into the water and sank quickly like a large stone.

The men crowded about the rail. "Get a rope," shouted Roldan, and his men rushed toward the rigging.

Mateo quickly took Paco's sword and thrust it into Roldan's face. "If any of you touch a rope, I will kill him."

The soldiers looked at each other, each waiting for the other to make a move.

Diego ran over. "Francisco, you have won! It is over. Now we must bring him up or we are no better than they."

Mateo never took his eyes off Roldan. "I'm sorry, Diego. They have made their decision and now they must pay for it."

"Look, in the water," cried Miramor, "he moves!"

The men turned away and rushed back to the rail to look over the side. Garcia could be seen below, slowly waving his sword aloft as great silvery bubbles left his mouth and floated upward. In the brightly lit depths, his polished armor shone like mother-of-pearl. Turning, he used the sword as a staff and began walking in the direction of the beach, clouds of silt spreading out behind him. The soldiers leaned over the rail as they cheered and screamed encouragement. After a few moments Garcia stopped and looked round to get his bearings. The brown cloud of silt that had been following him now engulfed him, obscuring him. The shouting died.

Diego grabbed Mateo's arm. "Francisco, by all that's holy, throw him a rope!"

Mateo turned away from him and looked down with the others.

Garcia crawled out from the brown cloud, and the men erupted in cheers. Paco pushed through to the rail, pointing to the sandy beach. "That way, senor, that way. It is not far!"

Shouting began anew as Garcia slowly got to his feet. Evidently having seen Paco's outstretched arm, Garcia headed in the proper direction and the men roared in approval. Some of the men looked back to sneer at Mateo while others exchanged money as they bet on the outcome. Garcia lumbered along the sandy bottom, the shouting of the men growing in intensity as he moved further and further away from the ship, and then he dropped the sword. Falling to his knees, he crawled a few steps more as the shouting died and then he pitched forward, rolling onto his back. A single shining silver bubble the size of an orange left his mouth and wobbled its way to the surface as his arms came to rest, curled around like a babe's.

Miramor began crying, and Diego went to him, pulling him from the rail. "It's over, boy. Go below."

Mateo stared into Roldan's eyes. "And now I shall expect your full cooperation."

Roldan said nothing.

Mateo shouted to his men. "Ready the boat to take the horses ashore. We shall find some water and provisions."

The men left the rail slowly and reluctantly as they went about their tasks.

Chapter 7

Calling Crow sat in the middle of the canoe, paddling furiously as he watched the ominous dark clouds building. Runs Like Deer sat forward of him, the muscles in his back rippling rhythmically as they raced the squall for the land.

Calling Crow called back to his cousin, Big Nose, who was steering. "Can we reach the land in time?"

"Yes, I think so."

Calling Crow wasn't so sure as he gauged the distance to the land. A sudden gust of wind slammed broadside into the canoe, sending stinging spray into their faces. Looking downwind, they saw the same wind taking the tops off the white waves as it made a moaning sound. *"Aieyah,"* said Calling Crow quietly, as the image of his father's overturned canoe kept drifting into his head. He prayed to the Great Spirit to calm the waters as his heart throbbed in his chest like a large fish tossed into a canoe. For two days now they had been paddling steadily south and had seen no evidence of the cloudboats. He decided that if they survived the storm, they would look for two more days and then go home.

Two gulls suddenly appeared low overhead. They headed toward the land, but north of the direction the canoe was taking. Calling Crow saw it as a sign, an answer to his prayer to the Great Spirit.

"Turn about," he shouted to Big Nose. "Follow the gulls."

Big Nose quickly turned the canoe toward the disappearing gulls. A few moments later they saw the gulls sitting on the calm waters of a small bay on the other side of a thin spit of land.

"Paddle for there," said Calling Crow. Just then a hard rain came down, punching holes in the sea where it fell. They paddled quickly, barely able to make out the land on the now gray, featureless horizon. They continued their furious paddling, and when they were the distance of an arrow's flight from the beach the storm suddenly stopped. Runs Like Deer turned round and raised his arms, giving out a victory cry. Calling Crow and Big Nose joined in joyfully. Calling Crow was about to tell Big Nose to head in to the beach when he noticed a large group of gulls congregating on the water, some of them sticking their heads beneath the surface. Intrigued, he told Big Nose to steer for the spot.

As they approached, the gulls worriedly took wing, singly and in pairs, until there were none. Big Nose paddled the dugout in a circle while Calling Crow and Runs Like Deer peered into the depths.

"What is it?" said Runs Like Deer.

A dark mass could be seen resting on the bottom. As Calling Crow studied it through the undulations of the waves he saw that it was either a large man such as he had never seen before, or a spirit. It seemed to be moving ever so slowly toward the beach.

Calling Crow and the others leaned closer to the surface of the water to see it more clearly. It wore a great silver seashell on its head and a great mass of seaweed grew from its face, moving in the water like a ghostfish. Its eyes were dark and cavernous and expressed a deep sadness. Calling Crow and the others were not sure whether it was alive or dead.

Runs Like Deer extended the full length of his lance into the water to prod the thing. At that moment the surge picked up again, moving the thing forward a bit and turning the great head as if it were trying to look up at its tormentors.

"Aieyah!" said Runs Like Deer, drawing back to hide in the dugout. "It moves!" They watched in awe as it slid over the small rocks and continued its snail's pace toward the beach.

Calling Crow turned to Big Nose, who continued to maneuver the dugout. "Let us go in. We will wait for it there."

A short while later the form broke the surface of the water and did not move. They slowly waded into the sea toward it. Calling Crow held his knife outstretched; Big Nose put an arrow to his bow; and Runs Like Deer raised his lance to the ready. Runs Like Deer prodded the manlike thing with his lance as it lay on its back. Nothing happened.

"Let's pull it out of the water," said Calling Crow.

The other two grabbed the thing by its legs and they dragged it up onto the sand. It was very big. Big Nose jabbed at the gleaming shell-like skin. His lance glanced off with a loud clatter none of them had ever heard before.

"It has magic skin," said Big Nose.

"Aieyah," said Runs Like Deer.

"There are some openings in it," said Calling Crow. He took an arrow from his quiver and pushed it between two segments of the magic skin. A froth of blood bubbled out.

"It is like a man," said Runs Like Deer, "it bleeds."

"Yes," said Calling Crow, "and it is dead."

"I will make sure," said Big Nose. He walked off and returned with a rock the size of his fist. Kneeling down, he pounded the arrow into the creature's body. A powerful blow snapped the arrow off and the rock struck the strange man in the abdomen.

"Aieyah!" said Big Nose, as a large pink bubble emerged from the creature's mouth, reflecting sun and sky.

Big Nose jumped back, ready to attack, but the creature didn't move. The bubble burst, and Calling Crow knelt and pulled at the magic skin. A section of it came loose. He plunged his knife into the man-thing's purple flesh and it went deep. Nothing happened. Satisfied, Calling Crow got to his feet.

"That is enough," said Calling Crow. "It is dead and cannot hurt us or it already would have tried. Come. We must find a place to spend the night."

They camped high on the beach behind a huge fallen tree. Calling Crow pulled his bark blanket about him as he looked up at the mass of stars spilled across the black sky. Low on the horizon the Hunter could be seen stalking his prey, while the surf rumbled and hissed like a chorus of drums and chanting voices. The wind moaned steadily across the sand, and periodically an owl called out. It was all beauty, he thought, a song of beauty to the Great Spirit, but he could not truly appreciate it. The specter of the Destroyer waited just beyond the edge of his dreams, like an enemy in the darkness outside the glow of the fire, and it troubled him deeply. What did the strange creature down on the beach have to do with the Destroyer? If only in his vision he had been able to see the face of the Destroyer. Then he would be able to recognize it when he found it. He could never rest until he was sure that it had gone far, far away from his people and Tumaqua. He thought of these things for some time and then the sound of Big Nose's and Runs Like Deer's voices suddenly roused him.

"What do you think of the thing from the water?" said Runs Like Deer.

"I don't know," said Big Nose. "It is a bad thing. I am sure of that."

"Calling Crow," said Runs Like Deer, "what do you think?"

"Remember what Mennewah said," said Calling Crow. "He said that if the creatures fall from the cloudboats onto the land then they will die. Perhaps this one ventured onto the land and died before he could get back onto his cloudboat." As he said this, Calling Crow hoped that the cloudboats were truly gone and not just waiting in the sea out of sight. The other two men grew silent as they pondered Calling Crow's words. Soon they slept.

Despite their brooding thoughts, the night was good. The sea sang to them and an owl remained nearby, calling out all during the night, unafraid. In the morning they separated briefly to bathe in the sea and pray. When they came together Calling Crow led them down the beach to see if the creature was still there. The tide had pulled it back out into the surf, but it was still exposed and a small cloud of gulls covered it, screaming and flapping their wings.

"See?" said Calling Crow. "The gulls are eating it. Whatever it is, it is dead. Come, let us search for a stream."

They walked the beach for most of the morning and then Runs Like Deer spotted something in the sand ahead. When they drew near they saw it was the tracks of four men who had come out of the trees. By the looks of the footprints, they had grossly deformed flat feet, with no evidence of toes, and they had been carrying heavy loads.

They followed the tracks for most of the afternoon, pausing briefly in several places to rest. When the sun began to sink low over the forest, they came upon a large dune that stretched from the forest down to the beach.

"Let us rest here," said Calling Crow, and they sat down in a weed-filled depression at the base of the dune. Out of the constant blast of wind and sand, Calling Crow's skin warmed and tingled as he thought of the strange events of the past days. Who were the men who had left these prints? The Flathead People never came this far north. Perhaps the Mountain People were now hunting in this land. If that was so, he would have to meet with the Council of Old Men and the other braves to discuss it. As Calling Crow thought these things, he watched a line of pelicans slowly making their way up the coast. They flew angled out toward the sea as they struggled against the strong breeze.

"Listen," said Big Nose, "what is that?"

Calling Crow stood, exposing his head to the constant wind that filled his ear with noise, and listened carefully. There was a small sound in the wind, a different, repetitive sound. He looked down the beach from where they had come, as Big Nose and Runs Like Deer got to their feet and looked toward the tree line, searching for the source of the noise. It was a sound none of them had ever heard before. It had a deliberate quality, as if someone were chipping an arrowhead, but no rock made a sound like that. Calling Crow nocked an arrow into his bow. He looked at his friends. "It must be coming from the other side of the dune."

Calling Crow led the way up the dune. When they reached the crest they froze. At the bottom were a dozen or so of the strangest, manlike creatures they had ever seen. Resembling the creature they had found in the sea, they were pale of color and had long hair growing wildly out of their faces. Some were dressed in fine brown or tan skins cut from some unknown creature. Incredibly, one wore a garment more green than the greenest tree in the forest, while another wore a coat bluer than the sea seen from a hill on a summer day. Some of the creatures had the large silver shells on their heads, and they sat in the sand, talking and laughing. Calling Crow motioned Big Nose and Runs Like Deer to crouch down out of sight. When they were hidden, he turned to Runs Like Deer and said in a soft voice, "Take the canoe and go back to Tumaqua. Tell them we have found this Destroyer and his army of demons. Tell them to bring all the braves and we will kill him here!"

Runs Like Deer nodded grimly. He moved away and quietly crept down the dune. Looking back only once, he took off at a run. Calling Crow and Big Nose watched him in silence until he disappeared around the curve of the beach and then they crept back up again to watch the strange creatures.

"Aieyah!" said Big Nose. "Look!"

Calling Crow watched in disbelief as one of the creatures used a clawlike hand to remove a glowing coal from a smoking box. He then held the coal against a black rock and beat it with a club, producing the same striking sound they had heard earlier. Holding it close to his face to inspect it, he seemed satisfied. He then dipped it into a large gourd full of water and it bubbled and hissed.

"Like a hot rock dropped in a soup," said Calling Crow quietly to Big Nose.

Big Nose nodded, and they both continued to stare.

Another creature got to his feet and squeezed a skin of some kind back and forth, and it wailed and shrieked as if alive. Two others got up and danced as if overjoyed at its tortured cries. In astounded silence, Calling Crow and Big Nose watched these and the other activities of the strange creatures until the shadows grew long. They were about to back away down the dune to find a place to hide for the night when they spotted another strange creature far away on the beach. Approaching at an incredible speed, it raced through the surf, kicking up a froth. Calling Crow and Big Nose were so overwhelmed by the sight that they made no move to hide themselves. The creature was much bigger than the others and appeared to be half hairy-faced demon, half huge, four-legged beast. The top half had hair like fire and swung a long knife of some kind, while shouting an alarm in a loud squawking voice. When it drew closer the men below suddenly turned as one to look up at Calling Crow and Big Nose. The shock of discovery broke the spell that had frozen them, and they turned and ran down the dune.

"Quick," said Calling Crow, "into the trees."

As they ran for the tree line they heard horrible shrieks of laughter behind them. Calling Crow turned briefly and was relieved to see that the demon men were falling behind. Moments later his relief turned to horror. The large, four-legged creature was racing after them, gaining quickly.

Calling Crow's heart pounded in his ears as they ran for

the green safety of the forest. He ran faster than he had ever run before, but soon he could hear the creature's labored breaths and its hooves thudding in the sand behind them. He turned his head and saw that it was so close the man half could look him in the eyes. Big Nose nocked an arrow into his bow as they ran. He turned quickly and released it, the arrow going high over the creature's head. Calling Crow put an arrow in his bow. He stopped and turned, taking aim. As soon as he released it, he felt a surge of triumph, knowing it had gone true. Then, he watched in horror as the arrow glanced noisily off the creature's magic skin. Calling Crow drew his knife and stood his ground to fight, but the creature raced past him, knocking Big Nose to the ground.

Big Nose tumbled, throwing up a spray of sand, and the creature shrieked as it raced past. Calling Crow tried to get another arrow nocked, but the creature had wheeled about and was upon him almost immediately. Suddenly looming huge, it struck him with its flank, knocking him away as if he were a mere fly. Calling Crow sprawled breathless upon the sand. He struggled to his feet, looking about him for his bow, but the creature had already scooped it up. It now circled them. Big Nose struggled to get to his feet, and Calling Crow ran to help him. He heard a shout from behind and turned. The band of shouting demons would soon overcome them. Calling Crow stopped and again drew his knife. He screamed out a war cry and it filled him with strength as he waited for the demons and the charging four-legged creature.

The four-legged beast reached him first. It raised its long knife in the air. Again Calling Crow gave out a war cry. The huge creature thundered at him and he dodged to the side, but not quickly enough. The creature's flanks barely brushed him, but the force was enough to knock him flying. He looked to the sky and the sun broke into many suns as a thousand screams sounded in his ears. He struggled to his feet as the demon men surrounded him. Shrieking in their strange language, they prodded him with their knives and spears. Calling Crow lunged for one of them as others seized him tightly from behind. As his hands sought a white hairy throat, something crashed hard into his head and he fell back onto the sand.

Chapter 8

Diego spotted Miramor by the spring that fed the small creek. The boy had run away that morning and had not been seen all day. He sat in the shade of the trees with his feet in the shallow water. His head was down, and his body had an attitude of great suffering. Diego knew that only God's grace could relieve his sorrows, but the boy was a converted Moor, or Morisco, and not very knowledgeable of the Faith.

Diego pushed into the grove. "What is bothering you, boy?"

The boy shook his head. "Nothing, senor. There is nothing anymore."

Diego frowned. "Don't grieve anymore for the soldier, Garcia. He shall have a chance to stand before God and plead his case with Him. Perhaps he shall even get into heaven."

The boy looked at him hopefully.

Diego's face grew more serious. "God is merciful, boy. You must pray for Him to mete out some of His mercy to your Senor Garcia."

The boy stared off into the darkness of the forest. "I've forgotten how to pray. I no longer know the words."

Diego shook his head. "It is of no matter. I will teach you and then we shall get back to the boats. There are some who are worried about you."

Diego got down on his knees and the boy did the same.

"Lord God Almighty," Diego intoned in his phlegmy voice, "please be merciful to this boy's friend who shall soon come before you." Diego turned to the boy. "We shall now say the Lord's Prayer."

As the boy repeated the words after Diego, a column of men moved through the thick green forest, carrying sacks of fruit and clay jars full of water. Alonso Roldan, who was in the lead, spotted Diego and Miramor ahead by the stream. Those behind him were not placed to see them. Intrigued, Roldan held up his hand for the column to stop. From his vantage, he could hear the faint drone of Diego's voice as the old believer led the boy in prayers. Diego made the sign of the cross and got to his feet. The boy followed suit.

Manuel Ortiz tapped Roldan on the shoulder. "What is it? What do you see?"

"Quiet," hissed Roldan.

A moment later, Diego Vega and Miramor came out of the grove and walked off toward the beach, unaware of the men watching them.

Roldan turned round to Manuel Ortiz. "Let's go. Pass the word back."

The men continued walking along the forest trail till they found a sandy path. They turned and came out onto the beach. Their boots dug deep into the soft sand, and they carried their loads with great difficulty. Slowly they headed for two boats which were drawn up on the shore. Senor Alonso Roldan and his young friend and lieutenant, Manuel Ortiz, were empty-handed as they trudged along at the head of the little column. Ortiz turned his boyish face to Roldan.

"That cursed Mateo will not be back for a while. He thinks he can find where those two Indians we captured came from, but these monkeys leave no track a man can follow."

Senor Roldan nodded without looking at him. "Did they interrogate them?"

"*Sí*, they tried to, but they got nothing out of them."

Manuel Ortiz wiped his brow with the back of his hand. "What an utter waste of time this trip has been."

Senor Roldan nodded. "That it has, and for that and for Senor Garcia's death, Francisco Mateo shall pay. Though it takes me a hundred years, I shall make him pay!"

Senors Roldan and Ortiz and the column of soldiers reached the boats. The soldiers put down their heavy jars gratefully, some sitting down immediately in the hot sand to rest. Others went over to the smaller of the two boats where one of the Indians lay chained up.

Roldan walked over and leaned into the boat to look at the Indian. He was filled with contempt. The Indian was naked but for a strip of animal skin between his buttocks and a few feathers in his hair. Subhumans, they were as stupid as monkeys and as sullen and stubborn as mules. And they couldn't do half the work a black could do, which made them almost worthless. If it had not been for the meddling Fathers, the Conquistadors would have exterminated them all years ago. He turned to Ortiz.

"Where is the other bare-ass?"

"They have already taken him out to the ship for the barber to patch up. When Mateo's horse knocked him down, he must have landed on a rock. It opened up his head and broke his arm."

"It does not matter. One or two, it does not exactly make for a fortune."

"True," said Ortiz. "But what amazing specimens they are, eh? They are as big as blacks."

Roldan nodded. He was annoyed at Ortiz for telling him the obvious. He had already been calculating what he could get for thirty or forty as big as the two caught on the beach.

Roldan looked around and turned back to Ortiz. "Where are the rest of these fool colonists?"

Ortiz looked over at the boat. "There's Roberto and two other farmers. I don't know where Vasquez, the harelip, is. Pelagro, the fat Genovese, is on the *Hound*."

Senor Roldan turned aside and spat. "Come with me. We have work to do."

They walked to the other long boat which was half loaded with clay water jars. Roldan pointed to two coils of rope. "Grab the ropes and find Hotea the Indian to interpret for me."

Ortiz leaned into the boat and grabbed the ropes.

Roldan looked at the bright green of the forest behind them. "I'll find out where the rest of the bare-asses are hiding."

Calling Crow was lying on his back, tied down in a great canoe on the beach. In a rage he tried to free his hands from the cords which bound them, cords as hard as stone. Earlier, before they had put him in the great canoe, the big, fire-haired, four-legged creature and an old silver-headed demon had attempted to speak to him. Their voices were like dogs trying to speak like men, and he could understand nothing they said.

In anger and frustration Calling Crow again shook the cords like stone on his hands. The demon men leaned over the canoe to look down at him and laugh at his efforts. A very pale-faced demon man smiled, showing a tooth that shined like the sun. "*¿Cuál es su nombre?*" he said.

Calling Crow stared at his glowing tooth. "Release me!" he demanded.

The demon man thought this very funny and laughed loudly, turning to share something with the others. More pale hairy heads leaned down to scrutinize Calling Crow. The demon man with the shining tooth tapped himself proudly on the chest. "*Yo soy Roberto,*" he said. "*Ro . . . berr . . . to.*" Then he poked Calling Crow's chest.

"I am Calling Crow," said Calling Crow slowly, amazed at the exchange. Were these men? They seemed so strange and had such great powers.

Shining Tooth attempted to repeat Calling Crow's name and gave up. He moved out of view as he turned to talk to the others. Loud laughter followed. Suddenly a young man with hair like sea grass was looking down at Calling Crow. The others crowded about him.

Sea Grass Hair shouted and raised his long knife. Call-

ing Crow thought he was going to kill him, but instead Sea
Grass Hair sliced the cords tying him down and pulled
him roughly out of the canoe and to his feet. Calling Crow
looked about him for an escape route, but they surrounded
him. A short, smooth-faced man approached. His skin was
much darker than the others. Calling Crow's eyes widened
in shock as Dark Skin spoke to him using signs and some
heavily accented words from Calling Crow's own tongue.

"I am Hotea," he said. "These men are from a land
across the great water." Hotea slowly sounded the name of
the land. "Castile. They have come across the waters because their king has given them these lands to govern in
his name."

Calling Crow forgot his amazement as anger welled up
within him. He frowned and raised his arms, rattling the
stone ropes they had put upon them as he used signs and
some of his own words to reply. "Surely you lie, for how
can their king give away something which is not his,
something he has never laid his eyes upon?"

Hotea smiled sadly and said something in the harsh
tones of the others. Then Sea Grass Hair shouted menacingly at Calling Crow. Hotea translated. "He wants to
know where your village is."

Calling Crow looked at Sea Grass Hair and then at
Hotea. "I have no village." A great sorrow suddenly came
over Calling Crow as Hotea translated. Had the time come
for his tribe to perish? Was Sea Grass Hair the Destroyer
in his vision?

Hotea pointed at Sea Grass Hair as he spoke to Calling
Crow. "This man is Manuel Ortiz. He will kill you if you
don't tell him where your village is. You must tell him."

Calling Crow stared at the man called Ortiz for a few
moments. "I have no village."

Hotea translated, and Ortiz stepped forward and struck
Calling Crow in the face. Calling Crow grabbed for him
with his bound hands, and two men seized him from behind. There was a great deal of loud talking, and then another older man stepped forward and pushed Sea Grass
Hair out of the way. He spoke to Hotea. The others smiled

at his words and stepped back a few paces. Calling Crow wondered what the older man had said to make the others smile.

Hotea turned to Calling Crow. "This man is Senor Roldan. He has great medicine. He said that if you don't tell us where your village is, he will call down thunder and lightning upon you."

Calling Crow scowled as he spoke. "Not only are you all liars, but you are all crazy as well."

Hotea told Roldan what Calling Crow had said. Roldan then picked up a tall stick with many carvings on it and slowly approached Calling Crow. He set one end of the stick on the ground beside Calling Crow and knelt down. Calling Crow saw many strange dwellings carved into the stick. There was even a large buck deer carved there. Toward the bottom of the long stick a small piece of smoking kindling was attached. The man called Roldan smiled at Calling Crow and squeezed the stick. There was a clicking sound, like a branch snapped underfoot, and a moment later the tall stick erupted in thunder and smoke. Calling Crow jumped and ran, knocking one man down before the others pushed him roughly to the sand. Several demon men piled on Calling Crow to hold him on the ground. His heart beat like the wings of a captured bird and his mind raced. The demon men had great horrible powers but he must not tell them about Tumaqua. He must tell them something else; perhaps he could set them off on the wrong trail.

Someone drove his foot into Calling Crow's side and he looked up. The one called Roldan looked down at Calling Crow as if he were a diseased dog. Hotea repeated Roldan's demand that Calling Crow tell him the location of his village.

Calling Crow coughed as he spoke to Hotea. "My friend and I were taken prisoner by another tribe a long time ago. They took us far away from our village to this strange place and we have only now managed to escape. I am not even sure about where I am."

Hotea translated, and Roldan smiled. He spoke in dog-growling tones to Hotea. Hotea nodded and looked down at Calling Crow.

"Where do your captors live?"

Calling Crow pointed west. "It is three days' march into the forest toward the setting sun."

Hotea translated, and Roldan the demon man studied Calling Crow for a moment. Then all the demon men turned as one to look in the distance.

Calling Crow watched through red, angry eyes as two of the huge four-legged creatures which had run him and Big Nose down earlier now raced toward him. They drew up a few feet away with hideous squeals and snorts, pawing the earth and throwing up a cloud of sand. Calling Crow watched in amazement as the top fire-haired, manlike half of one creature disengaged itself from the lower four-legged half. Then Calling Crow realized that each of these things was really two separate creatures, one a huge demon dog, the other a demon man riding on the top.

Hotea said to Calling Crow, "That is Senor Mateo. He is the chief of these people."

The fire-haired demon man who was called Mateo glanced briefly at Calling Crow before turning to speak to the demon man called Roldan.

Calling Crow could tell by the exchange between the two men that Roldan was Mateo Fire Hair's bitter enemy. Fire Hair addressed Roldan in angry, barking tones, and then Roldan responded in words that were colder than the water at the bottom of the sea. Calling Crow could see that each of the two men wanted very much to kill the other. The other demon men moved away suddenly, and Calling Crow saw a big canoe moving quickly through the surf toward him. Rising from its center was a tall thin tree, and hanging from this was a great skin which blew in the wind. When it drew close, a dozen demon men quickly pulled down the skin and jumped out to pull the canoe up onto the shore. Fire Hair issued orders, and the men secured many ropes to the demon dogs, pushing and tugging them into the center of the great canoe. Next, rough hands seized Calling Crow and he was lowered into the other ca-

noe. He tried to raise his head to see where they were going, but the sides of the canoe were too high to see over
and the effort caused him great pain. He blacked out and
awoke for a brief moment later to see a demon dog being
hoisted up the side of a great cloudboat by many ropes as
it snorted and wailed.

The demon men roughly pushed Calling Crow down
into the belly of the cloudboat. It was dark, but his nose
told him they were putting him into some kind of animal's
pen. His body felt afire and he was very weak from some
kind of spell they had cast upon him. As his eyes adjusted
to the darkness, he saw a figure lying not far away. He
crawled through the dry grasses lying on the ground. It
was Big Nose. As Calling Crow's eyes adjusted to the dim
light, he saw that red spots covered his cousin's face and
his mouth hung open in the heat.

"Aieyah," said Calling Crow. "Big Nose, are you well?"

Big Nose said nothing, and Calling Crow put his hand
on his brow. It burned like a rock exposed to the summer
afternoon's sun. He, too, must be under the powerful spell
of the demon men. Calling Crow shook Big Nose again
and, getting no response, crawled back over to the door of
the pen. He tried to undo the cords that secured it, but they
were as cool as stone and just as strong. Suddenly the
cloudboat groaned and leaned over dizzyingly. Calling
Crow knew they were moving and a horrible thought
struck him. What if they somehow found his village of
Tumaqua? The thought sickened him and he crawled back
over to Big Nose. He lay his hand on Big Nose's head. It
was cool to the touch now.

Big Nose opened his eyes slowly. "What spell is this
they . . ."

Calling Crow leaned closer as Big Nose closed his eyes
and his voice trailed off. Calling Crow listened closely, but
the only sound he heard was the creaking of the big trees
woven into the belly of the cloudboat. Calling Crow shook
him. "Big Nose, what is it?"

Big Nose grabbed Calling Crow's arm and his eyes

opened wide. They seemed to look through Calling Crow. "Forgive me ... I am leaving you alone in this place."

As Calling Crow looked down at his friend, a fly landed on one of Big Nose's watery, sightless eyes. Another fly lit on his cheek, rubbing its back legs as it circled in a death dance. Calling Crow cried out in sorrow, but the spell the demon men had put upon him strangled the sound in his throat.

For a long time he lay unmoving in the darkness. Then, the one called Hotea and an old gray-haired demon man opened the gate to his pen. They brought food for him, but Calling Crow was too weak to eat it. When the demon men saw that Big Nose had died, they carried him out and Calling Crow felt as if they had taken his spirit away as well. He lay back and felt himself spinning down, as if into the bottom of the cold sea.

Chapter 9

Miramor, the ship's boy, climbed the stairs from the gundeck, his bare feet slapping the oaken beams. The lamp he carried created a wobbly pool of yellow light around him, the only light visible on this night. The moon and stars were completely obscured by a low layer of thick marine clouds. Still groggy from his sleep, he tried to remember the dream he had been dreaming only a few moments ago when he had been awakened for his watch. It was the vineyard; he remembered lying in the grass at the edge of Senor Gaspar's vineyard, the sun warming his skin, while he and another boy watched a column of ants moving across the ground like the brave soldiers of De Sole, the great Conquistador. As Miramor headed for the ship's rail to feel his way forward, he wondered if they would ever get back to Santo Domingo. All the things that had happened crowded into his head suddenly: Garcia's drowning, the horrible man, Mateo, the kindness of old Diego. When would it all end? he wondered. When would they go home?

Reaching the rail, Miramor heard the faint sound of the surf in the distance and turned to look. "By all the saints!" he cried. "Why, there must be four dozen of them or more!"

There, in the distant blackness, dozens and dozens of fires burned brightly.

It must be a village of hundreds, he thought, as he watched the flickering lights reflected on the rolling black waves. He ran toward the stairs leading up to the poop. "Indians!" he cried. "There are Indians on the shores!"

After the sun had risen halfway to its zenith, a fair breeze began to blow off the land. The sailors and soldiers on the decks of the *Guadalupe* and the *Speeding Hound* congregated in groups and watched the shore. They were pointing and laughing at about a dozen Indians who had ventured shyly out of the trees as far as the water's edge. To the amusement and delight of the men, the Indians were almost naked, the men wearing only a thin loincloth over their genitals and the women only a skirt of grass or weeds, leaving their breasts exposed. The Indians could be seen pointing back at the ships and waving. Even though there were dozens of small dugout canoes drawn up on the beach, the Indians made no attempt to come out to the ships.

Senor Francisco Mateo stood next to Diego. Diego's hand was wrapped in a rough woolen bandage. The barber had wrapped the burns in some spiderwebs he'd found in the below decks and that had sped up the healing process. Both men were silent as they took in the scene. After a while Mateo turned to Diego. "They are not as big as the two fellows we caught at latitude thirty-two," he said, "but they still appear bigger and stronger than the Arawaks."

"*Sí,*" said Diego, "they evidently have a good life here and plenty to eat."

As Mateo watched the Indians on the beach, he worried about Diego's state of mind. He could see a storm brewing in there. "Diego," he said, trying to gauge the man's mood, "how many do you think there are?"

Diego's eyes narrowed as he took account of the village. "Based on the number of huts, I would estimate at least two or three hundred."

Mateo laughed quietly. "And all of them almost as naked as the day they were born."

Diego frowned. "What need have they of clothes? Did Adam and Eve wear clothes?"

"No," said Mateo, his tone becoming more serious, "and neither do little children need clothes. But once they're baptized and grow up, then they're better off with them, eh?"

"They would be better off if we put to sea right now and left them alone."

"Ah," said Mateo, "you think too much." He laughed good-naturedly. "If this is allowed by the Council of the Indies, then I shall lose no sleep over it."

Mateo watched Diego, knowing the man was intensely sad. But it was a misplaced sadness. It could not change the world. "Diego, their world is rapidly coming to an end. It is far better that we find them than some of the others, eh?"

Diego sighed. "I was very wrong to agree to such a thing as this. If there were a way home I would leave now."

"Come," said Mateo. "Your sadness is uncalled for. Our prayers have been answered. Now these soldiers will no longer cause trouble. And those Indians on the beach, why, even they will benefit. They will have to work, but so does every peasant in Castile. But they will be baptized and taught God's laws."

Despite his own words, Mateo felt Diego's melancholy infecting him. He looked at the Indians and tried to shake it off. They were more victims of their own primitiveness than they were of the colony, so why should he feel bad about this?

Mateo patted Diego on the back. "You and I, my friend, we shall be much richer than when we left Santo Domingo."

"*Sí,*" said Diego, "we shall receive our thirty pieces of silver."

Mateo was about to reply when one of the sailors called up to them that the boats were ready.

Mateo and Diego climbed into the first boat, and it was lowered with a great deal of squeaks and clatter and shouted orders. The crowd of Indians on the beach thinned as the boats neared, and by the time they landed, there were only a couple of dozen left. These were old men and women who stood close to one another with fearful expressions on their faces.

Mateo led his men up toward the dwellings which were scattered among the trees at the edge of the forest. He formed three squads of four men each, one arquebusman and one crossbowman among each. He addressed them on the sand under the hot sun.

"Fan out and search at least a league into the forest. The others may have cleared out for good, or they may be hiding, waiting to strike. Use your arquebuses to signal if you come under attack."

The men nodded grimly and walked off.

Mateo led the way up into the village. He stopped before the first of the huts. In the topmost branches of a tall pine tree just behind it, a large blackbird crowed a warning at them, as if left behind by the Indians with instructions to guard the village. Mateo and the others laughed at its threatening tone and went inside.

The hut was a simple affair, its circular walls made of woven cane, with empty racks or shelves upon which the natives evidently slept. From a pole running across the top hung a few small animal skins. Finding nothing of interest, they walked outside and into the next hut.

"Over here," said a small mestizo colonist named Rodriguez. He spoke softly in a voice one would use in church. "Look at this." He stood before a sort of tapestry with smooth colored stones woven into it. It was a scene of half a dozen Indians surrounding a stag, shooting arrows into it. He softly ran his hand over it. "This is better than many of our own frescoes, is it not?"

"*Sí*," said Diego, "it is very beautiful. Something like this takes much intelligence and skill."

Mateo gave the fresco a quick look and laughed. "It is quite rudimentary, if you ask me." As he walked off to inspect a skin hanging from one of the rafters of the hut, a runner came in.

"Senor Mateo," said the man, out of breath, "we found something, a hut off by itself . . ." The man coughed, his eyes wide with fear.

"Well," demanded Mateo, "what of it, man? Speak!"

The man quickly made the sign of the cross. "Senor, it is filled with unspeakable horrors!"

Mateo nodded grimly. "Lead the way." He followed the man, and Diego and the others hurried to catch up with him.

Chapter IO

In the blackness of the hut, a colonist held a torch aloft while another held a crossbow at the ready. In the flickering light, Senors Francisco Mateo and Diego Vega stared grimly at the neatly piled stack of bones at their feet, while all around the shadows shimmered with menace. Both Mateo and Diego had cloths tied round their mouths.

"This is all the evidence we need," said Mateo. He nodded at the bones. "According to the Council of the Indies, if the Indians are cannibals they can be legally taken to work the plantations. See how neatly they've chewed the meat from the bone."

The two colonists laughed nervously and continued their surveillance of the shadows.

"But, Francisco," said Diego, "this does not prove that they are cannibals!"

Mateo's voice roared, echoing back and forth in the dark hut. "Diego, for the love of God, what more proof do you need? Surely they are smart enough not to let us catch them at such horrors."

Diego blinked his large sad eyes nervously. "Francisco," he said, "cannibals have never been reported this far north. Besides, there are tribes which prepare their dead in this fashion, picking all the flesh from the bones."

"I don't believe it," said Mateo loudly, "why would they . . ."

The rectangle of light at the far end of the hut blinked as one of the men came in. He hurried up to Mateo.

"Sir," he said, "their chief has arrived with the rest of his people. There are dozens of braves and even more women and children."

"What name does he go by?" said Mateo.

"Ahopo."

"Let's go meet him," said Mateo. "This is what we came here for."

Mateo turned to Diego. "Take a couple of men with you and transfer the big Indian down to the bilge."

Diego was abhorred by the order. The bilge was the darkest, dampest, most stinking part of a ship. Every crumb of food that was not eaten, every drop of sweat, every turd and drop of piss that did not go over the side ended up in the bilge, mixing with the rock and sand of the ballast there. It was full of bad air that could kill even a healthy man. Diego protested. "Francisco, he is still sick of the Indian pox, for him to sit down there for hours, why, it would kill him!"

Francisco Mateo frowned as he considered this. "Very well. Leave him in the goat pen for now, but when you see us coming back out to the ship, take him down to the bilge and chain him good. I don't want him warning the others when we bring them aboard."

Mateo and his men stood in the shade cast by a thatched hut. His crossbowmen and arquebusmen were arranged protectively around them. Across from them stood the chief of the village, Ahopo, and a dozen of his top warriors. The rest of his people were scattered in a large, milling, curious crowd. Ahopo was a large man, a full head taller than Mateo. Like his men, he was naked but for a loincloth, and his skin was decorated with many tattoos. Geometric bands of them encircled his biceps, chest, and legs, giving the appearance of a garment. He also wore a large necklace of shells and stones around his thick neck as a symbol of his rank.

Hungrily clutching a gourd cup of wine in his big hands, Ahopo smiled at Mateo and tilted it to his lips. Many of the women and children were trying on clothing and beads. Four criollos were busy passing gourds of wine to the women, most of whom were already drunk. Out in the sunny, bare-dirt village center, girls of six or seven years played with cloth dolls they'd been given, and dozens of boys in their early teens, brows furrowed in rapt concentration, traded among themselves for glass beads and rings of brass and iron. A woman in her teens unabashedly canted her hips and urinated, her water running down one leg to form a dark muddy pool at her feet. Around the periphery of all the activity, small groups of Indian men squatted, their loincloths puddling on the ground, as they laughingly pointed and commented on the goings-on.

Mateo took a small sip from his gourd of red wine, not wanting to come under its spell. He looked back at Ahopo and saw him stagger as he went off to refill his cup with wine.

Mateo turned to one of his men who knew some of the Arawak tongue and was familiar with Indian hand signals. "Now, let us get them out onto the ships. Tell them we have more gifts for them out there, or tell them we will take them to see their dearly departed in the nether realm. Such a tale worked for Gaspar de León down along the Main."

A while later, Ahopo raised his arms and began shouting at his people in a loud gruff voice. When he finished, they gathered up their new things and began moving down to the beach and the canoes. When all the Indian canoes were loaded, Mateo gave the signal to push off. When the flotilla was halfway to the ships, Mateo and the men in his boat looked back to see a drunken Indian in the lead canoe fall into the sea with a loud splash. Mateo smiled and turned round to his men. "When we get aboard, break out two or three more casks of wine. Keep their cups running over and them making merry. Then get as many to go below as you can. Our task will be easier that way."

The men nodded grimly, knowing a fight probably lay ahead.

Chapter 11

Calling Crow's throat was raw and he felt as if he were on fire. He lay on the dry grasses, barely able to move. How long ago had Big Nose died? he wondered. How long had he lain here? He could not say. His fever brought him many dreams and evil spirits, and he was growing weaker by the day.

He pulled himself up and drank from the calabash of water they had left with him. The cool water brought some relief, and he remembered how they had taken him up out of the belly of the cloudboat one day and walked him around. That was when he had seen a strange thing. A demon man sat on the edge of the cloudboat, leaning way out. Calling Crow had watched, perplexed, and then a turd dropped from the man into the sea. They seemed to be men! They had great medicine and they looked like hideous spirits, but they seemed to be ordinary men. The realization had given him some hope that perhaps he could escape.

Calling Crow heard people coming down into the belly of the cloudboat. It was the one that could speak, the one called Hotea. He was carrying a stick that burned and gave off light. Behind him came the old sad-faced man with gray hair and a young man with a long knife who was wearing magic skin. The light from the burning stick flashed off the young man's magic skin like sunlight off of silver fish lying in the bottom of a canoe.

Gray Hair spoke to Hotea, and Hotea said, "We have to put you down into the very bottom of the ship."

Calling Crow tried to muster his strength. "So, why is the old fool telling me this? Why does he not just put me down there?"

Hotea pushed in front of old Gray Hair. Speaking so rapidly Calling Crow could hardly follow him, he said, "The old one feels badly about all of this. He wants you to pray to his god with him first."

Calling Crow laughed in disgust. "I will not. I want nothing to do with his god. I want only to return to my people."

After Hotea relayed Calling Crow's words, the young man in magic skin grabbed Calling Crow by the arm, yanking him to his feet. They took him out of the animal pen and down further into the cloudboat. From the terrible stench, Calling Crow knew he was truly within the bowels of the cloudboat. The young man attempted to put a heavy black ring around his neck. Calling Crow fought him as best he could, but he was weak and couldn't put up much fight. Then old Gray Hair started squawking in his strange voice, and the man removed the heavy ring. Instead, they bound Calling Crow's hands behind him with hide thongs. They went away, leaving Calling Crow in a darkness he

had never imagined possible. He tried to free his hands,
but they were bound too tightly.

After a while, Calling Crow heard many noises from
above. He thought he heard children running and laughing.
Then a steady drumming started up, and he heard people
singing. A horrible thought suddenly threw him into a
panic. Had the cloudboat reached his village of Tumaqua?
Were his own people up there now, singing and dancing
while the demon men prepared to destroy them? He started
pulling at the cords feverishly. He discovered that they had
loosened some and that he could slide them up and down,
rubbing them against the tree they'd tied him to. He
worked feverishly as the drumming swelled.

The noises filtered down to Calling Crow in the blackness
and the sweat poured from him as he worked the thongs up
and down against the tree behind him. He felt them loosen
further and pulled as hard as he could. One of the thongs
popped as it broke, then another. With a cry of anger, he
broke the others. He crawled on all fours in the dark until he
found the jagged hill leading up. With the sounds of people
singing and shouting to guide him, he came closer and
closer to them. The dim shapes of the many trees growing
through the cloudboat began to appear in the darkness
around him. He looked about and saw another of the strange
jagged hills leading up. Without making a sound he crept up
and the light grew brighter, the sounds louder. He moved
toward another of the jagged hills and saw people in the
daylight above. He looked around for a weapon and saw a
clublike stick sitting on the ground. Picking it up, he moved
stealthily up the hill. As he came out into the light, he saw
that these were people, not demons, but they were not his
people. They appeared to be either crazy or under a spell of
some kind. Some of them sat in a stupor; others stood about,
laughing and talking loudly.

Calling Crow moved out among them, and they seemed
not to notice him. They were all drinking a drink as they
watched some of the demons. Three of them made strange
music from pieces of wood they held and stroked as two

others danced a crazy dance, stamping their feet so loudly they sounded as if they were made out of stone. Calling Crow looked around and saw the fire-haired demon called Mateo standing with Hotea Who Speaks. They were watching quietly while other demon men passed about calabashes of the strange drink the people loved so. A young woman staggered by Calling Crow, and he grabbed her arm.

"Why have you all come out here?" he said to her as he looked around anxiously.

"Ahopo, our Chief, has brought us here to enjoy the many gifts of the People From the Sky."

"Where is this Ahopo?" said Calling Crow.

The woman looked round, almost falling as she did. She pointed at a very large man who was sitting down with some others watching the dancers. From the back he looked like a large tree stump growing up from the cloudboat.

Calling Crow pushed through the milling crowd of people, trying to keep out of sight of the demon men who were scattered here and there watching. Movement from above caught Calling Crow's eye and he looked up. He saw many of the demon men in the upper parts of the cloudboat trees, some of them with the medicine sticks which brought down thunder and lightning. Some of the demon men pulled and tugged at the great skins which normally hung from the trees. Calling Crow had seen them do this before when they had brought him up from the belly of the cloudboat. The demons would drop them in order to make the cloudboat move through the waters. Calling Crow moved faster now. He must get close to the one called Ahopo and warn him.

Across the open space on which the dancers stamped and clapped and yelled, two of the demon men suddenly recognized Calling Crow. They started for him, going around the people, rather than through them, so as not to raise an alarm.

Calling Crow shouted at Ahopo. "This is a trap! Flee while you can. Flee!"

Some of the people nearby looked up at him from where they sat as they pointed and laughed crazily. Two boys who were sitting at the top of one of the jagged hills that go down began looking around nervously.

Calling Crow saw more of the demon men closing in on him from behind. He yelled over to the big man called Ahopo. "You, Ahopo! Take your people from here quickly before it is too late."

Ahopo jerked awkwardly about. He was struggling to get to his feet when the thunder sticks exploded all around. Many of the people fell down in fright as wild screams erupted. The women and children ran quickly for the jagged hills that go down, trampling one another in their haste to get away. The braves looked about in fearful astonishment as they got unsteadily to their feet. Picking up their wooden lances, they ran at the demon men, but the thunder sticks erupted again and they fell down, many of them red with their own blood. Others who were not hurt trembled on the ground, too frightened to move. The demon men moved in quickly to tie them up and push them below. Calling Crow knocked a demon man to the ground with his stick and ran over to Ahopo and his men. He pointed to the back of the cloudboat. "Over there is where they steer the cloudboat, much the same as we steer a canoe, but they do it with a big pole. If we can take it away from them, we can make the cloudboat go back to the land."

Ahopo looked around quickly and saw that his men were being pushed back on every front. He shouted for those around him to follow him, and about a dozen men rushed with him toward the rear of the cloudboat. Calling Crow followed them. "There!" he shouted, indicating the demon man down in a hole in the cloudboat who was moving the big pole.

"Kill him!" shouted Ahopo, and two of his braves dove into the hole. One knocked the demon man to the ground and the other smashed his head in with his club. Standing, he put his hand on the pole awkwardly as he waited for orders from Ahopo.

Calling Crow was about to tell how he had seen the demon men operate the turning pole, when he and the others saw Fire Hair Mateo and some demon men running over. Three of the demon men were armed with the long, sharp knives and three of them carried the long thunder sticks. They immediately attacked with their long knives, and Calling Crow fought hard alongside Ahopo and his warriors, managing to drive them back. Then the thunder sticks erupted all at once in a blinding cloud of smoke and fire. Calling Crow's ears rang loudly as he coughed chokingly, and he did not know if he was alive or dead. Dazed, he spotted Ahopo in the acrid haze. He, too, appeared stunned, but was still on his feet. Three of his braves, however, lay sprawled on the blood-splattered ground. Calling Crow felt as if he were in a dream as he watched one of the braves slowly pick himself up off the ground. The man's bloodied, purple innards were hanging down and he clutched them tightly to his stomach. Moaning loudly like a ghost, his eyes unseeing, he staggered to the edge of the cloudboat and fell over into the waters. Calling Crow then saw a flash of movement. Ahopo's big form moved swiftly across the short distance between the braves and the demon men. He quickly jabbed his lance into Fire Hair Mateo's back and dove over the edge of the cloudboat into the sea. The demon men swarmed forward. Calling Crow was knocked up against the edge of the cloudboat, and his heart raced when it looked like he, too, would go over into the waters. He was then thrown roughly to the ground and one of them tied his arms tightly behind him. As they jerked him roughly to his feet, he saw that Fire Hair was still standing, although he looked weak. He and the other demon men were looking into the waters. Calling Crow looked over. He saw Ahopo's large head pop from a wave. He gave it a shake like a dog and swam powerfully for the shore. Closer in, the gutted brave who had fallen out of the cloudboat swam slowly with one hand, holding his billowing innards to his stomach with the other.

* * *

Calling Crow was put into a large animal pen packed tightly with a great many people. Some of them clustered around two of the holes in the wall in order to look out upon the world. They would turn round every so often to shout back to the others about what they saw or did not see. Men, women, and children all stood jammed together, looking dazed and confused. Others lay on the straw that was strewn about, their eyes glazed in fear.

One of the men pushed through the crowd and came over to Calling Crow. "What people are you?" he asked, using his hands and his own strange-sounding language.

Calling Crow recognized him as one of Ahopo's personal braves. "I am Muskogee," he said.

"What do they call you?" said the man.

"Calling Crow. And by what name are you known?"

"I am Tencheehee. How did you get here?"

"They captured my friend and me. They put us deep inside this place. We got sick and my friend died." Calling Crow looked over at a man who doubled over to vomit violently. "Why did you and these people come out here?"

Tencheehee spat sideways onto the wooden deck. "They tricked us. They gave us a drink they call wine. It is bad medicine. It made us crazy and then we were easily fooled."

Calling Crow looked at the man and said nothing.

Tencheehee bristled with anger. "Do you think we are cowards? We fought! You saw us! But it did no good, for they have the powerful medicine sticks that make thunder. What terrible things they are! When we ran at them, many men dropped dead before they could get close enough to fight."

Tencheehee turned away from Calling Crow momentarily to call over to the people looking out at the world. "Do you see anything?"

One of the men turned round and shouted in a worried voice, "No, just the big waters." He noticed Calling Crow and left the hole in the wall and came over. Standing beside Tencheehee, he stared wildly at Calling Crow. "You! What are they going to do to us?"

"I don't know," said Calling Crow, put off by the man's lack of composure.

The man looked around furtively. "I think they are going to eat us!"

"No," said Calling Crow. "I don't think so."

"Well, they have penned us up like dogs to be fattened!"

Tencheehee turned back to Calling Crow. "I think they are demons. They are taking us far out into the big water so that we will fall off the end of the earth."

"*Aieyah!*" said the other man. "That is what it is. They are demons and are taking us to the underworld!"

Calling Crow lay asleep on the dry grass when suddenly the cloudboat leaned over violently. He awoke as all around the people moaned in pain and fear. Calling Crow was vaguely aware of a difference in the air. The weather was changing! With a sense of foreboding, he got to his feet and made his way to the two holes in the wall which looked out. Calling Crow stuck his head out and a gust of wind whipped his hair. In the distance he saw a dense black mass of clouds on the horizon. It colored the sky above it and the sea below.

"Is it coming our way?" Calling Crow asked the man keeping a vigil at the other hole.

The man's eyes narrowed grimly as he nodded.

The cloudboat raced down a deep sea, and Calling Crow felt light-headed and dizzy. A few large drops of rain rattled down against the side of the cloudboat as the sky darkened. All the people in the animal pen were awake now. In the dim light they looked about worriedly. Again the cloudboat rolled way over, and a collective moan filled the air.

"Pray to the god Hurracane!" shouted someone from the gloom. "He is angry with us all!"

Wind and water slammed into the ship with a raging roar. Down in the helmsman's shelter, Diego braced himself against a beam as he stood behind the helmsman. Both men looked out at the lightning-streaked blackness. A wave smashed over the bow, threatening to pull the ship down into the foaming black water. The helmsman cursed as he fought the shuddering whipstaff which controlled the rudder. Lightning flashed close by and Diego looked up. Even with the sails trimmed, the wind howled ominously as it blew through the rigging. Diego made the sign of the cross and climbed up onto the quarterdeck. On his knees, he peered down into the shelter at the helmsman. "Keep her before the wind," he shouted. "I am going forward."

Jagged lightning streaked down from the night sky to the ocean's surface. In the flash, Diego saw stark fear in the helmsman's face. Thunder crashed like a cannonade, and Diego thought, God help us, there was no better seaman than this man, and if he is frightened then things are a lot worse than I thought.

As Diego made his way carefully along the rail, he tried to put the image of the other man's frightened face out of his mind. He thought of the Indians locked away in the blackness of the hold. Surely they were frightened half to death. There was nothing he could do about their horrible confinement, but at least he could go down and try to calm them. He thanked God his wife, who was an Arawak Indian, was not here to see them penned up like cattle.

He pressed up firmly against the bulkhead as he made his way along the length of the ship. He was shocked to suddenly notice a figure before him in the darkness. His name came from the blackness and his blood ran cold. A gust of wind tore past him, past the darkened figure, and he heard a flapping sound. Large leathery wings spread out and then tucked back in. He almost jumped overboard as the dark figure called his name again. A distant flash of lightning lit the scene, and relief flooded through him as he recognized Miguel Pinzon, a farmer. Pinzon got down on his knees, his helmeted head bowed. His large hide cape flapped about him.

Recovering, Diego moved closer. "Miguel, are you all right?"

Miguel called out in a loud tearful voice, "Diego! Hear my vow. If the Lord God will spare me, I shall go on a pilgrimage to the holy land. I swear it! As soon as we land I shall make my plans." Miguel put his head in his hands and cried spastically.

Diego started around him. Miguel grabbed his leg. "Please, senor, hear my confession, hear my sins so that I may attain forgiveness!"

Diego broke away. Lightning flashed and he saw that there were other pairs of men kneeling about on the deck, hearing each other's confessions. The sight frightened him to the core of his soul. The ship careened down the back of a wave, and Diego thought it might go straight to the bottom, straight to hell! What if the Council of the Indies, the Pope, and the Bishops had all been wrong about this business of slavery? What if it truly was a sin against God? That would explain the terrible storm which now threatened them.

A rogue wave smashed into the ship from starboard. Diego fell to his knees as the ship's timbers groaned like a huge beast in its death throes. With a roar, the sea washed quickly over the deck, and Diego worried that they were taking on too much water. The ship was not riding well. No longer was it able to slough off what the sea threw at it. Diego got to his feet and quickly headed for the ramp to the gundeck. As he approached the Indian pen, he noticed a crowd of men at the forward part of the gundeck. As he drew closer, he could hear their angry voices over the sounds of the storm. A colonist named Rodrigo Escabar ran up to him.

"It's Senor Roldan, sir. He is trying to talk the men into throwing the Indians overboard so the ship will ride better in the storm."

The thought dazed Diego like a blow to the head. He approached the throng of men. All around them, hammocks swung violently from the beams. He pushed through the crowd to the front and shouted at Senor Roldan. "What kind of talk is this? It is madness to propose such a thing!"

Roldan was only momentarily distracted by Diego's words, and continued his address to the crowd. "It is the only way!" he shouted. "Come, we haven't much time!"

"*Sí,*" cried another colonist, glaring angrily at Diego, "*he* would have us drown along with the savages."

A chorus of angry agreement broke out, and Diego flinched at its vehemence.

"Let's go then!" yelled Roldan.

Diego turned and started back toward the stairs. Francisco Mateo was sick from a wound inflicted by an Indian lance, but the key to the armory was in his cabin. With arquebuses and crossbows, and some of the other colonists, perhaps they could stop them.

Roldan's voice cried out behind him. "Seize him!"

Two men grabbed Diego, pinning his arms behind him. "You cannot do this!" he shouted. "This is a crime against God!"

"Shut up, fool!" shouted Roldan. He turned to his men. "Let's go!" He pushed past Diego and the mob followed him. Some of the men held back at a distance in fear of what they were about to do. Diego was pulled along behind them.

"In the name of God," he shouted, "don't do this thing!" The men's faces were haunted with fear and they didn't hear him as they followed along.

Upon reaching the main pen, Manuel Ortiz unlatched the gate. With drawn swords, he and four men pulled a dozen frightened Indians out.

The man holding Diego released him in the excitement. Diego stood on his toes to see over the crowd. *"Madre de Dios,"* he cried. A woman with a baby held tightly in her arms was among those pulled out.

"Out of the way, out of the way," yelled Roldan and Ortiz as they forced the Indians along at swordpoint.

Pushed up onto the deck in the driving rain and wind, the Indians tried to run back into the hold of the ship, but were kept back by the swords of the men.

"Quickly," shouted Roldan, "do it now. Throw them over."

The men holding the Indians hesitated, none of them wanting to be first.

"Do it or we are all dead men!" shouted Ortiz. He grabbed an old man and pried him away from the arms of the others. The man screamed as Ortiz shoved him roughly back to the rail. Ortiz pushed him over and he disappeared into the blackness of sea and air. The mob was emboldened.

"Come on," shouted a colonist, "let us be done with it now."

"Overboard with the others!" shouted another. "Throw them all over!" They grabbed two more Indian men.

"No!" shouted Diego. "For the love of God, don't do this." His words were whipped away by the wind.

The Indians fought back but were pushed ruthlessly over the rail, disappearing into the black water. Two men seized the woman holding the baby, and Diego was filled with repulsion. He pushed wildly through the crowd, knocking men out of the way. "Spare her! For God's sake, spare her and the child!"

A soldier armed with a crossbow stepped before him. Kneeling to steady himself on the swaying deck, he aimed it at Diego's chest.

Diego's heart stopped. "Please," he cried, "please."

"Go ahead," said the soldier, "save her."

Diego looked at the crossbow and couldn't move. The men holding the woman watched for a moment and then pulled the screaming woman toward the rail. Diego watched in horror as they pushed her and the babe over. He fell to his hands and knees.

"Now, the others. Hurry!" shouted Roldan.

The mob was charged with a fury as wild as the storm as they pushed past Diego, trampling him. Unable to get to his feet, he crawled to the rail and held on, vomiting violently.

The women and children screamed in terror as they waited for the demon men to return and drag more people out. Calling Crow watched the dimly lit area by the pen opening. Keeping his back against the bulkhead, he was grateful for something solid as the cloudboat rocked back and forth crazily. All around him in the dark, people were wild with fear. A great stench filled the hold from the many people who had gotten sick, and it seemed as if every man, woman, and child in the hold was crying in his ears.

"Why did they take them?" a man said over and over. He had been repeating the words ever since some of the people had been pulled roughly from the pen. Calling Crow thought that perhaps the demon men really did mean to eat them after all. A loud noise erupted from behind, and he felt the shock as the large demon dog that Fire Hair had ridden earlier screamed and kicked at the walls of his pen. A woman screamed insanely, raising the hairs on Calling Crow's neck.

The cloudboat shook violently, as if in the jaws of a great sea beast, and the screams crescendoed. Calling Crow waited for the jaws to crush the cloudboat, expecting at any moment to see great white teeth descending down upon them. He heard new shouts of alarm, and the demon men, led by Fire Hair's Enemy, reappeared at the door to the cage, carrying their thunder sticks. With a howl of fury, they pulled the cage open and charged in. Three men ran at the demon men and immediately fell down dead as the thunder sticks erupted in smoke and fire. Two of the demon men dragged off the bodies as Fire Hair's Enemy shouted orders in his horrid voice. More demon men

poured in, and two women threw themselves onto their
knees, begging for mercy. The men seized them roughly
by their hair and began dragging them up to the top. Calling Crow said a prayer to the Great Spirit and blotted out
the horrified screams. He must fight and die bravely.
Screaming a war cry, he ran at the nearest demon man.
The man's face blossomed in fear as Calling Crow threw
him onto the floor. Then he grabbed the woman the man
had been dragging out and pulled her back. Two demon
men seized him. Again he screamed out a war cry and
slammed one up against the timbers. Then others struck at
him with their fists, knocking him to the ground. Many
more of them came and seized him, carrying him up to the
top.

Out in the world, under the stormy night sky, Calling
Crow couldn't believe his eyes. In the intermittent flashes
of lightning, he saw the sea boiling and bubbling like a
soup pot with a rock fresh from the fire thrown in. Several
demon men grabbed a woman and dragged her to the edge
of the cloudboat. The old Gray Hair who had wanted Calling Crow to pray with him earlier protested, but the men
ignored him. They pushed the woman into the sea, and she
disappeared immediately into its black mouth. Calling
Crow felt his strength leave him and fear rushed into the
void. They were going to throw him into the sea! The sea
would swallow him up just as it had his father!

A man was thrown over next, crying piteously. Then
more women. The wails of the people were louder now
than the boiling waters and the shrieking winds.

The men dragged Calling Crow to the rail. Panting for
breath, he fought furiously. Somehow he managed to break
away when the cloudboat almost turned over in the wind.
He ran for one of the trees growing from the cloudboat
and began climbing up. Some of the demon men started up
after him and he kicked at them, keeping them at bay. Off
a ways, they continued dragging more people up from the
pen and throwing them into the boiling black waters. Their
screams distracted Calling Crow, and he didn't see the demon men coming at him from both limbs of the tree. They

pummeled him, attempting to pry his arms loose, while another came up from below and pulled on his legs. A demon man ripped Calling Crow's medicine bag loose and threw it into the sea. As it disappeared, Calling Crow felt the last of his strength leave him. Without his medicine he was powerless. How could he ever prevail against such demon men as these?

They began to pull him down. He couldn't think; he was like an animal trapped by hunters. Someone hit him on the head with something hard and he felt weak. As they dragged him to the edge he saw a man who had been pushed overboard, clinging to the cloudboat with his hands, screaming for mercy as he tried to climb back in. A demon man swung his long knife down, cutting one of the man's hands off and it fell onto the deck as the man disappeared over the side. Another demon man stabbed an old woman before picking her up and heaving her body over. All around people were screaming and dying. Calling Crow cried out as they dragged him to the edge. The black waters reached up hungrily for him. They were pushing him, punching him, when suddenly they stopped and he crawled back down to the deck and clung to it as if it were his mother and he a scolded child. Fighting for breath, he looked up. Fire Hair and some others stood there. They carried thunder sticks and the strange little bows, and Fire Hair's Enemy and the other demon men seemed suddenly cowed in their presence. Even the wind died down somewhat and the sea grew calmer. Fire Hair shouted angrily at the demon men, and they began taking people back down inside the cloudboat.

Back in the pen, Calling Crow was grateful for the dark. He felt a great shame for having been afraid. He lay on the straw, breathing heavily like an animal run down in a hunt. One out of three of the people had been thrown into the sea by the horrible demons. In the darkness around him, not one of those who were left spoke. He put his hand where his medicine bag had hung and as his fingers closed around nothing, a great sorrow filled him. His medicine was gone and it was the end of him. All about him in the blackness were the endless sobs of the others.

Gray light appeared on the horizon as the wind moaned over the decks. The worst of the storm had passed, but the ship still heaved heavily beneath the unsteady feet of the men. Diego Vega stood to the rear of the crowd as they faced Francisco Mateo and his officers. Paco Nacrillo had his arm about Mateo to help support him. Mateo shouted at the nervous mob. "Where is Roldan?" he said.

"Here!" came a shout. "We have him."

Mateo coughed weakly. "Tie him to the mizzenmast."

Three of the colonists dragged Roldan's struggling form to the mast and quickly tied his hands high. A man brought a lantern up close to Mateo, bathing him and the others in its yellow glow.

"Diego Vega," said Mateo, "come forward!"

Diego was startled out of his stupor upon hearing his name. He moved slowly through the crowd toward the dull light.

Francisco Mateo nodded weakly in greeting. "Diego, I want you to administer the punishment. Give him twenty lashes as hard as your arm will allow."

"But, Francisco, I have no experience with whippings."

None of the men said anything as they shifted uneasily in the early morning darkness.

Mateo coughed, then said quietly, "Diego, you were representing me when you tried to stop him. By disobeying your orders he disobeyed mine. Therefore you shall administer the whipping. I command it!"

Roldan shouted out angrily, "Mateo! I saved this ship!"

Mateo ignored the shout. Instead, he nodded at a man who held out a whip to Diego. His head bowed with grief and pain, Diego took it and turned to face Roldan. Roldan turned and smiled, as if to unnerve him. The look had no effect; Diego felt dead inside. He drew back and lashed the man on the back.

"Is that all the strength you have in that tired old arm?" said Roldan. His men laughed nervously.

"Diego," said Mateo quietly. "Give him full measure. Nineteen more."

"*Sí,* Francisco," said Diego tiredly.

Diego lashed Roldan two more times, and Roldan's voice boomed out, "Either he is a coward or else he is tired. I don't know which it is." Again the soldiers laughed.

"Coward?" cried Diego. "*You,* who kill women and children, call me a coward?" He lashed Roldan's back repeatedly without stopping. The men watching twitched visibly at the sound of the blows.

Diego's breath came heavily, and he paused to rest.

"Indian lover!" said Roldan hoarsely. His voice was still full of venom. "Indian lover, I shall make you pay for this."

"Shut up!" screamed Diego in a rage. He lashed Roldan as hard as he could. "Shut up!" Diego moved closer, lashing Roldan as he screamed at him. "You shall burn in hell for what you have done, do you hear?"

One of the colonists came up behind Diego and put his arms around him. "That is enough, Diego. It is finished now."

Sobbing, Diego dropped the whip. He allowed the man to lead him away.

Chapter 13

The *Guadalupe* and *Speeding Hound* rode low and sluggishly in the turquoise sea as they approached the island of Hispaniola. It rose out of the sea like a colossal, moss-covered rock. The Indians locked in the dark, battened-down holds of the ships did not see the huge mountains,

deep verdant green with tropical growth; they did not see
the sheer black rock cliff face where the earth had fallen
away, swept now by a white cascade of water moving in
the breeze like silk. As the ships drew closer, the Indians
did not see the palm-dotted, white sand beaches, nor the
gently rounded hills covered with green cane which undu-
lated in the breeze and the tiny, insectlike horse and cart
which moved slowly along the red mud scratch of a road.

As Senor Francisco Mateo gave the order to furl the
sails, his men were already bringing the Indians up from
the below decks. The *Guadalupe* bumped gently into the
stone quay, and many of the Indians, weakened from lack
of food and water, fell to the decks as a collective moan
rolled across the ship. Men leapt onto the ship with ropes,
and others in the rigging called out loudly as they secured
the sails.

As Mateo supervised the division and unloading of the
Indians, Jiminez de Longana, a minor official who worked
for the tax board of the Council of the Indies, came down
the quay. Tightly clutching the handhold rope stretched
across the boarding plank, Jiminez was as pale as the
trimmed sheets as he made his way aboard. Beneath his
wig, Jiminez's fat face was red and sweating by the time
he came up to the poop carrying a leather folder full of paper, stamps, ink, and candles.

Mateo nodded at him and led the way into his cabin.
Jiminez followed, breathing laboriously.

"Sit, please," said Mateo tiredly, hoping the man would
be swift with his business.

Bowing, Jiminez took a scarf from his pocket and
dusted off the chair before sitting. "Now," he said, puffing
himself up with a great breath, "how many Indians did
your ships bring in?"

"Let us just say, thirty-six," said Mateo.

"I see," said Jiminez, winking.

According to the charter of the colony of Hispaniola,
the colonists were required to give to the Crown as a tax
one fifth of any gold, goods, or Indians they acquired. Of
course, everyone, from the lowest farmer up to the colo-

ny's governor, routinely understated their accounts to de-
crease their tax. The wide extent of the cheating imparted
a sense of security, and there was even a saying in the islands about it: *The King is blind and far away and there's
money to be made today.*

Jiminez set his papers on the end of Mateo's desk.
"May I?"

Mateo nodded almost imperceptibly.

Jiminez bent and scribbled his calculations on a piece of
paper. He looked up at Mateo and waved his quill with a
flourish and a wink. "With a catch of thirty-six, the Royal
Fifth would come to five men and two women."

Mateo shook his head. "For this vessel, one man and
two women. You will find them waiting below. When the
Hound docks, you will take the same from them."

"You drive a hard bargain, sir." Jiminez scribbled some
more onto his paper. Without looking up he said in sing-
song,

> "Paper, stamps, and sealing wax,
>   Without them Kingdom would collapse."

"I am sure," said Mateo, "I am sure."

Chapter 14

Despite his fatigue and despair, Calling Crow was amazed
by the strange sights as he marched along the wide path,
tethered behind the others. The demon people lived in
square houses with sharp edges. There were even some
that looked to be made of stone. He thought that might account for their badness, for only round shapes gave power.

All along the path the demon people pointed and laughed at Calling Crow and the others who were tied up with him. The demon women were dressed up in skins from their feet to their necks. Even their heads were wrapped up, and Calling Crow wondered how they could stand the heat. Here and there among the crowds they saw people who were as black as night. Some of them were also tied up in the cords like stone. Two large demon dogs passed, followed close behind by a crowd of demon people in a thing which floated above two magic hoops which went around and around. By far, though, the last thing they saw was the most fantastic. At the edge of the town they came to a woman made of stone who stood in a pool of water. She held a pot from which an endless stream of water poured, splashing at her feet. Most of the people were afraid when they saw this thing and refused to go near it. Fire Hair's Enemy and the other demon men laughed and, through their interpreters, told the people to drink all they could of the water, for they would get no more for a long time.

"Don't drink the water," said an old man. "They are trying to trick us. It is a bad magic which has turned this woman to stone!"

When the interpreter heard this, he told the demon men and they laughed. "Look," they said, as they dipped their hands in the water and drank, "there is nothing wrong with this water."

"Don't believe them," shouted the old man.

Fire Hair's Enemy went over and dragged the old man to the pool, forcing his head under the water. Sputtering and coughing, he was forced to drink.

Calling Crow held back with the others, but after a while, seeing that the old man seemed unharmed by the water, and feeling overcome by his own thirst, he and the man he was tethered to slowly approached the pool and drank. Slowly, all the others overcame their fear and drank the water.

"It is called a 'fountain,' " said the interpreter. "It is the Fountain of the Maid."

Then the demon men were cracking their whips and

pulling the people to their feet. Forming up into a column, they marched through a hole at the base of a large wall and left the town behind.

They walked for the rest of the day past field after field of crops for which Calling Crow did not have names. One of the older men in the group fell over dead, and Calling Crow and the others asked to be given time to prepare him for his journey to the netherworld. The demon men told them to sit and rest while they talked it over. While the women wailed for the dead man, the demon men talked quietly among themselves, watching the people warily. After a short while they were again cracking their whips and shouting for the people to get up. The relatives of the dead man clung to his body, but the demon men pulled them to their feet. They left the dead man behind for the dogs.

It was night before they reached the place where they would stay. Untied from the others, Calling Crow was pushed into a small house of logs and mud. By the light of a small fire, he saw an old man sitting on the ground, chanting out a prayer. Three other men slept about the hut. They were all dressed in strange skins like the demon men, yet he could tell they were not demon men, but rather of the people. Calling Crow lay back in exhaustion. As the old man's chant filled the warm air, Calling Crow closed his eyes and found himself back on a hunting trip in happier days. It was the first time he had hunted with Sun Watcher and Birdfoot. Sun Watcher had already killed a buck deer, and Calling Crow and Birdfoot had yet to catch any meat. They stopped at a beautiful pond under the shade of a big oak tree. Sun Watcher and Calling Crow went off to find firewood. After a while they heard the happy trill of Birdfoot's flute. He played the "Song of the Rainbow Vision," one of the favorite tunes of their village. When Calling Crow and Sun Watcher returned, they saw Birdfoot sitting on a large rock in the middle of the pond, his image mirrored in its smooth waters. Oblivious to everything, he played his flute prayer to the spirit of the pond.

Calling Crow heard much shouting. Someone kicked

him as he lay in a stupor. In the dim light of dawn, he sat up to see a man stooping to go out the entryway. He looked around the hut. It had no openings save for the entryway, and the ground was strewn with bulrushes and food litter. Two men sat against the wall, watching him curiously. One had a full moon face and large eyes. He was very thin, almost like someone who had been dead for a week. The other was fatter, with very wide shoulders and a small head on a short, thick neck. Another very thin man lay against the far wall with his back to Calling Crow. The old man Calling Crow had glimpsed the night before sat in the center, eating. In the growing light, Calling Crow saw that the demon men skins they wore were filthy and the men were very dirty. Then Calling Crow noticed his own filth and he felt bad.

He looked at the man with the full moon face. "Is there a stream nearby where I can bathe?"

The man scowled. "You speak very strangely. What people are you?"

"Muskogee," said Calling Crow. "You also speak strangely."

The man seemed friendlier. "Yes. I am of the Guale People. The Spanish do not let us bathe but once every moon. They say daily bathing will make us sick."

"That is crazy," said Calling Crow.

The man nodded slowly as his wide-shouldered friend smiled. "They are crazy. And they stink, too." He threw some of the strange skins they wore at Calling Crow.

Calling Crow ran his hands over them in awe. He had never felt such skins. "What skins are these?" he asked.

"They are not skins. They are clothes. The Spanish make all the people wear their clothes. Put them on like we have or they will beat you."

Calling Crow looked at the others to see how the clothes went on. He pulled them on, and the two men showed him how to secure the bottoms, which they called breeches, with a drawstring. The old man said nothing as he watched and chewed slowly.

The moon-faced man said to Calling Crow, "I am Born

In Storm." He pointed to the man next to him. "This is No Neck. What do they call you?"

"I am Calling Crow. I am a Chief."

Born In Storm and No Neck laughed loudly. "A Chief?" said Born In Storm. "Where are your people, Chief?"

"They are far across the big water. The demon men came in their cloudboats and took my cousin and me away."

Born In Storm and No Neck laughed again. Calling Crow did not know why they laughed, but it was just another strange thing among many. Then Born In Storm took out a bright red stone and began fingering it. He saw Calling Crow watching and he held the stone up to a shaft of sunlight streaming into the hut. The stone sparkled and shined brilliant red, like a star. Calling Crow could not take his eyes off it as the man turned it about in the light.

Born In Storm held out the red stone to Calling Crow. "Here is some Spanish magic for a Chief. Someday soon you will need it."

Calling Crow took it, and it cut into his finger. He dropped it in shock as blood beaded on his fingertip. The other men laughed. Calling Crow carefully picked up the red stone again and examined it closely. Born In Storm and No Neck lost interest and said nothing. Calling Crow looked around. The sleeping man against the wall didn't move. The old man had finished eating and sat watching him, but said nothing.

Calling Crow crawled to the center of the hut and held the magic stone that cut like a knife up to the light.

"Put that down and eat," said the old man. "Soon *El Animal* will come and that will be very bad."

"El Animal?" said Calling Crow.

"Yes. That is the Spanish word for the four-legged beasts and they call one of the guards by the same word. He is of the people, but he has gone over to the Spanish. He is very big and likes to use his whip. The four-legged beasts must hate him as much as we do, for his name is an insult to them."

Calling Crow smiled at the old man's words.

The old man held out some food. Calling Crow took it and bit into it, finding it strange, but not unpleasant. "What is this food?" he asked as he chewed.

"Cassava bread. The Arawak People are very fond of it."

Calling Crow's brow furrowed. "Ara-wak?"

"They are the people who originally lived in this place," said the old man. "They are the Arawak, but the Spanish call them the Taino, or Gentle People. That may explain why there are hardly any left. The Arawak are small like the Caribs, and they look like them, too, but the Caribs are fierce and sly. Many who have not bothered to learn the differences between these two peoples have paid for their laziness with their lives."

"Isn't there meat?" asked Calling Crow.

The old man frowned as the two other men laughed loudly. "This island is full of their runaway animals and their offspring," said the old man, "but they tell us there is no meat. Not even for the sick or the nursing mothers. They want to keep us weak."

Calling Crow looked over at the sleeping man. "Why doesn't he get up?"

"He is sick with what we call the Spanish disease. One can get it merely from being around the Spanish. I went to the spirit world to bring his spirit back, but it did not want to come because this life among the Spanish is worse than death."

Born In Storm and No Neck went out the entryway. Calling Crow got to his feet and went over to look at the sick man. He had the same marks on his face as Big Nose had had on the ship before he died. "Both I and my friend had that same sickness. He died on the cloudboat, but I got well again."

"You had the Spanish disease and lived?" The old man's eyes grew wide with wonder.

Calling Crow nodded.

"You must have a very strong spirit guide. Very few who get the Spanish disease survive it."

Calling Crow looked at the walls of the hut and saw

himself as he was before, strong and happy. "I lived because I had my medicine bag with me, but I have since lost it."

"I will make you some medicine after a while," said the old man.

Someone began shouting outside. "Come," said the old man, "it is time to work."

"What kind of work?" said Calling Crow.

The old man shook his head. "You will find out soon enough."

Again Calling Crow held up the magic stone to the light. It glowed red like fiery blood. "What is this?" he said to the old man.

"It is not magic. The Spanish call it glass and use vessels made out of it to contain their drinking water and their wine."

"Why did he give it to me?"

"In case you want to leave this place."

"I do not understand."

"If you wrap it in some bread and swallow it, you will die. It is one of two ways out of this place."

"What is the other?"

"Cassava plant root. If you do not soak it properly and take the poisons out of it, it will kill you. Many choose to go that way."

"There must be a way to escape."

"That is what everyone says when they first get here."

Calling Crow felt a deep pain inside of him. Could the old man be right? Sadness began to push through him like the wind through the trees. To never be able to find his way back to his people . . . it was worse than death.

Calling Crow wrapped the glass up in a corn husk he found lying on the dirt floor.

The old man handed him a small medicine pouch made of smooth skin. "Here, you can put it in here. Later I will make you some medicine so you will have some protection."

"Thank you." Calling Crow tucked the pouch into his breeches. "What is your name?"

"I am Little Bear of the Guale People. I am a medicine man."

They went outside and joined a bunch of people who were lined up. All the men were dressed in the strange Spanish cloth. The women wore skirts of it and even covered their breasts with it. Little Bear picked up a basket from some that lay on the ground.

"Take a basket and follow me," he said to Calling Crow.

They walked toward a field where people were digging, making a big hole. Many Spanish stood about on the edge of the hole, some of them with large dogs tethered to their hands. Calling Crow stared at the dogs as they passed. He had never seen such big dogs as these. They had broad, powerful chests which tapered down to their sleek hindquarters. Their snouts were long and tapered, too, and they looked like they could run like the wind. The dogs barked continuously at the people and would obviously attack if the Spanish let them free.

A big man who did not look Spanish began shouting loudly at them to hurry. Little Bear turned to Calling Crow. "He is the *cholo* I told you about, the one they call *El Animal*."

"What is this word, *cholo*?"

"It means people who have gone over to the ways of the Spanish. It is a bad word."

"Hurry up, you dogs," said *El Animal*. "It is time for your baptism."

"What is he saying?" asked Calling Crow.

"The Black Robes are coming to pour water on the heads of those who have just arrived. We must go over there." Little Bear lifted his scrawny arm and pointed to a cluster of people under a tree.

Calling Crow looked over at them. They were standing before a tree with no leaves or branches which had another smaller tree lashed across it. "What is that?"

"They call it the Cross. The Black Robes plant them all over this land and worship them."

"Black Robes?"

"The Spanish medicine men. They call themselves

priests. Some of our people call them Men Without Wives."

Calling Crow shook his head as they started walking over.

When they joined the crowd of people, Calling Crow saw Fire Hair's Enemy among the Spanish. The man sat on a tree stump not far away while another man cut the hairs from his head and face with two small knives. Anger pulsed through Calling Crow as he watched and remembered the night on the ship. He could still hear the screams of the people as they were pushed into the sea. Calling Crow turned to Little Bear. "What is that one called?"

"That is the one they call Roll-dahn. He is a very bad man. Stay here."

Calling Crow watched Little Bear move closer to where Roldan was sitting. Little Bear squatted down as if to rest and quickly took some of Roldan's hair and tucked it under his breeches. He moved slowly back to Calling Crow, a withered old man, unnoticed by anybody.

"Why did you take his hairs?"

Little Bear shook his head. "Be quiet now. The Black Robes are coming."

"Why do you go for the baptism, too?" he said. "You did not just arrive."

"It is better than work, and I like the cool water on my head."

Father Luis was a short man fattened by middle age. His tonsured head and full face were reddened from his days in the sun and he sweated heavily under his black woolen robes. As he walked along with Father Sabastian, a young priest from Santo Domingo assigned to help him, he felt very tired and sad. Senor Alonso Roldan's pit mine was a short distance away and even now he could see the poor unfortunates working there under the hot sun. According to the Council of the Indies, captured hostiles and cannibals could be worked under such conditions a full year before being released. The great majority of them did not live that long, however. Father Luis shook his head sadly at the sight. Of all those who were allowed to have Indian laborers, the soldiers were the worst, and of all the soldiers, Roldan was the most unyielding to the priests' suggestions and the harshest overseer.

Fathers Luis and Sabastian walked past two breastplate-encased soldiers holding crossbows. As they passed, the soldiers laughed lecherously at some joke. Father Luis looked away. The crudity of the soldiers and their potential for violence frightened him. He had seen firsthand the fruit of that violence when he was a boy of six. He had been running and playing in the street with the other boys, when the soldiers in their armor and bright red scarfs came riding through their village after one of their many campaigns against the Moors. He and the other boys ran alongside of them, begging for coins. They smiled and laughed as they looked up admiringly at these powerful Christian soldiers. There were a few coins thrown, but Luis got none. "Me, me!" he shouted at a bearded knight in a shirt of mail. The knight smiled and lifted a small bundle wrapped in cloth he'd been carrying. He tossed it in the dusty street. It rolled like a cabbage down a side alley as the soldiers rode on in a cloud of dust. Luis raced after the bundle with the other boys hard on his heels. Just as he reached it another boy kicked it out of his grasp and went chasing after it. Infuriated, Luis ran after the boy and threw him on the ground where he bloodied his knees and hands and began crying loudly. Luis ran to the bundle which had come to rest in the gutter and triumphantly picked it up. He quickly peeled the clinging, wet cloth wrapping to reveal a horrid bearded face. The skin was yellow and purple in places, the almond-shaped Oriental eyes open, and the mouth smiling ghoulishly. A foul odor came from it.

He threw it down in horror as the other boys came running up behind him. For months afterward he had hardly slept. For years afterward the face's wicked smile had lived in his dreams, the death's head trophy of the Castilian knight. Only in the church, in the warm light of the candles before the beautiful painting of the Madonna and child, had he been able to free himself from that face, and in gratitude he would devote himself to the Faith forever after.

"Here we are," said Father Sabastian, as they reached a barren patch of ground with a wooden cross as tall as a man planted in the center. Nearby was a table and a water trough. The closest tree was a hundred meters away.

Father Sabastian held up the gleaming brass cross he was carrying. "Where do you want me to put this?"

Father Luis pointed to the head of the table, and Father Sabastian gently set the cross down. Father Luis said, "Bring the Indians up. I will bless the water."

As the young priest walked off, Father Luis made the sign of the cross over the trough and prayed softly, his lips moving rapidly.

Father Sabastian returned with only six Indians, all men. Father Luis sighed as he saw them; they were dressed in the shabby, undyed woolen breeches and shirts that had become their standard dress on the island and they looked sickly.

He looked at Father Sabastian. "I thought there were many needing baptism?"

The young priest shook his head. "There are, but the guard said to baptize these and then he would send the rest of them."

"Very well." Father Luis thought the old Indian in the group looked familiar. "Father Sabastian, ask the old one if he has already received his baptism."

Father Sabastian put the question to the old man and listened to his reply. He turned back to Luis. "Yes."

"Have him start back and let's begin with the others."

Father Sabastian spoke to the men, and they formed into a line. The old man didn't budge.

"Let us begin," said Father Luis.

Father Sabastian's young face frowned in seriousness as he dunked the oaken bucket in the trough and filled it. As Father Luis recited the liturgy, Father Sabastian poured the water slowly over the first Indian man's head and then moved to the next. The old Indian stubbornly remained, watching the ceremony from a few feet away. After all of the men had had water poured over their heads, Father Luis stepped back and picked up the cross.

He faced the men solemnly and made the sign of the cross over them. "I christen all of you Roberto." Not being able to take the time to enable each to choose his own Christian name in the mass baptisms, this was the method they usually employed. Father Luis was not happy with the arrangement, but it was necessary to ensure that there was enough time to give all of them the most important thing, which was the Sacrament itself.

The Indians stood around, not knowing that the ceremony had been concluded. "That is all," said Father Luis in the few words of Arawak that he knew. "Finished."

The Indians stood where they were.

"What is the matter?" said Father Luis. "Why aren't they going back?"

Father Sabastian talked to the tall Indian who had been baptized first. He turned to Father Luis. "He says the old one told them not to go back until he, too, is baptized."

"Tell the old one that you are only baptized once."

Father Sabastian nodded nervously and translated. He looked back at Father Luis. "He wants to know if the ceremony makes one holy?"

There was no shade and Father Luis felt as if he would faint in the heat. Then he saw the big ugly overseer they called *El Animal* hurrying toward them. He looked back at Father Sabastian. "Of course! Tell him, yes. Here comes the overseer!"

Father Luis looked at the old man as Father Sabastian translated. The old man glared at him stubbornly.

"He says," said Father Sabastian slowly, "that if that is the case he would like to be baptized again."

Father Luis felt his frustration getting the better of him. *El Animal* walked up to them. "What is the holdup?" he said.

Father Luis grew nervous as he looked up into the big man's eyes. They did not call him *El Animal* for his kindness. If he told him the old one was holding them up, he would beat him severely. "We are almost finished," said Father Luis.

El Animal smiled down at Father Luis. "Good. I will wait."

Father Luis wondered how many men had died due to this brute's sadistic touch. He nodded at Father Sabastian. "Let us do the old one. You say the prayers. I want to christen him myself."

Father Luis filled the bucket up. Young Father Sabastian's eyes grew wide as Father Luis slowly poured the entire contents of the bucket over the old man's head. The water soaked him, making a puddle of mud at his feet. Father Luis looked at him sternly, and the old man smiled broadly. Father Luis had to smile in return.

"Now they can go back," he said.

Father Sabastian spoke to the men, and they began walking back to the pit.

Father Luis turned to *El Animal.* "Where are the others to be baptized?"

"They have to go work now. You come back." The man began walking away.

Father Luis quickly walked round and blocked his path.

El Animal's small black eyes burned into Father Luis's brain. "I say you come back!"

Father Luis felt fear creep into his belly. He wondered how the soldiers controlled someone like this, how they disciplined him.

Someone shouted at them, and Father Luis turned.

Roldan was walking over.

El Animal ran quickly to him like a naughty child. The turnabout amazed Father Luis.

"He wants to baptize the rest of them," said *El Animal*, "but I have already sent them back into the pit."

Roldan looked at Father Luis in annoyance. "Can't you come back and do the rest tomorrow?"

Father Luis swallowed. Perhaps he *should* come back next week, he thought. After all, if he insisted on this, he could frustrate his other requests to provide the Indians with the Sacraments. But then again, this first Sacrament

was the most important. What if one of them died of the
pox? What kind of priest was he to put them in jeopardy
of not being able to enter the kingdom of heaven? "I have
other duties," he blurted out. "I will be busy tomorrow."

"Well, come back next week then. They have already
waited too long for you and they have work to do."
Roldan and *El Animal* started to walk away.

"No!" said Father Luis loudly. He was surprised by the
vehemence in his voice. "Some of them are sick, I'm told.
Next week could be too late. They must be baptized today!"

Roldan started back. He put his hand on the pommel of
his sword and smiled coldly. Father Luis's heart pounded
in his chest. Roldan looked into his eyes and saw the fear
there. He seemed pleased. He turned to *El Animal*.

"Bring him his precious Indians, but get them back in
the pit the moment he's through."

"*Sí*, Senor Roldan," said *El Animal*.

Roldan gave Father Luis a last icy look before he
walked off. Father Luis was angry at himself for letting
the other man see his fear, but at the same time he was
glad they would bring the other Indians up for their baptism. That was more important than any pain or shame he
might feel. He sighed and went back to the trough.

Chapter 15

The day after the baptism, Calling Crow and Little Bear
walked down into the muddy pit with the others. Little
Bear said to Calling Crow, "How did you sleep last night,
Roberto?"

"Why do you call me that?" asked Calling Crow.

"Because that is the name the Black Robe gave you yesterday." Little Bear pointed to an old man walking beside them. "And him, too, and the boy over there, and me."

"That is crazy!" said Calling Crow angrily. "I have a name. How can they give me another?"

Little Bear nodded. "We told you they were crazy."

A woman came and laid her basket down in front of Little Bear. He picked up a flat stick and began putting mud into her basket. He looked up at Calling Crow. "Now that you are baptized, you are a child of their god, and when you die you will go to the place He lives, which they call heaven. I don't believe it, though." The woman picked up the basket, put it on her head, and walked off.

"Why do they have us remove the earth?"

Little Bear frowned. "To get the yellow metal from it. It is a thing they love even more than their own god. You see, they speak of love of god, but when the talk rolls round to yellow metal it is obvious what they really love. For god they talk, read their books, and bend their knees in prayer, but for yellow metal they would crawl through fire, or slay a thousand of us."

Calling Crow wondered about this and found it confusing. After all, the Spanish had very powerful magic, like their cloudboats, their thunder sticks, and their long knives. These made them very powerful. Why their hunger for yellow metal? It did nothing and had no magic. Their love for such a thing made them seem crazy. It was all very strange.

A young man with a scarred back put down his basket in front of Calling Crow. Calling Crow ignored him and looked at the muddy earth at his feet. "I don't see any yellow metal in this earth."

"It is there," said Little Bear as he shoveled dirt, "in small pieces like the sand on the beach. How they get it out I . . ."

"You!" came a shout. It was *El Animal* standing up on the edge of the pit. He glared down at Calling Crow. "Stop talking and start shoveling or you will feel the kiss of my whip!"

Concern stilled Little Bear's face as he called over in a low voice, "Use one of those flat sticks and fill his basket with dirt."

Calling Crow took the stick and did as Little Bear said. The man put the basket on his head and walked off. A woman put her basket down and Calling Crow began filling it. Then *El Animal* turned and walked off a ways.

"Don't work too hard," said Little Bear. "There is not enough food for that. Work slow."

"Yes," said Calling Crow.

The woman took her basket and went off. Then an old man as skinny as a walking corpse put his basket in front of Calling Crow and he began filling it. He did not put too much in it, for he was afraid the old man would not be able to lift it. He stopped a moment to watch as the man put the basket on his head and walked to the edge of the pit. As he attempted to climb out he lost his footing on the muddy bank and dropped the basket. *El Animal* saw him fall and rushed over. He hauled the man out of the pit by his hair and threw him on the ground. Taking out his whip, he began thrashing him. Calling Crow put down his stick and started for him, but Little Bear blocked his way. "No, go back to work. You cannot do anything."

El Animal struck the man again and again until he rolled away and down into the safety of the pit. His chest smeared with blood and mud, the man picked up his basket and came back to Calling Crow. Calling Crow leaned on his shovel, watching in anger as *El Animal* walked off. He thought, it was true what Born In Storm had said. Here they truly were worse off than the dead. Then he thought of Little Bear's words the morning before, but could not believe them. Surely one could escape from these horrors. He would do it, he told himself. He would escape soon.

Little Bear touched him on the back. "Work! Fill his basket or we will all get in trouble." Calling Crow picked up his shovel and continued working.

Salty sweat burned into Calling Crow's eyes and his

head and body ached badly. He lost his footing and nearly fell into the mud. Suddenly he heard beautiful voices singing, like happy spirits from another world, and he thought it must be a dream. He continued working like the others as the singing grew louder. He looked around and saw a strange procession go by on the big path not far from the pit. A Black Robe led a group of children along, singing as they went. All the people in the pit turned slightly to watch them as they passed. They were not Spanish and they did not dress in the Spanish style as the *cholos* did. Calling Crow turned to Little Bear. "Who are they?" he asked.

"They are the sons and daughters of *Caciques*."

"What is this *Cacique*?"

"That is the Spanish word for a Chief."

"Where are they going now?"

"The Black Robes have a special school for them. They treat them well, for through them they rule the people."

"I am a Chief."

Little Bear leaned on his shovel. "I heard you say that earlier. They will never believe you."

"Still, I must tell them." Calling Crow thought that if he could get out of this place, away from all the Spaniards with thunder sticks and fighting dogs and into a Black Robe school, then perhaps he could find a way to escape. He saw *El Animal* walking back toward them. He put down his shovel and walked to the edge of the pit.

Calling Crow called up to the man, "I am Calling Crow of the Muskogee People. I am the *Cacique* of my village."

El Animal frowned in disgust. "You are crazy. Get back to work."

Calling Crow did not move.

El Animal uncoiled his whip. "I will teach you, fool."

The whip whistled through the air, stinging and cutting painfully across Calling Crow's chest. He did not cry out and glared at the man in fury. Again the whip cut into his bloodied chest and he managed not to cry out. His chest heaved in pain and fury as the man drew the whip back. The whip cracked across the distance between them like black lightning, and Calling Crow held up his arm as the leather wrapped stingingly around it. He pulled on it, trying to pull the man down into the pit. "I am *Cacique*!"

El Animal cursed loudly, digging his heels in as he leaned backward. Roldan and two Spanish guards rushed over.

"What is going on?" demanded Senor Roldan.

"He says he is a *Cacique*," said *El Animal*, "but I say he is a fool." *El Animal* pulled hard on the whip and fell backward as Calling Crow released it.

"*Cacique*!" shouted Calling Crow in fury. "I *Cacique*!"

El Animal got to his feet and coiled the whip for another strike.

"You are a fool," said Roldan. He turned to *El Animal*. "Give me that!" Roldan grabbed the whip. He struck at Calling Crow, the whip cutting him across his legs. Calling Crow grabbed for it and missed. Roldan struck again, the whip cracking like a shot. "Bring the hounds," he shouted.

All the people stopped their work to watch as a dozen Spaniards rushed over, their snarling dogs straining at their ropes.

"I am *Cacique*!" shouted Calling Crow in fury as he looked up at Roldan. "*Cacique!*"

He was suddenly aware of the dogs. Too many to count, their eyes were fixed on him as they snarled, their sharp white teeth snapping. He stepped back a few paces involuntarily. He was only dimly aware of the Spanish talking; all he could see was the snapping teeth.

"Tell him to get back to work or he is dog meat," said Roldan.

"Fool," said *El Animal*, "if you don't go back to your digging you are food for the dogs. Do you hear me?"

Calling Crow tried to talk and could not. He could not move. All he could do was watch the eyes and teeth of the dogs. The Spanish knelt and began untying the ropes of the snarling dogs. Then Born In Storm and No Neck ran up. Born In Storm put the shovel in Calling Crow's hands and began pulling him backward. No Neck shouted up to the Spanish as they pulled him backward, "Please, senor, he is young and crazy! Please!"

"Enough," said Senor Roldan. He tossed the coiled-up whip at *El Animal*. "Now get them all back to work or I will use it on you." He walked off with a half dozen men clustered tightly around him.

In the pit Calling Crow's shame was greater than his pain. He could not look at any of the people about him as he worked.

"Do not be ashamed," said a voice.

It was Little Bear. Calling Crow said nothing and did not look at him.

"We are all afraid. All the people in this pit are afraid. All the brave ones are already dead."

Chapter 16

Senors Alonso Roldan and Manuel Ortiz rode at a trot along the sea road. Nearing the city, they were forced to slow their pace as they maneuvered around the many strollers and loiterers in the road. Passing the still-uncompleted Cathedral de Santa Maria la Menor, they rode up a cobblestone road to the smooth stone wall of the *Cabildo*. A half dozen horses were tethered in front of the Roman arch portico of the building.

The two men quickly dismounted and tied up their horses. Roldan led the way as they walked under the cool portico and down a half flight of steps. They walked round to the back and knocked at a set of large doors. A servant girl opened the door for them, bowing slightly as they entered.

Roldan and Ortiz stood in the marbled corridor till the

girl closed the door. "We are here to see the governor," said Roldan. "He is expecting us."

The girl nodded and walked down the hall to where two large soldiers in polished breastplate, holding tall halberds, guarded another pair of wooden doors. The girl opened the doors for them, and Roldan and Ortiz entered. The governor sat at his desk, which was situated in the middle of the surprisingly small office. He wore a red velvet doublet with a ruffled collar, and his fat face and bald head were beaded with sweat.

"Governor," said Roldan, "thank you for receiving us."

Governor Toledo nodded. "What have you to tell me?"

Senor Alonso Roldan was reassured at the sight of the man. He was a loyal Peninsular official. Now justice would be done.

"Governor, I have knowledge of one of your subjects who has broken the laws."

"What was that?" said Toledo. He took his quill from the inkstand and looked round for paper.

"Governor, it was a man known as Francisco Mateo. He underreported the number of captive Indians he brought back from the Floridas so as to pay less tax. The tax man himself seems to have been complicit in this, too, I might add."

Governor Toledo sighed. "Hardly a unique crime, I'm afraid. It happens quite a bit. But, I shall have someone look into it."

As Toledo's quill scratched on the paper, Roldan frowned. Toledo did not look like he cared much that the Crown was being cheated.

Governor Toledo smiled at Manuel Ortiz. "I suppose you are a witness to this great crime, too."

Manuel Ortiz nodded.

Governor Toledo scribbled some more and then looked tiredly at the two men. "This is what could not wait until tomorrow?"

Roldan felt his anger rising. "No, Governor, there is more, something very serious."

"Get on with it, man."

Roldan nodded. "Several months ago, I and some of my men were witness to a certain Senor Diego Vega, committing the act of sodomy with a Moorish boy named Miramor."

Governor Toledo put down his quill and sat back. His face grew very red. "Conchietta!" he yelled at the door, and the servant girl entered.

"Come here."

The girl walked over and leaned close. The governor whispered something in her ear, and she immediately left the room.

Governor Toledo looked back and forth between the two men and finally settled on Manuel Ortiz. "I suppose you witnessed this, too, eh?"

Ortiz nodded.

The sound of many boots sounded out in the corridor and a squad of six soldiers dressed in breastplate and carrying crossbows burst into the room. They immediately seized Roldan and Ortiz by the arms.

"What is the meaning of this?" demanded Roldan.

"Senor," said Governor Toledo slowly, his face still beet-red, "you are either mad or else you are a liar! Diego Vega is a good man and true. I know this because I came over with him on the *Galician*'s second voyage twenty-five years ago! I don't know what you hoped to gain by attempting to savage his reputation, but you shall not succeed!"

Governor Toledo looked at the soldiers. "Throw them out of here!"

The six men dragged Roldan and Ortiz quickly down the corridor. Their angry shouts echoed off the marble walls as the soldiers wrestled them through the doors. Pushing them up the stairs, the soldiers threw them roughly out onto the street where they fell into the dust.

Bleeding from the nose, Roldan got to his feet and dusted himself off. He walked straight to his horse, mounted, and rode off. Manuel Ortiz hurriedly dusted himself off and mounted his horse, racing after him.

Ortiz did not catch up with Roldan until they had passed

through the gates of the city. Without a word, they rode slowly along the red dirt of the valley road. On either side of them the cane rose up like a green wall, stopping the slight breeze, which moved the tall tops of the cane. The air in the road was like an oven, and both men were soaked through with sweat. As they rode along, Roldan could not put the thought of what had just happened out of his mind. The ignominy of it took his mind back to the ship and his flogging, a flogging for saving the ship! The pain he suffered that night was nothing compared to his shame at having had to face his men afterward. The shame burned in him now, even hotter than the noon sun which beat down on them from high above.

Manuel Ortiz came abreast of Roldan and slowed to a trot. He spat out a mouthful of dust and looked over at Roldan. Roldan's eyes were glazed as if he were drunk. They rode in silence for a while. Finally Ortiz said, "Senor, what can we do?"

Roldan looked off into the distance. "Nothing at present. But there will come a time. I will just have to wait for that time, that is all."

Ortiz nodded. "God! Who would have thought it, Diego's coming over with the governor? There must be some . . ."

"Shut up!" snapped Roldan. He reined up his horse and turned angrily to the younger man. "Your prattle angers me and it changes nothing."

"Sorry, Senor." Ortiz avoided Roldan's eyes, and they rode on.

Again Roldan reined his horse to a stop, causing Ortiz to ride past him. He turned his mount round and rode back as Roldan dismounted and tied his horse to a tree at the edge of the road.

"What is it, sir?" said Ortiz, quickly dismounting. He held the reins of his horse.

Roldan ignored him as he walked into the field. Ortiz tied his mount to the same tree and stood watching in silence.

"Come!" roared Roldan, and two lizards in the shade of a nearby rock skittered away at the sudden noise.

Ortiz hurried over to Roldan, who had stopped at a rock as big as a sow. "Sir?" he said tentatively. "What is it?"

Roldan turned to him. "Hear my oath," he said in a hoarse, solemn voice. "You shall be my only witness!"

"Yes, sir." Ortiz watched intently as Roldan drew his knife and knelt before the rock.

Roldan stared at the mountains in the distance. "I, Alonso Roldan, swear before these mountains and this rock, and with Manuel Ortiz as my witness, that I shall have my revenge against Francisco Mateo and Diego Vega, even if it should take me a thousand days!"

"It is witnessed," said Ortiz.

Roldan lay his hand on the rock and quickly sliced off the smallest finger of his left hand.

Ortiz frowned as he watched the thick red blood pulse from the stub. Roldan picked up the finger and placed it on a cloth handkerchief. He solemnly handed it to Ortiz. "Keep this as proof of my vow."

"Yes, senor." Ortiz stole a last furtive look at the finger before wrapping it up and putting it in the top pocket of his doublet.

Roldan got quickly to his feet, his left hand dripping blood onto his tan breeches and white hose.

Ortiz took a rag from his breeches pocket. "Senor, allow me?" He tied it firmly around Roldan's left hand, staunching the flow of blood. He had barely finished when Roldan strode over to his horse and mounted. Without a look back, he dug his spurs into his mount's side and bounded down the road.

"Senor, wait," said Manuel Ortiz, as he raced for his own mount.

Chapter 17

Diego and his wife, Lomaya, crossed the street. The sun was bright as a smith's forge and the people in the thick black shadows of the buildings were almost invisible. As Diego and Lomaya walked in the bright heat, Diego noticed the people in the shadows watching them closely. He looked away nervously and when he looked back, he saw that they were Indians and that there were very many of them. A young mestizo came out of a house and some Indians attacked him. He crawled out into the hot street, leaving a trail of blood in the tan dust. An Indian ran out and struck him hard with a club, the blow bashing in the back of the man's head like a melon. Diego gripped Lomaya's arm and they backed away as a mob of Indians began forming. "Quickly," said Diego, pulling Lomaya around, "let's run."

They ran in the direction of the jungle. As Diego pushed into the cool green safety of the thick jungle, he heard shouts behind and turned. Someone had spotted them and was now pointing them out to the others. Diego pulled Lomaya along behind him. As they ran, the vines caught at their clothes, as if trying to hold them back. Lomaya screamed and Diego turned to see that the vines were really large snakes hanging from the trees. One of them had seized Lomaya's blouse and held her tight. He pulled his sword and chopped it in half as the others hissed and snapped at them.

They ran on and soon his leg and hip stiffened and ached so badly that he had to slow down. Lomaya pulled at his arm. "Please hurry! They are gaining!" Painfully, he ran on, sweeping the vile serpents out of their way with his sword. He tripped on a log and fell on the soft dank earth. He managed to roll onto his side and sit up. Lomaya knelt before him, her face a blur of tears. She screamed at him, "Please, get up!"

Diego closed his eyes and when he opened them, Lomaya was gone and in her place, one of the men looked menacingly down at him. Diego raised his sword, but a blow from one of the men knocked it painfully out of his hand. A crowd gathered now around him. With great sadness, Diego recognized Lomaya's face among them. Then her face changed into the face of the woman who was tossed into the sea with her babe in her arms. The man looked from her to Diego and smiled menacingly. He raised the cane knife for another blow.

"No!" said Diego, raising his arm. The man's blade cracked into his forearm, severing his hand but for a thin strand of flesh. It swung hideously, uselessly from his wrist as warm blood dripped onto his face. Hot pain throbbed through him. "Please!" he cried as they laughed at him. "No!"

The man swung again and the blade cracked deep into the bone of Diego's upraised arm, breaking it. Diego moaned deeply as the other man stabbed him in the groin, and he felt his water running out of him as pain paralyzed him. Blood and sweat stung his eyes, blurring his vision. One of the men aimed a blow at Diego's head, and he couldn't move his arm fast enough to fend it off. It cracked into his skull, setting up a loud ringing.

"Diego! Please, Diego!" It was Lomaya. Her voice came through the hot night air. "Diego, you are dreaming!" She held a candle and looked down at him in the bed. Her long hair framed her frightened face in the candlelight. "What is the matter?"

He sat up in the bed, drenched with sweat. A slight breeze moved through the open window, chilling him. He pulled his breeches on and headed for the doorway.

Lomaya held the candle before her, shielding it with her hand. "Where are you going?" she cried. "Come back to the bed. You are still sick with fever!"

"Leave me. Leave me be." He ran out of the room and

into the kitchen. By the light of the moon, he jerked open the wooden door of the pantry and took out the bottle. He bit down hard on the cork and pulled it out, spitting it across the room. Tilting the bottle back, he drank from it so quickly that it ran down his neck. He was vaguely aware of Lomaya crying in the other room as he ran out into the night.

Later he heard her come out into the garden, in the silvery moonlight. He was lying up against the wall, the empty bottle by his side, and she knelt and took his gray head in her arms. He spoke her name, and she kissed his forehead. She rocked him back and forth as she chanted a prayer to Mary the Mother and another to her ancestors.

He felt so sad. "It is too late for prayers," he said in a thick voice. "What we have done is against all of God's laws, it is too much for prayers!"

"No," she cried in a frightened voice, "don't speak so. Go to see the good priest, Father Luis. He can help you. Of all of them, he is the closest to God."

Diego said nothing.

"Will you go?" she said.

"All right," said Diego. "I will go tomorrow."

Chapter 18

The hole in the thatched roof of the hut emitted a steady stream of smoke. Inside, four men sat around a fire, their heads just beneath the ceiling of smoke hovering in the damp air. Calling Crow had been here for six moons now. A high log palisade surrounded the entire place. During the day the Spanish soldiers were everywhere, and at night they let the killing dogs roam freely. No one dared leave their hut for fear of being ripped to pieces.

Calling Crow watched Little Bear, who sat chanting close to the fire, shaking his rattle rhythmically. Off a ways, the other two occupants of the hut, Born In Storm and No Neck, sat drinking the wine they had purchased that evening.

"Cacique," said Born In Storm, "why did you not buy any wine?"

"Because it is bad," said Calling Crow. "I saw a whole village of people easily taken by the Spanish because they were under its influence."

"It is either this or following the Jesus path," said Born In Storm.

Calling Crow ignored him. The Spanish gave the people a small amount of their money at the end of every week for their labor. When they had first given him some money he didn't understand. Here they were, penned up like dogs and forced to work, yet they gave them a reward. Some said that the Spanish were required to do this by their *Cacique* across the big water. But later, when he saw how most of the people spent the money on wine, and what it did to them, he understood why the Spanish did it so willingly. The people who bought and drank the wine went crazy for a while. They forgot who they were, and where they were; it dulled their pain and made them sleep. After he had been here for three moons he grew very sad and he was going to take it, but Little Bear had convinced him not to. He had told him that the wine would blot out his dreams. Without dreams, a person could never make contact with their guiding spirits. They could never be free. Little Bear did not drink the wine and so neither did Calling Crow. Instead he bought some extra cassava bread and fruit with his money.

The fire flared suddenly and mysteriously and Calling Crow looked over. Little Bear's eyes were half closed, but his face still wore the same determined look it had when he had started chanting after they had finished their work. With one hand he shook the rattle, its sound threatening and hypnotic like a snake's, and in the other he held a *shemi*, a tiny, doll-like talisman he had fashioned out of Roldan's hairs and some feathers and bones. Calling Crow knew there were other things inside it, too, but he did not know what they were. With the rattle, Little Bear was going to call the spirits into the shemi. Then they would kill Roldan. Calling Crow felt a tiny pang of happiness at the thought of Roldan falling down dead. Then his heart burned as he thought of Fire Hair Mateo. He was the one Calling Crow most wanted to see dead, and someday he would kill him. He would keep himself alive for that day.

Little Bear let out a wail, throwing his head back as he prayed rhythmically.

Calling Crow thought, What was the point of killing only one Spanish? What they really needed was to kill the entire race of them. Then these other people could go back to the way they were, instead of living like penned-up dogs. Calling Crow would be stuck in this place forever, though, unable to get back to his people and Tiamai across the big waters. But at least he would be free to roam the forest alone and lament, to climb a hill and see the earth spread out before him while the wind moved his hair and birds sang.

"Heyah heyah, hokah heyah," came Little Bear's prayer to the spirits. The rattle hissed in the darkness, calling.

Calling Crow thought of his village of Tumaqua. He summoned up the memory of the hunting trip with Sun Watcher and Birdfoot, and again saw Birdfoot out on the rock playing his flute. Try as he might, however, he couldn't remember the song. Not being able to bring the song back bothered him, and he looked away from the fire and into the blackness of the hut, his heart growing heavier. What about his beautiful young Tiamai? Did she still wait for him? More likely she was now mourning him as dead and another brave would soon take her for a wife. Were Sun Watcher and Birdfoot off on a hunting trip? Was Mennewah the Shaman at this very moment chanting a prayer under the same night sky full of stars? Or were they all gone, victims of the Destroyer, as he had seen in his vision?

"Hey, *Cacique.*"

It was No Neck. He and Born In Storm had moved back against the far wall of the hut.

Calling Crow looked over at him.

No Neck tilted the bottle up to his face. "*Cacique,* come and drink with us."

"I do not want to drink," said Calling Crow.

"Then come and talk with us. Or is a *Cacique* too high in rank to talk to ordinary men like us?"

The men laughed.

Calling Crow said nothing. That was not true. He did not feel superior to them, despite their bad manners. They were all the same here, all slaves.

Outside a dog began barking, then another. Soon every dog around the compound was barking and howling. Calling Crow and the other men listened in silence. It was someone attempting an escape, thought Calling Crow. The heavy thud of Spanish boots passed the hut, and the dogs began to quiet down.

Calling Crow went over and sat next to the two men. Neither said anything. Born In Storm held the bottle in front of Calling Crow's face. Calling Crow was saddened that Born In Storm was drinking more. He had grown to like the thin man, and they had talked many times. But now he was coming more under the spell of No Neck and the wine.

"Tell us about your village, Calling Crow," said Born In Storm.

"It is too painful to talk of them while I am kept here."

No Neck laughed loudly, and then Born In Storm joined in.

Hearing his friend's cold laugh saddened Calling Crow. He wondered about the wine's effect on the people. It made some of them weak and pitiful; it made others cruel and evil.

"Tell us about your people," said No Neck. "Why did you run away and leave them?"

Calling Crow got to his feet. "You are both good men when you are wide awake, but now that you are drinking wine you act crazy. If you were not so firmly in its embrace, I would pound you both to a pulp."

Calling Crow walked back to his side of the hut. Little Bear continued chanting, unaware that there was anyone else in the hut, and Calling Crow knew he must be deep inside the spirit world.

Someone grabbed Calling Crow from behind, his arms locking around his neck. As he pulled him backward, Calling Crow spun about and drove his elbow hard into his assailant's face. He briefly saw No Neck's face in the flickering light, blood streaming from his nose as he staggered backward. Like a ghost in the dim firelight, Born In Storm's frail form rushed at Calling Crow. Calling Crow easily threw him onto the hard dirt floor where he cried out in pain.

Calling Crow waited for him to get to his feet. He remained on the ground, moaning like a woman in labor. Saddened, Calling Crow turned to go back to his own side of the hut. Shrieking like a swooping hawk, No Neck's heavy form suddenly crashed into Calling Crow, dragging him to the ground. Twisting sideways, Calling Crow was aware of a third figure moving silently in the flickering light. Had someone else entered the hut to join them in their attack? Then Little Bear brought a clay jar full of water down on the back of No Neck's head, shattering the jar like an egg and dousing him with water. No Neck collapsed in a heap beside Calling Crow and Born In Storm.

Little Bear stared down at Born In Storm in cold, silent fury, and Born In Storm lowered his head and crept back to his side of the hut. Little Bear prodded No Neck with his foot. He did not move.

"It is the wine," said Calling Crow. "They are not bad men."

Little Bear nodded.

"Thank you for helping me," said Calling Crow.

"I did not do it for you, but for No Neck," said Little Bear, smiling. "He badly needed a bath."

No Neck came out of his unconsciousness.

Little Bear looked down on him sternly. "You must re-
place that water for me before morning."

Saying nothing, No Neck moved back into the darkness
on his side of the hut.

The singing of the birds in the trees at the edge of the
huts awoke Calling Crow. As he listened to their song, he
thought that if they had to stay in this bad place they
would not sing. He sat up. In the feeble light of dawn he
saw Little Bear sitting by the ashes of the night's fire. No
Neck silently left the hut, his face frozen in shame or
drunken pain. Born In Storm remained sleeping as the
light slowly filled the hut. Calling Crow walked over and
shook him. He moaned but did not move.

Calling Crow sat back down beside Little Bear. "He
must have drank more wine after they attacked me."

Little Bear shook his head. "No. He is dying. He swallowed some pieces of blood glass last night. I saw him. He
did it because of his shame at attacking you."

Calling Crow sighed and put his head in his hands.

"Do not grieve for him," said Little Bear.

Calling Crow raised his reddened eyes to him. "Say
nothing, Little Bear, please say nothing."

Chapter 19

Diego tied up his horse outside the church and walked
round to the hut in the back where Father Luis lived. He
saw Father Luis and Father Sabastian loading some supplies on the back of an ass. Their old Indian servant,
Miguel, was helping them.

"*Hola*, Father," said Diego as he walked up.

Father Luis smiled. Father Sabastian nodded to Diego as he walked off into the hut.

"Why have you come?" said Father Luis.

Diego struggled for the right words. How did one speak of such horrors as he had witnessed in the bright light of day? He smiled sadly. "I have been feeling bad lately about some things which have happened."

Father Luis smiled. "To feel bad on occasion is no sin."

Diego nodded. "Yes, Father. But it has affected my faith. It is becoming weak, I'm afraid."

Father Luis laughed. "I see. Then I must reacquaint you with the power of prayer."

Diego said nothing.

Father Luis went on. "We are going to the mountains on a harvest, but you can come along and we will talk when we can." A "harvest" was the term the priests used to describe their treks into the foothills to convince the runaway Indians to come back to the missions with them. From there, the runaways would be returned to their overseers, but only after the priests had received assurances that they would not be punished.

The asses were soon loaded, and the little expedition left the mission. Miguel led the asses, which were tethered head to tail, out to the road. Diego and Fathers Luis and Sabastian followed along behind. They soon reached the foothills, and the column wound its way up a thin trail. Father Luis turned round to Diego, who was bringing up the rear.

"So, what is it that is troubling you so, Diego?" he said.

Diego was breathing heavily and took a moment to reply. "When I went out on Senor Mateo's ship, several Indians died that did not have to."

Father Luis frowned. "I'm told that many were infected with the Indian pox, that they were dying even as they were being brought off the ships."

Diego struggled for a breath. "That is true, but that is not what I meant."

Before Father Luis could answer, Miguel halted the column. He walked back to them. "There they are," he said, pointing up to where the trail reappeared after disappearing around the curving spine of the ridge line. About a half dozen Indians could be seen walking slowly. Four of them looked to be middle-aged men and there was an older couple bringing up the rear.

"Let's hurry," said Father Luis. "They are not too far now. We can catch them."

As the pace picked up, Diego could barely keep up, let alone talk. A short while later they rounded the curve of the trail, but the Indians were nowhere in sight. Father Luis raised his hand to call a halt.

They stood silently as they scanned the surrounding vista.

"They have vanished," said Diego.

"Into thin air," said Father Luis, as the men looked around. A rock fell, clacking noisily. They looked over to where a sheer rock face rose steeply to the crest of the hill. The Indians had climbed up, using gaps in the rock as handholds and footholds. Diego and the priests ran over to the base as Miguel brought the asses over. The Indians were about fifteen meters up, but had an equal distance to go before reaching the crest and freedom.

Father Luis said to Diego, "Tell them to come down. We will help them."

Diego called up, relaying the message in Arawak.

"We've had too much of your help already," said one of the men. "Leave us be."

Diego turned to Father Luis and shook his head. "They won't come down."

"Keep trying," said Father Luis.

Diego repeated his plea.

"Go away. Leave us." The words floated down on the hot, still air.

"They won't listen," said Diego, "it is no use."

Father Luis grew angry. "No wonder you are having doubts of faith, if you give up on things that easily." He knelt down in the dirt and rocks. Father Sabastian and Miguel also knelt. Father Luis looked up at Diego. "Kneel and pray with us and I'll show you the power of prayer. Together we shall win with prayer."

Diego knelt down with the other men. Above, the Indians moved higher up the rock face. They were now about the height of a house, but they still had a ways to go and the angle was becoming increasingly steep.

Diego felt a great pity for the Indians. To be so desperate as to want to go to the mountains where they would surely die, it was very sad. He hoped the priest's prayers would be answered.

The Indians reached a point about the length of a man from the top where they could climb no further. They clung there, their faces expressionless.

For a long time, no one said anything as the men prayed silently, while above the Indians clung motionless to the rock. Then Miguel stood up suddenly. "Something is happening," he said. "I think they are up to something."

Diego looked up and saw that the old couple were agitated. The four men, evidently relatives, were trying to calm them, but were having no success.

Father Luis looked over at Diego. "Talk to them, find out what is going on."

"Yes, Father." Diego got to his feet and looked up. The Indians were talking excitedly, but he could not hear what they were saying. He said to Father Luis, "I think they are getting ready to come down."

Father Luis smiled triumphantly and got to his feet. "I told you! See what prayer can do?"

Diego watched the old couple press their bodies against the wall as they turned round. Then, without warning, the old man jumped and crumpled on the rocks below.

"Madre de Dios!" shouted Father Luis. He made the sign of the cross and ran to him.

Unable to look away, Diego watched the woman prepare herself.

"No!" he shouted.

She jumped and landed not far from her mate, the soft sound of her impact sickening him. Diego sat down in the dust. He put his head in his hands and cried.

Chapter 20

The big black crow flew low over the pit as it looked down at the people working in the mud. Calling Crow could not take his eyes off its straight, arrowlike flight as its wings flapped powerfully and silently. Lighting in a distant tree on a rise leading up to the mountains, it cawed repeatedly. Its rasping voice was the only sound in the world other than the tiny clink of metal tools on earth and stone and the shuffling feet of the bearers. The other people, drugged by their pain and fatigue, were unaware of the bird, but Calling Crow could not take his eyes off it. Lately a plan had come to him. He had been buying scraps of meat with the little Spanish money he had. He hid them high up in the roof of the hut, and he would use them to lure the dogs off, enabling him to make it to the wall and over. He had been memorizing the layout of the compound and the habits of the soldiers, and he had wanted more time, but now there was this noble bird telling him he would have to leave tonight. It was the time of the bitten moon and would be very dark, and that made Calling Crow feel more bold.

Calling Crow carefully shoveled a load of dirt into a woman's basket. As she put it on her head and walked off, he looked around at the Spanish. They were everywhere, too many to count. There were almost as many as the people, yet despite their hunger for the yellow metal, they did not dig in the pits. Instead, most of them loafed, or played at their gambling games. But, there were always some watching the people work, and these were the ones with the dogs and thunder sticks. From the very first day it had been obvious to Calling Crow that escape during the day was impossible.

The crow called to him for quite some time and then, growing impatient, flew off toward the hills.

Calling Crow had noticed that Little Bear was different today. Earlier he had said nothing, seeming not to see Calling Crow as he passed him in the pit. Even now, later in the day, he worked like a younger man, strong and steady.

The heavy thudding of hooves distracted the people in the pits, and they looked up to see Roldan riding by on his horse. Calling Crow saw Little Bear stop his shoveling to watch. Calling Crow had seen the same thing many times this day. Whenever Roldan passed, Little Bear would stop what he was doing and watch him. He was waiting for Roldan to fall down dead.

The sun burned in the sky overhead like a raging fire. As Calling Crow filled a woman's basket with dirt, she fell in a faint. He lifted her face out of the dirt as the *cholo* guards rushed over. Anger burned within him like the embers of a fire as their shouts abused him. Always it was the same, whenever anyone fainted or was hurt, their shouts would fill the air: "Keep on working! Leave them! Keep on working!" Then they would wade into the pit with their whips and thunder sticks and drag the person off where one of the Black Robes would pray over them.

For a long time Calling Crow worked and twice he thought he would faint, too. Then he saw some people climbing out of the pit and heading up to the shade of some trees. Then others followed. It was time to eat. Every day when the sun was high, the people would gather, and soon after the Spanish arrived with a wagon full of cassava bread. There was never any meat, of course. Calling Crow had not had meat since before his capture.

Calling Crow walked over and touched Little Bear's shoulder. "It is time to stop and eat." Together they climbed out of the pit and moved in among the people to sit in the shade of the trees. They said little as they waited, for they had very little strength left to talk. As the heat rolled off the pit in rippling waves, they waited for the cassava wagon. They waited a long time and still it did not come. Even the Spanish guards looked about, talking quietly among themselves as they wondered when it would arrive. Finally all the people's heads turned as a column of dust was spotted down the main road. A few minutes later Roldan and another man rode up on horses. There was no cassava wagon.

They quickly dismounted, and Roldan handed the reins of his horse to the other man. Roldan approached the Spanish guards and the *cholos*. The people watched as they argued loudly. Then *El Animal* approached the people. "There is no food today," he shouted. "Go back to work now."

From the middle of the crowd, Calling Crow and Little Bear could not hear what they were saying. Then the word started spreading through the crowd in scared, murmured voices. "No food today. They say we must go back to work."

People around Calling Crow and Little Bear began to slowly get to their feet. Calling Crow was startled as Little Bear stood suddenly and shouted at them, "Everyone. Stay here! Do not move until they give us food. Stay here!"

People looked from him to each other and to the Spanish as they tried to decide what to do.

"Stay here," shouted Little Bear. The people closest to him sat back down. The sitting down rippled from the middle of the crowd all the way out to where the Spanish stood, like the waves from a rock tossed in a calm pool. Only Little Bear was standing now, a withered old man with a fierce, determined face, looking as if it were carved from rock.

"Get up," demanded one of the Spanish guards. "On your feet!" He kicked the man nearest him, and the man grunted in pain and fell onto his side. The people remained sitting and squatting, their eyes fixed nervously on the earth at their feet.

"Stay here until they feed you," shouted Little Bear. He looked over at the guards. "Yes, we are your slaves, but we are not dogs! You need us to do your work so feed us." He turned back to the people. "It is all right. They will not kill you."

Calling Crow watched the Spanish arguing loudly up at the head of the people. He saw Roldan signal some soldiers who stood off in the distance. They started over, their dogs straining at their ropes.

"Little Bear," said Calling Crow, "sit down. They are bringing the killing dogs."

Little Bear did not look down at him. "Let them. I cannot live this way anymore. I thought I could, but I cannot. I had a dream last night. In the dream my father came to see me here and I could not look at him because of my shame. I will be going to the spirit world soon, and I want to be able to look him in the eye. So if I have to die today, at least I will do so standing up, with the sun on my back and the green hills filling my eyes."

The snarling dogs practically pulled the soldiers along. Then the soldiers in the front used their whips and clubs on the people, opening a path to Little Bear. Roldan shouted to his interpreter, and the man said to Little Bear, "Tell the people to go back to the pit."

"No, they are too weak to work. They shall not move until you feed them."

Calling Crow saw fearful realization blossoming on the interpreter's face as he told Roldan what Little Bear had said. Roldan's face turned red with hot blood as he began shouting in a rage. Calling Crow watched in growing horror as the two men holding the dogs knelt and began untying them.

"Old man," said the interpreter, "please tell these people to go back to work or else they will surely kill you."

Little Bear said nothing as he looked off at the hills. A handler released his dog. With a quick lunge, the animal leapt at Little Bear's throat. Little Bear looked down at the last possible moment and brought his hands up to his face, but not before the animal's jaws had closed on his neck. The weight of the dog knocked him backward and then the other was on him as the people screamed and moaned in horror. The two dogs and Little Bear writhed on the ground. Calling Crow tried to pull one of the dogs off, and it turned quickly, biting him on the cheek, and then the

Spanish beat him with whips. Calling Crow fended off the blows as best he could and then some people grabbed him from behind and dragged him backward, down toward the pit. Calling Crow found the shemi that Little Bear had made lying half-buried in the mud where somebody had stepped on it. Tears filled his eyes at the sight of it, and he left it there and moved off to join the others at work.

Calling Crow waited in the darkness of the hut until No Neck's ragged breathing settled into a loud, rattling snore. He then pulled himself up on a crosspiece of the roof and got down his bag of meat scraps. He listened carefully to the sounds of the compound. Some soldiers approached and Calling Crow silently sang a prayer in his head to pass the time as they moved off.

Finally he went out into the night and moved quickly along the damp ground. Overhead, he was relieved to see only the light of a few stars visible above the scattered clouds; if he moved well he would be invisible to the soldiers. He walked the compound, turning where he had memorized, until he reached one of the pits. There he poured out the pungent meat scraps. There was enough to keep the dogs busy for a while. He listened to the loud racket the crickets and frogs were making. They would also help shield him from the dull ears of the soldiers. It was the crow spirit's protection, he told himself hopefully, as he headed in the direction it had taken.

He stopped after a while to listen for the dogs and heard nothing. Hopefully they were busy enjoying the meal he had provided them. Earlier he had also rubbed some medicine that an old man had given him over his body. The old man had said that it would make him invisible to all dogs. Calling Crow prayed that it was so as he made his way to the wall. He quickly and silently climbed it and walked to the stream where the Spanish got their water. Reaching it without incident, he said a quick prayer of thanks and moved quietly along the sandy bank.

Calling Crow walked swiftly but silently. He was able to follow the curve of the creek by the outline of the few

trees along its bank against the faint starlight. He stopped
for a moment and listened as he stood still as a tree himself. He was ready to move again when he heard a voice.
The voice was no more than a few feet away, and he could
tell from its intonation that it was asking a question. Another voice on the other side of him answered. Calling
Crow broke out in a sweat. He was between two soldiers
who had evidently camped outside the compound. They
were talking as they lay down and waited for sleep to
come! One of the voices said something, and the first
voice broke out in a loud laugh, and then the other joined
in. Calling Crow slowly crouched close to the earth. Moving slower than a snail, he put one foot down after another,
fearing all the while that he would step on one of the soldiers. Finally, after a long time, he was sure he was away
from them and increased his pace.

The underbrush grew thick and Calling Crow was
forced to move down the bank and walk in the ankle-deep
water. He was well away from the soldiers when he heard
something following him back on the bank. He moved
faster and heard it crashing through the brush behind him.
He wondered why the medicine the old man had given
him was not working and thought that perhaps this was a
spirit dog. He heard a scrabbling of claws on wet rock and
nervously began moving out toward the deeper part of the
creek. He was too late; a throaty growl reached his ears,
raising the hairs on his neck. He ran wildly as a splash
sounded behind him and then iron jaws closed around his
leg, causing him to cry out. He whirled about, and the
creature released its grip and then lunged at his face. Calling Crow caught it by the skin about its head and managed
to hold it off while it snarled and snapped, its claws ripping his chest raw. With a powerful shake, the dog broke
free of his grasp and bit down hard on his arm. Letting out
a moan of pain, Calling Crow grabbed for the dog with his
other arm. He lost his footing on a mossy rock and fell
into the knee-deep water on top of the dog. The dog released him, and he quickly wrapped both arms around its
neck, pinning its head under the slowly moving water.

Calling Crow raised his head into the warm night air as the dog shook and clawed at him as it tried to free its head. He held it under until it stopped moving and then released it. In the feeble light he saw it slide away, turning slowly in the sluggish current. Calling Crow got slowly and painfully to his feet. He felt like shouting out a victory cry. He was free! He stood in the middle of the stream, listening to see if anyone had heard the sounds of the struggle. There was only the gentle sigh of the water, and he moved back to the bank.

After walking and running half the night, he found a hole in the earth in which to sleep and hide in the light of day. Crawling on his hands and knees, he moved way into the back and lay down as a deep sleep settled over him.

He heard the dogs first. They did not bark or snarl; there was only a steady sniffing and pawing. Then he heard the voices of the soldiers. They were at the entrance of the hole. He heard them talking and laughing loudly. "Come out," said the interpreter. "Come out now or we will send the dogs in after you."

Calling Crow felt a great anger as he crawled out into the morning light. To have been free, if only for a night, had been a joy and now he was a captive. He charged the soldiers, and they hit him with sticks and fists. He did not feel any pain. What was the pain of a blow compared with the great pain in his heart? They took him back to the camp and whipped him for a long time. He laughed at them and insulted them. Finally, when he could stand no more and cried out in pain, they were pleased and stopped. They then threw him into the pit with the others.

Calling Crow worked as slowly as he could. Twice he fell to the ground in a faint, but the others helped him to his feet before *El Animal* or one of the other guards saw him.

That night in the hut he was too sick to eat. He lay on the ground in front of the fire while No Neck watched him from the other side of the hut. He thought of Tiamai and wished he could be with her. It had been so long. He tried to remember her and realized painfully that he could no longer see her face.

"Cacique," said No Neck. "Come, drink some of my wine. It will help you to forget what you have become."

Calling Crow did not want to drink wine, but he could not stand his pain any longer. He crawled over and drank thirstily from No Neck's jar. They sat in silence for a long time, listening to the sound of a woman and child crying in the next hut. No Neck passed out and fell onto his side in a stupor. Calling Crow drained the rest of his jar and crawled back over to the wall. He took the blood glass out of the small medicine bag Little Bear had given him and held it up to the light of the fire. It glowed red like the setting sun. It seemed on fire, like his heart.

Chapter 21

In the dim light of the cane-walled, thatch-roofed hut, Father Luis shifted in his chair and reached around to scratch his back. The intense heat of the afternoon made him sweat badly, and the moisture made the wool fibers dig into his skin like a thousand tiny knives. Sighing heavily, he looked down at the paper on the table before him. How to begin? he thought. How to put over forty years of pain and suffering and death down onto a single piece of paper?

He looked out at the bright sunshine and wondered where Father Antonio was. He was firmly on the landowners' side regarding the Indian question and it would not do to have him see the letter. Father Luis rubbed the feather quill against his cheek pensively. If he wrote this letter . . . and if the wrong pair of eyes in Castile saw it, then there could be much trouble for him. He was arrayed against some very powerful interests on the island, many of them in the Church.

Father Luis struggled to fill his lungs with the hot stifling air and prayed momentarily for a slight breeze to wash through. He watched to see if the nearest tree would move in answer to his prayer, and he immediately felt foolish and said a quick prayer of apology. He thought of his visit to Roldan's mine and the sufferings of the native people there . . . to think that the Lord would cool him off by virtue of a slight demonstration of His power was not only foolish, but arrogant as well.

Father Luis shooed a fly buzzing him. He touched the quill to the paper. As he wrote, he saw hope glimmering in the wet ink trace the quill left behind:

> *Only after having beseeched the* encomendero *landowners on at least a dozen separate occasions, and even our own Bishop Cavago at least three times, all to no avail, do I dare write these lines. Most of the* encomenderos *continue to treat the Indians brutally, or to sanction that treatment, ignoring all the stipulations of the Council of the Indies on these matters. I will relate several incidences herein to document what I mean . . .*

Finishing, Father Luis folded the paper neatly. He tilted the sealing wax candle, dripping a glistening crystal-clear bead of wax onto the seam. When it congealed into a milky pearl he pushed his ring into it and, as he did, felt his own fate sealed by the action. So be it, he thought. Once his friend, Father Cuneo, the King's confessor, received this it was all in God's hands.

Father Antonio came into the hut, and Father Luis quickly tucked the letter up his sleeve.

Father Antonio hoisted a leather pouch onto the table. "I've been looking all over for Miguel," he said tiredly, "and he is nowhere to be found. You shall have to take the mail to the ship."

Father Luis nodded. "Perhaps he is down at the reservation."

Father Antonio frowned. "Probably. He is slipping back into the old ways. You better have a talk with him."

Father Luis didn't say anything. This was something he tried not to think about. It wasn't just Miguel, but many of the Indians. He had a horrid suspicion that, if left alone, they would all soon slip back into their old ways. It was a most disturbing thought.

Father Luis went out into the bright light and stopped for a moment to allow his eyes to adjust. As he walked around the church, its high adobe walls and arched portals gave his troubled mind some succor. Building this church had been one of his biggest achievements. It would withstand the hurricanes which yearly wreaked havoc on the island's flimsy cane dwellings and would be here long after he was gone.

Father Luis urged the ass down the mountain road with steady, gentle kicks. He wanted to get to Santo Domingo and do this quickly before he thought about it too long and changed his mind. When he came to the dull green olive trees which lined the last stretch of road into the city, he could hear shouting and laughter. As he entered the shade of the trees and his eyes adjusted, he saw with a sinking heart that a group of soldiers appeared to be sprawled about in the dirt, blocking the road as they drank wine and gambled.

When Father Luis could see their faces clearly, his breath quickened. Their horrid weapons, no doubt stained with the blood of innocents, lay about, arquebus, halberd, and crossbow, their sharp steel swords. The closer he got, the more their talk abused his ears. They were an embarrassment to Christianity. They knew the Lord's holy commandments yet they behaved like beasts. Even the most warlike Indians of the new world were saintlike compared to these, for the Indians knew not of God and His laws.

"Father," said one of the soldiers mockingly. He had his hand on his sword as he advanced.

Father Luis felt his pulse quickening. He thought of

turning about and telling Father Antonio the ass had bruised a hoof on a rock and he couldn't get to the ship on time.

The soldier stepped in front of the ass, and it stopped, waiting patiently.

"What do you want?" said Father Luis. He looked back over his shoulder. There was no one coming in either direction.

"Won't you have a drink with us, Father?"

The other soldiers watched with leering drunken faces.

Father Luis's face grew red as a beet. "Stand back and let me pass," he said, a quaver to his voice. "I have business in Santo Domingo."

The man swayed drunkenly and took the ass's halter in his hand. "What's the hurry, Father?" He looked back at the others who lay about, one of them throwing some dice onto the dirt. "We want you to gamble with us."

"Can you not see I am a man of God?" Father Luis tried to put as much anger as possible into his voice, but was unnerved at the pleading quality of the result.

"Then dismount and we shall bend our knees in prayer together instead."

A bellow of rough laughter followed, and another man got to his feet and started over. Father Luis's heart pounded in his chest. He swallowed hard. He felt like a swine being pushed into a holding pen before a holiday feast. Please, God, he prayed, give me the courage to do Thy divine will.

"Let me pass," he said, this time managing to put more anger into his words.

The man held on to the halter and came around the side of the ass.

Father Luis felt as if his heart would stop. *Madre de Dios.* He jabbed his heels into the ass and the animal jerked forward in fright, bumping the drunken soldier. He staggered backward and fell on the ground as the others laughed. Father Luis, his face taut with fear, looked straight ahead as the ass trotted by. Thank God! he thought, when he was safely out of the shaded area. He turned quickly around for a look and saw that they were not following him. Thank God!

Father Luis soon approached the city gate. Made of reddish adobe brick, its high walls had crumbled in places, and bushes and weeds sprouted from the exposed earth. The wall stretched about two cable lengths, with turrets at either end and a high Roman arch in the center. Father Luis passed beneath the arch into the shade and the noise of children playing in the waters of the Fountain of the Maid. He paused to drink from the fountain as a mule train passed, the slow-moving animals tethered head to tail.

Father Luis started out again through the red dust streets of Santo Domingo. He saw the half-naked children playing in the dirt, saw the diseased men and women begging, and wished he had never been transferred to the colonies. He was a man of God and he wanted to help these people, but he could not. Not really. He was not a politician. He was not cut out for all this courtly intrigue and skullduggery. He frowned slightly as the ass plodded along. Perhaps he should just forget about the letter.

He soon came out upon the wharf area. The resinous smell of tar mixed with the salty aroma of the sea as he rode past a great carrack which was careened over against the stone quay for bottom cleaning and caulking. Sturdy ropes secured it to iron posts in the quay, and its masts were supported by heavy timbers. A raft of logs lashed to the hull rose and fell slightly in the swells, its wetted wood glinting dully in the afternoon light. No men were working on it. He rode on to two ships tied up together. In front of them, several tall stacks of casks waited to be loaded onto the ships. The fragrant sweet smell of cane sugar filled the air, and Father Luis looked up at the men moving about on the ships. They were Francisco Mateo's ships, and he spotted him leaning against the rail talking to another man. Mateo looked down and waved.

Father Luis nodded and looked away. He didn't like the man; he was part of the problem here. Indeed, of the two shiploads of captives he had brought in a few months ago,

many of them were already sick or had died from the Indian pox.

Father Luis approached the last of the caravels tied up
along the quay. He could tell by all the activity going on
that she was the *Esmerelda*, the ship which would take the
mail to Castile. Gangs of mestizos and Indians rushed
about to finish loading her before she left in the morning.

He tied up the ass and walked up the plank. Halfway
there he retrieved his own letter from the sack and tucked
it in his robe. He gave the sack to the guard and walked
back down. His cowardice weighed heavily on him and he
felt very sad. He tried to tell himself that the feeling would
pass after a while, but he knew that it would not.

Someone called his name. It was Senor Domenico Grimaldi, one of his parishioners. He sat with some other men
at a table under a tent top on the other side of the casks.

Despite the hot weather, Grimaldi wore a heavy wool
cloak about his shoulders. He smiled as Father Luis approached. Aged and badly weakened by fevers, Grimaldi
had only come to the colony three years earlier, but his
constitution was poor and he had never been able to withstand the tropical weather. Now he was going back to live
out the rest of his life in peace at his estate in Lisbon.

"How are you, Father?" he said.

Father Luis looked down at the table. "Not very well."

Senor Grimaldi took Luis's hands. He looked deep into
his eyes and smiled. "Well, please take care of yourself,
Father. The Indians love you and they depend on you very
much."

Luis's eyes grew moist. It was as if God were speaking
to him through his friend. What had he done? He, the only
chance the Indians on this island had, and he had abandoned them. He tried to smile at Grimaldi and said nothing.

Grimaldi smiled and held up an empty cup. "Won't you
join me in a cup of beer?"

Father Luis shook his head and looked around furtively.
"No. Listen, Domenico, I want you to take something
back for me."

"Of course, Father," said Grimaldi.

Father Luis took the letter and handed it to him. "Give this only to Father Cuneo at the palace in Castile. Show it to no one else, do you understand?"

"Of course, Father Luis. Just as you say."

Father Luis got to his feet. "I must go now."

Grimaldi clapped him on the back. "I will miss you, Father."

Father Luis leaned close. "And I, you. God loves you, Domenico."

As Father Luis rode off, he looked out at the harbor. The calm sea was a beautiful shade of blue, like the virgin's gown in the church paintings, and a cool breeze came off of it, refreshing him. The color and fresh air filled him with hope. He looked out past the stone breakwater at the many small, lateen-rigged fishing boats bobbing in the gentle waves. Finally, he thought, something would be done about these great injustices, and that change would be his legacy. Instead of leaving only a church of stone, he would have changed the lives of thousands of Indians forever. A smile broke out on his large round face and for the first time in a long time he was truly happy.

Chapter 22

Calling Crow shoveled dirt into the woman's basket. "Are you of the Guale People?" she asked him, but he didn't hear her. He, like all the others in the pit, was entranced by the smell wafting over them, and he could think of nothing else. The smell came from the raised bank at the edge of the pit where some Spanish guards were roasting a large animal over a fire. Everyone knew it was for the Spanish only; they had never given the people meat, except once when some rotten scraps were mixed in with their cassava bread. The people told Calling Crow that this animal was a pig, and all morning the sweet scent of the pig meat and the crisp smell of its fat dripping onto the fire had tickled and teased everyone's nostrils cruelly until meat was all anyone could think about. They talked of it in angry, muffled tones; some of the older, weaker ones even wept as they worked. Calling Crow thought that No Neck, who was working close by, would go mad. He had not taken his eyes off of it and had fallen down several times because he had been walking backward to keep the pig in sight. Then, Roldan's younger helper and another Spanish carrying a crossbow came to the edge of the pit and pointed at Calling Crow, No Neck, and an old man called Big Heart.

"You and you and you! Come with me."

Calling Crow, No Neck, and Big Heart climbed up the bank of the pit and followed the two Spanish to the horse-drawn wagon the Spanish transported food and supplies in. Ortiz indicated that they should get in. As Calling Crow pulled himself in, Ortiz kicked him in the buttocks. Calling Crow turned quickly to fling himself onto Ortiz, but No Neck and Big Heart grabbed him from behind, pinning him to the floor of the wagon. Ortiz said something in Spanish and scowled, going round to the front of the wagon. Calling Crow felt paralyzed by his rage and shame. No Neck and Big Heart only let Calling Crow up after the wagon began moving, and it was then that Calling Crow decided that he would swallow the blood glass that night and leave this place for the netherworld.

As the wagon swayed and bumped past fields of towering cane, No Neck and Big Heart laughed and talked quietly about how much wine they could drink, about how much wine Calling Crow had drunk the night before, about which woman was lying with which man. Calling Crow said nothing as he watched fields of grass pass by. Finally they came to a plantation full of flowering cassava

plants. Among the orderly rows, many black slaves
worked at digging up the roots with many-pointed sticks.
The slaves sang as they worked, one man who had perhaps
been their Chief in their native land calling out a line of
their strange song, after which the others would repeat the
phrase in a thick, organlike harmony. As he listened, Calling Crow forgot his own sadness as the pain and suffering
in the singing filled the air. There was something else in
the music, a bright hopeful lilt running through the refrain.

The wagon turned in a road and pulled up toward a
large, thatch-roofed, open-sided hut where black women
could be seen preparing the cassava by squeezing it in
long skin bags hanging from the roof of the hut. The
wagon stopped, and Calling Crow and the others were
made to load many baskets of cassava bread and fruit and
vases of water and wine. When they finished, Ortiz went
off. Calling Crow and Big Heart sat in the shade of the
wagon under the watchful eyes of the crossbow-armed
Spanish, while No Neck, who had come to this place
many times, walked over to talk to the black people. He
came back a few moments later and sat down heavily,
something concealed under his tunic. When the Spanish
guards wandered around to the far side of the cart, No
Neck produced a red glass Spanish bottle. He took a sip
and rubbed his lips appreciatively.

"Is it wine?" said Calling Crow.

"No, it is better, stronger. It is cane liquor."

"Give me some," said Calling Crow.

No Neck handed Calling Crow the bottle, and he tilted
it up and drank hungrily.

"That is enough," said No Neck, "too much." He
laughed as Calling Crow handed the bottle back to him.
"This is not wine, Calling Crow. Soon you will know
that."

They sat in the shade silently, and Ortiz and the other
Spanish came back and ordered them into the wagon. The
wagon had not gone far when Calling Crow felt his head
open up and a multitude of angry, shouting demons rush
inside. He leapt to his feet and rushed forward to attack

Ortiz. Grabbing him from behind, he tried to pull him back into the bed of the wagon. No Neck and Big Heart pulled Calling Crow backward while the Spanish guard hit him repeatedly in the face. Suddenly the wagon jumped violently and Calling Crow was thrown out onto the road. The wagon stopped, tilted up at a crazy angle, and Calling Crow crawled to one of the wheels as No Neck and Big Heart called to him. He heard the Spanish cursing him angrily as he grasped the wheel. They beat him, but he didn't care. He held the wheel tighter and it began spinning, moving around faster and faster, more cruel Spanish magic.

Calling Crow watched No Neck and Big Heart picking up the bread and fruit from the road. He heard a horse coming and saw Roldan dismounting. Roldan barked angrily at Ortiz, both men pausing several times to glare over at Calling Crow.

Roldan cursed and grabbed the coiled-up whip from the bed of the wagon. He stepped back and extended the leather coil to its full length. Then, with a quick snap, he lashed it out at Calling Crow. Calling Crow flinched at the biting pain. He held up his arms and the next blow cut into them. He saw something coming down the path from the hills. At about the distance an arrow would travel, a Black Robe rode closer on a small horse. They continued to beat him, and he knew then that they would kill him. He would not live out this day. The words that Little Bear had taught him came to him suddenly and he called out, "Father, I *Cacique! Cacique!*" *Caciques* were not supposed to work in the pits. If he could possibly get out, he would be in a position to help the others. The Black Robe evidently did not hear him, and the whip continued to bite into his back, each blow draining the life's blood from him. Calling Crow got to his knees and crawled out into the road. A gust of wind blew a wave of dust across the road and into his eyes. Again he called out loudly, "I *Cacique! Cacique!*" He looked up as Roldan continued to beat him and saw that the Black Robe was not going to stop. The man must have heard him and was going to do

nothing. Quickly, angrily, despite the red-hot stinging of
the whip on his back, he began scratching into the dirt
road the image of the crossed sticks that the Black Robes
worshiped. In his own language he shouted at the Black
Robe, "I put the cross of your craven religion in the dirt
where it belongs. I piss on your cross!" As Calling Crow
reached for the rope tie of his breeches, a hard blow
landed on the back of his head.

Father Luis saw the wagon and men over by the edge of
the cane field as a few big errant drops of rain struck his
face. He heard the crack of a whip plainly, but kept his
eyes straight ahead. It was more of those horrid soldiers.
Hopefully his letter would change much of what they did
on this island. But, in the meantime, he could not inter-
vene in every instance of abuse. Thunderheads were building over the green hills in the distance. A big rainstorm
was coming. He'd better hurry. He had to teach a catechism to the Indians in his charge.

He heard a deep loud, awful voice that seemed to be
calling him. "Father, I *Cacique! Cacique!*" it cried loudly.
It was a horrible voice, full of pain and rage, almost like
that of a great animal taught to speak like a man. The
voice came again and again, stabbing to the soul of Father
Luis as he kept his eyes straight ahead and tried to ignore
it. It must be one of the soldiers, he thought, trying to play
a joke on him. He must fix his mind on something else.
What was it that Father Marcos had said about a new theory that was going around? According to the theory, the
Christ had visited this new world, perhaps after rising
from his sepulchre. After all, there were many stories
among the Indians on the Main about the bearded white
God who had appeared to them. And had not Cortés in
New Spain conquered the Indians there, poor souls, because they had thought him their bearded white God returning to them?

"Father!" The voice was piercing and soul-rendering in
its pain. Father Luis halted the ass and looked over. In the
quickly darkening light, he saw one of the Indians crawl-

ing about in the dirt of the road as the overseer stood over
him, whip in hand. Those terrible soldiers, thought Father
Luis. Had they no respect, no fear of Him who rules over
all, Spanish and Indian alike?

Father Luis jerked the halter of the ass and looked away
as the ass started forward again. Pity. But God would
surely punish the soldiers for these abuses.

A great flash of lightning lit up the sky and once more
Father Luis looked over at the men. His breath caught in
astonishment. The Indian had scratched a life-sized cross
in the dirt of the road! It was a miracle, as if God Himself
was working through the man! A concussion of thunder
rolled across the land, rumbling in Father Luis's chest cav-
ity, and another lightning bolt whip-lashed across the darkening sky, shattering it into a thousand pieces. The Indian
screamed out something unintelligible, the loud voice so
horribly tortured, it stopped the ass in its tracks. Father
Luis sat watching the scene, unable to move. The overseer
stooped over the Indian and brought the hard wooden handle of the whip down on the back of his head. He collapsed onto the crude cross on the ground as cold rain
began pouring down all around in a torrent.

The rain broke the spell over Father Luis, and he
quickly slipped off the ass and hurried over. He saw that
it was Roldan and one of his men. "What in God's name
are you doing?" he shouted.

They said nothing as they dragged the Indian toward the
wagon, leaving the smear of a trail in the mud. Roldan
looked back at Father Luis. "This is none of your affair.
We are merely disciplining him."

"Discipline?" said Father Luis loudly as he followed
them. "I wouldn't discipline a dog as poorly. Leave him
be!" They dropped the Indian, and Father Luis knelt down
in the mud beside him, slapping him on the face. There
was no response.

Father Luis looked up at Roldan and Ortiz. They were
smiling! "I heard him say he is a *Cacique*!" he shouted
over the sound of the rain. "You are not allowed to work

Caciques. They and their progeny are supposed to be sent to the mission schools."

Roldan spat in the mud. "He is no *Cacique.* He is simply lying to get out of work."

Father Luis looked at the slowly disappearing cross scratched in the muddy earth. "Well, for certain he is a Christian and because of that I shall take him at his word."

Roldan frowned in annoyance at Calling Crow's still unmoving form. "It is like the old saying: 'The devil takes refuge behind the cross.'"

"Who are you to be a judge of such things?"

Roldan said nothing, and Father Luis turned to No Neck and Big Heart, who were watching. "Is he a *Cacique?*"

"Yes, Father," said No Neck, looking nervously over at Roldan. "That is what he has told us."

"That settles it, then," said Father Luis. "I'm taking him with me."

The rain came down steady now as the thunder and lightning moved off into the distance. Father Luis turned to No Neck and Big Heart. "Help me with him." Together the three men carried him over to the ass and slung him facedown across the animal's back. The ass shifted uncomfortably for a moment, moving its hoofs as it adjusted to the heavy load.

Roldan walked over to him. "By what authority do you do this?"

Father Luis took the cross from around his neck and held it out. "By His!" he shouted. "And if that is not enough for you, you can go before the Cabildo of Santo Domingo and plead your case with them!"

Roldan smiled evilly. "Very well, Father," he said.

Father Luis turned away and took the bridle of the ass. He led him back toward the path.

"Now we shall have to work the others even harder, Father," Roldan shouted to Father Luis's retreating form. He struck No Neck hard, knocking him into the mud. He whipped Big Heart while shouting at the priest's back. "Now you must do his work, too, you dogs."

Father Luis did not turn around as he led the ass toward the ox track.

Calling Crow heard Birdfoot's flute playing in his dream. He could not see him, however, nor could he see Sun Watcher, or his village of Tumaqua, or Tiamai. Sadness welled up in him as he realized they were gone from him now. There was only the haunting music moving like a brightly colored snake through the white mist of his dream. Just before he woke, he realized that Roldan's blows must have knocked all the memories out of his head.

He woke in a place where they kept animals. Without opening his eyes, he could smell their food and droppings. He opened his eyes and saw the Black Robe sitting next to him. Calling Crow was surprised at how fat the man was. He smelled very bad, too.

"I, Father Luis," said the Black Robe, using signs and some of Calling Crow's own words. "What name you?"

"Calling Crow."

"Tell me how you came to this place?"

Calling Crow told the Black Robe about the girl he loved who was called Tiamai, and how he had planned to marry her, how Caldo had died, and how he had killed Many Skins Man and become Chief.

The Black Robe was very upset when he heard about Many Skins Man's death. "Bad!" he said. "Very bad!" He waved his hand over Calling Crow as if to chase away flies. "Go on."

Calling Crow told him about going after the cloudboats, about his capture and how Big Nose had died.

"Where your village?" said the Black Robe.

Calling Crow grew suspicious. "At the other end of the sea."

"Ha!" The Black Robe laughed heartily and jabbed Calling Crow with a fat finger. "You no say where. You think I slaver, eh? You funny man."

Calling Crow said nothing further.

The Black Robe got up from his seat. "You worry no

more, eh? You have home this place. You have father, too. God is father. Holy Mary is mother, and Jesus is savior! Jesus is Lord! Don't worry."

Calling Crow tried to focus on the man's face, but his eyes watered, blurring his vision. He fell back into a deep sleep.

He woke a long time later, his nose telling him there was food nearby, meat. The fat Black Robe had left it in a wooden bowl beside where Calling Crow lay. Calling Crow knocked the bowl onto the floor in his haste to eat it. It was good, and he left the animal place and walked out into the sun. The light hurt his eyes, and he stumbled into the shadow of a large hut made of stone. He walked along, feeling the walls, till he found an opening. Now his eyes could see, and it was a very pleasing sight after the dirt and filth of the mines and the mine's hovels. This house of red rocks and weathered wood beams, mud smeared over all, felt good to him. It was like waking after death. He slowly ran his hands over the walls as he walked along on a path of smooth rocks.

There was peace here. He stepped across the threshold. The wind came in behind him, moving his hair while the leaves swirled on the rocks outside the door like skittering bugs. Inside the walls it was cool and peaceful and dim. He moved in further to the center and after a while he saw the beautiful woman on the wall and the man attached to the tree. He realized it was the Jesus and Mother Mary that the Black Robes prayed to, and he sat down before them and stared.

Chapter 23

In the sad, half-light of the church, Senor Francisco Mateo looked up at the pulpit at the beef-red face of Father Luis. The father was livid, and Mateo saw spittle flying from his lips as he continued his angry harangue of the landowners.

" '. . . And the Lord said, I have surely seen the affliction of my people which are in Egypt . . .' " Father Luis looked up, catching Mateo's eye. "This land here is as cruel a place as Egypt was." He continued reading. " '. . . and have heard their cry by reason of their taskmasters . . .' " Father Luis looked slowly round the congregation. "That is you! '. . . for I know their sorrows.' " He said this last softly and again looked round at the congregation. "Has any one of you ever tried to ponder the sorrows of these people who labor for you? I don't think so. 'And I am come down to deliver them out of the hand of the Egyptians, and to bring them up out of that land unto a good land and large, unto a land flowing with milk and honey . . .' "

A portly man next to Mateo coughed, his phlegmy hacking echoing loudly off the stone walls.

Father Luis sighed heavily as he waited for the man to stop. "The Lord's meaning is obvious. Surely you can see that the Indians of these lands share a similar plight." He paused for a moment, the only sound in the church being the scratch of a boot on the stone floor. "Be it hereby known, as the servant of the Lord, I shall not sit idly by while even one of the Indians in your *encomiendas* is mistreated in any way!"

Unable to contain himself, Mateo called out, "Are you now trying to tell us how to run our businesses?" Without turning her black lace-shrouded head, his wife squeezed his hand in warning.

"Yes," cried another man. "You should stick to teaching the Gospel, that is all!"

Father Luis slammed his meaty hand down on the pulpit, causing some of the women in the front row to jump. He leaned forward as he looked at Mateo. "This *is* the Gospel. His Gospel! And He is speaking to you! Now, hear me carefully. I shall withhold the Sacraments from any member of this congregation whose treatment of the native peoples goes against the rules of the Council of the Indies. Then I shall recommend excommunication to the Bishop."

A hush fell over the people. For Catholics, excommunication was the most serious punishment there was, worse even than earthly punishments.

Mateo smiled coolly, but inside he was troubled. To be cut off from God's grace and condemned to the fires of hell for all eternity was a frightening thing to contemplate.

An old gentleman in the rear of the church got up and quietly left. Several hollow coughs echoed through the cool church. Three men and their wives got to their feet and quickly walked out. Mateo considered walking out; he couldn't sit and listen to much more, but again, as if reading his thoughts, his wife squeezed his hand in warning.

Father Luis looked down at the congregation, his face shaking in anger. "And now," he said, "let us close the service with the Lord's Prayer."

Mateo stayed in his seat until all had left the church. His wife had been deeply disturbed by the father's threats and had left with her father. Now Mateo's anger built as he thought of the injustice of it all. The colony needed Indians to work the plantations and mines, and he had provided them. And there had been ample evidence that they were cannibals, and therefore taken legally, all according to the rules of the Council of the Indies.

Father Luis walked out of the sacristy, and Mateo got to his feet and approached him. The father looked haggard and did not seem surprised to see him.

"What would you have us do?" said Mateo quietly.

Father Luis turned. "What?"

"The Indians must work for the greater good of the colony and Spain. To make them work we must push them. Don't you see?"

Father Luis shook his head tiredly. "No. I do not see. I see no need of beatings, starving people into submission . . ."

"These things happen rarely. They are the exceptions to the rule!"

"One exception is too many."

Mateo scowled and moved closer. "Ah, you have never had to run a business and turn a profit; you've never had to bring in a crop." Mateo wanted to rein in his anger, but he could not. "What do you know of these things?"

Father Luis looked at him as if he were mad and then turned away from him.

Mateo heard a noise in the rear of the church and turned. An Indian with his back to them ran a polishing cloth along the wooden frame of a painted panel. Something about the man looked familiar, and Mateo walked back. Father Luis followed him.

The Indian turned round, and Mateo recognized him as the man he had captured on the beach. "You!" he said. "You are the one from the beach."

Father Luis translated Mateo's words.

Calling Crow shook his head. "Tell him I was on his ship, but I am not that one."

"He said you are wrong," said Father Luis.

Mateo advanced on Calling Crow. "He lies! He is the very one I took from the beach! What is he doing here?"

Father Luis stepped between the men and looked at Mateo. "What of it? It makes no difference now."

Before Mateo could answer, Calling Crow faced him. Calling Crow's face was a burning mask of hate as he said in his own language, "The man you took from the beach died long ago!" He quickly walked outside.

"How dare he shout at me like that!" Mateo followed Calling Crow outside and grabbed him by the shoulder. With a blur of speed, Calling Crow spun around and threw Mateo to the ground.

The two men rolled about, each trying to get his hands around the other's throat. Mateo brought his knee up between Calling Crow's legs, and Calling Crow sucked in his breath in pain.

Breathing rapidly, Mateo got to his feet. Calling Crow pushed himself to his knees. Looking up at Mateo, he said in his own language, "Kill me now, Fire Hair! For if you do not, I will surely kill you one day."

Father Luis appeared beside Mateo and hit him across the side of his face. Mateo turned quickly as Father Luis continued to slap at his face again and again.

"If you were not a priest . . ." Mateo cried out in rage.

"Don't you threaten me, you who breaks God's laws and the laws of this land!"

"You must be mad!" said Mateo. "What are you talking about?"

"He is a *Cacique* and you sold him to Roldan and his animals! That is against the rules of the Council of the Indies."

Mateo wiped at a small trickle of blood which ran from his nose. "A *Cacique*, eh? I don't believe it."

"Yes, a *Cacique*, and now a proper Christian."

Mateo turned away from Father Luis and looked down at Calling Crow. Embers of hate glowed in the Indian's eyes. "You are blinded by your own wishes for these people, Father. He is as Christ-like as a snake in the grass."

Father Luis's voice rose in pitch. "How dare you talk that way here! Leave at once!"

Mateo did not move.

Father Luis's cheeks shook with rage. "Go now, do you hear me? You are wrong, man. Wrong, I say, like the others. So much of what you and the others have done on these shores in the name of God and King is terribly, terribly wrong!"

Mateo's eyes burned into the other man's. He turned quickly and walked off.

Calling Crow went into the church to pray. He walked through the quiet coolness and sat down in the front row

before the Jesus on a cross. He thought of the people in
the pit, of No Neck and Big Heart and the others, and he
felt ashamed for having left. He was sure Roldan would
have killed him, but still he felt shame. He would ask Father Luis if he could go to the pit with him to help the
people.

The cool air and the rich strange smells of tallow candles and incense filled his nose, and a peace came over
him. Now that he was out of the hands of the soldiers and
under the loose control of Father Luis, he began to think
of escape. The priest seemed to be a good man, but who
could tell with these Spanish? There was no telling how he
would be later on. Calling Crow decided to use his new
freedom to carefully plan an escape to the mountains. Others here had told him that there were people living free up
there. This time, however, he would plan very carefully so
he wouldn't be captured like before.

Getting to his feet, he respectfully placed his offering on
the altar and sat down again. He prayed very hard for the
people in the pit, but he felt no power from the prayer. Sitting at the Jesus's feet, he squeezed the spirit bag Little
Bear had given him, hoping its medicine would combine
with the powerful medicine of the Spanish gods. He
prayed more and still he felt nothing. He looked at the
bright red blood running down the Jesus's face, at the long
hair on his head, his upcast eyes, the spear hole in his side
and the blood pouring from it. He could not understand
this religion. If the Jesus had all the magic that they said
he had, and if the priests had that same magic, and if they
were against what happened in the pits, why could they
not stop it? And this Father God—if he, Calling Crow,
were now *His* child, why had He let them do those things
to him? And surely Little Bear who had been baptized
many, many times was His child, too. But did it help him?

Perhaps the Jesus wanted to show them how brave and
proud he was and how their torture meant nothing to him.
That must be it, he thought. Feeling better with this new
understanding, he prayed again, staring hard at the Jesus.
He prayed this way for a long time, and then he saw the

Jesus in war paint and feathers. *Aieyah!* He had great power! Calling Crow thought of Fire Hair Mateo's hand on his arm earlier. He felt his kick. If he had the power of the Jesus, Fire Hair Mateo would be dead now.

Calling Crow stared at the Jesus awhile longer and then closed his eyes to pray for his escape. He prayed for a long time and then he slept.

The gentle slap of Father Luis's sandaled feet on the stone floor woke Calling Crow and he opened his eyes. The father came up behind him and spoke.

"I am sad to stop you praying, Roberto, but I want you to run fast for me."

Calling Crow was momentarily confused by the father's words. They communicated using a mixture of signs, Calling Crow's own language, and Spanish, and sometimes there were things they could not quite get across to each other, things which turned very strange in the telling.

Calling Crow said, "Yes, Father. I will do it. Tell me, if the Jesus has great power and you are a friend of the Jesus, could you ask him to help the people in the pit?"

Father Luis smiled sadly. "Every day I ask him, Roberto."

Calling Crow was puzzled. "Why must you ask him again and again?"

Father Luis laughed. "Sometimes others are talking into his ears and he does not hear my words."

"Ah," said Calling Crow. It did not make much sense to him, but he was tired of the confusing talk and so he said nothing more.

Father Luis nodded. "Roberto, I want you to go to the town."

As Calling Crow waited for him to go on, his nose was troubled by the priest's bad smell. It radiated out with the heat from his large fat body. Why did he persist in wearing the heavy black robes? Calling Crow wondered.

Father Luis glanced up at the altar and a look of horror came over his face. "God of the sky, forgive us," he cried loudly. He quickly grabbed the hare that Calling Crow had earlier snared and placed on the altar as an offering. Holding it at arm's length, he extended it to Calling Crow. "Please, no put this on altar."

Calling Crow took the limp hare and looked at him. "Why, Father?"

"If the Chief Father in town saw this, he would have you whipped!"

"Why? I have done nothing wrong."

Father Luis shook his head in exasperation. "Please, Roberto. Never do this bad thing again, eh?"

"Yes, Father." Again Calling Crow felt confused. He did not understand why the father did not think his offering worthy, but perhaps he would learn in time.

Father Luis handed Calling Crow one of the pieces of thin skin which the Spanish insisted *said* things. Calling Crow had already held one up to his ear and heard nothing.

"Here," said the father. "I want you to take this letter to Bishop Cavago. You remember I showed you the big stone house he lives in?"

Calling Crow nodded.

"Remember, you must give it to no one except the old Chief Father who has no hair on his head." Father Luis touched the tip of his nose. "And he has a melon growing here."

Calling Crow frowned. "I do not understand."

"He has a mark on his nose, round like a small casaba melon."

"Ah," said Calling Crow.

They walked out of the church together, Father Luis's hand on Calling Crow's shoulder. Calling Crow's skin crawled at this affront, but he knew the father was merely ignorant of the ways of his people and so he said nothing.

Father Luis paused and looked up at the sun. "You should not return today. The sun will go away before you get halfway back. Stay with the Chief Father's servants and come back in the morning."

Calling Crow walked down the road at a good pace. The afternoon sun warmed his back and cheered him. He walked fast, delighting in the sights of birds flying and bees gliding low over the clover of the meadow. The shadows were getting long when he arrived at the wall of the city. He paused at the Stone Pouring Woman to drink. Delighting in the coolness, he wanted to stay, but went straight to the big stone house instead.

Chapter 24

Juana of the Arawak People was awake. She lay still in the bed as the Bishop slept beside her. His eyes were closed, and she took advantage of the moment to look closely at his features. The blemish on his nose, a bulbous growth, was wrinkled like a melon. All that remained of his hair, a few long grayish strands, grew just above and behind his ears, like the hair on a corpse. These Spanish were very different from her own people, she thought. The old ones had more hair on their faces than on their heads.

Satisfied that he was asleep, she pulled her robe about her and sat up. As her feet touched the floor, his eyes opened and he touched his sweaty hand to her face. She cursed inwardly. She should have lain still longer. Then maybe he would have gone to sleep.

"Is Pedro still giving you Spanish lessons?" he said. Senor Pedro Barrameda was the majordomo, a Spanish who ruled over all the servants. Despite the Bishop's orders, he treated Juana with contempt, but only when the Bishop was not around.

"He says he is going to, but he never does."

"I will talk to him tomorrow."

"*Sí.*"

The Bishop turned her head with his hand and looked into her eyes. "Don't be in such a hurry, child."

"I have to go back to the reservation. I have work to do there."

"Is work more pleasing to you than lying with me?"

Juana's stomach turned at what she must say. "Of course not. You know it is not so."

The Bishop smiled and a knock came at the door.

Juana's heart beat rapidly as he sat up. Hopefully it was someone calling on him.

He got out of bed and quickly pulled the gown about his broad, hairy body. He opened the door a crack.

Juana could hear old Senor Barrameda's voice, dry as a fallen leaf long in the sun. "An Indian messenger has arrived with a letter."

"Well, where is it?"

"He would not give it to me. I know it is for you because I could clearly see your name on it, but he would not hand it over to me."

Bishop Cavago's voice rose in annoyance. "Why not?"

"I do not know. He is either deaf, or else he cannot speak the language. I think he is also nearly blind, too, for he studied my facial features most carefully."

"Thank you, Pedro. I will be there in a few minutes."

Bishop Cavago closed the door and watched Juana get out of the bed and pull her slip on. As she started through the door into the rear of the apartment, he called to her, "I will talk to him tomorrow about your lesson."

With some effort, Juana managed to smile and went into the other room to dress.

Bishop Cavago walked to the courtyard door. He was surprised by the sight of the messenger. He had never seen an Indian so large of build. "I am Bishop Cavago," he said.

Calling Crow studied the man carefully before handing him the letter.

Bishop Cavago ripped it open impatiently, glaring at the big insolent Indian as he walked off in his curious, wolfish gait. He glanced down at the signature and felt a twinge of anger. Father Luis again. He might have known. He read the letter quickly and balled it up. First he had been quoting scriptures to him, his own Bishop! Then he had angered most of the *encomenderos* on the island by placing himself between them and their Indians. Now, he was threatening the *encomenderos* with excommunication!

Bishop Cavago watched the small groups of Indians huddled in the shade of the courtyard. He smoothed the letter out against his gown and put it in his vest pocket. Well, he would have to do something about Father Luis before too long, perhaps that mission down on the Main where the Caribs were still proving so bothersome. At any rate, he could not allow him to take matters like this into his own hands.

Calling Crow saw one of Father Luis's native servants, the one called Miguel, sitting in the courtyard of the Bishop's house with some other men. He walked over to him.

"Grandfather, are you staying the night here?"

"Yes. I stay the night. And you?"

"Yes. I will stay."

"Are you hungry?"

"Yes."

Miguel got slowly to his feet. "Come. I know where we can get meat."

As Calling Crow and Miguel moved out onto the hot street, they found themselves in a crowd of people. The women talked loudly among themselves as the men walked quietly. A shout of warning came, and the crowd quickly moved to the side to get out of the way of an approaching Spanish on horseback. Calling Crow was shoved against a slender woman walking beside him and instinctively grabbed her to keep her from falling. She dropped the sack she was carrying, and he stepped on some of the fruits that fell out of it as he fought to keep his balance. The people shouted angrily at the rider as the dust from his mount floated through the air, obscuring them from one another and grinding in their teeth. Someone made a joke that the Spanish was in a hurry because he must be right off the boat from Spain and, having eaten of some red peppers for the first time, desperately needed water. Some of the people laughed at this, and Calling Crow looked around for Miguel. Someone hit him on the arm. It was the woman.

"You mashed my fruit to a pulp with your big feet!"

Calling Crow looked down at her. Since he had been in this place, he had learned enough of the local dialect to be able to understand her.

She wore her hair pulled back in the Spanish fashion. Her face was proud and her skin had a glow to it which drew the eye. As she knelt in the street to pick up her food, he could see that beneath the Spanish cloth, her breasts were firm and her hips rounded nicely. He felt bad at noticing this, however, for he was reminded of Tiamai.

The woman flashed an exaggerated hostile look at him. "Since you knocked these out of my hand, you should help me pick them up."

Calling Crow made no move, and the woman handed him the sack of fruits. "Take these over there," she said, pointing to a cool spot of shade cast by a tree.

Calling Crow walked over and, turning, spotted Miguel watching him from a distance. The older man's face darkened with displeasure, and he quickly turned and walked away. The woman walked over to him and held the fruits out. He held the bag open as she placed them inside. He handed the bag to her.

"What people are you?" she said.

"I am Calling Crow of the Muskogee People."

She smiled and then frowned. "I have never heard of those people. What do the Spanish call you?"

"Roberto."

"I am Juana. I am of the Arawak People."

A group of laughing children ran past them through the dusty street, their laughter rising above the dull drone of the adult voices like the songs of brightly colored birds. Juana smiled at them and then turned her attention back to Calling Crow.

"Where do you live?"

"Outside the city," said Calling Crow absently as he looked around for Miguel. He wondered why he had walked away. "I live with a priest called Luis. For a Spanish, he is a good man."

"Yes. I have heard of him."

A vendor walked by with a basket full of shiny red and green peppers. Calling Crow remained where he was as Juana inspected the peppers.

"There will be dancing tonight at the Napatuca reservation," she said. "Why don't you come?"

"I must talk to my companion first." Again Calling Crow looked around for Miguel and could find him nowhere. He turned back to speak with the strange, attractive woman named Juana but she had joined the crowd on the street. He watched her walk away. She walked proudly, he decided, like the daughter of a *Cacique*. She turned round to look at him and smiled.

Calling Crow walked back in the direction he and Miguel had come from and saw him standing at a row of small reed-thatched, palm frond–roofed vendor stands. Each one housed baskets piled high with fruits and vegetables. He walked up to Miguel.

"What did she say to you?" asked Miguel.

"That there will be a feast and dancing at the reservation tonight."

Miguel's eyes turned to slits. "Stay away from her."

"Why?" said Calling Crow.

"*Why?* You sound like the Spanish! See how she dresses? See how she wears her hair? She is not of the people anymore. That is why. You should stay away from her."

Calling Crow said nothing out of respect for Miguel's greater years, for that was the way of the people. But he knew that Miguel must be wrong somehow. For in just a short time this woman had touched something in his heart. He knew she wasn't a bad woman. He thought of staying away, however, for after all, thoughts of Tiamai still saddened him. Then a loneliness greater than that sadness welled up in him. No. The more he thought of this attractive woman, this mysterious Juana, the more he knew he must go.

Later that day, Calling Crow wandered past the reed-thatched huts of the reservation. Down by the beach, the drums beat steadily, like the heart of the village. The sound filled the people with a sense of joy and expectation. A group of six men and two women stood around a cook pot in front of a hut. They were looking over at Calling Crow as he passed and some of them laughed. One of the women waved him over.

"What people are you?" she said.

"Muskogee."

She turned back to the other woman. "So big, eh?" She said something that Calling Crow did not understand and they laughed again.

He turned away from them to watch the people walking by.

"Have you eaten?" the woman asked him.

"No."

"Sit."

Calling Crow stood watching the people as she walked over to the cook pot. He saw her quickly pull some hot meat from the pot and put it in a gourd bowl.

She brought it back to him. "Here."

He thanked her as he knelt and pulled a piece of the hot meat from the bone. "What meat is this?"

"It is pig. It was brought here by the Spanish."

"It is very good."

The woman smiled. She went back to stand with her group, but she continued to watch him eat, smiling at him.

Calling Crow watched the people milling around. Down at the beach he could see the small figures dancing in a line. Then he saw Juana walking alone up the path from the beach. He liked the way she moved. He looked at her, and she saw him and started toward him. The woman who had given him the meat ran up and grabbed the gourd bowl from him angrily. She glared at him before dashing back to her group.

Juana stood before him.

He got to his feet to stand beside her. He liked her smell. It was like the earth at night after a rain.

"You came," she said.

"Yes." He felt a little sad for a moment. Tiamai was gone from him, but here was this woman who was strong and pleasing.

"Where is your friend?" she said.

"He did not want to come." He could tell by the look in her eyes that she knew what Miguel had said. They stood silently for a while, watching the people walking about.

"I do not understand," said Calling Crow. "Why are these people free, while others are chained in the gold pits?"

"Aieyah," said Juana, shaking her head. "It is difficult to explain. I think it is because of the Black Robes. They have spoken to the Spanish *Cacique* across the waters on the behalf of this village. But the village must still pay a tribute to the Spanish."

"What do they pay?" asked Calling Crow.

"They paid gold at first," said Juana, "but then the gold ran out."

"And now?"

"Every day the village must send a hundred men to work." She pointed to a place where there was a smolder-ing firewell. "They assemble there every morning to be taken to the place where they will work that day."

Juana studied Calling Crow for a few moments and then grabbed his arm. "Let's go down to the beach and watch the dance."

As she led him away, two Spanish soldiers and a Black Robe came out of a hut. They were followed by a smiling man who, given his many adornments, Calling Crow as-sumed was the *Cacique* of the people of this reservation. He felt anger burning in him as he watched the *Cacique* smiling up at the Spanish in subservience.

"We outnumber them all," Calling Crow said to her qui-etly, "and yet we are enslaved. Why can't we drive them back into the sea?"

"No. That is what everyone thinks when they are first brought here. They are too strong, however."

"Perhaps. Why don't more people run away to the mountains?"

Juana looked at him curiously. "And live like hunted rabbits?"

"Not like rabbits, like men!"

Juana smiled at him and tugged him by the arm. "Come, forget about that for a while."

They walked down to the mass of people by the beach bonfire. Calling Crow joined the men on one side while Juana joined the women opposite them. When the line of women came and danced before him and the other men, she pulled him out of the line and danced around him. As the others smiled at him, he watched her, his face expressionless. She is very beautiful, he thought, she moves as gracefully as a deer.

Chapter 25

The sun was a small white ball high above as the two men raced on their horses down the red dirt road alongside the canebrake. Inside the dense green of the cane an invisible army of insects ground out a cloud of rhythmic noise, unheard by the riders in the thunder of the horses' hooves. One of the men was Francisco Mateo. His good friend, Senor Diego Vega, had become seriously ill, and Mateo had secured the services of a Senor Balboa, the best physician on the island, to rally him. Mateo and Balboa rode without speaking until they came to the road leading up to Diego Vega's *estancia*. As they started up the road, Senor Balboa, a short bald-headed man, reined in his mount. Mateo pulled up alongside him.

"Before we go inside," said Balboa, "tell me what has been done for him of late."

"His cook has been making him some soups and his wife has had an Indian healer giving him some potions; she is Indian, you see. None of this has yet turned the tide of his sickness."

Senor Balboa nodded grimly and they rode on.

An old Indian manservant walked hurriedly from the *estancia*, waving at the two men as they rode up. Mateo and Balboa dismounted, and Balboa called out to the servant, "Where are they keeping him?"

"The kitchen," said the man.

"Good, good," said Balboa, "the ventilation is better there." He looked at Mateo. "Bad air will only aggravate a fever. Thank God his Indian wife knew enough to do as she has."

Senors Mateo and Balboa followed the old servant through the house and into the kitchen. They saw Diego Vega lying on his back on a table. His Indian wife, Lomaya, leaned over him, rubbing his forehead with a cold compress. Standing off to the side was an ancient, white-haired Indian shaman wearing a ceremonial mantle of feathers and bones.

Lomaya bowed a greeting. The shaman seemed not to notice the two men.

Mateo nodded slightly. "This is Senor Balboa, a physician."

Lomaya nodded her head nervously. "This is Yomo. He is a healer and he is of my people."

Balboa looked at the shaman suspiciously as Mateo leaned his large hairy head down to listen to Diego Vega. His breathing was loud and labored. Hopefully he could be saved from death. Mateo turned to Lomaya. "Senor Balboa is an excellent physician, Lomaya. He has also ministered to my own wife. If anyone can save Diego, he can."

"Thank you, Senor Mateo," said Lomaya haltingly in her Arawak accent. She smiled sadly. "But Yomo has been ministering to Diego for several days. You need not have come."

Balboa shook his head. "Senora," he said, "we shall give Diego the very best that our own superior civilization has to offer, and, God willing, we shall rally him!" Balboa turned to an Indian woman servant who was looking on. "Please take the senora into the parlor. This might upset her." He looked at the shaman. "And tell him that he is no longer needed."

Mateo was about to add something when Diego coughed and muttered incomprehensibly. They stood waiting to see if he would continue, but he lapsed back into unconsciousness, the rasp of his breathing filling the room.

Balboa looked over at the shaman, who had not moved. "Did you tell him he could go?" he asked the woman servant.

"Yes," she said, "but he wants to watch."

Balboa scoffed. "Whatever for? He wouldn't understand any of it." He smiled encouragingly at Lomaya and hoisted his bag upon the wooden table by the window. "Very well." Laying his knives, bulbs, bleeding cups, and charts out, he moved over to stand beside Diego.

"Senor Balboa," said Mateo, "perhaps you could explain what we are going to do in order to reassure Lomaya."

Balboa nodded. "Senora, I am simply going to reduce the pressure on Diego's insides. He has too much of the wrong kind of humors built up in his system."

Lomaya looked down on Diego's supine form and made the sign of the cross. She left with the servant, but Yomo the Shaman remained standing by the door, never taking his eyes off of Diego's unconscious form.

Balboa had Mateo help him remove Diego's clothing. He then gave Diego an enema, using a bulb made from a sheep's intestines to deliver the purgative. Shortly afterward Diego began groaning in pain. Balboa ordered a servant to bring in a wooden tub, and they lowered Diego into it.

Mateo watched in awe and not a little distaste as Balboa inspected what Diego had passed.

Balboa looked up at him. "From this I have learned that there is a great deal of filth lodged around his liver."

"How can you be sure?" said Mateo. "I mean, don't all men's . . ."

Balboa shook his head confidently. "No. It is an indication of imbalance. If one ate the proper things, in the proper balance, at the proper time of year, then one's stools would smell and resemble a freshly baked cake from the oven."

Mateo frowned. He doubted all of this, but he dared not give voice to his doubts. After all, his own wife, Felipa, swore by the doctor's methods and had him bleed her on a regular basis. "I see," he said finally. He looked over at Yomo, who continued to watch the treatment. Yomo's incredulity had given way to wide-eyed interest. Mateo turned back to Balboa. "Well, what else is to be done for him? There must be some other ways to help him."

"There are," said Balboa without looking up from his work as he mixed some things in a bowl. "More purgings using some powders I have devised."

The servant helped Balboa bathe Diego, and they lifted him back up onto the table.

"The procedure seems to have helped him some," said Mateo. "He is moaning much louder."

Balboa glanced at Mateo sternly. He then looked over at Yomo, who was worriedly watching the proceedings. Balboa turned to the servant. "Where are his waters?"

The Indian looked at him questioningly. "Senor?"

"His piss pot, man! Bring it to me."

Incredulity spread across the man's features, and he went to fetch a covered clay pot from behind the door.

"Are you going to inspect that, too, in order to judge his condition?" asked Mateo.

"No."

"What are you going to do with it?" said Mateo.

"I am not going to do anything; he is going to drink it." Balboa looked over at Mateo. "Don't worry. This is the latest medical technique from the courts of Europe."

Mateo frowned sadly as Balboa lifted the top from the

pot and poured a draught into a wooden cup. "Help me lift him up."

They pulled Diego to a sitting position. Yomo watched intently and the Indian servant solemnly made the sign of the cross as Balboa poured the urine down Diego's throat. Diego sputtered and coughed spastically as they lay him back down.

Balboa picked up one of his knives. "Now I shall bleed him." After consulting a large chart depicting a naked human form, he made an incision just below Diego's left elbow. Then he quickly made an incision on the same spot on the right arm. Again, the Indian servant made the sign of the cross and Yomo's eyes grew large as they watched.

Mateo handed Balboa his bleeding cups and watched in fascination as he squeezed and attached them to Diego's pale skin. Together they watched them slowly fill with blood.

When Balboa had finished, Diego lay like an alabaster statue. Balboa looked at Mateo. "We can do nothing further."

"It is finished, eh?" said Mateo. "Good."

Balboa eyed Mateo curiously. "Not finished. Now it is time to pray."

Mateo helped Balboa pack up his bag. They left Yomo and the servant with Diego and went out to the parlor. Balboa joined Lomaya and her servant on the couch.

"How is he?" said Lomaya.

"He is still in a faint," said Balboa. "Let us pray." Balboa bowed his head and the women followed his example.

Back in the kitchen, Yomo took some crushed brown herbs from his bag and put them in Diego's mouth. Diego began working his jaw and swallowed several times. Yomo sang quietly as he moved his hands over Diego's face, neck, and chest, feeling the spirit there, manipulating the skin and bones as he pushed and pulled it out. Diego belched loudly, and Yomo tilted the man's head to the side. A stream of vomit erupted and shot into the tub on the floor. Yomo reached in his pouch and brought out some green seeds. He put them in Diego's mouth, one at a time, as he sang, holding Diego's mouth closed till he swallowed them. Yomo sang his prayer to the four directions, shaking his rattle. Then he stopped. He nodded solemnly to the Indian servant and exited through the kitchen door.

The only sound in the parlor was the creak of the floorboards as Mateo paced the floor while the others sat with bowed heads. Minutes and then hours rolled by in the still house.

Finally a servant entered the room. "He is awake and hungry," he proclaimed.

"He is?" said Mateo in wonder.

The man nodded happily.

Lomaya rushed off to the kitchen.

"Praise God," said Balboa. "Praise God!"

Chapter 26

Calling Crow took Juana for his woman. Thoughts of Tiamai still tinged him with sadness, but he could not deny himself this woman who was here and wanted him. In the beginning he would wait till evening when Father Luis was busy praying with the other Black Robes in the church and then he would leave and meet her on the beach. He tried to take her away to the mountains, but she would not go. Still he came to see her and he became happy. His memories of his home village remained, but they were no longer leaping flames in his mind, but rather red embers under a covering of soft gray ash. Such was the power of this woman, Juana, that even his dream of

the Destroyer seemed like it had never come to him. Now
his heart was full of her and it was very good. They lay
many nights there on the beach, entwined in each other's
warmth on sand that still held the heat of the sun, looking
up at the heavens as the sea sang its many sacred songs to
them. Then the rains came. Calling Crow had never in his
life seen so much rain. Juana's people told him that it was
the way it should be, the way it had always been, and that
it was good, but still it was very strange to him.

Juana took him to a secret place she knew near the sea.
There, inside a thick grove of palmetto, Calling Crow built
a small hut for them. They brought skins and blankets to
lie upon, tallow candles, skins full of water, Calling
Crow's spirit bag, Juana's treasure bundle full of things
from her people, and a finely carved wooden Jesus on a
cross. They planted corn, and there was plenty of small
game to be found in the surrounding forest. Calling Crow
dug a firewell in the hut, and the smoke from their fire
rose to the thatch-palmetto roof, dissipating in a gentle
fog, instead of rolling up in a telltale column. Oftentimes
they managed to sneak away and they had many happy
nights and mornings there.

They sat before the small fire, its smoke filling and
warming the hut. In the flames they saw reflected their
love of each other. Calling Crow stirred the flames occasionally while Juana sewed some clothes in the Spanish
fashion. They did not speak, for there was no need. After
a time Juana got to her feet and turned down the skins of
the pallet. She stepped out of her gown and lay down waiting for him. He damped the fire down and went to her. After they stopped moving against each other, they lay side
by side in the shapes they had made in the earth and felt
the warmth of each other.

One damp morning after Calling Crow had quietly returned to his hut behind the mission church, old Miguel
came in. Calling Crow was very tired and, hearing him,
raised his head. "What is it, Grandfather?"

"Father Luis was looking for you." Miguel looked back

out at the churchyard. "He was going to take you to Roldan's pit again, but he could not find you."

Calling Crow felt bad. He had gone once to help with the baptisms, and he had convinced Father Luis to bring along fruits for the people to eat. It had been good, and he was looking forward to going again. "Ah," he said, "I will go next time."

Miguel frowned. "You have been seeing that woman, haven't you?"

"Yes."

Miguel's voice was gruff. "She is no longer of the people."

Calling Crow sat up and said nothing.

"Stay away from her. If you do not, you will become like the Spanish and lose your soul."

"Ha," said Calling Crow, "being so long in this strange place I have already lost my soul."

"She is a *chola*."

"Why, because she is a servant to the Chief Black Robe? Many of the people are servants to the Spanish. It is better than being a slave, or being dead."

"No!" Miguel's hoarse voice took on a great strength. "It is much worse than that. She lies with the Chief Black Robe!"

Calling Crow felt as if Miguel had jabbed a cold stone spear through his heart. "How do you know this?"

"Three others who live in that house have told me this. So I know that it is so."

Calling Crow got to his feet and walked outside. He thought he heard Father Luis calling him, but he continued walking. His heart was on fire with a great anger, and he walked along the roads until he neared the jungle. As he headed across a pasture, warm rain came down and washed over him, but it did not soothe him. Instead his anger flamed up into a fire so hot that even the seas could never put it out. He entered the jungle and moved quickly through the foliage. Big drops of rain splattered down on the wide glossy leaves. Soon he came to the hills near the sea. He passed their corn patch and headed for their hut in the palmetto grove. The fire had died down, and Juana lay among the skins. She lifted her head as he entered the hut.

He stood looking down at her, saying nothing.

Juana looked at him worriedly as she got to her feet. She pulled her dress on. "Did you come back to work on the corn?"

He said nothing.

"Why do you look at me that way? Tell me."

"Because I see you for the first time, Black Robe woman."

Juana's expression collapsed as if she had been struck across the face. "Who told you that?"

"Miguel. He said there are others who say that it is so."

She turned away to pick up the water skin. He advanced and turned her around to face him.

"Is it true?"

Her face looked at him as if she could not believe he would treat her so. "Is what true? I love you! That is true."

"Did you lie with the Chief Black Robe?"

She said nothing and he shook her. "Did you lie with him?"

She would not look at him. "I love you only."

"Why did you do it?"

"I did it only for others."

"What kind of answer is that?"

"It is true. To save my uncle and my brother. They were going to kill them for striking a guard. The Bishop said he would intercede if I did what he asked."

"And did he?"

"Yes."

He pushed her away, and she fell backward onto the soft sand. "I shall kill him," he said. "I could sneak into his house and do it."

"No, Calling Crow," she yelled at him, "don't do this thing. I will lose you." Her face an angry mask, she grabbed him about his legs as he started for the entrance to the hut.

He didn't seem to be aware of her as he moved away, dragging her through the sand. She cried out angrily, her eyes shining with tears as she clung to his leg. "Don't do this thing to us. Don't do it."

He said nothing, reaching down to pry her arms from him. Once free of her, he moved quickly toward the entrance.

"Would you kill our child also for your revenge?"

He stopped and turned to her. "A child? How do you know it is our child?"

She looked deep into his eyes. "I ate of some medicine an old woman of my people prepared for me every time I was with him so I would not have his child." She touched her belly. "It is *our* child."

He sat down suddenly in the sand as his strength left him. She came to him and put her arms around him. "Please understand, my love. I did what I did with him only because I had to. I did it for my family."

"Where are your brother and your uncle now?" He spoke tiredly, as if in a daze.

"They ran away to the mountains. Uncle died, but my brother still has not been captured."

Calling Crow threw back his head. "Oh, Great Spirit, deliver us from these Spanish!"

Juana put her hand on his face. "We will be safe. We can find peace. Our child can have a happy life. We are a part of this new world now."

"Woman, I am in their world, but I can never be part of it."

"Yes, you can. Calling Crow, you are a strong man, I know, and brave. But if you take from this new world what it offers, you can be much stronger."

"What are you saying?"

"Those who fight against the Spanish ways are not happy. Those who fight can only run away or be killed. Those who take on the Spanish ways become stronger, don't you see? To hunt the deer in your land that you have told me about, you must learn the way of the deer. You must wear the skin of the deer. It is the same with this. You must learn their ways. You are wise. You see how things are. Do I lie about these things?"

"You talk too much," he said, but in his heart he was thinking. What she said might be true, but he didn't think that he could do these things.

"If you would learn the ways of the Spanish then we could have a better life here. So could our child. He could become a part of the new world."

To even consider this hurt him too much and so he said nothing.

She went on. "Why don't you learn their language? Father Luis would teach you."

"Why should I learn their language?"

"You could be one of their interpreters, and then we would have a better life here. You could make the lives of the people better."

He got to his feet. He was confused by all of her words. "That is enough talk for now."

"I will wait for you here tomorrow," she said.

He said nothing as he walked out.

On his way back to Father Luis's church, he saw the people who had come up from the reservation, sitting about on the streets of the town, waiting for food to fall from a wagon, or waiting for a chance to steal. He saw them rush to get out of the way when one of the Spanish rode past on their large horses. He saw their children begging. This contrasted with how fat and healthy the *cholos* and their children looked in their Spanish clothes. The Spanish had great power. She was right in that. It was as if he was seeing right for the first time in a long time. The Spanish were such strange, brutal people, and he could not understand how the Great Spirit could let things come to this, but he could not hide from what his eyes showed him: the Spanish had great power and great medicine. It was so, and the ones who took on the Spanish ways as their own grew more powerful and seemed to prosper. Their women and babies were fat, and some of them even had the horses and carts of the Spanish.

Later that afternoon he arrived back at the mission church. With a heavy heart, he went inside and saw Father Luis praying alone up in the front.

Calling Crow walked up behind him.

Father Luis turned and smiled expectantly.

"I want to go to the *Cacique* school and learn more of the speech of your people."

Father Luis raised his hands to the Jesus on the cross and smiled warmly. "Thank you, God, for hearing the prayers of someone with weak faith, such as I." He turned to Calling Crow. "Roberto, my son, I shall take you there tomorrow."

Chapter 27

Just past the big whitewashed arch that separated the small room from the big one, Calling Crow sat on the straw-littered floor with three other Indian men carving crucifixes from blocks of wood. He noticed that the two priests had finally begun working on the big forge, and he put down his carving and walked over to watch them. They had been building the thing for as long as he had been coming to the *Cacique*'s school and had only recently finished it. He had watched them make the mud bricks, and the rack inside for the crucible, as well as stitch together the bellows. Earlier this day he had watched some men bring in baskets of the strange earth they used to make Spanish iron. Then they had begun feeding the fire. They worked all morning, and the thing was very hot, almost as hot as the sun, it seemed. Now they were about to make Spanish iron, and Calling Crow very much wanted to see how it was done. He stood silently behind the priest who was moving the wooden pole coming out of the forge up and down. Sweat ran down the man's tonsured head in the intense heat, and the bellows wheezed like a man with a knife in his chest. The other priest prayed as he worked, his mouth moving as he paused from time to time to peer into the hot insides of the forge. Calling Crow strained to hear what medicine prayers the priest said in order to make the iron, but he could not hear because of the sucking noise of the bellows. Someone suddenly grabbed Calling Crow on the shoulder, and he turned. Father Luis's red sweaty face smiled at him. Calling Crow was pleased to see him. The father had been very good to him.

"Que piensa de la escuela?" said Father Luis.

"Me gusta mucho," said Calling Crow slowly.

Father Luis clapped him on the shoulder. "Father Gomez tells me you are learning faster than any of the other students."

Calling Crow nodded.

"Good," said Father Luis. "I would like you to go to the market for me."

"Yes. I will go," said Calling Crow.

Outside, Calling Crow looped the halter over the ass's head and then checked to ensure that the pack frame was secured to the animal's back. As he started down the road, Calling Crow looked back to see Father Luis waving good-bye. He returned the wave. This trip to the market had become Calling Crow's weekly chore. Calling Crow especially liked the trips because they gave him and Juana a chance to meet in the light of day. They met at the Stone Pouring Woman at the plaza.

Calling Crow went slowly through the streets, careful of the many people and animals racing here and there. He was always amazed at the sights of so many people and carts in one place, so many big fine horses. He saw them now as noble animals and was amazed at how frightened he had been of them when he had first seen them and thought them demon dogs.

Calling Crow spotted Juana ahead. She was sitting alone on the edge of the fountain, and his heart was made heavy by the language of her figure. She was slumped over, weighed down by a heavy spirit. When she saw him approach, she straightened up and tried to appear happy, but gave up when she saw that he knew.

"Why are you so worried?" he said as he led the ass toward her.

She looked around at the people passing by and waited till a woman who had stopped to dip some water out of the fountain with her hands had finished and moved on. "The Bishop says he is going to send me away on the packet ship which leaves in the spring for New Spain. He is worried that the baby will soon show, and he doesn't want talk in his house."

Calling Crow felt a great anger as he thought of this man who had used her for so long. His anger turned to fear. He couldn't let them take Juana away from him. "We could go to the mountains," he said. "You could find someone to guide us."

"And spend all our time moving and hiding while the soldiers hunt us? No, Calling Crow, we cannot. Think of the baby. Up there it gets very cold at night and there is little food. The baby would not survive. We can't do it."

"We must. We cannot let him send you away."

She looked around worriedly as his voice grew louder.

"We should have run away earlier," he said. "I should not have allowed you to change my mind."

They fell silent as a group of people came to drink from the fountain's cool waters. When they left she pulled him by the arm to sit down. He remained standing, holding the ass's halter.

"I know what we can do," she said.

"What is that?"

"We could go to the Floridas."

"How?" he said. "By walking on the water like the Jesus?"

"No," she said. "It can be done."

"I thought it could only be done by the Spanish in their large ships."

She shook her head. "My people did it for generations in big sea canoes long before the Spanish came here."

"Then we shall just take one of their sea canoes and go."

"There are no more."

"Woman," said Calling Crow, "why do you tell me these things if there are no more sea canoes?"

"Because," she said slowly, as if thinking of the task at hand, "there are still a few old men left who know how to make the sea canoes and how to read the winds and seas."

"Who are they?"

"One is old Blue Bird who is far away up in the mountains, and very sick when last I heard. The other, old Red Coat, is in my village."

"Would he make one for us?"

Juana thought for a moment. "It is very dangerous, but he might."

"What is the danger?"

"If the Spanish catch us, they will put us all in the pits for trying to escape."

"Do you think Red Coat will do it?"

"He is very unhappy with the way things have become. Let us go and find him now."

Calling Crow carried one of the iron Spanish axes as he and Juana followed the bowlegged old man named Red Coat through the jungle. Red Coat had had one of the young men of the reservation steal the axe. As they moved beneath the tall palms and other trees, scores of unseen birds kept up a great chatter above. Up ahead, Red Coat walked purposefully, despite his lopsided gait, as if he knew exactly where to find the tree he wanted, as if the tree was calling him. They crossed a small clearing, and as they went again into the thick growth, the old man stopped suddenly before a tall, stout rubber tree. "Here it is," he said. "This tree will take us across."

Even though Calling Crow could smell the sea, it might be too far to drag such a big tree. "How far is it to the sea?" he asked Red Coat.

Without a word, the old man walked off, and Calling Crow and Juana followed him. They did not have to go far. Just beyond the grove of trees, they came out onto a beautiful white beach which sloped gently down to the lapping waves.

Red Dog smiled at Calling Crow as if he were an impatient child. "When the canoe is ready, it will be much lighter. I will get some others who can be trusted to help us drag it down to the water."

They went back to the tree, and Red Coat knelt and sang a prayer to the tree's spirit, asking it to forgive them for cutting it down. He told the spirit how they needed the tree to cross the big water to take Calling Crow and his woman home to his village and people. When he finished, he got to his feet and turned to Calling Crow.

"You can begin."

As Calling Crow chopped at the base of the tree in the thick jungle heat, he was quickly covered with sweat. The steady rhythmic crack of the axe echoed into the green thickness of the jungle and it was the only sound, the birds having already retreated far away. Several times Calling Crow stopped and asked Red Coat if he were making too much noise, and Red Coat shook his head. As Calling Crow worked quickly he marveled at the magic of the Spanish iron axe. With it he was able to cut halfway through the tree in the time it would take to start a fire. He remembered a time long, long ago when he and two others had taken most of the day to cut through a tree much thinner than this. That part of his life seemed almost to have never happened now.

He continued chopping. Finally the tree squealed as it leaned slowly sideways, then began falling faster. As it crashed through the branches of the surrounding trees, Calling Crow looked at the axe in his hands and thought how much more powerful the Spanish iron was than the simple stone and wooden clubs and stone knives of his people.

The earth shook when the tree landed, and Calling Crow heard the sound as a song. It was the song of their release. It would be like the stories of the Christ rising from the dead. He and she would leave these people who had many things, but who lived as though they were dead. He and she would go back to his own people, and they would live like human beings again.

Chapter 28

Senors Alonso Roldan and Manuel Ortiz sat under a shade tree not far from the pit. A soldier named Diaz ran up to them.

"A great fleet arrives from Spain!" he said.

"When?" said Roldan.

"Now," shouted Diaz. "There are many sails upon the sea."

Roldan quickly got to his feet. "Go get the horses," he said to Ortiz. He turned back to Diaz. "Tell *El Animal* to keep things running smoothly. We will be back when we find out what is going on."

A short while later Roldan urged his horse along the road which climbed to the heights. Ortiz rode behind him as the road circled higher and higher. They reached the crest where the deep blue sea met the pale blue sky with a thin mist of clouds compressed in between.

Roldan and Ortiz dismounted and went quickly over to where some others were sitting on some rocks, looking out.

"There," said a young boy, pointing with a slender brown hand.

Roldan looked down. The fleet moved slowly, at least two dozen ships in all. From the heights they looked like the carved toys boys set upon ponds and streams around the island to play with. With their sails billowed out, the tiny ships pushed into tiny white bow waves, leaving thin white wakes behind. As Roldan watched them in silence, he marveled at the wonder of it all. Here they came, he thought, if they'd had fair winds, all the way from Spain in probably a month's time. He hoped there would be mail from his family aboard one of them.

A clatter of hooves sounded on the ground behind them, and Roldan and the others turned to see a rider dismount. It was another soldier from the town.

The man ran over quickly. His face was lit with excitement.

"It is De Sole!" he exclaimed as he looked at the others. "De Sole!"

"How do you know?" said Roldan.

The man's eyes were glazed in wonder. "One of the ships docked yesterday on the other side of the island and a rider has come over to tell the governor."

"De Sole," said Roldan slowly and reverentially, remembering all the fantastic tales of the Conquistador's brave deeds, the stories of the mind-boggling amount of treasures he brought to the King in ships so fully loaded they threatened to sink. "Why is he coming here?"

The soldier's face was still flushed with excitement, "It is a great day for the New World! The King has made De Sole governor of this island, and he is going to lead a great expedition to conquer Florida. He will be governor of all the lands he conquers there, too!" The soldier shouted to the others, "Long live the King!" He turned and raced back to his horse and rode off.

Roldan put his left, three-fingered hand on Ortiz's shoulder. "Do you realize what this means?" he said, his eyes blazing.

Ortiz looked confused. "It is good, I am sure. There will be opportunities for those who want to go along to Florida."

Roldan shook his head. "Yes, yes, but not that. Now De Sole, a true Spaniard, is governor of this island; Toledo is out! Now Mateo and his old friend, Diego, are vulnerable. Soon we will have our revenge! Come, let's go into the town!"

* * *

Juana moved among the stalks of corn, looking for ear-worms and pulling them off quickly. How tall and beautiful the corn is, she thought. The rich green color was like a song and was a good omen of their coming voyage. She heard the steady chopping rhythm of Calling Crow's Spanish axe as he worked in the thick grove of palms not far away, and the smell of the coals he constantly ladled into the log's hollow reached her nostrils. Despite these two very telling signs, she was not worried. The surrounding jungle was very marshy, and there was nothing here that the Spanish wanted. Many of the men from the reservation hunted near here and they would warn them if any Spanish got too close.

As Juana pulled another worm from a stalk of corn, the sounds of Calling Crow's axe again brushed her ear and she smiled. Powerful and steady, that was the way it had been last night, too.

A gust of warm wind moved her hair, rustling the corn-stalks noisily, and she put her hand on her belly. She was very happy now. The baby would be born across the water in the Floridas, safe and free.

Again a gust of wind carried the smells of the sea to her nose, and she realized it was reminding her that if she wanted clams for their dinner she would have to go to the beach now while the tide was still out. She left the corn and started walking along the solid earth path which wound through the marshy jungle. Soon the wind was blowing harder and the smell of the mud flats was very strong. When she came out into the clearing, she saw many large Spanish ships on the water. Wider than any she had seen before, and with masts like the tallest trees, they moved slowly, their full sails decorated with red crosses and some symbols which she did not know. Slowly and soundlessly they made their way toward the harbor around the island. She watched for a few moments and then hurried back to get Calling Crow.

They went back down and watched the last of the ships. It was now so close they could make out the tiny figures of men up in the rigging as the ship gradually disappeared around the curve of the island.

"What does it mean?" said Calling Crow.

"I don't know," said Juana. "They always come in this way when they come from Spain, but never have I seen so many come at one time."

"Let us go into town and find out what it means," he said.

They carefully covered the canoe with many branches, totally obscuring it from whoever might wander by the grove. Then they entered the jungle and picked up the trail, walking swiftly without speaking. The sun had reached its zenith. When they finally reached the dusty streets of Santo Domingo, the sun was beginning its descent to the sea.

All people, Indian and Spanish alike, were in a great state of agitation. Lone men on horses raced here and there as they delivered messages, while the other people all moved in the direction of the main road to the harbor.

Juana called out to an old man who was hobbling along in front of them. "Where have all the ships come from and what are they here for?"

The old man stopped. "Their great warrior, De Sole, has arrived with many men to make war on the People Across the Waters."

"The Floridas?" said Calling Crow.

The man looked at Calling Crow, curious about this man who was so ignorant. "They say," he went on sadly, "that this De Sole has killed more people than there are grains of sand on the beach. With their iron swords, he and his men chopped down all the Apalachee People as easily as if they were stalks of corn. And now he comes to kill again."

The old man shook his head sadly. "Who can ever understand these Spanish?" Calling Crow and Juana watched him hobble away until he was lost in the crowd.

Juana looked at Calling Crow to hear what he had to say about all this, but he said nothing. For a long time they stood, thinking of the implications of what they had heard,

as the people walked around them, hurriedly heading for
the harbor road.

Finally Calling Crow turned to Juana. "Let us go and
see this De Sole." They joined the river of people flowing
along the road. After a while they spotted a man they
knew from the reservation sitting up on the roof of one of
the stables along the road. Calling Crow called to him and
the man told them to climb up. Calling Crow lifted Juana
up to him. He climbed up, and they could see the masts of
the ships in the harbor bristling upward like a forest of
trees stripped of their leaves. Other people climbed onto
the roof until there was no more room and then the people
began lining the sides of the streets, kept out of the middle
by many soldiers with swords. The excited people spoke
all at once like a flock of birds until there came a great
sound which frightened them. It was like the footsteps of
a mighty giant, and it came from the direction of the
ships—*romph, romph, romph-romph-romph*. The sound
grew louder and louder as the people anxiously glanced
down the road and at each other. A man gave out a shout,
pointing into the distance. A great column of men appeared coming up the road. At the front of the column,
many men in bloodred clothes angrily pounded on large
white drums. The men all brought their drumsticks down
at the same time, making one great sound.

After they passed, word spread that the Spanish who
was called De Sole was coming. He appeared, riding on a
great white horse, which danced proudly for the people on
the streets. Calling Crow could not take his eyes off him.
Covered in shining Spanish armor, De Sole had sharp gray
eyes like a hawk as he looked quickly about him at the
many people in the streets. Calling Crow stood up, attempting to keep him in sight, but he moved on. More soldiers came by, led by another group of drummers beating
their drums with one loud voice, and then so many soldiers came by packed tightly together in the street that
they looked to Calling Crow like the river of fighting ants
he and Juana had once seen passing across the floor of the
jungle.

There were too many Spanish for Calling Crow and Juana to count. Row after row of them passed, many of them armed with the tall thunder sticks, some of them struggling to hold on to the large, snarling, killing dogs which panted and pulled at their cords, and all of them armed with the long iron swords. At one point they raised their swords suddenly, as if with one hand, and the mass of gleaming iron caught the setting sun and reflected its angry red fire into the eyes of the people, blinding them. Many cried out in fear, thinking it some new Spanish magic.

Calling Crow and Juana stayed up on the roof long after the soldiers had gone. As Calling Crow thought of De Sole and his many men, he remembered the old man's words: "De Sole has killed more people than there are grains of sand on the beach!" A terrible thought came to Calling Crow. Fire Hair the Enslaver was a mere boy compared to this powerful Spanish. Might this De Sole be the Destroyer of his dream? He thought back to his dream and to his horror and sadness at the sight of his beloved village of Tumaqua dead and abandoned.

As Calling Crow remembered his dream, a storm began moving in from the sea. He and Juana could smell it as they sat in silence.

Finally Calling Crow spoke. "This is very bad. This De Sole might be the Destroyer I have dreamed of."

He helped Juana down onto the street just as the first drops of rain began pelting them.

"You go back to the Bishop's big house for now. I will find Red Coat, and we will work on the canoe tonight. Now we must work every night. Perhaps we can finish it before De Sole and his soldiers leave for the Floridas. Then we can warn the people over there that he is coming."

They moved silently down the street, blending into the shadows of the gray buildings.

Chapter 29

Down at the harbor, the rain began with a few big scattered drops striking the wooden planks of the ships heavily like hammer blows. Then it grew quickly to a groaning roar, as if a celestial organist had pulled out all the stops to swell a chord. After a while, the drops decreased in size and velocity and the sound of their collision with the earth became a gentle, steady sigh.

Three figures emerged from the largest of the ships tied up at the quay, one of a new type of construction called a galleon. Her name was the *Isabella*, and she was the flagship of the Conquistador, De Sole.

The first of the three men to approach the gangplank was a soldier, Lieutenant Vasco Guzman, a veteran of De Sole's campaign against the Apalachee Indians, and one of his most trusted lieutenants. Guzman wore a black woolen cape over his half armor and breeches, and his head was protected from the rain by a comb morion helmet of the shape which distinguished Spanish soldiers around the globe. After quickly and easily crossing the gangplank in the dark, he turned when he realized the other two men hadn't followed him. Silently cursing his stupidity, he quickly retraced his steps and took the older man's arm.

"Excuse me, Holiness," he said, "how forgetful of me. Allow me to help you across."

Father Toribio Mendoza, one of the half dozen Inquisitors assigned to the royal court of Spain, looked gravely at the soldier from under the hood of his black robe. Normally he would have reprimanded the soldier for his bad manners, but his mind was on much more important matters. He had just traveled halfway around the earthly orb because of a certain Father Luis's accusations against the *encomenderos* of Santo Domingo and Bishop Cavago. Soon he would be confronting them personally, and he began recalling the particulars of the letter to his mind— some Indians, who were not cannibals, and who had not acted hostilely against the King's subjects, had been taken as slaves; Indians had been whipped to death; some were ill-fed, poorly clothed, and overworked, but much, much worse than that, supposedly many of them had not been baptized and properly instructed in the Faith.

Father Toribio extended his hand, allowing himself to be led across the gangway as the rain soaked down deep into the fibers of his woolen robe, chilling him. Behind him, Father Mariano Pacheco, a young priest straight from the monastery of Santa Marta, followed along, his hand on the older priest's elbow as if to assist in steadying him, but in reality, to help himself pass over the black abyss of water below.

When all were safe on the solid stone of the quay, Lieutenant Guzman turned to Father Toribio. "Holiness, it is not too far. We can walk there in a quarter of an hour."

The old man bowed his hooded head gravely, and they moved down the street. They walked past a long row of darkened warehouses and turned onto a street lined with small houses and closed-up shops. They were suddenly startled at the silent approach of two figures in the darkness, a rather tall native man and a handsome native woman. They passed without a word, and Lieutenant Guzman turned round to the two priests.

"A strapping big fellow, eh? I've never seen an Indian so big."

The Inquisitor gave him a blank look, and they continued on their way, sloshing through large puddles of cold rainwater. Finally Lieutenant Guzman turned into a doorway, and the priests followed him in. He pounded hard on the thick wood of the door and then turned to look with the two priests at the rain coming down on the dark street. The door was opened by an old Spaniard, shielding the flickering flame of a candle.

"What is it?" he said.

Lieutenant Guzman reached under his cape and handed the man a piece of paper stamped with an official seal. "Father Toribio Mendoza, Assistant Special Inquisitor to the Court of King Charles, to see Bishop Cavago."

The servant attempted to read the paper in the dim moving light. He then tried to get a look at the two hooded figures standing behind the soldier in the dark. Giving up, he nodded nervously. "Follow me, please."

He led them through a hallway into a large parlor lit by a dozen candles. Several paintings hung on the walls, and the rich aroma of flowers filled the room. Embers glowed dully in the fireplace beneath a crust of gray ash.

The servant turned and bowed deeply, pointing to the three couches which were arranged to face the hearth. "Sit, please." He then knelt and threw two logs onto the embers. He fanned them and a large flame sprang up, bathing the parlor in a warm glow. He got to his feet. "I will get the Bishop."

Bishop Cavago had many candles burning in his bed-chamber. There was such a heavenly vision in there that his eyes seemed not to get enough. The beautiful sight was on the bed—an Indian girl of fifteen years, reclining naked on her back, inspecting the image of her face in a small silver-plated mirror. She was a study in contrasts, he thought, her face cherubic with large brown eyes and just a touch of fat, her womanly body ripened like a sticky fruit full of sweet syrup. He marveled at that body, the small pearlike breasts, the pinkish-brown nipples, the sheen of the small black patch of hair on her pubis. It seemed like only yesterday that she had been just another snotty-nosed waif running wildly through the courtyard. Now . . . He put down his brush. Her flaring hips and flat belly beckoned him. She was such a pretty little thing. He thought of Juana and felt a sense of loss. Juana was more beautiful, and mature, capable of carrying on an intelligent conversation with him, unlike this one. But her condition would soon be obvious, and he had already made arrangements to send her south on the packet ship.

A loud knock came at the door. He waved over at the girl, and she got off the bed and went into the next chamber.

"What is it?" he said through the door.

"Come quickly, my lord."

Bishop Cavago felt a rush of annoyance. It was Pedro. As Cavago went to the door, Pedro said something else which was muffled by the thickness of the door.

Bishop Cavago opened the door and saw him walking off. "What in heaven's name is it, man? I asked not to be disturbed tonight!"

Pedro Barrameda nodded excitedly. "The Inquisitor waits for you in the parlor."

"What Inquisitor? Are you daft? There is no Inquisitor on this island."

"Yes, my lord. He came over with De Sole's fleet, and he says he has business with you."

"Mother of God," said Cavago as panic flooded through him. "Go back out to him. Hurry! Tell him I shall be right there."

"Yes, my lord." Pedro turned and quickly hurried back down the corridor.

Cavago went into the other chamber. "Go," he hissed at the girl. After she left, he pulled and tied his robe about him, rushing about to inspect the room. Satisfied, he stood before the mirror and brushed the gray wisps of his hair back along the sides of his head. Composing his face into an appropriate grave mask, he opened the door.

He had no trouble picking the Inquisitor out from among the three men in the parlor. Somber under his black hood, he remained seated. The soldier and the young priest quickly knelt in front of the Bishop, kissing the back of the hand he extended to them in turn.

The Inquisitor remained silent as the younger priest said, "Excellency, this is Father Toribio Mendoza, Assistant Special Inquisitor to the Court of King Charles. I am his assistant, Father Mariano Pacheco." He nodded to the soldier. "This is Lieutenant Guzman, of De Sole's army, who has graciously conducted us to your house."

Bishop Cavago nodded to the Inquisitor. He glanced quickly into the man's watery eyes, hoping to read in them something of his mission here. They were, however, large, sad eyes that calmly saw all, but gave away nothing.

Pedro brought a small wooden chair over and placed it behind Bishop Cavago. He sat down and faced the Inquisitor. "Holiness, welcome to my house. How may I help you?"

The Inquisitor spoke with a deep powerful voice which added to his authority. "Are you familiar with a Father Luis from the Higuey Mission church?"

Cavago nodded calmly. Inside, a foreboding tightened his stomach around the meal of beef and beans he had eaten earlier.

"Well," the Inquisitor went on dryly, "he has made several charges regarding the conduct of the local landowners and church officials toward the native peoples."

"I see," said Bishop Cavago as he assumed an air of concerned interest. Inside, Bishop Cavago was enraged. Father Luis! This could be very bad. His stomach churned like a freshly poured cup of beer. He must save himself.

The Inquisitor sighed deeply. "Father Luis related several specific incidences of severe beatings by overseers and some more general charges of lapses in converting the natives and failure to give them proper religious instruction."

The Inquisitor regarded Bishop Cavago with his large eyes as he settled back into the couch. "What say you to all of that?"

"Holiness," Cavago began, smiling warmly, "I think I can explain all of this satisfactorily. I have personally looked into one specific charge of physical abuse and found it to be politically motivated. I am very sorry that these complaints had to go all the way to Seville. They really don't amount to much, as you will see."

"I hope so. Father Luis says that you were notified by letter on two different occasions about certain abuses, but that you never responded."

Cavago's brow furrowed questioningly. Somehow he

would have to turn the tables on Father Luis. He would get back at him for this treachery! "If he says that he sent me the letters, then I am sure that it is so. However, I never received them."

The Inquisitor frowned, revealing a furrowed field of worries on his brow. "How is that possible?"

"I will explain, Holiness, but first let me attend to your needs. You must be tired and in need of nourishment." Cavago turned to Pedro, who was sitting in a chair in the darkened hallway. "Pedro, some hot tea for Father Toribio and the others."

Pedro nodded. "I will be right back."

Cavago turned back to the Inquisitor. "Holiness, let me see, how can I best explain this? Here on this island, most of us rely heavily on the Indians as runners and messengers, among their other duties. However, they are very childlike. This quality can be endearing, but when work needs to be done, frustrating. They are totally without self-discipline and have to be supervised in even the simplest tasks. Now, if Father Luis gave one of them some messages for me, perhaps the carrier simply threw them away and spent the time loitering in the marketplace with his fellows or else watching the construction of the cathedral. As far as conversations between Father Luis and me on this subject, we have had only two that I recall, and both times I thoroughly investigated his allegations."

"And what did you find?"

"Well, that there were beatings, yes, but the Indians were not treated any more harshly than would be a Christian peasant in Castile who has sullenly refused to do his work."

"But I'm told there was one beaten to death."

"Yes, Holiness, it was over at . . ."

Pedro returned with a silver tea service set upon a small table. He placed it between Bishop Cavago and the two priests on the couch. He poured a cup and handed it to the Inquisitor, who nodded his thanks.

Bishop Cavago went on as Pedro poured for the others. "The death was at the estate of Senor Manzano. An Indian was whipped there, and he did die later, but it was from one of the plagues which ravage the Indian tribes and not from his beating. I have a sworn affidavit from a physician on this."

The Inquisitor took a sip of tea and set his cup down on the saucer. "I see."

Cavago was suddenly struck with a thought. The Inquisitor's and his assistant's robes were damp and they must be quite chilled. He was missing an opportunity here. "Holiness," he said, "could I get you and Father Pacheco some dry things to wear?"

"Excellency, you are most kind," said Father Pacheco.

The Inquisitor nodded his thanks.

"Please follow me to my chambers," said Cavago. "You can change there." Cavago turned to Pedro. "Get a dry shawl for the lieutenant."

When they returned, the Inquisitor again took his seat on the couch. "I still have to talk to Father Luis about all of this," he said. "I don't understand how he could see so many problems where you see none."

Cavago smiled in chagrin. "He is—how shall I put it—an extremely nervous type of person. He loves his Indians dearly, but he sometimes gets so involved in ministering to their wants, that he forgets that Spaniards are Christian, too, and that they have wants and rights also. There has to be a balance here if the colony is to continue to prosper. I have been trying to strike that balance, and so to him I suppose I am not sympathetic enough to some Indian demands."

Cavago watched the Inquisitor's face for some sign that he had been able to deflect Father Luis's attack. The Inquisitor seemed deep in thought. "Perhaps His Holiness would like something to eat?" said Cavago.

The Inquisitor shook his head and appeared to relax a little. "More tea would be fine."

As Cavago poured the tea, a warm confidence began to suffuse him. He sensed he had done well and that the danger was passing. Still, he would not leave it at this. For good measure, he would take Father Toribio out to talk to

Senor Manzano. Yes, that was a good idea. And other landowners. But Father Luis! A cold anger welled up in Cavago. For all Luis's assumed piety and sackcloth suffering, he was simply a schemer. Perhaps he desired the bishopric himself. That must be it! Well, Cavago would meet his challenge and cut his schemes short.

Father Toribio got to his feet to look at the paintings on the walls. Yes, thought Cavago, the danger was definitely passing.

"How was your passage over, Holiness?" he said.

"Please call me Father Toribio. The passage was uncomfortable." Father Toribio shook his head sadly. "I could not accustom myself to the crowding and the movement of the ship. And the smells!"

Cavago nodded.

"But the Lord must have been with us because the captain told us it was the fastest, safest crossing he has made yet."

"Well, you shall stay here," said Cavago. "I have already instructed Pedro to make up a room for you and Father Pacheco."

A knock came at the door. As Pedro went to answer it, Father Toribio turned to Cavago. "You are popular tonight."

Cavago smiled.

Pedro showed two soldiers into the parlor.

"Yes?" said Bishop Cavago.

The elder of the two soldiers, a small but commanding man of trim, powerful proportions spoke up. "My lord, I am Senor Alonso Roldan and this is Senor Manuel Ortiz. We have important business to discuss."

"What is it?" said Cavago. He noticed with mild revulsion that the little finger on the man's left hand was missing.

"Well, for one thing, we have a report to make to Lieutenant Guzman here concerning a criollo colonist named Francisco Mateo and his failure to obtain a license for a slaving venture so he could avoid paying his tax."

"I see," said Cavago. "But Mateo's ship returned almost

eighteen months ago! Why are you just reporting this now?"

Roldan smiled. "My lord, we tried to tell Governor Toledo about this, but he was not interested."

Cavago nodded. "I see, but couldn't this have waited till the morning?"

Roldan shook his head. "That's not the main reason I'm here. I have a report for His Holiness, too, and I was told that I would find him here."

"What is it?" said Father Toribio.

Roldan frowned. "Holiness, it concerns one Diego Vega, a friend of the same Senor Mateo's, and a young ship's boy, a Morisco named Miramor. It is about some things which happened while on a voyage on the ship, *Guadalupe*."

Cavago's ears pricked up at the mention of Diego Vega. He was a good friend of Father Luis's.

"How do you know all of this?" said Father Toribio.

"We were on the ship, too, Holiness."

"I see," said Toribio. "Well, I agree with Bishop Cavago. I think you should come back in the morning."

Roldan nodded respectfully. "Yes, Holiness. I only rushed over because of the seriousness of these things."

Toribio frowned. "Serious, are they? Why are they so serious?"

"Well, Holiness," said Roldan, clearing his throat, "they are—how shall I put it?—most indelicate."

Father Toribio sighed tiredly. "I see. Well, go on and be quick in the telling. I shall take my rest in the morning."

Chapter 30

It was early evening as Senor Francisco Mateo sat before the great fireplace in his parlor and packed his pipe. He had spent the day supervising the rounding up of half his herd of cows in preparation for slaughter, and there had been many strays and much hard work. Now it was time to enjoy a smoke. He dipped a straw into the lamp on the table beside him and held it to the pipe. Drawing hard, he filled his lungs with smoke. Only a heartbeat later he felt his mind focus and his worries and concerns loosen their grip on him. What a wonderful herb tobacco was, he thought. It was better than any tonic in the Old World for relieving pain and hunger. When Christopher Columbus had first sailed into the Antilles, he found the local Arawak Indians smoking rolled-up sticks of it. Now Senor Mateo was one of the few colonists who smoked it on a regular basis, but there were more trying it every day. And one day, he thought warmly, every man, woman, and child in Castile would smoke it; he hoped so anyway, for he had two fields planted with it and planned to send a consignment of it there for sale.

Mateo drew more smoke into his lungs. Things were going well now. His good friend, Diego Vega, had recovered and was growing stronger by the day. Mateo looked round the parlor contentedly, running his eyes past a tall chest of drawers made of polished hardwood with stylishly wrought ironwork. He was staring at his favorite painting of a vaquero on a horse herding a dozen or so cattle through a field of scrub trees and cactus when he heard a shout. Andres, the cook's little mestizo boy, came running into the room.

"Senor Mateo," he cried excitedly, "there are soldiers in the courtyard!"

Mateo got to his feet and tapped his pipe against the stones of the fireplace. Heavy steps sounded in the corridor. Three soldiers in breastplate, one of them carrying a loaded crossbow, entered the room.

Mateo angrily confronted them. "Who let you into my house?"

The man in the lead ignored his question. "Are you Senor Francisco Mateo?"

Mateo nodded, too furious to speak.

"You will come with us."

"Where? Why?" said Mateo.

"You are to appear before De Sole," snapped the soldier. "That is all you need to know."

An hour later, Senor Francisco Mateo was escorted down the stone steps of the *Cabildo* by two burly soldiers. All the rage he had felt when they had led him away from his house had left him and now he felt tired and strangely empty. He thought of the charge against him, tax evasion, and almost laughed in disgust. There weren't enough jail cells in all of Spain to hold those who kept back a little of their tax. It was simply the way business was done here in the colony.

"Did you know that your friend, Senor Diego Vega, was charged with sodomy?" said the older soldier as their boots echoed down the marble corridor.

Mateo stopped. "What in God's name are you talking about?"

"They say that Diego Vega committed the crime with Miramor, the soldier's boy."

Mateo's face grew red. "That's crazy! Where did they get that idea?"

"Four who were on your ship have signed affidavits which were given to the Inquisitor."

"Who were they?" demanded Mateo.

"I don't know," said the man. "Soldiers, I'm told. Come on. De Sole is waiting."

Mateo boiled with rage as they continued down the corridor. Roldan! It had to be his doing! And all to get back at him. A black pall of grief came over him. Diego was all but lost. Sodomy was the most vile of heresies and ruthlessly punished with death by burning.

They came to the entrance to De Sole's chambers. Two soldiers in gleaming armor, with long halberds at their sides, stood on either side of the great opened doors. They seemed made of wax as Mateo and his two guards walked through the doors.

At a desk in the rear of the room, De Sole sat stiffly upright in a high-backed, ornately carved wooden chair with purple velvet padding on the seat, back, and arms. Even though De Sole was sitting, Mateo could tell that he was a tall man, with a soldier's thin, muscled frame. His mustache and goatee, along with his hair, were turning gray, but he still exuded strength. On the large walnut desk before him were a stack of forms, a candelabra, and an inkwell. De Sole was writing rapidly, his white quill moving jerkily.

Mateo bowed, and De Sole indicated a chair without looking up. The soldiers left the room, and De Sole put the quill in the inkwell and looked up. He stroked the point of his beard. "Yours is the case of the untaxed Indian captives."

Mateo nodded. "Excellency," he said, "the man who I am sure has brought these charges cares nothing about how many pesos of gold the Crown collects. He and I have a rivalry going back many years, and he is simply seeking to revenge himself upon me."

"Revenge or no, you are still guilty of tax evasion."

Mateo looked into the other man's eyes. There was something reptilian about them, the look of a tortoise perhaps, a snake. All Mateo's instincts told him it would be foolish to plead with this man.

"Excellency, what is to be done to me?"

De Sole silently studied him. "We will get to that in a moment. I am told you are an aficionado of the knightly games. Is that so?"

"In my younger days," said Mateo. "Why do you ask?"

"There will soon be a fair in my honor, with archery shoots, wrestling, a feast, a ball, but most important, jousting."

Fairs were held yearly on the island, usually at harvesttime, and knightly games were popular throughout the Spanish kingdom due to the many novels on the subject, the most famous of which was *Amadis of Gaul*. On the island, Mateo had distinguished himself as an excellent horseman and swordsman and won many prizes.

Mateo returned the other's stare steadily. "I still don't understand."

De Sole folded his hands. "It is quite simple. I quite enjoy the joust, and on the whole island there is only one who would be a worthy opponent for me in the coming games—you."

"And so you want to joust with me?"

"Yes," said De Sole. "Did you know that the ancient Romans allowed their slaves and convicts to fight their way to freedom?"

Mateo nodded. "Yes, Excellency. I have heard that. And you are allowing me the same privilege?"

A slight, icy smile broke the hard angles of De Sole's face. "In a sense. You do not have to prevail in the joust, only participate, and in so doing you will be excused from the usual jail term for tax evasion. You must only pay what you owe. What do you say?"

Mateo didn't like the arrangement; if he won, he could incur the man's enmity, and he was governor, but he couldn't let him win easily either. He thought of the slanderous charges against Diego and was struck with an idea. De Sole wanted this match very badly, and he couldn't force him to joust, not really. Therefore he might be inclined to throw in something more to get what he desired. "Excellency," he said, "I will do it on one condition."

De Sole's smile collapsed. "I am not used to granting conditions," he snapped.

Mateo said nothing.

"What is the condition?"

"Excellency," said Mateo, "are you aware of the charges against Senor Diego Vega?"

De Sole nodded.

"Excellency, it is a preposterous slander. Diego Vega would never do such a thing. It is all the cowardly machinations of the same soldier who is responsible for my being here before you today, Senor Alonso Roldan. Would you allow me to bring some reputable citizens before you, people you could question thoroughly about Diego's character? I'm sure that then you would quickly see that this is nothing but baseless slander and we could clear it up."

"Very well," said de Sole and his icy smile returned. He looked up at the guards. "Escort him to the tax man's office and after he pays his tax, release him."

Chapter 31

Bishop Cavago donned his large black sun hat and walked out of his house. He felt good, for he had managed to deflect all the charges Father Luis had directed against him and now the Inquisitor was off investigating other areas. Another bit of luck that had fallen to him was that De Sole had chosen him to be his own liaison to the Church on the expedition to the Floridas. This had been quickly communicated to the Inquisitor. And to top it all off, Father Luis was also going on the expedition, not staying behind with the Inquisitor as he had feared. Once they were over there, he would have to make some arrangement for him, perhaps put him in charge of some wild settlement to keep him busy. Now there was only one more possible threat to him—Juana. He couldn't very well go to the Floridas and leave her behind on the island with the Inquisitor. Some-

one might say something about the two of them, and if the
Inquisitor ever interviewed her, she might talk. He must
find her and take her with him.

Cavago climbed into the open coach of his carriage and
nodded to his driver. They moved off, bouncing along the
rutted street. Every day for the past week they had
searched a different part of the city. Today they went toward the wharf. The streets were crowded, and they rode
past strolling ladies and gentlemen, throngs of soldiers and
sailors still fresh off the ships, vendors selling their wares
of native baskets and mats woven from grasses, and the
ever-present swarm of begging children. One beggar, an
older mestizo man, approached the carriage when it
slowed to let a courier on a horse pass. Cavago gave him
a cold stare, turning the beggar's pleading countenance
into a sneer of hate. The horseman raced by, hooves
throwing up a cloud of red dust in the middle of the street.
The carriage began moving again, and as the air slowly
cleared, Cavago spotted Juana. "Quickly," he said, pointing her out to the driver.

The driver maneuvered the carriage to the side of the
street where Juana stood talking to a woman vegetable
vendor. The long, green skirt Juana wore could no longer
hide the life growing inside of her belly.

As the carriage drew up, Cavago saw the startled look
on her face. Juana quickly said something in her own language to the woman vendor and then walked over to the
carriage. A few Indians standing about stared at them in
curiosity.

"I haven't seen you in days, child," said Cavago.

Juana waited for him to go on, her face composed into
a pleasing oval.

"I shall be leaving with the De Sole expedition to the
Floridas." Cavago saw that she was pleased at the news,
and this evidence of her true feelings hurt him. He had
done much for her and had believed she had grown to
think well of him. Well, so be it, he thought. It was further
evidence that it would not be wise to leave her behind.

"When do you leave?" said Juana in a voice she often

used when they were around others, a voice that showed no emotion.

"Within the month. How would you like to go with me?" Cavago was sure of her emotions this time. The startled pain in her eyes was obvious, and it hurt him.

"It would be difficult for me now," she said slowly. "My uncle has been very ill on the reservation. I have been spending much of my time there, nursing him."

Cavago's anger hardened his voice. "I want you to go finish up the business with your uncle and be at my house tonight."

Juana looked as if she would faint. She said nothing.

"Don't mope so, child," said Cavago. He smiled cajolingly. "The voyage will not be so bad."

Still Juana said nothing, and he went on.

"Running away would not be wise, because, as we both know, I have many friends and spies on the island, and besides, you wouldn't want to hurt the child."

Juana nodded respectfully as the driver cracked his whip, moving the carriage out into the street traffic.

Juana felt like there was a knife slashing at her belly. She walked slowly and aimlessly through the streets. The happy warm thoughts that used to sustain her, thoughts of Calling Crow and their work on the big dugout, thoughts of their happy plans made by the fire in the hut, all these warm thoughts now grew cold like a fire on the beach swamped by a rogue wave. All she could see was the Bishop's horrible smiling face. She moved in a daze, unaware of the noises and movement around her. She stepped on a vendor's basket of wares, and he cursed her angrily. She moved on, unaware. Children began following her, laughing and shouting at her, but she did not respond and they grew fearful and let her be. She almost stepped in front of a galloping horse, but an old man grabbed her elbow and pulled her aside. Grabbing her by the arms, he looked in her eyes to speak to her and then hurried away in fright.

She walked on. Two men crossed the street carrying a large basket, and she almost walked into them.

"Crazy woman! Watch where you are going," one of them shouted at her loudly.

His voice was like a blow, and her mind was suddenly sharp. She looked at the man angrily and walked on to keep her meeting with Calling Crow.

Calling Crow was sitting in the shade of one of the few trees in the square. When he saw Juana approaching, he got to his feet. "What happened?" he said.

She walked over to the edge of the fountain and sat down. She dipped her hand in the water and wet her brow. Calling Crow sat down beside her.

"The Bishop is taking me with him on the expedition to the Floridas," she said. "It will leave within the month."

Calling Crow looked worriedly at the people walking and riding by. *"Aieyah!* And the canoe will not be ready for days and days! I should not have listened to you before; we should have run away. Now what are we to do?"

Juana held him tightly by the arm. "There is nothing we can do. I shall have to go with him."

He looked at her. "I would kill him before I'd let him take you away."

Tears rolled down Juana's cheeks.

Calling Crow looked at her and turned away. For a while he stared into the clear waters of the fountain and said nothing. He turned to her. "We shall have to get more of your people to help us with the canoe. Then perhaps we can finish it before the expedition leaves."

"But the more people you tell," she said, "the greater the danger that someone will talk."

"Then Red Coat will have to pick them very carefully. Take me to him now."

They got to their feet. Juana looked at their reflection in the pool. He was so brave and proud, she thought. But in the eyes of the Spanish, these were deadly sins for an Indian, never to be tolerated. Still, she loved him all the more for his pride and fearlessness. She dipped her hands into the water for a drink, and their image melted into rippling waves of light.

Chapter 32

Mateo tied up his horse at Father Luis's mission. As he walked past the church, the sound of many children rhythmically reciting a catechism echoed out of the Gothic windows into the hot, still air. He walked round the back and found Father Luis in his hut. The priest looked up at him tiredly from where he sat, writing at a table. He waved away a fly.

"Come in, Senor Mateo. What can I do for you?"

Mateo stood before the table, not knowing how to begin. "It is about Diego Vega."

Father Luis nodded. "I heard. It is unbelievable."

Mateo's voice grew angry. "Of course it is unbelievable; it is all lies! It is the work of Senor Roldan and his men. You must help me to expose them."

"Of course they are lies," said Father Luis, "but why did they say such terrible things about Diego?"

"Father, I'm afraid it is all to get back at me because of some things which happened on my ship some time ago. I made Diego give a whipping to Roldan. That is why he is doing this."

"But why a whipping? What happened? If you want me to help, you must tell me everything."

Mateo sighed heavily and sat down. An hour later Father Luis got to his feet and began pacing. He stopped and stared angrily at Mateo. "You should have come to me sooner about this!"

Mateo said nothing, hanging his head glumly.

"Roberto," called Father Luis.

Calling Crow came into the hut and stopped suddenly at the sight of Mateo.

"It is all right," said Father Luis.

Calling Crow remained where he was.

"Roberto, is it true that many Indians were pushed into the sea during the storm on the ship?"

"Yes, Father."

"Why didn't you tell me?"

"You never asked."

"But, Roberto, something so terrible, you must have wanted to tell others of it."

Calling Crow looked down. "Many terrible things have happened, Father. Too many to tell."

"Very well," said Father Luis. "And what was old Diego Vega's role in this? You know him; he is the one with the large head of gray hair."

"He is good, Father. He tried to stop them, but they would not stop. He is good."

As Mateo listened to the exchange, he was amazed. This was the near-naked wild man they had captured on the beach?

Father Luis interrupted his thoughts. "Senor Mateo, we will have a difficult time of this. The charges against him are so pernicious, so evil, that we will have to prove them false beyond the shadow of a doubt."

Mateo nodded tiredly. "Yes, Father. I will do whatever you say."

Father Luis smiled at him. "I will have Roberto go with me to the *Cabildo* and repeat what he has just said before the Inquisitor. He can tell them what really happened on that voyage."

Father Luis looked over at Calling Crow. "Will you do that, Roberto?"

"Yes, Father," said Calling Crow.

Father Luis nodded. "You can go now."

Chapter 33

The sun was beginning its climb into a clear blue sky. Calling Crow pushed through the chest-high bushes with Juana right behind him. Calling Crow and Juana had been working on the canoe every night now, and today they had been walking since before sunup. But, despite his fatigue, he felt good today. With the four extra men Red Coat had picked to help them, they had been making good progress on the canoe and would be ready to put off for Florida in days.

They came out into a boggy area and walked in the sun-warmed muddy water along the invisible path they had memorized. An hour later, as they neared the wall of coast forest ahead, Calling Crow stopped abruptly and Juana bumped into him tiredly. "What is it?" she said.

Calling Crow turned his head back and forth slowly as he listened. "Nothing. It is nothing."

They moved into the thick trees and bushes till they found their trail. After walking for a while they came to a thicket of flowering bushes. They pushed inside. Parting the leaves on the other side, Calling Crow and Juana looked out. The canoe sat alone in the quiet palmetto glade.

"I wonder why Red Coat's men are not here?" said Juana softly.

Calling Crow watched silently, saying nothing. Finally, he turned to Juana. "Let's go out." They pushed into the clearing.

It was very quiet as they walked up to the canoe.

"You gather more wood," said Calling Crow. "I will start the fire." Calling Crow knelt to blow on the coals of their old fire. Soon a tiny curl of smoke appeared. He sprinkled kindling on it and blew it into a flame. As he was putting on more kindling, he saw two soldiers walk out of the trees. They both carried crossbows, and one of them held Juana by the arm.

Calling Crow stood as they walked up to him. "Where are the others?" said the man holding Juana.

"There are no others," said Calling Crow.

The man scowled. He turned to his companion. "Scout around here. Be careful."

The soldier grunted in reply and moved off.

"Now," said the man. "Get that fire going good, and we will put an end to this canoe." He pushed Juana and she stumbled into Calling Crow. "You help him. Carry these sticks and logs and put them in the canoe."

Juana picked up an armload of the firewood they had stacked the day before. She dumped it in the canoe and started back for more.

Calling Crow looked around for the other soldier as he scooped up the burning kindling with a large curled piece of bark. As the soldier kept the crossbow trained on him, he dumped it on the wood Juana had piled in the canoe. The fire grew quickly.

"Now help her carry firewood!" said the soldier.

Calling Crow picked up an armload of stout sticks and carried them over to the canoe where Juana was.

"They have a hut back here!" came the voice of the soldier who had disappeared into the thicket.

The soldier guarding Calling Crow looked over, and Calling Crow dropped most of the sticks he was carrying and swung one stick as big around as his wrist against the man's helmet. The stick clanged off the helmet, breaking in half, and the man fell over.

"Juana!" he said. "Run!" They raced for the safety of the thicket. Clawing their way through, they came out into the trees. The crackle of the fire reached their ears as they ran.

Calling Crow and Juana ran till they reached the bog. They looked back over the trees and saw the black sooty smoke roiling skyward, carrying with it their hopes of escape and a new life. They were so saddened by what happened that they said nothing till they reached the edge of the town. There, many people were talking excitedly about the fair being held in De Sole's honor. Tired and hungry, and thinking that perhaps they could get something to eat there, Calling Crow and Juana headed for the fairgrounds.

They joined the crowd that was following a strange giant. A Spanish, he had legs as long as Calling Crow was tall, and he walked in a slow, steady gait, turning to wave and smile at all he passed. Despite his anger and despair, Calling Crow was amazed by the height of the man.

Two small boys dashed out of the crowd and ran under the man, one of them touching his leg. A smile appeared on the boy's face as he ran back to the crowd shouting, "They are sticks! He is walking on sticks!"

Calling Crow felt disgust and despair as the crowd broke into an excited babble of speculation. He turned to Juana. "Beneath the power of these Spanish, there are many tricks. There is no end to them."

Juana nodded sadly, and they moved on toward some shade trees. Against the trunk of one of them, a group of native men sat drinking Spanish wine from a bottle. Calling Crow saw others lying sick and unable to move and thought it very bad.

He turned to Juana. "I wonder who among your people has betrayed us. I must find Red Coat and talk to him."

"It may not have been betrayal," said Juana.

Calling Crow turned round to her. "Don't talk! You talk too much."

"I will talk," said Juana. She faced him angrily. "And you will listen to me."

Calling Crow's eyes blazed angrily. "No more."

Juana went on. "It is possible that the Spanish just stumbled onto the canoe. While they rarely go there, still it is possible. But it doesn't matter now."

Calling Crow said to her bitterly, "One of your people told. Don't defend them! Do you want to be with them or me?"

She said nothing, and he turned away. In the distance he

saw a sleek black horse tethered to a tree outside a red cloth house.

He turned back to her, his face an agonized mask of rage and sorrow. She was crying softly.

"Maybe you are right," he said. "It matters not now. We should go off to the mountains. At least there we could be together till the end."

Juana looked at him sadly and said nothing.

Calling Crow waited. "Well," he said, "are you going with me?"

She said nothing for a few moments, and Calling Crow's face twisted in pain.

Juana moved close to him and lay her head against his chest. "I go with you always and anywhere, my love."

Calling Crow put his arms around her and held her.

They walked to the red cloth house with the beautiful horse tethered outside. Calling Crow leaned against the fence of branches that had been constructed around it. A man walked out of the cloth house and up to the horse, and Calling Crow involuntarily tensed. It was Mateo. He patted the great animal on the neck as he talked to it.

Juana sensed his anger and touched his arm lightly. "Who is he?"

"Mateo, the one who brought me here. Remember I told you about him? Now they have put his friend in jail, the kind old Gray Hair called Diego." Calling Crow shook his head slowly in disgust. "These Spanish, they put the good in jail and let the bad run free."

Juana looked at him worriedly and turned to look back at the crowds. "I want to be alone for a while," she said. "I will find you later."

Calling Crow said nothing as she walked off. He watched Mateo pull his gray-colored chain mail leggings over his breeches. Then he put on a bright red doublet, and then armor and a hood. As the great horse nibbled the dew-wetted grass, Mateo covered it with body armor decorated with many bright red tassels. Looking up suddenly, he saw Calling Crow. Calling Crow met his gaze, wondering if he would ever be rid of him and his kind.

A boy ran up to Mateo, yelling excitedly that it was time for the joust. Mateo mounted the horse, and the boy took the bridle, leading him away.

Calling Crow had heard about the joust, and the thought of seeing either Mateo or De Sole skewered on one of the long lances like a roasted bird inflamed him with an angry hope. He walked back toward the playing field.

Up in the stands, crowds of colorfully dressed Spanish moved about, while the native peoples pressed up against the wooden fences that surrounded the field, their usually blank faces full of wonder and smiles. Calling Crow pushed into the crowd.

The drummers and trumpeters played a fanfare, and the crowd noise dropped to a collective whisper of anticipation. From between two tents De Sole appeared on his great white horse and raced out onto the field. Everyone in the stands got to their feet and cheered. De Sole was dressed in white and gold, carrying a pure white shield over his left arm, his sword held aloft in the other. His horse was decked with polished armor and golden tassels. He seemed an apparition to Calling Crow, brighter even than the morning sun.

Rearing his horse back, De Sole slashed at the sky with his sword, shouting, "Santiago!" He charged across the field, slashing the air aggressively, and the people around Calling Crow smiled appreciatively. Making a tight turn, De Sole raced back and stopped before the stands. Slowly, the cheering faded.

Another cheer went up as the black horse bearing Mateo raced onto the field. Mateo reined up beside De Sole. Calling Crow watched in rapt attention as Mateo pulled a metal helmet topped off with a bright red feather over his head.

Both men faced the stands. The drums rolled until the crowd grew quiet. Raising his arms dramatically, the announcer's loud voice boomed out, "Ladies and gentlemen, the first joust will be a pass, left to left, with shields." He looked solemnly at the two knights. "Begin."

The crowd fell into silent as Mateo and De Sole rode

off to opposite ends of the field. Turning, they steadied their mounts as they watched a gold pennant flying atop the pole before the stands. A page released it, and the pennant fell away, fluttering to earth. Calling Crow saw sunlight flashing off Mateo's mount's hooves as they threw clods of soft damp earth. The two knights raced toward each other.

Calling Crow pushed up against the fence. The thunder of the horses' hooves reached him as the two men closed. Mateo's lance drove into De Sole's shield, shattering it, but De Sole remained in the saddle. The two men turned round at the ends, and De Sole quickly leaned down to take the shield handed up to him by a maid before beginning his next run. As they quickly closed, De Sole leaned low at the last minute and clipped Mateo's helmet, sending it flying. The horns sounded a fanfare signaling the end of the first part of the contest, and the two rode back to the stands.

The announcer walked calmly out to the field as the two combatants attempted to calm their dancing steeds. He raised his arms solemnly. "The next contest . . . will consist of three runs . . . passing right to right across the barrier . . . without shields."

Juana pushed through the crowd up to Calling Crow. She had a woman with her, an older fat woman with a pretty face.

"Calling Crow," she said, "there is a way for us to get to the Floridas together."

Calling Crow looked at her sadly. "I thought you said you would go to the mountains with me."

Juana shook her head. "Listen, please. They are picking men to be bearers for De Sole in the Floridas, but they must understand the language of the Spanish. If you were picked as a bearer, we could both go, and when we were there we could run away together."

Calling Crow said nothing as he thought about it.

"This is my friend, Jomme," said Juana. "Her man, Wild Bird, works carrying for the Spanish. He is at the old warehouse in the city now and he can help us."

Calling Crow raised his hand for silence. He thought

quietly for a moment. "It is true," he said. "We would have a better chance of escaping in the Floridas." He looked at Juana sharply. "Why do you think they would pick me?"

"*Aieyah,*" said Jomme, interrupting, "all they have to do is get one look at you! You are so big! You could carry twice what another man could."

Calling Crow said nothing as he considered it. Juana grabbed his arm and shook him. "Calling Crow, Jomme says that the Spanish that Wild Bird works for is a good man. You must go to him and tell him that Jomme sent you. Tell him that he should hire you as a bearer and an interpreter."

Calling Crow looked at her, his eyes hard as stones. "If he does not choose me as a bearer then we go away to the mountains."

Juana nodded. "Yes."

A thunderous cheer erupted from the crowd, and Calling Crow turned back to the field. The gold cloth fluttered down from the pole. Sunlight flashed off Mateo's mount's shoes as he sped down the field. Calling Crow watched as Mateo's lance dug deep and held, flipping De Sole quickly and cleanly off his horse. De Sole landed on the barrier with a crash, shattering the wood. Calling Crow turned to Juana. "I have seen enough. I go now. Where do I find this man, Wild Bird?"

Juana shouted to be heard over the crowd. "On the main road, close to the harbor, there is a big house the same color as the Spanish skin. They have put much food and materials in there for De Sole's ships. Wild Bird should be there."

Mateo reined in Vailarin and dismounted. Quickly running back to de Sole, he saw with relief that the man's eyes were open and he was attempting to get to his feet.

Mateo extended his hand.

De Sole looked at it and frowned. With his mailed fist, he angrily smashed a piece of wood debris out of his way and sat up. Without looking at Mateo, he pushed himself to a kneeling position. "They said you were quite good at these knightly games and they were right. I, however, am a soldier, and I haven't had the time to master all the tricks of it." De Sole got slowly to his feet and brushed some dirt and wood debris from his armor. "Well, you have won fair and square. You may go."

"Thank you," said Mateo. "About Diego Vega, Excellency. Remember what we talked about? When can I bring some good citizens of the island around to see you?"

"Why bring anybody around?"

"Excellency, you agreed to do that so I could show you that he is a good man."

De Sole's face hardened. "Enough! For a crime such as his, there can be no bargaining, no pleading."

Mateo felt his temper rising and could not stop himself. "Excellency, he is not guilty! This is nothing but slander! You must allow me to defend him from these false charges."

One of the squires reached De Sole and began hurriedly dusting off his armor. De Sole's face was livid as he barked at Mateo. "Shut up! One more word out of you, and you will go straight to jail."

Mateo's pulse was pounding in his temple, but he managed to say nothing.

"One more thing," said De Sole. "I want you to report to the *Cabildo* in the morning."

"Excellency?" said Mateo.

De Sole pushed away the boy who was brushing the dirt from the shoulders of his armor, knocking him to the ground. He turned to Mateo as some soldiers dressed in heavy armor lumbered protectively up to him. "Because of your slaving raid in Florida, you have a knowledge of that coast. I shall use you as one of my scouts on the expedition."

Mateo bowed, and his disgust and anger made him want to puke. "Thank you, Excellency."

Calling Crow ran all the way to the big house. He slowed to a walk when he spotted a man squatting outside the black rectangle of the doorway. The man did not look like one of the people. Big and fat, he sang to himself as he caressed a skin bottle of Spanish wine.

"Are you the one they call Wild Bird?"

The man spat and grabbed himself. "This is the Wild Bird here, man. Do you want to see it?"

Calling Crow ignored the insult. "The one called Wild Bird is picking men to go with De Sole. I want to go."

The man waved at him drunkenly. "They are all picked. Go away."

Calling Crow started toward the dark opening of the big house. The drunk man got to his feet and blocked his way. "Hey! You can't go in there."

Calling Crow pushed the man, and he fell backward. Ignoring the man's shouts and curses, Calling Crow looked around in the vast dimness, waiting for his eyes to adjust. Stacked up against the wall behind him were many pieces of trees. They were like so many bones, he thought. Juana had told him that the Spanish sent these chopped-down trees back to Spain where they made colors with them, which they put into their clothes. Calling Crow looked around. The large center of the building was empty, but on the far side he saw some big two-wheeled carts lined up. There was smoke from a fire on the other side of them, and voices.

He walked over. When he was halfway there he heard a sound from behind and turned. The fat drunk staggered into the big house and called after him. Calling Crow ignored him and continued walking.

He walked between two carts. They were arranged in a large rough circle, and there was a small fire in the middle. About two dozen Carib and Arawak men squatted in a group around the fire, while not far away two large mestizo or *cholo* men stood around another fire looking at a large piece of paper with their writings upon it. One of them had a beard.

Calling Crow looked at the carts. Many of them were loaded with the weapons of the Spanish soldiers: thunder sticks, swords, and long clubs, taller than a man, with sharp iron tips. In the cart nearest Calling Crow, there were many of these spears stacked up like the Spanish cane after the harvest. Some of the sharp tips of the spears stuck out from the bundles, ready to pierce anyone who foolishly stumbled into them.

The smaller, smooth-faced man walked over to Calling Crow. Calling Crow saw he was a *cholo*.

"What do you want?" said the *cholo*.

"I want to ask Wild Bird to hire me to carry for De Sole."

"He has gone somewhere. But you look like you could carry much. Go over there with the others."

As Calling Crow started over to the men by the fire, the loud voice of the other bearded man, a Spanish, boomed out. "You there! Where are you going?"

Before Calling Crow could say anything, the *cholo* spoke. "I told him to sit with the others. He is very big; he could carry much. He also speaks Spanish passably."

The big, black-bearded Spanish barked at him, "And I told you we had enough." He looked at Calling Crow in annoyance. "Get out of here. We don't need any more bearers."

The man walked back to the fire and again picked up the piece of paper. Calling Crow remained where he was. A moment later, the drunk from the door staggered into the circle formed by the carts. He walked up to the Spanish.

"Senor Galvez, I tried to stop him from coming in, but he snuck by me when I went to piss."

The bearded Spanish called Galvez looked up. "Never mind," he began, and then he saw Calling Crow.

"Go, you empty-headed Indian. Are you dumb? Get out of here."

Calling Crow ignored the man's insults and stood his ground. "I want to go with De Sole as a bearer," he said. "I am strong." Calling Crow pointed to the Caribs, who were avidly watching the exchange. "I can carry as much as three of them, and I can understand your language."

Galvez laughed. "No, you don't understand my language very well. I have already told you to go. Do you know what *go* means?"

Calling Crow stood and said nothing. Galvez looked at him in amused silence. No one said anything. A knot of wood snapped in the fire, releasing a hissing jet of gas. Galvez suddenly put down his paper and walked over to one of the carts piled high with bundles covered in cloth and tied neatly with cords. He picked up the handles of the cart from the ground and turned it slowly.

With the hint of a smile on his face, he yelled, "Santiago!" and began pushing the cart toward Calling Crow, slowly picking up speed.

Calling Crow stood his ground. When the cart was almost on top of him, he bent low to meet it, digging in the balls of his feet. He slid backward a few feet as he fought for a purchase in the dusty earth, finally managing to stop the cart. Galvez grunted and cursed as he attempted to push Calling Crow back further. Calling Crow sensed something behind and turned slightly to see the sharp points of the tall spears jutting out from another cart just an arm's length from his back. Shouting out a war cry, he slowly began pushing the cart back. The Caribs watched the contest intently, their hard faces giving away nothing about how they felt about the contest.

Calling Crow turned the cart as he pushed it back, maneuvering Galvez toward the small fire. "I shall roast a Spanish for my Carib friends to eat," he said loudly. "What do you think about that?"

"I say you are full of shit," said Galvez. He looked over his shoulder at the drunk who was watching the contest with the *cholo*. "Manuel, get over here."

The fat drunk ran over and put his shoulder to the cart alongside Galvez. The cart slowly began inching back toward the spear points. Galvez laughed through his heaving breaths. "Now we shall make an Indian pincushion out of you, how about that?"

Again, Calling Crow screamed out a war cry, shaking the cart roughly about the way a dog would a bone. The veins in his neck bulged as he managed to stop the progress of the cart an arm's length away from the spear points. Galvez and the drunk cursed as they pushed, the cart shaking violently, but not moving.

Galvez shook the sweat out of his eyes and looked back, calling to the *cholo*, "Agustine! Come and help us."

The *cholo* hesitated.

"Agustine, get over here now or I'll have you whipped."

The *cholo* walked over and began pushing. Slowly the cart moved backward, closer and closer to the spear points. Calling Crow felt one pierce the flesh of his shoulder like a bee sting. Summoning all his strength, he pushed back, but could not move the cart. He felt his strength running out of him, and the spear point jabbed him painfully again. Then an older Carib quickly and silently got to his feet. Slipping deftly under the cart, he surfaced beside Calling Crow and began pushing. For a moment nothing happened, but then the cart began moving slowly. Another Carib appeared suddenly, pushing on the other side of Calling Crow, and the cart moved back the thickness of a finger. Calling Crow let out a war cry, and three more Caribs got to their feet and ran over to push. The cart began rolling quickly backward against the Spanish. When they were within a foot of the fire they jumped out of the way, and the fat drunk and the *cholo* fell on the ground. The Caribs cheered as the wagon rolled over the fire, coming to rest a few yards beyond.

Calling Crow staggered as he coughed and fought for breath, but managed to stay on his feet. The Caribs formed a small protective group around him as they talked softly in their whistling speech.

The fat drunk staggered up to Calling Crow. "Now you get out of here, or I shall throw you out."

Calling Crow rubbed the wounds on his shoulder as he looked at the man in cold fury. Manuel, the drunk, staggered backward and looked over his shoulder.

"Agustine, come help me remove this savage."

Galvez looked over at Agustine. "Stay where you are."

Galvez dusted his pants off as he walked up to the drunk. "You and Agustine and perhaps a squad of soldiers could put this fellow outside, but not you alone. Now go outside and do not let anybody else in or you shall work for someone else! Do you understand?"

The man's large cheeks shook as he nodded quickly.

Galvez studied Calling Crow for a moment. "All right," he said, "that is enough play for today. There is work to do before the sun sets. Take your place with those fellows over there."

Calling Crow nodded and walked over to stand with the Caribs.

Chapter 34

A *long* high bench dominated the great hall of the *Cabildo*. A dozen black-hood-shrouded clerics sat behind the bench with the large figure of Father Toribio, the Inquisitor, in the center. Two soldiers wearing polished breastplate and holding tall halberds flanked the bench. Along the back wall, a row of large windows had been curtained to keep out the light of day. Several dozen candles burned brilliantly in the two large candelabra suspended from the ceiling overhead. About thirty men, minor officials, *encomenderos*, and soldiers, and one Indian off by himself, sat in a gallery of chairs which faced the bench. They talked among themselves in whispers as the priests waited for the inquisition to begin.

Father Toribio nodded at Father Pacheco, and the young priest rose to his feet. The noise in the great room died. Father Pacheco bowed his head. "We will begin with a prayer," he said in a thin voice, and he recited the Lord's Prayer slowly. Finishing, he said, "Long live the King!"

The men repeated the phrase, and Father Pacheco

climbed the stairs to the high bench. He faced the room. "Father Luis, you will be the first to speak. You may approach."

Father Luis got to his feet and approached the bench. His heart pounded in his chest as he bowed to Father Toribio. He must make the man see that this was a terrible wrong they were about to do to Diego Vega. "Holiness, I am afraid that we are about to start down the wrong path. I would like to be given an opportunity to prove that these despicable accusations have been dreamed up to cover up the real crime which occurred on Senor Mateo's expedition."

Father Toribio looked unperturbed. "And what was that, Father Luis?"

Father Luis's voice trembled with anger. "The deliberate drowning of eighteen Indians, women and children among them, by Senor Alonso Roldan and his soldiers."

Bishop Cavago got to his feet. "Holiness, this is the event which Senor Roldan related to me, and which I explained to you. It was not Senor Roldan who did this, but rather one of his men."

Father Toribio, the Inquisitor, frowned. "Is Senor Roldan here? Let him tell the story."

Alonso Roldan got up from his chair and approached the bench.

Father Toribio looked down on him. "Is what Father Luis says true?"

Roldan looked over at Father Luis. "It is true that it happened, but not in the way he says. I was on the ship, but I did not give the order to throw them over. It was the soldier, Alfonso Zamora. He and the other men did it because the ship was overcrowded and in danger of sinking."

"Is he in the gallery?" said Father Toribio.

A few of the soldiers shifted uncomfortably as the Inquisitor looked in their direction.

"No, Holiness," said Roldan, "he is dead. He died a few months after the ship returned."

Mateo leapt to his feet. "Holiness! This is all a pack of lies! Senor Roldan was the one who stirred the men up."

Roldan turned to him. "How do you know? You were drunk in your cabin when the ship was in danger of sinking. How do you know?"

"More lies!" shouted Mateo. "Diego saw what he was up to and tried to stop him."

"And you would have us take the word of a sodomite?" said Roldan incredulously.

Mateo started toward him. "You shall pay for all of this, you . . ."

One of the soldiers grabbed Mateo and pushed him back to where he had been standing. Father Luis took Mateo's arm and tried to calm him. A priest entered the hall and walked up to the bench. He whispered in the Inquisitor's ear and the audience waited.

Finishing, the priest walked away, his sandals softly slapping the marble floor tiles.

Father Toribio held up his hand. "There are two reasons why I will not allow this debate to go on a moment longer. One is that the man accused of the drownings is long dead, and the second, more important reason is that the Moorish boy has just confessed to the crime which he and Diego Vega are charged with."

A rustle of whispered speculation broke out in the gallery.

"Senors Mateo and Roldan," said Father Toribio, "take your seats, please."

Father Toribio waited till the hall quieted. "And now Senor Diego Vega will be given a chance to prove his innocence. Prepare to bring him out."

Father Luis hurried to the bench. "Holiness, if you will grant me a little more time . . . I have asked one of the Indians who was on that ship to come here today to testify. His name is Roberto, and he is sitting over there."

The men in the gallery turned to stare at Calling Crow as he got to his feet.

Father Toribio shook his head angrily. "No! That matter is closed. We are here for another matter." He looked at Calling Crow in distaste. "Ask him to leave the room now." Father Toribio addressed the men in the gallery. "You all must vacate the hall at this time."

After the men had left, Father Toribio turned to Father Pacheco. "You can bring Diego Vega in now."

Pacheco nodded and walked off. Father Luis pressed up against the bench. "Holiness, this test proves nothing about what happened on that voyage. It is cruel and demeaning. Please reconsider."

Father Toribio's red face shook with anger. "Nonsense! It has been used successfully in the royal court. If it is a good enough test there, then surely it is good enough here in the colonies!"

Father Luis rushed from the bench and hurried after Father Pacheco.

In another chamber of the *Cabildo*, Diego Vega's heart beat rapidly as he sat on the stone bench. Under the thick, loose-fitting woolen robes they had given him, he was sweating heavily, and the drops ran clammily down his armpits to chill his naked sides. His wife, Lomaya, sat beside him, wrapped in an identical robe, which, for some strange reason, the priest had also insisted she wear. Down the hall and inside the main chamber of the *Cabildo*, the Inquisitor and his staff were conferring before they called them in.

Diego glanced at Lomaya, but her presence did not reassure him. Nothing reassured him anymore, not even prayer, not since they had told him what he was charged with. He felt like a swine in a slaughterhouse. The charges were false, so wildly false that the only way he could understand it all was that it must be some kind of horrible mistake. It was also, he knew, a matter of divine retribution. God had decided to punish him in this horrible way for the unspeakable violations of His laws by the men on the ship that night. These mistaken men, with their horrible accusation, were merely God's instruments.

Lomaya touched his arm. "Look, the boy!"

Two soldiers, one on each arm, escorted Miramor down the corridor. As they passed, Diego and Lomaya saw many bruises on the boy's face. His eyes were glazed over, and he didn't even notice them as the two soldiers led him around the corner and out of sight.

Diego looked at Lomaya and quickly turned away. She was swept up in this horrible nightmare and would have to pay right along with him. His shame was only exceeded by his fear.

The slap of sandaled feet came on the stone floor. The young priest and the friendly figure of Father Luis appeared coming down the hall.

Diego and Lomaya got to their feet.

"It is time," said Father Luis. He looked at Diego sadly. "Just be honest in all you tell them and do what they tell you, Diego."

Diego nodded. "Of course, Father." Diego and Lomaya followed the two priests down the corridor and into the large chamber. The priests led Diego and Lomaya past a pallet of velvet covers laid out upon the stone floor. Diego glanced at the pallet as they passed, but took no note of it. With the two priests, he and Lomaya paused to stand before the bench.

Father Luis leaned toward Diego's ear. "Remember, just do what they tell you, and may God bless you."

"Thank you, Father," said Diego softly.

Father Luis and Father Pacheco walked off and took their seats at the end of the bench. The phlegmy scratch of someone's cough echoed off the stone walls.

From his lofty vantage, the Inquisitor fixed his large watery eyes on Diego. Diego thought he saw sorrow and mercy in them and that soothed him a little.

"Diego Vega?" said the Inquisitor.

"Yes, Holiness?"

"Do you know what you are being charged with?"

"Yes, Holiness. They told me."

"How do you plead?"

"I am not guilty, Holiness."

"After four witnesses have sworn to having seen you with the boy, you still insist on your innocence?"

Diego nodded. "Yes, Holiness. I am not guilty."

"Is that your wife?"

"Yes, Holiness." Despite the heavy robe, Diego began to shiver.

The Inquisitor turned aside to whisper into the ear of Father Pacheco. Father Pacheco watched Diego and Lomaya and then whispered softly into the Inquisitor's ear.

The Inquisitor again looked down on Diego. "Did you know that the boy called for a confessor and confessed to it? Did you know that?"

"No, Holiness." He and Lomaya exchanged horrified looks. Diego's voice quavered and cracked. "I don't know why he would confess to such a thing."

The Inquisitor leaned forward. "Perhaps because it is true?"

"No, Holiness. I swear before all in this room and God above that this thing never happened."

"Very well," snapped the Inquisitor in annoyance, "then you shall have to prove it."

"I don't understand, Holiness," said Diego, looking around the chamber nervously. Out of all the priests seated up on the high bench, only Father Luis would meet his eyes. He nodded slowly, as if offering encouragement.

"Behind you," said the Inquisitor, "do you see the pallet that has been prepared on the floor?"

"Yes, Holiness," said Diego nervously, still not quite sure what the Inquisitor intended.

The Inquisitor appeared angry. "Do I have to spell it out for you, man? There is a pallet. Your wife is at your side. Perform the marital act!"

Diego turned away in horror at the Inquisitor's words. Black shame spread through him as he looked down at the pallet. Without a word, Lomaya lay down on it, pulling the velvet covers over herself. She looked up at the ceiling as she quickly removed her robe underneath the covers. Diego got down onto his knees and turned back to look at the Inquisitor.

"Must all the priests remain, Holiness?"

The Inquisitor said nothing as he and the other priests avoided looking directly at him and Lomaya.

"Diego, please," said Lomaya in a whisper.

Diego turned to her and quickly slipped out of his loose robe. Pulling the covers up over his naked back, he lay be-

side her. Sweat beaded on his brow as he turned and
looked at her. "I am sorry for you, Lomaya," he said quietly. "None of this is your affair, yet you have to submit
to this. I am very much ashamed for you."

"Do what they want," whispered Lomaya worriedly.
She looked into his eyes. "It is all right."

Diego nodded. He lay his hand on her arm and moved
closer. After a while he discovered to his horror that his
machinery would not work. He quickly looked over his
shoulder at the priests, and they looked away. Turning
back to Lomaya, he strained harder but nothing happened,
and he felt as if he had died from his hips on down.

"What is the matter?" whispered Lomaya worriedly.

Diego shook his head as sweat poured from his brow. "I
don't know."

Lomaya ran her hand over his head.

Diego looked in her eyes and saw such deep sadness
there. "I love you, Lomaya." He lay his hand on her
breast, and she pulled him closer.

"And I, you."

They lay still, holding each other tightly.

"Enough! That is enough," came the deep voice of the
Inquisitor. "Pull on your robes and stand for sentencing!"

Diego felt a deep sadness and horror as he realized what
it meant. He turned his head toward the priests. "I am innocent," he said quietly. He began crying, his sobs echoing
off the walls.

Chapter 35

Calling Crow and Juana hurried to the open, paving-stone
place where the Spanish often held their religious and gov-

ernmental ceremonies. Two crosses had been planted up
on a raised stone platform, and the large crowd that had
gathered knew that this was where the Spanish would kill
Diego and the boy.

Calling Crow and Juana stood with the people while the
Spanish crowded closer to where some soldiers were piling firewood up around the two crosses. Calling Crow noticed Mateo's familiar head of red hair in the crowd.
Father Luis was with him, and they pushed through the
gawkers as they attempted to get closer to the front.

Calling Crow and Juana threaded their way through the
people to the edge of the inner crowd of Spanish and half-
Spanish.

"What is Father Luis going to do?" said Juana.

Calling Crow shook his head. "There is nothing he can
do. The Inquisitor has already found Diego guilty."

The crowd surged forward suddenly, pressing Calling
Crow and Juana up tightly against others. Heads turned
and people began pointing as a procession of black-robed
priests came slowly down the street. Three horse-drawn
carts rolled along behind them.

The soldiers took Diego and the boy from the first cart
and led them up the steps to the two crosses. They tied
them to the crosses, and then five other men with their
hands bound behind them were led from the other two
carts up onto the platform. These men wore strange,
pointed hats on their heads and were made to stand in
front of the planted crosses where the crowd pointed and
laughed derisively at them.

Calling Crow saw Diego looking wildly about. He
shouted angrily at the people that he was innocent. The
boy said nothing and stared blankly, as if unaware of
where he was.

More people crowded behind Calling Crow and Juana,
wedging them in tightly. Calling Crow saw the tall Inquisitor mount the steps. Father Luis and Mateo rushed over to
him. Father Luis argued loudly with him, and then Mateo
began shouting. Their voices reached Calling Crow and
Juana over the noise of the crowd, and they, too, began

shouting at the Inquisitor and the priests, "He is innocent!"
The people around them looked at them in amusement.
The Inquisitor quickly walked away from Father Luis and
Mateo, and then two soldiers pushed them back into the
crowd.

Mateo and Father Luis pushed over to where the soldiers were stacking the wood. Calling Crow saw Mateo
hand one of the soldiers a small leather pouch. The man
looked inside and then quickly tucked it in his doublet.
Calling Crow knew that it was gold. Father Luis had told
him the night before that Mateo might have no recourse
but to bribe the soldiers to strangle his friend. That way
the old man wouldn't suffer in the flames.

The soldiers continued to pile wood at the base of the
crosses as the priests mounted the steps to the platform.
The tall Inquisitor faced the crowd. His face was hard and
dark under the black hood. With raised arms, he quieted
the crowd and his voice rang out loudly: "Behold these
craven men, Diego Vega and Miramor the Moor, who have
been sentenced to die for the crime of sodomy, this bitter,
detestable crime, a thing altogether inhuman which causes
us to tremble with violent horror as we weigh its
gravity . . ."

"Yes," came a call from the crowd, "it is so!"

"Evil," shouted another voice. "Evil!"

The Inquisitor raised his hands for silence. "We cannot
doubt that the enormity of their crime makes it an offence
to the Divine Majesty." The Inquisitor jabbed a finger toward Diego and Miramor. "These two men here are like
beasts of burden which have no understanding of their
evil."

The Inquisitor faced the crowd again and raised his
hands. His eyes seemed to grow larger, and he pointed,
Calling Crow thought, straight at him. "The fact of their
guilt neither can nor should be questioned by any true
Catholic! Now, the fires of *His* justice will cauterize this
community and burn away the toxins of this despicable
sin. All kneel to hear the Lord's Prayer."

A younger priest stepped forward as the murmuring

crowd got to its knees. He read the prayer from a book in a droning voice. When the priest finished, the Inquisitor started down the stairs and the priest followed him.

The crowd's appetite whetted, it pushed forward for a better vantage.

Calling Crow and Juana tried to push out of the crowd as the soldiers crowded closely around Diego, obscuring him from view. One of them looked around nervously, and when they moved away, Diego's head hung limply. The soldiers moved over to the boy, and Calling Crow saw the big soldier place his large hands around the boy's neck. The boy's eyes bulged, and he struggled visibly against his ropes, then hung limply from his cross.

In the crowd, Father Luis made the sign of the cross. Then the big soldier touched his torch to the pyres. Flames quickly climbed the crosses and both men's clothing caught fire.

Mateo fell to his knees and began crying. Calling Crow was stunned by the sight. He'd never thought Mateo capable of tears. Then he thought about how Mateo had never shed a tear over Big Nose's death, or the people tossed off his ship into the angry sea, and this thought brought back some of Calling Crow's anger toward the man.

Father Luis placed his hands on Mateo's shoulders and attempted to comfort him. Calling Crow felt someone shaking him. Juana's face was wet with tears.

"Please, let's go," she shouted.

Calling Crow pushed through the crowd, making a path for Juana. The stench of burnt flesh reached their noses as they passed the many smiling, chattering faces. Soon they were at the edge of the crowd and hurrying away, but the smoke seemed to follow them. Carried by the land breeze, it moved in a low thin cloud overhead, obscuring the grand buildings as they passed them, the governor's mansion, through which passed the King's enlightened commands, the *Cabildo*, where the Spanish made their many laws to protect the people, and the cathedral, from which was dispensed their God's great mercy. All the grand buildings appeared dark and sooty through the smoke.

Chapter 36

Bishop Cavago looked out over the rail at the people gathered on the quay. He thought of how tiresome and dangerous the expedition would undoubtedly be, and of how content he had been in his house in the town. But, he told himself, the expedition would be good, too. It would present him with many opportunities, and he would have greatly expanded authority.

He heard a commotion behind him and turned to see one of the soldiers being chastised by Father Luis for shoving an Indian. There, he thought, was one of the opportunities. Father Luis could put his blind love for the Indians to better use in Florida. He would leave him there, not in charge, but as an aide to Father Salcido. And what about Juana? He really did not want to part from her. If he could keep an eye on her until the Inquisitor went back to Castile, and until she had the child, well, then, perhaps things could be as they once were. But if she was taken with one of these mission-tamed braves on the ship, as he suspected, then he would have to find out which one and get rid of him somehow. He would see.

He watched a small Indian dugout move away from the quay. The rowers, naked but for loincloths, dug their broad paddles into the calm sea powerfully as the solitary passenger, an official of some kind, perhaps a lawyer, held onto the gunwales with both hands, his head moving forward and backward with the strokes of the oars. Yes, thought Bishop Cavago as he filled his chest with the cool air, the benefits could definitely outweigh the discomforts. He would do his best to see that they did.

* * *

Senor Francisco Mateo stood with several other *enco-menderos* who had been impressed by De Sole to serve on the expedition. Not far away from them, De Sole and his captains talked excitedly, the wind tugging at their hair and beards. Bishop Cavago and some priests walked by and started down the stairs to the waist. Father Luis was among them, and he nodded sadly to Mateo as he passed.

Mateo looked back down on the quay to where his wife, Felipa, and her father stood. Felipa wore her best black velvet dress for the occasion. Mateo tried to smile at her, and giving up, waved dutifully before turning away to watch some sailors hauling on a rope. His weariness went to the bone, and he felt heavy and old. All his pride about the grand, just role of King and colony in the New World had been exposed as cruel illusion by Diego's miserable death.

Alonso Roldan and Manuel Ortiz walked up to De Sole and bowed in greeting. Mateo looked away in disgust. He had visited Diego in jail the day before he died, and Diego had raved about how all who had gone to Florida on his expedition three years earlier were cursed. Perhaps Diego had been right. Perhaps his curse was now unfolding.

Calling Crow carried a large clay jar of oil across the gangplank and onto the deck of the *Isabella*. Shouted orders and the occasional crack of a whip rose above the constant howling of the many dogs in the belly of the ship. Calling Crow followed a Carib carrying a sack of grain across the deck. The large sack obscured the man's body and seemed to have sprouted legs as it moved surefootedly down the ramp leading to the gundeck. Below in the interior of the ship, the barking of the dogs was much louder. Calling Crow saw them in the rear, all chained together, snapping angrily at the legs of a man who was walking past.

Calling Crow set the jar down with the others. He was pleased to see how long the rows of jars had grown, and how high the mounds of sacks, for he and the others were very tired of the work. He started up the ramp, passing others as they came down loaded like pack animals. He came out into the sun and looked about, hoping to see Juana. He knew she was already on the ship. She would stay in a cabin in the front of the ship with some of the other women, while he and the other bearers would sleep up on the deck.

Calling Crow walked around the ship's boat and spotted Juana and another woman by the rail washing clothes in a wooden tub. He walked over to her. The woman beside Juana averted her eyes, continuing her rubbing and wringing as Calling Crow looked at Juana.

"Are you well?" he said.

Juana nodded, looking around quickly. "Six of us are staying in there." She nodded to a door. "It is crowded, but at least it will be out of the weather if we have rain."

Calling Crow looked at her and felt many different feelings. Her belly was bigger now and that made his heart sing. Yet it could be the Bishop's child. The thought saddened him a little, but he would accept the child as theirs. They were leaving this crazy place, yet they would still not be free. He softly sang a prayer to the Great Spirit and to Father Luis's gods, the Mother Mary and the Jesus. *Aieyah!* He would miss Father Luis. He had been a good friend, despite his strange habits and ways.

He looked out across the harbor at the sea. They must get away from the Spanish as soon as possible after they reached the other side of the sea. They must, for once there he would never allow the Spanish to take them back to this place. If they had to die in the Floridas, then at least they would die together and their spirits would be together after death.

The other woman picked up an armful of damp clothing and walked away. Calling Crow moved closer to Juana. "We will run away the first chance we get. Keep your eyes on me, and I will tell you when it is a good time."

"How will we . . ." Juana saw the Bishop and another Black Robe approaching. "He comes," she said, going back to her work. "You must not let him see you talking to me. Go quickly."

Calling Crow joined the steady stream of men who were
walking back toward the quay to carry in more provisions.

Juana saw the priest and Bishop Cavago go up onto the
half deck where some others were talking. Then the
Bishop walked in her direction. He stood at the rail a short
distance away and looked out at the sea.

"Who was that?" he said.

Juana did not look at him as she wrung out a cloth into
the tub. "I do not know what he is called."

"What did he want?"

"He was looking for a woman who is not on this ship."

"Is that so?" The Bishop continued to stare at the sea.
Then he turned to her. "Well, there is no sense in catching
the eye of any of these fellows. They will more than likely
stay in the Floridas. You will be returning to the island
with me, of course."

Juana continued to avoid his eyes as she scrubbed a
shirt on the side of the tub. She was on fire with anger, yet
she dared not show any reaction. His eyes were all over
her while she worked, and she was greatly relieved when
two other women, each carrying a sack of dirty clothing,
walked over to use the tub.

The Bishop ignored them as he looked down at her.
"Juana, there is more washing in my cabin behind the
door. See to it."

Juana nodded as he walked off.

As the women dumped their clothing into the tub, Juana
watched Calling Crow walk by carrying another one of the
large stone jars. After he passed, there was a sudden star-
tling sound of thunder yet not a cloud was in the sky. The
thunder came again and again, and the women shrieked
and lay on the ground. Juana sat down slowly, breathing
through her teeth as she held her hand on her belly.

"*Aieyah*," shouted one of the women, her eyes clamped
shut, "what was it?"

Calling Crow ran over to them. "It is the ships in the
harbor. They are firing their big cannons for De Sole." He
knelt down beside Juana and spoke softly into her ear. "I
will be out here always. Stay away from him as best you

can. If he won't leave you alone, tell me and I will talk to
Father Luis. Perhaps he can help us. If he cannot, then I
will have to deal with him myself."

Many trumpets blew a fanfare. A Spanish soldier
shouted at the people. "Quiet! Quiet now!" Calling Crow
and Juana watched Bishop Cavago and the priests climb
the steps to the poop deck. The Bishop raised his arms to
give the blessing, and all got down on their knees. After
the blessing, the men got to their feet.

The heavy thud of three pairs of boots was heard on the
quiet deck as De Sole and two of his captains walked toward the poop. They quickly climbed the steps and turned
to look out upon the people assembled on the decks. De
Sole drew his sword and knelt on one knee. Looking skyward, he said in a loud, booming voice, "I, Juan Pinosa de
Sole, do hereby swear before all of you today, that I will
not take a razor to my beard until Florida is brought to
heel!"

"Hear, hear," shouted his captains, and all the men immediately took to cheering.

"Aieyah," said Calling Crow quietly to Juana. "It will
be bad for those people over there."

Juana nodded grimly.

De Sole went on. "How honorable a calling it is that we
Christian knights follow, for with the grace of God we
shall have the pleasure of winning over that great land of
Florida for the Crown. And all the inhabitants thereof,
their souls we shall deliver to the priests for eternal salva-
tion."

Calling Crow and Juana frowned worriedly as De Sole
got to his feet. Raising his sword high, he shouted. "Santiago!"

"Santiago!" roared the soldiers in unison.

A squad of arquebusmen fired their loud weapons all at
once. Juana flinched, and Calling Crow impulsively
wanted to hold her, but dared not. Black smoke drifted
across the deck in the mild breeze. The men on shore began pushing the big ship off the quay with timbers as the
sailors on board strained at the capstan. Slowly the main-

sail rose and billowed out in a gentle curve as the big ship turned about.

Chapter 37

The *Isabella* and the other ships of De Sole's fleet moved slowly into a small bay. Senor Francisco Mateo watched as the sailors shouted and rushed about lowering sail and readying the anchors. A dozen natives stood on the curve of sandy beach. As Mateo leaned against the rail to watch them, the smell of millions of flowers emanating from the shores filled the air like a breath from heaven. The smell did little to lift the pall of melancholy that hung over him, however. He did not want to be here. His last foray into the Floridas had cost him too much. A hollow thud sounded as a sailor wielding a large wooden mallet knocked loose the chocks holding the anchor. There was a momentary groaning rush of hawser through the hawse-hole followed by a large splash as the anchor entered the water.

One of De Sole's guards walked up to Mateo. "His Excellency would like to speak with you," he said.

As Mateo turned to start up the stairs, he saw Father Luis's Indian, Roberto, hanging about the washerwomen. Not having known he was aboard the ship, Mateo stopped and stared at him for a moment. The guard turned round to him. "Come quickly, senor. He is waiting."

Mateo was shown into De Sole's spacious cabin. Senor Alonso Roldan stood beside De Sole's desk looking down at a large chart spread out there. When Roldan noticed Mateo, he bowed slightly to De Sole and walked off a few feet.

De Sole looked at Mateo. "Senor Roldan says we are now in the area you had explored on your voyage. I told you when we left Santo Domingo I wanted you to report to me when the coast began to look familiar."

Mateo gave Roldan a steady look as he stepped around the desk to look down at the chart. It was a new chart, decorated with comely Indian maids prancing naked on the shores of Florida and friendly dolphins leaping from the waters. Mateo looked at De Sole. "Where are we, according to your reckoning?"

De Sole ran his little finger down the coast, stopping at a point. "Here, at latitude twenty-seven and a half."

Mateo shook his head. "I've never landed this far south." He pointed to a spur of land jutting out much further north. "This is where I left the coast last time."

De Sole sat back in his chair, eyeing Mateo suspiciously. "Then you are saying that Senor Roldan is a liar?"

Mateo turned to look at Roldan. "Oh, he is that, too, but in this instance it is probably just a matter of his not being able to read a chart properly."

Roldan's face turned crimson. "Excellency," he said tiredly, "he lies. I told you he would do nothing to help you."

Mateo glared angrily at Roldan, then turned back to De Sole. "Excellency, let him and me settle our score now and forever?"

De Sole sat back in his chair and folded his hands. "No. Not yet. Both of you are familiar with this land and the natives, so there will be no swordplay until I give permission. Do you understand?"

De Sole stared at Mateo as he waited for an answer. A soldier strode quickly into the room. "Indians, sir. A canoe full of them, coming out."

De Sole got to his feet. "Very well. Prepare a boat with a gun and meet them. Bring their *Cacique* aboard if he's among them."

The soldier bowed and walked out.

De Sole pulled on his sword. He turned to Mateo. "That will be all."

Mateo bowed and turned to Roldan. "Soon we shall settle our score."

Roldan's face remained impassive. "Sooner than you think."

From up on the foredeck, Calling Crow watched the people on the beach. They were nearly naked, free and happy as children as they watched the ships, while Calling Crow wore the plain wool breeches and shirt of the Spanish. They, too, would soon fall before the power of the Spanish and be forced to wear their rough clothing and work in their fields and mines. And there was nothing Calling Crow could do about it. But when he and Juana escaped, they could warn the people on their way north. Although they were very far from Tumaqua, they could get there. He was sure of it. His people traded with many other tribes from faraway lands. There would be trading parties going in the direction from which the cold winds blew. It would take many days of walking, but eventually they would find their way to his village. Then what? He had been thinking of this more and more lately. What would they find there? Would the village still be there? And who was Chief? He wondered if Tiamai was married. She should be; after all, he had been gone a long time. Most importantly, though, he had been worrying about whether or not he and Juana would be accepted. And would Juana be happy there? He hoped so.

The howling and barking of the dogs was very loud now. It sounded from between the boards of the deck. Despite his fear of the dogs, Calling Crow pitied them. Not once during the entire voyage had he seen any Spanish feed them. Now their hunger was driving them mad.

"They will curse this day for the rest of their lives."

"What?" said Calling Crow, turning to see Juana coming up behind him.

"The people on the beach."

"Ah," he said, nodding sadly, "yes, as well I know."

Juana stood beside him, a large basket of soiled clothing beside her. When a stream was located, she was to go ashore with the other women to wash it under the watchful eyes of some Spanish soldiers.

A loud guffaw erupted not far away where some soldiers were preparing to go ashore. They talked and laughed as they put on their armor and loaded their weapons. Below, as the ripe smell of the land permeated the hold of the ship, the barking of the dogs grew even louder until it sounded to Calling Crow like the hell the Spanish often spoke of.

Calling Crow turned to look at Juana. "Tell me again what you will do when you get ashore."

Juana looked around and saw that Long Hair Woman was out of earshot, loading up another big basket with some other women. She turned back to Calling Crow. "I will go with the other women washers, and I will wait till it is very quiet and the guard is not watching. Then I will sneak away and hide in the woods. When it is dark and the stars are clear, I will make my way to the beach where I will call like the owl. You will find me in that way."

Calling Crow looked at her. She was dressed in a gown of rough Spanish wool, but despite the shapelessness of the garment, her round belly showed through. He knew they must get away soon.

"You look very beautiful," he said.

Juana looked at him, her eyes moist with many days and nights of unshed tears. Calling Crow wished he could hold her, but he dared not for fear of someone seeing them.

"Do not worry, my love," he said, "soon we will escape and be on our way."

Juana nodded, too overcome to speak.

A shout went up, then a chorus of excited speculation among the Spanish. Calling Crow looked back at the beach. "Some of these foolish people are coming out in a canoe," he said.

"He has seen us," said Juana.

"Who?" said Calling Crow.

"The Bishop. He is watching us from up there."

Calling Crow turned and looked up at the priests gathered at the rail on the half deck. The Bishop looked at him, and Calling Crow cursed himself for letting the man see him with Juana. The priests climbed the steps to the quarterdeck and moved out of sight.

Later Juana watched Calling Crow climb down the rope ladder into the boat with the other bearers. As she smiled down at him, someone joined her at the rail. She turned, and her smile froze at the sight of the Bishop.

Juana looked away from the Bishop and back down at Calling Crow. Calling Crow had seen the Bishop, and his face darkened with hate. Juana raised her hand to wave, and the Bishop seized it tightly.

He pulled her away, back toward the mainmast. Juana yanked her hand away. "What are you doing? I am to help with the washing."

The Bishop shook his head and grabbed her wrist again. "Oh, no. In your condition it would not be wise."

"But, my lord," said Juana as he pulled her toward the stairs, "I was told to wash with the others."

Bishop Cavago squeezed her wrist painfully as he pulled her along toward his cabin. "If you love to wash so much, I shall have a tub put in my cabin for you, child."

"Why do you do this to me?" said Juana.

The Bishop's reddened face quivered. "Because I have given you everything, do you hear? You belong to me. He shall never have you!"

"What do you mean?" said Juana as he pulled her along roughly by her wrist. "He is of my people, that is all!"

The Bishop opened his cabin door. "Do you think I am blind?" he said. He pushed her inside, bolting the door from the outside.

As the cold dimness of the cabin enveloped her, Juana pounded on the door. She heard the Bishop's muffled voice. "Don't carry on so, child. Just clean the room up and I shall let you out when I've a mind to."

Juana slumped to the floor. She said Calling Crow's name a few times and cried softly.

* * *

On the boat ride to the beach, Calling Crow could see nothing but the Bishop pulling Juana away by the arm. Now he knows, he thought, and that would make escape almost impossible. Still, he must find a way. Perhaps he could get Father Luis to help them. He didn't know how far the good priest would go, though, or even if he would go against his own, especially his Bishop, to help them, but perhaps it was time to find out.

As soon as the boats ground to a halt on the sand, three soldiers carrying loaded crossbows began yelling at Calling Crow and the Arawak man who was called Ito. "Out!" they shouted. "Start the others carrying the supplies up onto the beach. Hurry!"

Stepping out into the warm surf, Calling Crow called to the other bearers, and they grabbed the many baskets and boxes and carried them up onto the dry sand. Up by the tree line, a group of native men, women, and children had gathered to see the Spanish. The children stuck close to and in between the legs of their mothers, who were naked from the waist up and attractive, with firm round breasts and long black, oiled hair. The men were small of build, but smoothly muscled. The men wore small rings of gold in their ears. The people were genuinely friendly to the Spanish, and Calling Crow knew from this that they had had no contact with them before.

Calling Crow put down another box on the growing pile on the beach. From the forest came the scent of millions of flowers. Butterflies flitted everywhere, and bees and hummingbirds buzzed and whirred about. Calling Crow decided that the village must be hidden inside the forest somewhere.

One by one, the boats pulled up on the white sand to unload their occupants and supplies before heading back out to the ships for more. Calling Crow and Ito worked with a group of bearers as soldiers shouted orders and formed up in ranks. Off a ways, a party of priests, led by the Bishop, assembled in an orderly group, their black robes in stark contrast to the bright silk scarfs of the soldiers and the nakedness of the people.

One of the soldiers guarding Calling Crow and the others told them to rest, and they sat down on the boxes. They watched two young priests move away from the others and carry forward a wooden altar upon which lay rich cloths of purple and gold. Then a procession of four other priests carried a large gold cross over and set it upon the altar. This done, the Bishop took his place in front of the altar facing the cross. De Sole knelt, and then all the Spanish and even some of the people of this place followed his example. Calling Crow and the others knelt.

As the crowd grew quiet, the barking and cries of the dogs could be heard. The mass began with the priests singing the liturgy in Latin while bells were rung and incense burned. The local people looked on in wonder and awe. When it was finished, De Sole turned and conferred with his captains.

A soldier stood and raised his arms solemnly. "All quiet for the reading of the Proclamation!"

As the soldier waved his hands for silence, Ito turned to Calling Crow. "Are they not going to have it translated for these unlucky people?"

Calling Crow shook his head. "Would it matter?"

"Here ye all," the soldier's voice droned out. "The Proclamation of the Council of the Indies! On this the eighth day of April, in the year one thousand five hundred and fifty-eight of our Lord, I hereby proclaim to all you native peoples of this place which we Spanish call Florida, that from this day forward, you are to render your obedience and loyalty to our sovereign King Charles. You are also to embrace the one true Catholic faith for the rest of your days on this earth, devoting your life to God's laws. Your failure to do these things shall cause you to incur the anger of your sovereign and suffer the grave consequences. So be it said."

The soldier rolled up the proclamation, and three trumpeters sounded a fanfare.

The local Indians cheered and raised their lances to the sky. Some of the soldiers looked at them suspiciously, unsure whether or not they were being insulting.

Calling Crow, Ito, and the other bearers picked up their boxes and followed the column of soldiers and priests. Led by one of the local Indians, they began moving into the forest to make their way to the village. As they entered the forest's shadowy coolness, the howling of the dogs sounded eerily behind them. The trail followed a raised bank and took them through a hot humid bog of mangrove trees, their roots rising from the black water like sea monsters. Calling Crow thought that it would be a good place to slip away, but not with Juana locked up on the ship. He would have to wait for another chance. After a walk of a half league or so they came upon a small village of palm-thatched huts raised on stilts. De Sole and most of his men were already there, along with Mateo and Roldan. Calling Crow and the others put the supplies down where the soldiers indicated and sat down to rest.

After a while Hotea, the interpreter, approached with one of the local Indians, a small man of about a hundred and twenty pounds. The man wore a loincloth and the small earrings that the others had sported. They talked excitedly, but Calling Crow was too far away to hear what they said. He could see De Sole studying the man intently. The man began to sidle away when De Sole reached out for his ear and grabbed his earring. The man ducked down, attempting to escape, but two soldiers quickly grabbed him. De Sole ripped the ring from his ear, and the man crouched in fear on the ground as his ear and neck ran with blood.

"Senor Roldan," called De Sole loudly, "bring your lodestone!"

"Look," said Ito, pointing back the way they had come. "Their *Cacique* is coming."

Four men labored down the rough slope of the trail carrying a sedan chair made of cane and thatch. The *Cacique* sat calmly inside as the men carried him past Calling Crow and Ito. Calling Crow and Ito saw that he was old and thin, evidently suffering from some kind of sickness. They watched him slowly get out of the chair and bow to De Sole. Instead of the loincloths that his men wore, the

Cacique wore a robe of animal skins and had a skin of some kind wrapped around his head like a Moor's turban.

"They're going to want him to tell them about the gold," said Ito.

Calling Crow nodded grimly.

A soldier came up the trail leading a dog. The animal lunged at Calling Crow, Ito, and the other bearers as it passed. Barking and snapping frenziedly, it seemed oblivious to the rope about its neck. A few moments later a low growl could be heard, and then the frightened cries of the *Cacique*. "They are using the dog to frighten him into telling them where they get the gold," said Ito.

Calling Crow nodded. Anger and disgust filled him. He must get Juana away somehow . . . and soon.

Two soldiers came back to Calling Crow and the others and began shouting.

"On your feet! We're going back. Back to the beach!"

As Calling Crow, Ito, and the others lifted their baskets and boxes, De Sole and his entourage passed them. Calling Crow saw Mateo and Roldan, and the old *Cacique* in their midst. The man looked frightened out of his mind.

Calling Crow and the others started down the trail as a babble of excited speculation broke out among the bearers.

"Did you hear?" said Ito from behind.

Calling Crow shook his head.

"We will sail north to find the Saturiba People. They are the ones who traded these people their gold. They are taking the *Cacique* to the ship to help guide them."

Calling Crow and Ito walked along the raised trail through the mangrove forest. They heard the sporadic thunderous booming of arquebuses.

"They are killing them!" said Calling Crow.

"Yes," said Ito. "The Spanish took their food, and they were foolish enough to fight back."

As they passed through the dark forest, disembodied screams traveled over the still black waters, sounding like the tortured cries of the souls in hell.

Chapter 38

Calling Crow crouched next to Juana under the canvas spread across the gunwales on the forward part of the *Isabella*. The soldiers had put up the canvas at the insistence of Father Luis, to protect the people from the wind and driving rain of the storm.

The ships had hardly sailed more than a few leagues north when bad weather had moved in. One sunny day the sky turned black, and an hour later wind and rain came hard out of the northeast. Soon Calling Crow and the others grew very sick from the heavy seas. The ships made a hard starboard tack for the first half of the day, changing at midday to a port tack, which they held till nightfall, often coming back to anchor only slightly north of and within sight of where they'd anchored the night before. Even at night the ships rocked violently at anchor, giving the people no respite from the storm.

The few Indian women who had been given cabins had come up onto the deck so that they could be with their men, for they were sure that the ship would capsize, and they did not want to die alone. Some people lay in pools of their own vomit, unable to move. Others sang their death songs.

As Juana huddled close to Calling Crow, she thought she saw the dark hooded figure of the Bishop up on the poop looking down at them. He had been locking her in his room frequently now, and it was only because of the storm that he had let her out. She looked back up for him and thought, what did it matter now if he again saw her with Calling Crow? They were all going to die soon anyway. What did it matter now? She wrapped her arms around Calling Crow and held him tightly.

Calling Crow shouted into her ear over the wind and the cries of the others. "Do not worry, the storm will abate and we will get away. There will be a chance again."

Juana shook her head sadly, her tears washed away by the driving rain. "No. It is all over now. Let us not pretend. I love you, but our love will have to wait till we pass over to the next world." In the fading light of the day, she saw a dark figure nearby. It was Father Luis, the priest who had been so kind to Calling Crow. He was kneeling to hear someone's confession. She spoke into Calling Crow's ear. "Calling Crow, we must prepare now for our deaths. I will make my last confession now, then you must do the same." She called out to the father. "Father, please hear my last confession."

Calling Crow moved away as Father Luis knelt down beside her.

Father Luis was so deeply agitated by the things the girl, Juana, had told him that he had had to make a great effort to concentrate as he listened to the confessions of the others. Now, as he made his way down the steps to the gundeck in the growing dark, he felt his anger growing red-hot. He had been planning to talk to the Bishop in the morning, but he knew he would not be able to sleep if he didn't confront him right away about what the girl had said. He went back up the steps into the wind and noise. Hugging the bulkheads, he made his way to the cabins at the rear of the poop.

He knocked on the Bishop's door. Nothing happened for a few minutes, and he angrily knocked again. The door opened suddenly and the Bishop's face appeared in the glow of a candle he was holding. A gust of wind snuffed it out, but Luis could still see his face in the light reflected from another candle inside the cabin.

"What is it?" said the Bishop angrily.

"Excellency, I have just heard a most tortured confession."

Bishop Cavago's face grew sharp. "And?"

"It had to do with you."

"What do you mean?"

"The native woman, Juana. She said that you had relations with her."

A distant flicker of lightning lit Bishop Cavago's face, and he blinked a few times. "She must be suffering from delusions. The storm is making them all a little crazy. They are not used to storms at sea."

Thunder rumbled and a large wave crashed sideways into the ship, the timbers groaning as they flexed with the shock. Father Luis shouted over the noise as he shook his head. "No, Excellency. Like the others, she believes she is face-to-face with the Eternity. She would not lie. She said that you forced her to do these things."

Bishop Cavago looked angrily at Father Luis. "And what are you going to do about this crazy accusation?"

Father Luis stared at the Bishop in anger. "Excellency, when we return to Hispaniola ... the Inquisitor will have to be told."

Bishop Cavago's face quivered in the dim light. "Get out!" He slammed the door loudly in Father Luis's face.

Slowly, over a period of two days, the winds lost their velocity and the seas calmed. The deck of the *Isabella* was crowded with people, Indian and Spanish alike, kneeling to offer prayers of thanks. By the time the fleet arrived in the area where the Saturiba People were said to live, the seas were a navigable choppy green with white combers. The ships moved up a channel between the coast and a long sandy island, bare but for some sea grass, and dropped anchor. On the shore, a white expanse of sand stretched several hundred yards to a forest of tall, ragged-looking palmetto trees and pond pine, cypress and sweet gum. Mateo pushed against the rail with the others to stare hungrily at the land. It appeared deserted, the only sounds being the sorrowful cries of a few curious gulls and the slapping of the waves against the hull of the ship.

De Sole, Captain Herrera, and Hotea, the interpreter, stood up on the poop deck. The frail-looking *Cacique* was with them. De Sole waved at Mateo to come up the stairs.

"Does this place look familiar?" said De Sole as Mateo walked up to him.

Mateo shook his head. "I've never been here before."

De Sole gave him a look which said he did not believe him, but Mateo didn't care. He was here because he had no choice, not because he wanted to serve the great, noble De Sole in his grand expedition.

De Sole turned to Hotea. "Ask the *Cacique* if this is truly the place. It doesn't seem inhabited." De Sole smiled. "Tell him that if he is mistaken I shall merely thrash him, but that if he has lied to me I shall throw him to the dogs below."

Hotea put the question to the *Cacique,* and the man's chin shook in fear as he replied. Before Hotea could translate his reply, one of De Sole's men began shouting, "Indians! Look there!"

They turned to watch several Indians emerge from the forest onto the sandy beach. First there were only five of them, then dozens more hurried down onto the beach. From a trail further down the beach, more appeared. Two steady streams of Indians crowded out onto the beach.

Captain Herrera said to De Sole, "They look like ants from a stirred-up nest."

De Sole nodded. "They were expecting us."

"How could that be, Excellency?" said Herrera.

De Sole watched the Indians through eyes like slits. "A runner would have made better time coming up the coast than we did with that wind and sea we were fighting."

Herrera nodded. "You are right."

"Of course I am right," snapped De Sole. He glared at Mateo and then turned back to Herrera. "Take Hotea along to interpret, and a dozen soldiers for protection, and put a boat ashore to see if you can talk to them. Tell them we want to trade with them. Bring some truck with you."

"*Sí*, Excellency," said Herrera, bowing smartly. He quickly walked off and began shouting orders to his men.

De Sole turned to Mateo. "That is what worked for you, isn't it? Lots of bright truck?"

Mateo nodded and said nothing.

A moment later, they watched the boat head out from the ship. Alonso Roldan joined De Sole at the rail, and Mateo turned away angrily. They watched the progress of the boat. Two soldiers stood in the prow, their tall arquebuses on stands, ready to fire. Oars dipping rhythmically, the boat was halfway to the shore when a native craft appeared from a hidden creek further up. Constructed of two extremely long canoes lashed together and filled with at least two dozen men, the rowers stood as they dug their paddles into the sea. The canoe raced at an impressive speed for the ship's boat.

A volley of arrows rose from the Indian craft like an angry cloud of bees. The arrows arced down, most of them missing the boat. They littered the surface of the sea like straw in the gutter after a rain.

"Quite thick, eh?" said Roldan to De Sole. "A man would be stung for sure."

De Sole nodded without taking his eyes off the boats. "Not if he was wearing fine Castilian mail and armor. Nothing the savages have can penetrate that."

"Sí, that is so."

The ship's boat drew within range and two puffs of black smoke erupted from it. Then the report of the arquebuses reached the ship. The two crafts drew closer.

"They are no longer afraid of the arquebuses," said De Sole.

"Yes, Excellency," said Roldan, "to their detriment."

The two boats closed, and sunlight flashed off armor and sword as barely audible shouts and cries floated back over the water. The ship's boat disengaged and headed back for the *Isabella*. Looking down from the high deck of the ship, Mateo and the others could see that the soldiers had captured two of the Indians from the canoe.

De Sole turned to Mateo. "Come along. Let's go down to the waist to see what they've caught. Maybe you can shed some light on what they say."

Mateo said nothing as he followed De Sole and Roldan down the stairs.

Soldiers milled about the waist, waiting for the ship's

boat to come about. Herrera and three other soldiers were the first to come aboard, dragging the two Indians up with them. Hotea followed closely behind. Two more soldiers climbed up, helping a third whose breeches were drenched in blood, an arrow having pierced his unprotected leg. As the two Indians were pulled, struggling, across the deck, one of them lunged at Mateo, shrieking angrily.

Mateo was temporarily taken aback by the sheer hatred in the other man's face.

De Sole called over to Hotea, "What was he saying?"

Hotea told him, "He said that Senor Mateo is the one who took all his people away."

Mateo watched the Indian warily as he struggled to break free of the soldiers.

"Your reputation precedes you," said De Sole.

Mateo bowed. "I'm sure it pales compared to yours, Excellency."

De Sole smiled and turned back to Roldan. "It seems their enthusiasm is not to trade with us, but rather to attack us. Lock those two away for now."

Roldan nodded and walked off.

De Sole shouted to one of his officers. "Antonio! Have the ship's master prepare the signal pennant for an artillery barrage. We shall have to run them off the beach so we can land."

Antonio ran off and another officer hovered at De Sole's side. De Sole looked at him. "Prepare the men. We will go ashore in an hour's time."

"Sí, Excellency." The man ran off.

De Sole turned again to watch the mass of natives gathered on the beach. One more of the lashed-together canoes had ventured forth, but stayed well out of range of the ship.

Down in the bilge, Alonso Roldan kicked one of the two captured Indians as he and a soldier attempted to tie the struggling man up. The man still had plenty of fight left in him. Finishing, Roldan looked over in the dim light at Hotea and a soldier who were still tying up the other Indian.

The soldier got to his feet, and he and Hotea headed for the stairs.

"Wait a minute," said Roldan. Despite the stench of the bilge, he wanted to question the Indians. His mind still burned with the image of the one Indian fairly foaming at the mouth as he shrieked at Mateo. Roldan turned to Hotea. "Hotea, ask him what happened to the people of his village after the bulk of them were taken away by Mateo."

Hotea put the question to the Indian, and he talked at great length. Finally Hotea turned to Roldan. "He said that they went to live with the Saturiba People."

"What about the big *Cacique*, the one called Ahopo? Did he survive?"

Hotea questioned the man and then relayed his answer. "He said that Ahopo eventually became *Cacique* of both tribes. This was after the Saturiba *Cacique* was killed."

Roldan studied the Indian carefully as he recalled the man's earlier fit of rage against Mateo. Ahopo also would be eager to get his hands on the man who sailed away with most of his village. Roldan smiled as a plan began forming in his mind.

Hotea looked at him inquisitively. "What is it, senor?"

"Nothing for now. Let's get out of this stink."

Chapter 39

Up on the foredeck, Calling Crow and Juana watched the strange-looking double-hulled Indian canoe paddling back and forth as the men aboard it attempted to get a good look at the ships without getting within range of the guns. As Calling Crow watched, his heart was still troubled by their own problems. How and when would he and Juana make their escape? It was more dangerous now than he had anticipated and sometimes he despaired of their ever getting away. A loud clatter from above interrupted his thoughts. He saw a signal flag moving up the mast. He stopped one of the *cholos* hurrying by. "What does the flag mean?" he said, pointing to it.

The man smiled haughtily. "It is an order to prepare to bombard those stupid people on the beach."

"A bombardment!" said Juana in horror. She and Calling Crow looked at the beach as the *cholo* hurried off.

"Calling Crow, a bombardment would kill them all. What can we do?"

"Let's go get Father Luis," he said. "Maybe he can stop them."

They found Father Luis alone in his cabin. He blinked at the strong light as he opened the door. "Yes, children," he said, "what is it?"

"Father," said Calling Crow, "they are going to bombard the people on the beach with the big guns!"

Father Luis made the sign of the cross. "Just a minute."

Calling Crow and Juana followed Father Luis as he headed for the stairs to the waist. He turned to them. "You better stay here."

Father Luis hurried down the stairs and spotted Bishop Cavago talking with Fathers Tomas, Juan, and Miguel. He hurried over to them.

"They are going to bombard the natives," he said.

"No!" Old Father Tomas quickly made the sign of the cross.

"How do you know?" demanded Bishop Cavago.

"One of the Indians just told me," said Father Luis.

"Since when does De Sole consult with the Indians before he does something?"

Father Luis forced himself to maintain the proper respect toward the Bishop. After what the girl, Juana, had told him, it was very difficult. "Excellency, they know what is going on. One of them overheard it. We must put a stop to it."

Bishop Cavago quickly walked off and the other priests followed him. They found De Sole surrounded by his captains and soldiers. Bishop Cavago and the three priests pushed through the crowd.

De Sole bowed slightly when he saw Cavago. "My lord Bishop?"

"Excellency," said Bishop Cavago, "I think that we should be given the opportunity to attempt to convert these natives before any military action is taken."

A loud clatter sounded nearby and De Sole turned to watch a soldier lead one of the horses up the ramp. He looked back at the Bishop. "Very well. But please use all possible haste, for we have to get our forces ashore before darkness."

"Thank you, Excellency." Cavago turned round to Father Luis and the other priests.

"Perhaps we should take some soldiers with us," said Father Miguel. A young priest in his mid-twenties, he blinked his large brown eyes nervously. "Just in case."

"No," said Bishop Cavago. "That would enrage them. Only one of us should go. That way the natives will know we mean them no harm. Then, when they are calmer, we can all go ashore."

The priests grew quiet as the implications of the Bishop's words sank in.

"Father Luis," said Bishop Cavago in a kindly voice, "don't you agree?"

Father Luis tried to keep the fear out of his eyes. He knew what the Bishop was planning, but he could not stop him. "Yes, Excellency," he said.

"Well," said Bishop Cavago, "perhaps you should go. After all, you have had the most success with the Indians."

The other priests kept their eyes on the wooden deck boards.

"I will go, Excellency," said Father Luis. "I would like

a few minutes alone in my cabin to pray and prepare myself."

Bishop Cavago nodded grimly. "Of course."

Father Luis knelt in the dimness of his cabin as he prayed before the crucifix on the wall. A cold storm of fear and anger raged in his belly. As he prayed, he could not overcome his hatred of the Bishop. He cried out for forgiveness and strength, but the face of Jesus on the small cross in front of him remained twisted in its own pain, giving him no succor. The fear continued to grow inside of him. The Indians were furious. He could not even hope to calm them, let alone convert them. For what felt like a long time he prayed for strength to overcome his fear, while the many sounds filtered dully into his cabin: the tramp of feet, shouts, the clatter of weapons and armor. He thought of his happy life on the island of Hispaniola and the child who became his first baptism there. He had been sent to the new territories on the northwest side. The Indians there had been very hostile and suspicious. On Father Luis's third visit to their village, the *Cacique* had angrily ordered a sick child to be brought to him. "The child is dying anyway," he had said, "so you can have him for your god. Maybe then you will stop bothering us." Father Luis baptized the child, and did everything he could for him, but he had the Indian plague and didn't last. But all the while the child's father stayed with him, and Father Luis had a chance to tell him of God's greatness. The man eventually converted and became a good friend. Then others in the village converted one by one, family by family, until the entire population became Christians. As he thought of these things, he felt the fear losing its grip on him. He had saved many native people from their pagan ways and eventual damnation. The thought filled him with warmth. Then he was struck with a terrible thought. What would happen to Roberto and Juana if he were killed? They would be at the Bishop's mercy.

He opened the door and called to one of the Indians going by. "Bring Roberto and Juana to me. Hurry!"

The man ran off, and Father Luis closed himself back up in the comforting darkness of the cabin. He found some paper and sat down at the table. He wrote down all that the girl had told him. He was signing it when a loud pounding came at the door.

He opened it to Roberto and Juana. He quickly handed the note to Juana. "I have put down everything you told me on here, and I have signed it. When you get back to the island, put it someplace safe."

Juana nodded nervously.

"If the Bishop bothers you again, you tell him of this, and that you will show it to other priests. Tell him you will give it to the Inquisitor. Do you understand?"

Juana nodded sadly. "Thank you, Father."

Father Luis smiled sadly and shut the door. Someone shouted in to him, but he seemed not to hear. His fear was becoming smaller. After all, he had long done God's work. He had made many conversions, a small stream of souls who would someday make their way into God's great heaven. Even recently he had saved Roberto from the soldier's mine and started him on the right path. Now there were all those other natives out there on the beach, all of them waiting for the ugly weight of original sin to be lifted from their shoulders.

Father Luis felt the warmth of his love for these people filling him, lifting him. His heart was on fire with love, and as he continued to stare at the crucifix before him, the rest of the room dropped out of sight. He could see only the crucifix before him and Jesus's tortured uplifted face. He took the crucifix from the table and, holding it outstretched before him, walked outside.

Father Luis walked to the rear of the ship. Roberto suddenly stepped in front of him. A soldier grabbed Roberto roughly by the collar, but Father Luis shook his head and the man moved away.

"Father," said Roberto in his heavy accent, "please don't go. They are very angry and they know nothing of the commandments. I fear for you."

Luis smiled at him. "Don't be afraid. Don't you see?" Luis glanced skyward. "This is *His* way."

Roberto looked at him in disbelief, saying nothing. Luis smiled and blessed him before walking on. Then Senor Francisco Mateo took his arm. "Is it wise, Father?" he said. "I mean, the natives are extremely agitated. Perhaps you should wait."

Father Luis lay his hand on Mateo's shoulder. "I will be all right. Have faith in the Lord."

Mateo looked down at the deck. "Father, thank you for all you did for Diego. I know you really tried to save him and I appreciate it. I am sorry for the disrespect I've shown you in the past. I'm sorry for all the things I've done. Please forgive me?"

Father Luis made the sign of the cross over him and smiled. "I forgive you, Francisco, but more importantly, God forgives you. Go with the Lord."

Mateo nodded sadly and backed away.

Father Luis walked to the rail. He held tightly to the sailors who helped him climb down into the boat, which was bobbing gently on the sea. As his lips moved silently with the prayers he was saying, he was vaguely aware of Mateo arguing loudly with the Conquistador above. He heard the Conquistador say, "We do not interfere in the matters of priests." Then the boat pushed off from the ship and moved away.

The boatmen looked at him, their faces pinched with fear, as they pulled at their oars. He prayed hard, feeling the love of God well up in him. They fell away out of sight, and there was only the face of Our Lord on the cross, suffering so that all mankind, Spanish and Indian, would regain admittance to heaven. Luis heard someone shouting and realized that they wanted him to get out. Holding the crucifix with one hand, he climbed out of the boat into the chest-high water. The sand scratched between his toes as the warm water billowed out his robe. Up on the beach he saw the many natives watching him. He walked toward them, wondering at the angry looks on their faces. God is love, God is mercy, he prayed. Their eyes were wild with anger, but miraculously, they let him pass. He moved into the crowd, praying wondrously to the Christ on the cross. Love filled him dizzyingly as he watched their faces. He heard a rush of wind behind his ear, like the beating of the wings of the Holy Ghost, and then the Indians too fell away from view.

From the deck of the *Isabella* they all watched the tiny black-robed figure of Father Luis wade ashore. No one spoke as he approached the mob of angry Indians. He could be plainly seen walking among them, and then one man ran up behind him and brought his club down squarely on Father Luis's head. He dropped to his knees as if to pray and then fell forward onto his face. The others closed around him, and their clubs could be seen rising and falling in a fury.

The fathers quickly made the sign of the cross and knelt on the deck to pray. Calling Crow and Juana squatted back down with the other Indians under the shade of the canvas. Calling Crow began crying. *"Aieyah,"* he said between clenched teeth. "What god is this who would let such a thing happen to him?"

"No," said Juana tearfully. She put her arms around him. "You mustn't say such things."

Twenty feet away Bishop Cavago made the sign of the cross as he watched Juana put her arms around the big oafish Indian. Cavago's face twisted into an angry mask, and he turned and went toward his cabin.

At the rail, Mateo shouted angrily over at De Sole and Roldan. "What has been gained?"

De Sole stared back at him coldly. "Don't push your luck too far, Mateo, or I'll put you ashore next." He turned away and shouted to one of his men. "Give the order to begin the barrage."

Immediately the crew came to life. Soldiers ran to the rails to watch, while sailors ran to their posts, and the settlers and Indians quickly got out of their way. A red flag moved quickly up the mast, and violent explosions rippled suddenly from ship to ship. Great puffs of smoke gushed from the sides of the ships and quickly rolled toward the land in the breeze. The first volley of shots landed in the water, sending up dozens of seawater spouts as if a pod of whales had surfaced there. The natives seemed in shock, unable to move, and the next volley landed among them. Here and there paths appeared as several shots knocked through them like bowling balls through pins, then many shots were landing among them, sending up great geysers of sand. They fled for the forest in a mob as great leafy green branches fell from the trees and then the brown trunks of the trees fell over. A shot found the canoe that had earlier ventured forth and violently shattered it and its occupants like a giant hand crushing a leaf. Flotsam bobbed in the swells where the canoe had been. The barrage continued after the beach had been deserted, the noise rumbling among the ships like thunder during a quick summer storm.

Chapter 40

In the early morning, Calling Crow sat with the others in the sand under the shade of an open-sided palm-thatched shelter. He, along with many other people, had built over a dozen such shelters as part of the large Spanish camp on the beach. Not far away from Calling Crow some runners squatted out in the hot sand. Runners was the name the Spanish gave to bearers and servants who had attempted to escape. These two were chained together at the neck, and a soldier armed with an arquebus stood guard over them. Their presence served as a reminder to Calling Crow that he would have to be very careful. Elsewhere, soldiers stood in groups of four or five, armed with loaded crossbows and arquebuses. There had been several Spanish killed by Indians who had run out of the jungle, fired their arrows, and quickly disappeared back inside.

Calling Crow watched some bearers carrying baskets of food from the boats over to stack them under another shelter close by. Spanish soldiers would guard them tonight, but perhaps he could sneak there under cover of darkness to steal some food for his and Juana's journey. That is, if they ever got away. Juana was several shelters up the beach, and Calling Crow could not go to her. At night the soldiers kept guard, and already two men had been killed by the deadly crossbows as they attempted escape.

Calling Crow's friend, Ito, called over to him from where he sat with some others. "Your woman is coming."

Calling Crow saw Juana looking about as she walked under the shade of the shelter.

"Where have you been?" said Calling Crow as she walked up to him.

Juana looked back the way she had come. She sat in the sand next to him. "The Bishop won't let me out of his sight. I only managed to sneak away because he had to go into the bushes to relieve himself."

Calling Crow looked at the sand at his feet. "Keep yourself ready. Soon we will have a chance to go. You must be ready at any time."

Juana nodded.

The people looked up as one of the priests walked into the shelter. "We are celebrating mass further up the beach," he said. "We will start in a few minutes."

Calling Crow did not move as some of the people got to their feet. Juana got to her knees and dusted the sand off the back of her gown. "Come, Calling Crow, let's go receive the mass."

Calling Crow pointed to the runners. "Do you think they will want to receive mass, too?"

Juana looked down at the sand sadly. "What does that mean? I want to go to pray for us to have luck. That is all."

"Pretend you are sick, or something," said Calling Crow

angrily. "Don't go. I don't see why, after all that has happened, you still wish to do these Spanish things!"

Juana touched his arm. "Don't be that way. Just because of the bad ones, that does not mean that the religion is not true. Think of Father Luis."

Calling Crow turned to her angrily. "I have. I have thought a lot lately about what happened to him, despite his goodness. That is why I will have no more to do with their ways. And neither should you!"

More of the people got to their feet and walked off to go to the mass.

Juana walked off a few feet. "I will talk to you when I return."

Calling Crow looked up at her. "You are not Spanish. Why do you go?"

"Yes, I am not Spanish and neither are you, but we have both been with them so long that we now share some things in common, despite the wickedness of some of them."

Calling Crow scowled at her. "I have no Spanish in me. And soon I will have nothing to do with them. Or any of their creatures! Go away."

Juana flinched at the vehemence in his voice. She walked off.

Calling Crow got up and walked over to sit with his friend, Ito, and some other bearers. He said nothing as the other men looked at him. Calling Crow fell asleep in the cool shade, and then a squad of soldiers walked up and began yelling at him and the others.

The squad leader, a fat, older Spanish with a full beard, kicked Calling Crow's foot. "On your feet!"

As Calling Crow and the others got up, one of the soldiers said, "There has been a great battle. You will all be required to carry back the brave Spanish soldiers who have been wounded."

Calling Crow and Ito and the others joined a long column of bearers as they moved quickly into the jungle. Spanish soldiers armed with loaded crossbows were spaced one to every eight or ten bearers. As they moved

down the trail, Calling Crow listened to the squad leader
and a young boyish-looking soldier discuss the battle. The
boy's face was taut with fear.

"How many dead were there?" he said.

"Dozens," said the squad leader. He slapped at a mos-
quito on the back of his neck. "The Indians shoot their arrows as well as monkeys might, but there were scores of
them and our soldiers were simply overwhelmed."

The young soldier added nothing as his eyes resumed
their intense scrutiny of the jungle.

"What did they say?" said Ito softly to Calling Crow.

"That there were many soldiers killed."

The old Spanish squad leader glared over at Calling
Crow. "Stop your gibbering or I'll have you whipped here
and now!"

Calling Crow stared straight ahead as the fat Spanish
walked beside him, glaring angrily at him. Finally the man
moved back to the head of the column.

The trail came to an end at a great swamp. The two
Spanish consulted for a few minutes and then descended
into the ink-black water. Soon they were up to their waists,
and Calling Crow saw that if the guards grew careless, and
a man moved quickly enough, he could possibly escape
and be out of range of the deadly crossbows before they
reacted. But, of course, he could not leave until he managed to sneak Juana away.

They pushed through the still water, sending ripples out
ahead and sideways. Occasionally one of the men tripped
on a hidden root and cursed angrily. As the column
crossed the swamp, leeches appeared as if out of nowhere
on the necks and arms of the men, and periodically they
passed through thick clouds of flies and mosquitos which
bit them hungrily. At midday, they reached solid ground in
the form of a muddy bank. They picked up the trail and increased their pace, moving through a forest of sandy soil
sprouting giant ferns and bushes. The heat rose up from
the ground like an oven, and many men stumbled and
weaved weakly. Finally they emerged, sweating and exhausted into a large clearing.

The sandy soil was dotted with sparse bushes no higher than a man's knees. Corpses of men and horses littered the ground, and small knots of Spanish soldiers sat in the heat, resting and nursing each other's wounds. Men on horseback moved about the clearing, relaying messages and taking stock. As the column of bearers moved across the field, Calling Crow saw that most of the bodies were Indian. Many had been mutilated, their limbs hacked off and their insides pulled out. The bearers were silent as they walked along, repulsed by the grisly sight.

The column approached one of the larger groups of wounded, and Calling Crow spotted Mateo cradling the head of another Spanish that had died. Mateo did not see him, staring instead out into the distance as if in a daze. The column halted and Calling Crow and the others stood in the hot sun while the Spanish divided up the bearers down the line into work parties of a dozen men or more. A Spanish soldier rode past on a great horse. He paused to drink some water from a leather bota, and Calling Crow and the other bearers watched him thirstily. The man spat out a stream of water and corked his bota, looping the string of the skin water bag over the horn of his saddle. He rode off and Calling Crow and the others stared at the dark stain the water made in the sand.

One of the men behind Calling Crow called over to the old Spanish squad leader, "I need some water."

"There is no water," said the man.

"There will be water in the forest," said Ito angrily.

The squad leader walked over and punched Ito in the face, knocking him down. Calling Crow helped him to his feet as the man glared at them. He walked off to consult with some soldiers.

"Water!" said the bearer behind Ito. His voice was a croak.

The squad leader turned to look at them, but said nothing.

Calling Crow heard a sound. The man behind Ito dropped to his knees. He pitched forward onto his face and lay still.

Calling Crow called over to the squad leader. "Give us water!"

The man came back and glared at him. "No water." He turned to the men in the back. "Pick him up and let's get moving."

"No!" said Calling Crow. "We are not going anywhere till we get water."

The squad leader struck Calling Crow in the face. "Shut up, you!" He pushed Calling Crow, but Calling Crow would not move.

Calling Crow sat down and the other bearers followed his example. He looked up at the squad leader. There was no wind and the sun blazed like fire. "We will not move until we get water. We are not dogs. We are men!" Calling Crow felt dizzy and saw two suns in the sky. He had to shut his eyes to keep from falling over.

"Hernon!" shouted the squad leader, and the other soldier came over. "Help me get them on their feet."

The young soldier looked surprised. "What happened?"

"Never mind. Go get one of the captains. We'll put the dogs on them. That will get them moving."

"Here is some water."

The voice was familiar to Calling Crow and he looked up. It was Mateo. He handed a bota to the squad leader, and the man threw it at Calling Crow's feet. "Take a swig and pass it back. Then get on your feet."

Calling Crow ignored it. He looked up at Mateo. "I don't want your water."

Mateo frowned. "Very well." He turned to the squad leader. "They can't very well carry for you if they are not watered. There is a small pond just the other side of those trees over there." He pointed west at the distant tree line. "They can get water there."

Mateo walked off, and the squad leader shouted at Calling Crow. "On your feet! You'll get your water now and a whipping later! On your feet, all of you."

Calling Crow and Ito picked up the unconscious man. They walked slowly toward the tree line, carefully threading their way through the many corpses.

Ito said softly to Calling Crow, "Have you ever seen so many dead?"

"No," said Calling Crow absently. His thoughts were of Juana and worrying about her safety.

"Aieyah," said Ito, "these Spanish are truly demons. When my people were at war with the Yah-hee People, we would fight all day until we were tired, and only one, or maybe two men would die. But these Spanish, they wipe out one or two *villages* in a day!"

"It is so," said Calling Crow somberly. As he looked around, he thought of what the Spanish would do to the people in his own village of Tumaqua if they ever found them.

They reached the tree line and pushed back into the forest. About thirty yards into the thick growth they came to a wide pond of black water. It was a little cooler under the trees, and very quiet. A woodpecker rapped at the decaying hulk of tree not far away and the crickets kept up a steady soothing cadence. In the center of the pond, two men were bathing, surrounded by a dozen or so soldiers holding crossbows and arquebuses at the ready. As Calling Crow and the others came to the bank, the squad leader turned round to them. "Drink all you can, for we will not stop for water till we arrive back at the beach with the wounded."

As Calling Crow and the others fell to their knees to drink, the squad leader asked one of the soldiers who the bathers were.

The response hung in the still, dry air. "That is the great De Sole and one of his captains." The soldier's voice was reverential.

"He must have worked up quite a sweat slaying Indians, eh?" said the squad leader, laughing.

The soldier said tiredly. "Oh, he does not do it for the cleansing, but rather because this waterway might be the river Jordan which gives the power of life. The Indians say that it flows somewhere through this land and that all who bathe in its waters will never grow old."

Calling Crow splashed the warm water over his face and

neck. He looked over at Ito. "May the great De Sole get his ass bit off by an alligator!"

Ito laughed loudly and crazily. "Ah, Calling Crow, that is good, very good."

The squad leader looked over at them angrily. "You better get your fill of water. There will be no more."

Ito reached down to drink more. "Oh, brother alligator, have your afternoon meal now, we implore you!" He laughed again, rolling onto his side.

Calling Crow sat down on the bank in exhaustion. A beautiful blue swamp fly buzzed by and stopped to hover a few feet away. It stared at him with its two big black eyes, then turned gracefully and buzzed away. Calling Crow thought how beautiful it was in its freedom. A moment later the guards were yelling at them to get up. They led them back to the clearing.

Calling Crow and Ito were made to carry a Spanish soldier with half an arrow broken off inside his chest. The man's face was already covered in sweat from the poisons inside of him, and he kept up a low steady moaning as they walked toward the jungle.

"Do you think he will live?" said Ito.

"No," said Calling Crow, adding nothing further. His mind was on Juana again. He must locate her quickly at the camp without attracting attention. There would be no moon tonight, and it would be a good night to go.

Chapter 41

It had been early morning when the Spanish messenger arrived back at the expedition's base camp on the beach. Having run all the way from De Sole's village headquarters, he was exhausted and had to be fed and rested before he could deliver his message. Bishop Cavago went to the largest hut, which served as a headquarters and a church, to hear the young soldier address the crowd. "Excellency De Sole wants all the Spanish women to begin boarding the boats to the ships," he had said. "They will sail for the island today." The men and women present broke into excited speculation as the Bishop thought about what an opportunity the news presented him. He couldn't watch Juana all the time, and now that they were no longer living on the ship, he couldn't keep her safely locked up.

"What about my husband?" cried out an older woman. Her cry was echoed by others, and a new round of speculation ensued.

The messenger held up his arms. "There is not time to answer all of your questions now," he said in a confident voice. "Most of the force is intact, and those that have been wounded are being brought back here now by Indian bearers. Do not worry. Everything is under control. Now, please pack up your things. We must begin the boarding at once."

The Bishop walked outside and headed for the boats to talk to one of the sailors he knew who went back and forth from the ships to the beach.

In the afternoon, as the offshore breeze started up, Bishop Cavago walked down the beach to where Juana and a dozen or so other Indian women were weaving palm thatch for the roofs of the huts. The wind whipped his thin hair about as he waved at her to come to him. Juana put down her work and walked over.

"Come with me," he said.

They walked down the beach till they came to the main group of huts. People walked back and forth through the soft sand from the huts to the boats with bundles of clothing and supplies.

"What is going on?" said Juana as they approached one of the boats.

"Much, I'm afraid," said Bishop Cavago. "His Excellency, De Sole, says it is too dangerous here, and we are taking the precautions he has ordered."

Several barefoot men surrounded one of the boats that was loaded with people. They struggled to push it into the surf.

"What do you want of me?" said Juana.

"Just to talk for a while." They watched the men bend their backs, lifting and pushing the boat at the very moment a wave ran under it; it floated free. Bishop Cavago waved at one of the men, and he came over. The man quickly scooped Juana up in his arms and carried her toward the boat.

"I'm sending you back to my house," called out Bishop Cavago. "It is too dangerous for you here."

"No!" screamed Juana, beating on the man's back. "Please!"

The man quickly waded out into the surf and handed her up to two others who leaned out of the boat to take her. Juana's screams mixed with the wind and spray as the men dug their oars into the sea. The boat moved forward and a large wave smashed into it, thrusting its bow up. It splashed down, and the rowers fought the strong surf, winning as they pulled free of the white froth and out onto the gentle blue rollers. Soon Juana's screams were gone and there was only the hiss of the waves and the call of a hungry gull.

Calling Crow and Ito came out onto the beach at the base camp as the sun was sinking low. The Spanish had died on the litter, and now Calling Crow and Ito and some bearers sat in the shade not far from the wounded. Calling Crow was surprised at the agitated activity of the Spanish. Four Spanish boats headed out to the ships, while on the shore, soldiers were loading settlers and bundles of belongings into other boats pulled up on the sand.

Ito asked a man sitting in the sand what was happening.

"De Sole has sent all the women back to Santo Domingo until it is safe here. Then they will come back to stay."

Calling Crow's heart felt as if one of the iron bolts from the Spanish crossbows had pierced it. He looked down at the man, demanding, "Is he sending our women back, too?"

"No. Just the Spanish women."

Ito pointed to a hut further down on the beach where many native women worked at weaving thatch. "Maybe your woman is down there."

Calling Crow ran off toward the hut and Ito followed him. The women looked up at them when they arrived. Calling Crow did not see Juana, but he recognized one of the women who had been washing clothes with her. "Where is the woman called Juana?" he asked her.

The woman looked up from her weaving. "She went with the Chief Black Robe, and he put her on one of the boats going out to the ships."

"When?" demanded Calling Crow.

"A while ago," said the woman. "She is probably on the ship by now."

Calling Crow turned and ran in the direction of one of the boats that was being loaded up. Ito ran after him, grabbing him and attempting to pull him back. Calling Crow threw him to the sand and reached the boat just as a group of barefoot soldiers pushed it off the sand and into the water. The oars gleamed wetly as they curled through the air and dipped into the foaming surf. Calling Crow ran out into the waist-high surf and tried to pull himself into the boat. The soldiers on the boat laughed at him as the waves pounded against him. Someone stood and struck him on the head with one of the long oars. Seawater filled his nose and mouth, and he felt as if sharp claws were raking his throat and lungs. Rough hands grabbed him and dragged him onto the sand, where he was beaten. When he awoke, he lay under one of the shelters, chained to Ito.

Chapter 42

Senor Francisco Mateo had not shaved in weeks, and now his beard was dirty and knotted. His doublet was soiled with the blood of those he had killed and those he had consoled as they lay dying. Now he exited one of the huts in the deserted village. He asked two soldiers walking by if they had found any food. The men shook their heads and walked on. Mateo followed them a few paces back, his stomach growling. They might be lying. The soldiers shared anything they found among themselves first, bringing food back to the general pot only after they had their fill.

De Sole's army was out of provisions. Much of the cassava bread that had been brought from the island had been damaged by water during the storm, and it had been three weeks since the ships had departed for Hispaniola. Resupply ships would need at least three more weeks to make the return voyage. The last good meal the soldiers had eaten was a week earlier when they had dined on the last of the horses killed in the first battle. Although some food stores had been seized in the first village they had captured, that had been quickly eaten up. Now De Sole's finely trained, disciplined fighting force was merely fighting to stay alive, raiding villages further and further inland for their food stocks.

Mateo followed the soldiers as they walked into the little square in the center of the village. They heard angry curses. "Over there!" said one of the soldiers, pointing to one of the larger huts. They went inside and Mateo followed them. The hut had evidently once served as an Indian granary, but was now empty, all the maize and other foodstuffs having been hastily cleared out by the retreating

Indians. Dried cobs of maize and maize kernels littered the
floor. Mateo walked over to two soldiers who were arguing in the corner. Before them on the ground sat a covered
basket which the Indians had evidently not been able to
carry off in their haste.

"Have you found any food?" said Mateo.

The younger of the two men looked at him. "Yes. The
Indians have left you some as a present." He kicked the lid
off the basket.

Mateo looked inside. It was half filled with red, yellow,
and purple grains of maize, with two large turds sitting on
the top.

Mateo eyed the man coldly as he considered killing
him. He cared not of the consequences. Every day it
looked more and more as if none of them would ever go
home. He cared about nothing anymore.

Chapter 43

Calling Crow sat in the sand as the sun burned down on
his head. Inside there was fire and pain and the image of
the hurt look on Juana's face the other day when he had
angrily sent her away. Ito sat just behind Calling Crow. A
chain ran from the iron collar around Ito's neck to the one
around Calling Crow's. There were two other men simi-
larly chained sitting further back. Not far away the Bishop
and the *cholo* who served him were putting their altar
things in a large wooden box. Two soldiers with loaded
crossbows waited for them to finish. The *cholo* called *El
Animal* stood with them.

The Bishop put the top on the box and turned to the soldiers. "We're ready."

El Animal walked over to Calling Crow and the others. "On your feet. Pick up the boxes."

Anger welled in Calling Crow as he remembered the *cholo* from Roldan's pit. As Calling Crow hoisted the heavy box onto his shoulder, the Bishop walked over. He smiled at Calling Crow and called over to *El Animal* and the soldiers. "Keep an eye on this one. He is very crazy. He ran away and they caught him trying to swim back to the island."

The soldiers laughed and they began walking. They entered the forest and moved quickly down a well-defined trail. No one spoke, and Calling Crow's pain and sadness washed over him in waves as the chain swung back and forth between him and Ito. They walked in silence for a long time, the tramp of their feet and the clinking of their chains the only sounds. Calling Crow was covered with sweat when they reached the village which served as De Sole's headquarters. Soldiers sprawled against the huts, overcome by the heat. A few played cards, most slept. Calling Crow and the others walked tiredly through the main square. They were halfway to the end when angry shouts and screams filled the air. Calling Crow turned to see many braves racing toward them. They overwhelmed the Spanish soldiers in the square and ran into the huts to attack any they found there.

The soldier at the head of the column yelled, "Into the hut! Quickly!"

A flight of arrows whizzed through the air about them, and the two bearers who were behind Calling Crow fell dead. Ito tripped and fell, and Calling Crow helped him to his feet. Arrows flew about them as they ran into the hut. Calling Crow looked out at the square and saw that it was now full of braves. Many Spanish lay dead, and it looked as if the others had already fled. Calling Crow looked around the hut. It had only the one entrance they had come in, and a window at the opposite wall. One of the soldiers and the Bishop and his *cholo* were over by the window, piling up things against it, while the other soldier and *El Animal* worked feverishly at the entrance, piling up baskets and sticks against it.

The soldier pointed his crossbow at Calling Crow and Ito. "Get over here and help us."

Calling Crow and Ito went over and began stacking boxes and baskets up. A moment later several braves reached the entrance and began jabbing their lances in, trying to stick them. One of the braves pulled at the boxes and sticks as he tried to get in. The soldier aimed his crossbow, and the brave screamed as the bolt pierced his head. He fell backward. Another brave rushed up, fighting to get in. The man jabbed his lance in, almost sticking Calling Crow in the chest. Calling Crow backed away as several more braves rushed over and began ripping away the sticks and branches. The soldier dropped his crossbow and rushed forward with his sword. He stabbed through the baskets at the brave straight ahead, not seeing the one who was off to the side with a long lance. This brave jabbed in and stuck the soldier in the belly. He sank to the floor. Ito suddenly leaned against Calling Crow, grabbing him. Calling Crow turned and saw the bloodied point of a crossbow bolt protruding from his chest. It had struck him from behind. Calling Crow turned as Ito slid to his knees and pitched forward. Over at the window, the Bishop had his foot in the stirrup of the crossbow as he attempted to reload it. The Bishop's *cholo* continued to stack things up against the window. The soldier that had been with them lay dead.

Calling Crow left *El Animal* to defend the entrance as he reached down and took the dead soldier's sword. He advanced on the Bishop quietly, dragging Ito's inert form along behind him by the chain.

The Bishop looked up and saw him. "Hernando!" he said to his *cholo*. "Get him."

The *cholo* picked up a sword lying nearby and ran at Calling Crow. Calling Crow hoisted Ito's inert form in front of him as the *cholo* struck and the sword pierced Ito's body. Calling Crow used the few seconds it took the man to withdraw his sword to deliver a killing blow to his neck.

Calling Crow crept closer to the Bishop as he struggled

with the crossbow. The Bishop threw it at him. Calling Crow dodged it, and the Bishop grabbed a large brass cross out of the box and backed up. Calling Crow turned quickly to see what *El Animal* was up to. One of the braves had managed to grab the big man by the hair. Leaning way back, he was pulling *El Animal*'s head out as far as he could while another brave sawed his fat neck open with his stone knife.

Calling Crow pulled Ito's body up close behind him, pulling in as much chain as he could. He lunged at the Bishop, swinging the sword hard and fast. The Bishop managed to parry the blow with the cross. He moved quickly around, and Calling Crow barely managed to get out of the way as the cross whipped the air where his head had been. The Bishop continued to circle him, swinging the heavy cross with both hands as he tried to trip Calling Crow up in the chain. Calling Crow lunged at the Bishop, but the chain brought him up short, putting him off balance. The Bishop stepped in to deliver a roundhouse with the cross, knocking the sword out of Calling Crow's hand.

Calling Crow lunged on the ground after the sword, and the Bishop raised the cross to strike. Calling Crow grabbed his leg, pulling him down. The Bishop fell on his back across a wooden box and his eyes screwed up in pain. Calling Crow got to his feet.

Outside, a fanfare of trumpets sounded. Calling Crow saw De Sole and a dozen of his horsemen race into the square, swinging their iron swords as they slashed at the startled braves. Many soldiers with arquebuses emerged from the forest and opened fire.

The Bishop raised his head weakly and looked at Calling Crow. "You think I put her on the ship, don't you?" he said.

Calling Crow was momentarily stunned at the mention of Juana and did not move.

Bishop Cavago shook his head. "She *wanted* to go back."

For a moment Calling Crow's angry words to Juana came back to him. Would she go back because of that? No, he told himself. She would not. "You lie," he said.

"You think she wanted to run away with you and live like an animal in the forest?" The Bishop tried to smile. "She asked me to put her on the ship."

"No!" screamed Calling Crow. All the pain he'd suffered at the hands of the Spanish filled him. "You go to your hell for the liar you are!" He raised the sword and with both hands drove it into the Bishop's chest. Placing his foot on his throat, he pulled it out.

He looked outside. The Indians raced for the sanctuary of the bushes and trees, quickly disappearing.

Calling Crow threw the sword across the hut and sat down beside Ito's body. A soldier ran up and stuck his head in the entryway. He made the sign of the cross as he saw the blood-splattered smock of the Bishop and the dead soldiers. He looked over at Calling Crow briefly and then ran off.

Chapter 44

Rain soaked into the hair of Senor Alonso Roldan, running down his neck and into his doublet as he and his friend, Manuel Ortiz, moved into the bushes. Ortiz walked ahead, using his sword to hack at branches and vines. Roldan followed close behind. Over his shoulder he wore a leather arquebusman's sack, which they used to carry the heavy lead shot they required. He had another use in mind for it.

"Hold up a moment," he called out to Ortiz.

As Ortiz looked around nervously, Roldan turned once more to look back at the half dozen huts visible in the steady rain. They looked like rotted haystacks or piles of debris. Roldan thought with disgust that they were not a fitting place for Castilian men to live.

What Senor Alonso Roldan never would have thought possible had happened. The great De Sole, the man of whom legends had been written, was now bogged down in that wretched little village. His force had been cut in half by casualties and desertions, and the remaining men were almost starving, looking more every day like the savages they were fighting than Spanish men. He, Alonso Roldan, was determined not to be a part of this great tragedy. He still had his wits, his strength, and he had a plan. His plan was to deliver something from that miserable camp back there to the Indians, something that they would very much like to have and would probably pay for handsomely. More importantly, the very least he would get out of the trade would be safe passage overland for himself and Ortiz to Veracruz. Surely his trade was worth that much to them. And they *could* get to Veracruz overland if they didn't have to worry about the savages attacking them along the way. There were risks with the plan, he thought grimly, but the miserable look of the huts gave him all the resolve he needed to do this thing.

Another rivulet of rain found its way down his neck and into his doublet. Cursing, he turned round and nodded to Ortiz. They moved off.

They walked for hours before finally coming out of the thick bushes before a boggy clearing. Roldan looked up at the gray sky. Never had he imagined it could rain so much. Even back on the island he had never seen so much rain. He thought longingly of the dry heat of Estremadura where he had grown up, and he had to push the pictures out of his head. There were more important things to think about for now. He followed behind Ortiz as he descended into the waist-high water.

They waded through the bog for over an hour, and when Roldan was sure they were far enough away from any patrols De Sole might have sent out, he began calling out the word Hotea had taught him, *wakara*, or friend.

The steady tempo of the rain increased suddenly, the

drops making coin-sized splashes in the black water as the two men pushed on determinedly. They walked for most of the day without seeing any Indians.

Roldan pointed out a tall pine growing from the banks of the bog. "Let's rest there under the tree." As they sat down to rest, Roldan wondered where in hades all the Indians had gone. It was possible they had retreated, but he thought that unlikely. Perhaps he'd simply gone off in the wrong direction.

He looked up at the sodden gray sky and calculated that he could make it back to the village before dark if they left soon. Then tomorrow they would try again to the northwest. Roldan was about to get to his feet when Ortiz called softly to him.

"Over there, there is an Indian watching us."

Roldan looked where Ortiz pointed. He saw a barely clothed native about fifty feet away inside the bushes.

"Wakara," Roldan called out to him.

The man said nothing, continuing to look at them quietly.

Roldan got to his feet. As he did he heard someone behind them. He turned as five men ran up to them. Ortiz immediately pulled his sword.

"No," said Roldan, "don't do anything. Leave it to me."

The Indian men grabbed them roughly by their arms, pulling them along toward the thick of the forest.

Roldan tripped on a root, falling onto his knees. The Indian men yanked him to his feet. *"Wakara,"* said Roldan angrily, *"wakara*, damn your heathen soul!"

The Indian men made some joke in their own language and laughed.

It was fast growing dark when they reached the Indian village. Roldan and Ortiz were thrown into a hut.

Ortiz cursed the Indian who roughly bound his hands behind him.

Roldan shook his head. "Say nothing."

Both men sat down with their backs to the wall while they waited. Finally three men entered the hut. One of them carried a torch. In the flickering light, Roldan recognized the big man, and his heart beat faster. There was no mistake. It was indeed the *Cacique* Ahopo, the one whose village Mateo had captured three years earlier.

The man holding the torch said in bad Spanish, "I learned to speak your language while a slave. Why have you come here?"

Roldan bowed slightly to Ahopo while Ortiz watched warily. "I wanted to speak with the great *Cacique* Ahopo," said Roldan.

The man translated for Ahopo, who was looking at Roldan closely in the poor light. The two Indians spoke quietly for a minute and then the interpreter said, "Very well. What do you wish to say?"

"Tell him that I can produce the man who took away his people on the ships a long time ago."

Ahopo became very agitated at the news. He moved closer and Roldan found the man's great size formidable.

"He also wants you to deliver this other Spanish *Cacique* who has come," said the interpreter, "the one who calls himself De Sole."

"That I cannot do," said Roldan. The very suggestion of it angered him. Gaining his revenge on Francisco Mateo was one thing, but betraying De Sole and his soldiers was quite another.

The interpreter moved closer to Roldan. "Why do you do this?" he demanded. "What do you want?"

Roldan indicated the thick leather strap of the arquebusman's sack over his shoulder. "I want gold, as much as you can put in this bag."

Ahopo and the other man smiled when they heard this. They talked amongst themselves for a few more moments, and the man took the bag off Roldan's shoulder.

"That is not all that I want," said Roldan.

"Yes? What other do you want?"

"After I give you Francisco Mateo I want one of your people as a guide and a safe passage to Veracruz for my friend and me."

The Indian men talked at length, and Ahopo regarded

Roldan silently for a few moments. He nodded to the interpreter.

"It is agreed," said the man. He spoke to the other brave, who cut the cords binding Roldan's and Ortiz's hands.

Roldan rubbed his wrists as he regarded the Indians warily.

The interpreter spoke again. "When will you bring him here?"

"Within the next five nights."

The interpreter spoke quickly with Ahopo. Ahopo looked once more at Roldan and left the hut.

The interpreter frowned at them. "You may go now."

The rain fell in a fine mist as Alonso Roldan and Manuel Ortiz walked up to the hut which served as De Sole's headquarters. Wood smoke seeped through the palm thatch of the roof, giving the hut the appearance of a huge pile of fresh horse manure steaming in the early morning cold. Roldan turned to Ortiz. "Wait here. I will talk to him alone."

Ortiz turned and stood with his back to the hut.

Roldan went inside. A soldier stood guard at the entryway, while in the middle of the hut, another soldier armed with a loaded crossbow stood stiffly near the fire. De Sole sat a few feet away at a crude table on which two candles shed quivering pools of light. He was busy writing in a large volume with a quill pen and did not look up when Roldan bowed before him. Moths and insects flitted about the candles.

Roldan waited for a few moments, listening to the pop and hiss of the fire and the scratch of De Sole's quill on the paper. De Sole continued to ignore him. "Excellency," said Roldan finally, "I would like a word with you."

"Yes. Speak. I am perfectly capable of doing this and listening to you at the same time."

"Yes, Excellency. I think I have located a sizable cache of Indian food."

"Is that so?" De Sole still did not look up from his writing.

Roldan waited a few moments. A large moth flitted into the flame of one candle, flaring the flame briefly as it sizzled and fell to the table.

"What is sizable?" said De Sole.

"Several bushels of maize, Excellency. Enough for perhaps a hundred men to live on for a fortnight."

De Sole scoffed. "Hardly worth going after since we will be moving to another location in three or four days. One of the Indians has confessed that there is much gold four days march from here. My men would rather catch game along the way and go get gold."

"Excellency, I would still like your permission to go and get it."

"Very well. Go get it."

"I will need some Indian bearers."

"Take what you need." De Sole looked up from his writing. "Is that all?"

Roldan shook his head. "One more thing, Excellency. I should like to take Mateo with me."

De Sole waved away one of the moths with the quill. "Why?"

"He knows the area well."

"He told me that he does not."

"He lies. He and his men traveled all over this country in search of Indians."

"Well, he is no good to me. Take him."

Chapter 45

Calling Crow was chained together with three other bearers. They squatted in a line under the watchful eyes of Alonso Roldan and Hotea, the interpreter. Both men carried loaded crossbows. Roldan walked away, and a moment later his friend, Manuel Ortiz, exited the hut carrying an iron pan full of parched maize. Standing before one of the Indians he told him to take a handful, for they had much walking and carrying to do. Then he stood before Calling Crow. Calling Crow did not look up at him, nor did he take any of the maize. He did not want to eat. And with Juana gone back to that place, he did not want to live. Let them kill me now, he thought, I am ready.

Ortiz sneered at him. "You'll be begging for food later. Then you'll get only the whip." He moved on to the next man.

Calling Crow saw Roldan approaching with Mateo. For some reason, Mateo was without his sword.

Mateo caught his eye. "It appears our fates are somehow intertwined," he said.

Calling Crow ignored his crazy talk.

Roldan began shouting at the bearers. "On your feet! We are going now. On your feet!"

As Calling Crow got up, Mateo laughed sarcastically and said to Roldan, "You are all armed to the teeth. You must expect to encounter some difficulty on this patrol."

Roldan's face was expressionless. "There is no need for your talk. Just begin walking. Too much talking can be dangerous."

Calling Crow watched the exchange intently, and Mateo again caught his eye. "You see," he said, "our fates really are tied closely. Don't you think?"

Calling Crow looked away in disgust. Mateo really had gone crazy if he thought he wanted to engage in conversation with him.

Ortiz and Hotea took the lead. Roldan waited till the column moved out before falling in behind Mateo.

The rains had stopped, but the skies were still gray and impenetrable. They entered the bog, the walk slowing to a tiring, sloshing torture. Through a red haze of pain, exhaustion, and sadness, Juana's face appeared before Calling Crow again and again as he walked. He tried to shut out the visions, but he could not, and he cried out involuntarily. Ortiz jabbed him awake with the point of the bolt in his crossbow.

"One more word out of you and I'll take the whip to you."

Calling Crow was too dazed from pain and exertion to react.

After marching for most of the day, they reached the edge of the bog and climbed onto solid land. With the feel of the earth beneath his feet, Calling Crow's dreamlike state began to dissipate.

They started across a flat plain of weeds, dotted here and there with a few pine trees. At about the distance of three crossbow shots, the plain melded into a jungle area.

As they drew closer to the jungle, Calling Crow turned to look back at Mateo. Roldan was a few paces behind him with the crossbow pointed at his back. Roldan nervously watched the direction from which they had come, and Calling Crow realized that Roldan had brought Mateo out here to kill him. Calling Crow was not surprised by this. He knew these men hated each other, and he had seen much Spanish treachery already. What was a little more? Suddenly the tree line ahead exploded with sound. Dozens of braves emerged from the trees howling with rage. They rushed at Calling Crow and the others. To Calling Crow's amazement, Roldan, Ortiz, and Hotea did nothing as the men drew closer. Mateo turned to run, and several braves grabbed him from behind and shoved him to the ground. They piled on him and roughly bound his hands.

Calling Crow watched in bewilderment as the braves left Roldan, Ortiz, and Hotea unmolested. They walked behind, while the braves pushed Mateo and Calling Crow and the other bearers ahead of them toward the jungle.

The village was almost invisible in the thick jungle foliage, having been recently constructed of newly cut, still-green palm thatch. As they entered, a mob of noisy people milled about them. The women and children fingered the clothing of the Spanish and the bearers. Calling Crow wondered what sort of arrangement Roldan had made with them. Then their *Cacique* emerged with his entourage

from one of the huts. Calling Crow recognized him as
Ahopo, the big man who had jabbed Mateo with his lance
before jumping over the side of the ship. As Ahopo and
Hotea talked, Calling Crow realized what had happened.
Roldan and the others were delivering Mateo to Ahopo. In
return, they would get gold.

Ahopo and an attendant walked over to Mateo. Ahopo's
eyes lit up with delight as he recognized him. He pulled
Mateo roughly away from the others and ordered two
braves to hold him by the arms. Ahopo then looked over
at Calling Crow and the other bearers.

"Release them!" he demanded.

Three braves tried unsuccessfully to undo the iron ring
around Calling Crow's neck.

Ahopo spoke to Hotea. "Tell Roldan to release him."

Hotea translated the command, and Roldan took the key
from the pocket of his doublet. He quickly unlocked the
ring, and it and the chains fell loudly to the ground. Calling
Crow felt drunk from the freedom. He grabbed at Roldan,
but two braves pushed him back. Calling Crow rubbed his
neck and squatted on the ground to see what would happen.

Ahopo turned back to Roldan and the others. Roldan's
gaze was steely, but both Ortiz's and Hotea's eyes flitted
about the milling throng of braves like flies.

"We would like to be on our way now," said Roldan.

Hotea translated the request.

Ahopo nodded. "We will pay you now," he said.

"What did he say?" said Roldan worriedly to Hotea.

"He said he would pay us now."

Ahopo raised his hand. His braves quickly put arrows to
their bows and unleashed a cloud of arrows. Two of them
found their mark, striking Hotea and Ortiz. Only Roldan
got off a shot from his crossbow, which went deep into the
belly of one of the braves. The other braves rushed
Roldan, jabbing their lances at him. He pulled his sword
and swung at one man, taking off the point of his spear.
The other braves laughed.

Ahopo called out a command, and a young brave who
looked to be sixteen or so screamed and ran at Roldan.

Roldan nimbly sidestepped him, swinging his sword around to nearly sever his arm from his shoulder. Screaming, the man fell to his knees, and the other braves argued angrily amongst themselves about who would get to fight the Spanish next. Ahopo pointed to one brave, and he stepped away from the group, backed off a bit, and threw his lance. The lance pierced Roldan's thigh, and he cursed as he pulled it out. Blood quickly stained his blue breeches, sticking the material to his thigh. Ahopo shouted, and another brave rushed in with his lance. Roldan sidestepped the man but lost his balance as he put his full weight on his bad leg. Another man took advantage of the distraction Roldan's pain caused him to run up and jab his spear into his shoulder, quickly pulling it out and running off.

Roldan groaned loudly as he fell to his knees. Instead of rushing in to press their advantage, the braves gave Roldan time to recover, wanting to prolong their sport. When Roldan got to his feet, another brave ran forward and threw his spear. It pierced Roldan's groin, and he cried out and fell backward. Lying on the ground, he quickly jerked it out. He moaned loudly in pain, and the braves laughed loudly, speculating among themselves. They looked over at Ahopo expectantly. The big man frowned in disappointment and then nodded.

Screaming, a dozen braves rushed at Roldan. Again and again they stabbed downward, their sweating, muscled backs rippling from the effort.

Ahopo looked back at Mateo. His eyes bore into him as if he were vermin.

Ahopo then turned to Calling Crow and the other bearers. "Do any of you speak his language?"

Calling Crow got wearily to his feet.

"Tell him he shall live," said Ahopo, "but he shall live as a slave for the rest of his days. This way he will know what it is he has done to our people."

Calling Crow delivered the message to Mateo, relishing the fear and sadness he saw in the other man's eyes.

"Now," he said, "everything is turned around, Mateo. How do you like it?"

Ahopo shouted to his braves. "Put the chains on him."

Two braves held Mateo's arms, while a third attached one of the chains they had taken off the bearers around his neck. Ahopo came over and took the chain, giving it a painful yank. Mateo grabbed for it, holding back as Ahopo pulled him along. Ahopo yanked the chain, and Mateo lost his balance, falling to his knees. Laughing, Ahopo turned and ran, pulling Mateo through the dirt. An old woman rushed over from the side of the trail and kicked Mateo and the crowd howled with laughter. Mateo fought to hold onto the chain as people kicked and struck him. Calling Crow ran along, unable to turn away from the spectacle. Ahopo called for help, and two more braves grabbed the chain, dragging Mateo along until he lost consciousness.

Chapter 46

Calling Crow was in the village of the Saturibas for only a few days when a woman befriended him. Her name was Cochilima, and she was one of the most attractive women in the village. Her long, scalloped hair flowed over her breasts all the way down to her hips, which were full and inviting. Having lost Juana, Calling Crow was sad and wanted no one and nothing, yet because this woman pursued him so persistently and cooked for him, he went with her and lived in her house. They became lovers, and she begged him to tell her his story, but he would not, saying only that it hurt him too much to speak of it, which it did. Always, after their lovemaking, she would implore him to talk, but he would not and eventually she gave up. She made up for his quiet moods by talking enthusiastically, filling up the nights.

She told him everything about her life in the village and all the changes that had come to pass. She told him how life had been under Chief Callos, and how things had changed when the others had come to live with them. It was four turnings of the skies ago when Ahopo and his people arrived. They were welcomed and became of the people, but shortly afterward many people became sick. People began dying and there was much fear and worry. The people were angry with Ahopo and his people, thinking them somehow responsible. Then one day, Ahopo discovered in the hut of the medicine man, Tupac, a spell bundle containing one thing of each of the people who had died. They were small things of small value—a bone auger, a tiny clay figurine, a favorite feathered fishhook—but their purpose was clear: with them Tupac had cast his spell.

The village decided to hold a council and decide Tupac's fate, but before that could take place, Ahopo discovered Tupac sneaking away one night and killed him with a single blow from his club. Wonderfully, magically, the deaths stopped soon after and life became good again. It was then that they lost Callos. He and two braves had gone into the forest with Ahopo to seek a vision when tragedy struck. They were attacked in the night by the demon people, and only Ahopo and one of the braves returned alive. The brave limped for ever after, and having been struck a blow to his head which also drove away his man's mind, he was left with only the mind of the little boy he had once been. Ahopo had become Chief, having been given the sacred mantel by Callos as he lay dying on that fateful night.

Calling Crow got up from where he lay with Cochilima in her hut. He walked out onto the porch and sat down. Father Sun would be up shortly; the birds had already started singing. He had been in this new place with the Saturiba People for over two moons now. In the beginning, he had intended to go north to find Tumaqua, but despite his new freedom, his heart was very heavy from the loss of Juana and he had never begun the journey. He felt as if his soul had wandered from his body.

Cochilima called softly to him, but he did not go to her. Instead he sat and watched the outlines of the village take shape in the growing light. He saw the huts raised on stilts, the game pens, the hard-packed earthen courtyard. He saw the dogs tethered to the feeding pen. Then, as the light grew stronger, he noticed a familiar figure curled up with the dogs for their warmth. It was Mateo. His clothes were tattered rags now, and his red hair and beard had grown so much he resembled a four-legged beast more than a man. Still, Calling Crow's anger began to build within him as he watched the sleeping figure and thought of all the things that had happened to him since he had first seen this man on his high horse that day long ago. He thought it would have been better if Ahopo had killed Mateo as he did all the other Spanish that day. Then he realized that Mateo was the reason he was still here. Mateo was his last tie to that other world. When Mateo died, he would be free.

Calling Crow noticed two small shapes moving under a hut. He saw that they were boys when they ran out from beneath one hut and under another, drawing closer to the sleeping Mateo. They emerged in the diffused light, one of them armed with a stick. A dog sniffed them and lifted its head to bark softly, but Mateo continued to sleep. The boys waited till the dog quieted, and then they crept closer. When they were close enough, the larger of the two struck Mateo sharply on the back with the stick. Mateo raised his head and growled at them, and the boys backed off, laughing nervously. Mateo looked around furtively to see if there were any of the village adults up. While his head was turned, one of the boys threw a rock which struck him in the head. Mateo's leg had been damaged the day he was taken prisoner, and he got to his feet and ran after them in his peculiar, rocking-back-and-forth limp. He did not go far when the chain about him ran out, pulling him up short. He cursed impotently, and the boys howled in delight.

Calling Crow watched Mateo touch his head where the rock had struck him, bringing his finger down before his face to see the red blood. He moaned in pain and walked back. Lying down carefully, he pulled the chain back and curled it up beside him. He looked around once more before nestling up against the biggest of the dogs.

Mateo sat in the shade of a hut listening to the chanting in the distance. Most of the villagers were in the big hut singing their prayers, but there might be one or two about. He knew that one of the two soldiers they had brought back was still alive and he wanted to see him. He had managed to loosen and pull up the post they had chained him to, but he dared not run away until he was sure he could get far enough away. The last time he had gotten lost, and when they caught him they had almost beaten him to death.

He crawled as far as the chain would allow to look down the muddy street. No one was about, and he decided to go to the soldier.

He pulled the stake up and quietly gathered the chain up in his hands. He crawled under the hut, coming out by the back. He passed three more huts and then crept out into the street. The two men were tied up on poles just ahead near the firewell. As he crept closer his hope died, for both of them looked long dead. He stared at them silently, at the many burns and gouges on their bared skin, at their limp heads hanging down. One man suddenly opened his eyes, and Mateo was startled. The man said nothing for a few moments.

Mateo shook his head. "Is it bad?" he asked.

The man blinked, his only movement. In a voice like a rusty gate he said, "Give me water, fool."

Mateo looked around and saw a calabash of water sitting on a rock not far away. He quickly went and got it and held it up to the man's lips. Most of it ran down his chin, but he managed to get some in him. He set the calabash down.

The man coughed and the ropes suspending him creaked at the movement. "We were down to two dozen men," he said weakly, ". . . no food."

Mateo was suddenly aware that the chanting had stopped. "What about De Sole?" he said.

"Dead," said the man in a croaking voice. "We buried him in the river so the Indians wouldn't find him." The man opened his eyes again. "Give me more water."

Mateo looked down for the calabash and, as he did, saw four boys running up to him. They began shouting an alarm, and Mateo looked over to where the jungle edged up against the huts. It beckoned him, but he knew he would not make it and he remained where he was.

The boy in the lead ran up and struck him with the shaft of his lance, knocking him down. Then the others began beating him. He tried to fend off the blows as the boys shouted for the others to come. Holding his hands over his eyes, he heard a new commotion and looked up at Father Luis's Indian—he'd forgotten his name—throwing the boys out of the way. As one of the boys rolled in the dirt, the big Indian kicked him and spoke gruffly to him in their language. The boy got to his feet. He and the others backed off.

The big Indian grabbed the chain out of Mateo's hands. Mateo held the chain where it attached to the collar around his neck, and the Indian pulled him to his feet.

"You!" said Mateo, holding back. "You again."

"I have a name, Mateo! I am Calling Crow."

"Why don't you let them kill me, Calling Crow?"

Calling Crow jerked the chain angrily. "I don't know. Don't ask." As the gathering crowd watched, Calling Crow pulled Mateo along back toward his hut. A small group of boys followed him, laughing and shouting.

Chapter 47

Calling Crow looked back at the rear of the hut where Cochilima was sitting while she ate her soup. She looked up, meeting his eyes, and he looked away. Her loud voice bothered him now, as did the infrequency of her bathing, although she bathed as regularly as the others in her tribe, which was still more than the Spanish. He realized that he never should have agreed to move into her hut; he could never forget Juana. And he should not have stayed here with these people when they freed him. He could never be a part of them. They were stupid. They had no Council; instead they slavishly did whatever Ahopo told them.

Calling Crow tried to capture Tiamai's face in his heart. Try as he might, he could not. There was only one face in his heart now and that was Juana's. And she was back on that island of despair where he would never again set foot.

Cochilima said something to him, but he did not answer. Instead, he looked out at the packed earth of the street and saw Mateo being led away by three women. They were evidently going off to dig for roots. Calling Crow thought about how these people did not grow corn, nor any other crop. They kept a few dogs, but relied mostly on what Mother Earth gave easily. Their constant digging about for roots reminded him of the swine the Spanish kept.

One of the women whacked Mateo with a stick, showering abuse on him. Her words drifted up on the hot, still air. "He has been fucking the dogs so long that now he has fur, too!" Her words brought laughter to the others, but Calling Crow's face remained composed. Seeing his enemy abused in these ways no longer gave him pleasure. He thought of Father Luis and his strange teaching of mercy. Was that why? But it was Luis's mercy which had

sent him to his own death. Then again, it was also Luis's
mercy which had saved Calling Crow from the gold-
hungry soldiers. But for what?

The sticks in the floor squeaked, and Calling Crow
turned as Cochilima threw the calabash of scalding hot
soup at him. He got quickly to his feet as she jumped at
him, her nails scratching bloody trails in his face. He
pushed her away, and she fell to the floor.

"I cook for you and you ignore me, you Spanish slave!"

Saying nothing, Calling Crow walked back and took the
skin cape he had traded game for and his lance.

"Yes," she cried. "Take your cape. You will not sleep
here tonight."

"Yes," he said. "I will not." He tied his spirit bag to the
rope tie of his breeches and quickly jumped over the rail-
ing to the ground. Standing by the stilts of the house, he
listened to her screams turn to sobs. He felt bad for her,
but he knew sadness, too. He opened his spirit bag and
looked inside at the black iridescence of a crow's feather,
the blackened dried-up finger of Roldan, the piece of black
cloth he had taken from Father Luis's cloak on the beach
the day of his death. He said a prayer and walked out into
the slowly falling rain. The sky was obscured by warm
sodden clouds. It would be dark soon. He decided to sleep
in the common hut used by the unmarried men.

Calling Crow lay on his back in the blackness of the hut
listening to the shouts and laughter of the braves as they
amused themselves with the latest Spanish captive. There
hadn't been any soldiers brought back to the village for
one moon, and he had thought them all long dead. But just
today a trading party had brought this one back. Calling
Crow was amazed by the man's strength. He had faced the
combined tortures of most of the young men in the village
from when the sun went down till now. Dawn was coming
and the man was still alive. His moaning was deep and
penetrating. For a long time Calling Crow had been able
to keep it confined to only his head, but now it went down
into his heart. He got to his feet and went out into the hot
night.

He saw them over by the firewell. There were only ten or so, the others having evidently gone off to sleep. As Calling Crow approached the edge of the fire's glow, the men acknowledged his presence with looks of welcome. Calling Crow stood off a ways. A man picked a piece of firewood from the fire and advanced on the captive where he hung from the pole. He touched the glowing end to the man's chest but got no reaction. The others laughed. "He won't favor you with a cry," said one of the onlookers.

"We shall see," said the man. He turned angrily to the hanging soldier and jabbed the glowing stick at the man's genitals. The man shook spastically, moaning deeply.

The onlookers laughed. Calling Crow closed his eyes for a moment. Beneath his eyelids he saw another scene which had been coming back to him often now: from a distance he saw the boat moving through the surf under the bright sunlight, saw Father Luis climbing out with the cross held high, saw the man run up behind him, raising his club, saw it smash down so hard the father's knees jumped out from beneath him. Calling Crow felt the urge to lash out; he felt his heart would leap out of his chest if he did not move. He walked swiftly out of the shadows and picked up a club. The others smiled at him as he walked past them. He delivered a quick powerful blow to the captive's head and his cries stopped. He dropped the club and the others looked at him angrily as he walked back into the darkness.

Chapter 48

With the others, Calling Crow watched the confrontation. Mateo had evidently gotten confused in the night, and sunrise found him sleeping in the middle of the village square. Now Moscoso, one of the senior braves, screamed down at him angrily, the tendons in his neck standing out like bowstrings. "Out of my way, Spanish dog!"

The crowd quickly grew as others heard the commotion. Mateo opened his eyes and laughed strangely as he got slowly to his feet. Moscoso stared at him, his eyes bulging. He pushed Mateo violently, sending him sprawling. He then walked off.

The people laughed as the weakened Mateo struggled to get to his feet. He looked round at the women and children and bulged out his eyes in a pantomime of Moscoso. They drew back in fear and the men who had gathered laughed loudly. Mateo saw Calling Crow in the crowd and called over to him in a loud friendly tone.

"Calling Crow! How do you like your new home? Are you not glad to be free of the Spanish?"

The people frowned as they tried to make sense of the Spanish language. They watched Calling Crow to see what he would do.

Calling Crow pushed through the crowd and up to Mateo. "These people are like the saints of your religion when compared to you Spanish."

Mateo laughed. "That is good. You are funny. But what of Father Luis? Was he also so bad?"

Calling Crow stared at him angrily and said nothing. The people who were watching grew bored and began drifting off.

Mateo said, "You know, he came to me in my dream last night. He spoke of you. Do you want to know what he said?"

Still Calling Crow said nothing.

"He said that you would help me to escape." Mateo laughed.

Calling Crow continued to stare. He frowned in disgust as Mateo's laugh grew shrill and crazy.

Mateo turned and began hobbling away, turning to laugh once more before he disappeared into a patch of shade cast by one of the huts.

* * *

Calling Crow was troubled by the encounter with Mateo, for he, too, had been thinking of Father Luis, and Mateo's dream disturbed him greatly. The spirits came to one in dreams and their wishes must be acted upon. This was the way of his people. But Mateo was a Spanish, and was it the same for them?

Calling Crow thought about it for days and decided he must be alone and seek a vision for the answer. He left the hut where he had been sleeping and went out into the morning stillness. Looking around to see that no one had seen him, he moved into the jungle. After walking most of the day, he found a proper place by a small stream just before Father Sun began his descent over the forest. He made a fire and gathered many rocks, putting some of them in the ashes, stacking others beside the fire. He cut down some long pine boughs and began building a sweat house. When the house was completed and the rocks hot, he used some sticks to pick some of them out of the fire. He carried them into the hut and sat on his haunches, looking skyward as the heat rose and the sweat ran off of him. He put some tobacco in his pipe and, lighting it with an ember, blew sacred smoke in the four directions, singing the song for a vision to the Great Father.

He returned outside into the night air again and again after his many sweats. Finally Calling Crow fell down in exhaustion. He left his body there where it lay and went walking down a deer path till he came to the edge of the sea. The wind whipped his hair while waves thundered and hissed in the blackness, becoming visible when they broke, phosphorescent ghosts rushing at him. He walked into the sea, his total lack of fear surprising him, and then he was beneath the waves and the noise, moving slowly through the cold water. The sea bottom sloped downward at a steep angle and he went down and down, instinctively knowing where to go, until he came to a large cave. He entered and surprised a huge fish, which almost knocked him down in its haste to get away. After it was gone, he continued on into the cave until he saw some people in the

distance. They all sat on rocks in a semicircle facing him.
With his back to Calling Crow, but facing the people, a
man sat on a large seashell. As Calling Crow approached
closer he saw that the people were all old ones who had
passed on, some of them from his own village. As he
looked at their faces, he saw the Chief of Tumaqua, Caldo.
Caldo nodded in greeting, and Calling Crow looked at the
other faces. He saw his friend, Little Bear of the Guale
People, who had been killed by the dogs. Little Bear
smiled, warming Calling Crow's heart. Calling Crow's
eyes moved on and suddenly looked into the face of his
long-dead father. Tears of joy filled Calling Crow's eyes.
His father smiled at him and pointed to the figure in the
center. The man turned slowly round to him and Calling
Crow saw it was Father Luis. Saying nothing, the father
smiled and slowly nodded his head.

Calling Crow opened his eyes in the blinding light of
day. The heat of the sun beat down on him, baking him
like a fish on a hot rock. He could tell from the light that
it was just past midday. He walked stiffly down to the
nearby stream, bathed, and began walking back to the village.

Chapter 49

Calling Crow parted the bushes and looked over to where
the women talked and gathered berries. Mateo was tied
round the neck with a rope, and an old woman held the
other end. Calling Crow backed away out of sight and
pushed through the bushes. He walked till he could no
longer hear their talk, and then he sat on a rotted log. He
had been thinking of his vision for the past two days. It was

always in his head. He thought he heard a voice calling him and got to his feet. Pushing through a thicket, he suddenly caught sight of the sea, wide, blue, and beautiful. He suddenly knew what he must do. He hurried back to the women.

Walking up to the old one with the rope, he said, "I want to borrow this Spanish monkey for a while. I have spied some nice fruits up in a tree and I want him to fetch them for me."

The woman laughed at his words as she handed the rope to him. As Calling Crow led Mateo off, he kicked him hard when he stumbled over a root, shouting viciously at him.

When they were out of sight, Calling Crow put his arm around Mateo's waist, helping him as he hobbled along on his bad leg. "Hurry," said Calling Crow, "we must get as far away as we can before they realize we have gone and tell the men."

When Mateo heard this, his eyes welled with tears. "Why are you doing this?" he said.

"Because Father Luis told me to. Don't talk. We must get far away before nightfall."

After they had walked for several hours Mateo collapsed into unconsciousness. Calling Crow put him over his shoulder and continued on. When the sun sank low in the sky, he moved into a thicket of shrubs. He made a sleeping shelter, scooping together a large quantity of dead leaves to keep them warm. As he covered him with the leaves, Mateo suddenly awoke and sat up. Both men said nothing for a long while as they stared into the dying light, listening to the calls of the birds and animals.

"Where are you taking me?" said Mateo finally.

Calling Crow looked at him. "I do not know. We will just go as far as we can go and then wait for a long time. When they have stopped looking for us, we can begin moving again."

"No," said Mateo, "no more waiting! You can leave me here if you like and I will try and get home. But if I have to, I would rather die here than spend more time waiting."

"What would you do on your own?" said Calling Crow wearily.

"I would try to signal a ship."

Calling Crow said nothing for a moment. Spanish ships had brought him nothing but suffering. "Do you think there will be a ship?"

Mateo coughed weakly. "There will be many, one after another. I am sure of this. By now they must have guessed what has happened to the De Sole expedition and they will be searching for whoever has survived."

Calling Crow thought for a long time. Then he said, "I will help you to call a ship, but we should get much further away from here before we try."

"Yes. You are right."

They fell silent for a long time and then Mateo said, "Do not worry. If we find a ship I will not let them . . ."

Calling Crow suddenly held up his hand for silence. "They come for us," he said quietly, grabbing his axe. He got softly to his feet and crept off into the growing darkness.

Mateo sat listening to the strange animal sounds. He shifted his weight, trying to see better through the shrubs surrounding him. He heard a snap, as of a branch being stepped upon, and saw someone approaching in the dim light. When the man drew closer he saw that it was Moscoso. The man smiled as he approached, saying nothing. Birdcalls floated through the dark trees in an odd serenade as Moscoso drew his knife and got down on his hands and knees to crawl into the shrubs. The light was just about gone now, and Mateo could see only the lighter roundness of Moscoso's face as he crawled forward. A thud sounded, like a melon being broken over a knee, and a warm mess splattered against Mateo's face. He heard Calling Crow's voice say softly, "The others are still about. Say nothing."

Mateo heard Calling Crow dragging the body off a ways and then he was soundlessly beside him in the shrubs. They both listened to the strange birdcalls in the blackness. Finally they were gone.

"They will not be back tonight," said Calling Crow.

"Thank you," said Mateo.

Calling Crow said nothing.

"Was there not anything about Hispaniola that you found good?" said Mateo after a time.

"Only Father Luis, one old man who has died, and one woman."

"Tell me about the woman."

Calling Crow's voice was reverential. "There was a native woman who lived at the Bishop's house. Her name was Juana, and she was my woman. She was going to have my child."

"Did she die?"

"No more talk of it," said Calling Crow angrily. "No more!"

In the morning, Mateo saw Moscoso's body lying a few feet away, his head covered in blood.

Calling Crow said, "It is time to walk."

Mateo tried to get to his feet but could not, being too weak. Calling Crow went out to the sea and collected some crabs and clams. He brought them back into the jungle and cooked them over a small fire. After Mateo had eaten he was able to walk and they began pushing through the thick of the quiet jungle. Before the day was gone Calling Crow was again forced to carry Mateo. This night when they stopped, they camped on the beach and Calling Crow lit a fire to signal any Spanish ships which might be sailing by. In the morning Mateo was again too weak to move. Calling Crow made another meal of crabs and clams and, this done, hunted in the forest till he found a medicine tree. He stripped some bark from it and pounded it with a rock till it was edible. He fed it to Mateo, and they spent the day resting and the night with another signal fire. The next day Mateo was better, and they again went into the jungle to continue walking. Calling Crow came upon an anthill around midday. He removed his clothing and had Mateo do the same, setting the bundle on the top of the anthill. Toward dusk when the ants had feasted on all the vermin in their clothes and gone away, they put them back on and continued walking. Again they slept on the beach with a signal fire going.

The next morning a ship appeared on the horizon. Calling Crow blew on the embers and threw on some dew-soaked leaves to send up some smoke. Not too long afterward he saw the tiny ship's boat making its way toward them.

Calling Crow stood on the sun-bright beach with Mateo, watching the sailors on the small boat quickly furl the sail as the surf carried them swiftly toward shore. The boat ground on the sand, and three men immediately jumped out and pulled it up high on the beach.

An old man dressed all in black got out and approached them. When the man saw Mateo they embraced and Calling Crow looked on.

Mateo clasped the man's hands and looked over at Calling Crow. "I never thought I would set eyes on another Spaniard again."

The old man nodded.

"Why were you in these waters?" said Mateo.

"To search, of course," said the old man. "When none of De Sole's men were there when his ships returned, they asked for all possible help. What happened to De Sole?"

"De Sole is dead."

"Dead?" said the old man in disbelief.

"Yes," said Mateo, "buried by his own men. I spoke to one of his soldiers before he died." Mateo nodded toward Calling Crow. "He helped me to escape."

The man looked at Calling Crow and then back to Mateo. "Come, senor," he said, "we must get you back." He pulled Mateo toward the boat.

Mateo stopped and turned to Calling Crow. "You must come with us." He turned to the old man. "We must take him with us or they will kill him."

Calling Crow remained where he was. "No, I don't want to go back there."

"What about your woman?" said Mateo.

Tears reddened Calling Crow's eyes at the thought of seeing Juana again. But he could not go back to that place. Not when he was this close to getting home.

He shook his head. "I will not go back there."

"Then we shall take you home to your village," said Mateo.

The old man looked at Mateo in alarm. "Senor, you must come back to the ship now to see a physician."

Mateo's voice took on some of its former force. "Yes. But we must take him to his village. I remember the latitude. We can get him there."

Calling Crow did not move. The thought of soon seeing his own people was too much to resist. "I will go," he said.

As he was rowed out to the ship, Calling Crow's heart was being torn in two. Although he longed to go back to Tumaqua, being in the company of the Spanish again was overwhelming. Could he really trust Mateo?

On board the ship, a priest said a mass for Mateo and the others. Calling Crow sat behind them, his head bowed as he waited. Afterward Mateo disappeared below with the priest. While they were gone Calling Crow grew more worried. The sailors raised the sails and the big ship slowly began moving. Calling Crow watched the trees on the land slowly blur into a bright green smear at the edge of the water and he was struck with a terrible thought. Could Mateo be the Destroyer after all? Was he only taking Calling Crow back so he could learn the location of Tumaqua? He told himself it could not be so, yet the thought would not leave him.

Mateo and the old man approached. Calling Crow turned from the rail to face them.

Mateo said, "I ask you again to come back to the island with us. I have some influence there. I will make sure you are allowed to live your life free."

Some of the Spanish sailors looked curiously at Calling Crow. He stared into the distance as he thought. He could go back to try and find her. The Bishop was no more and she would be free of him. But he was free and so close to Tumaqua now; his long journey was nearing an end. As he stood on the strange rolling deck of the ship, with all the

Spanish eyeing him closely, he felt foolish and vulnerable.
"No," he said, "I want to go back to my people."

Mateo nodded his head sadly. "Very well, my friend,
and so you shall. I believe I can find that place where we
met on the beach so long ago, but you will have to guide
me to your village from there."

Calling Crow felt the fear come alive in him again. He
could not lead them to Tumaqua. "No," he said, "take me
to that place where you found me and I will make my way
from there."

Mateo smiled sadly. "I see that you still do not trust me
and I have only myself to blame for that. Very well, I shall
take you as close as I can to where I found you."

Calling Crow jumped out of the ship's boat and pushed
through the waist-deep water. When he reached dry sand,
he paused to look back at the ship. He could not make out
the faces of the tiny figures along the rail, and he turned
and walked into the forest.

Calling Crow stayed out of sight among the trees until
late afternoon of the next day when the ship sailed off. After it had disappeared, he went deeper into the forest and
began walking north.

For five days he walked carefully through vast unknown
lands. He kept to the thickest part of the forest, following
the game trails, and as he walked he thought about what
he would find when he reached Tumaqua. He knew that
there would be a new Chief, but who? He was Chief, but
they probably thought him long dead. What would happen? And Tiamai would be married, too. Despite his love
for Juana, he wondered to whom. He did not like to think
these thoughts, but they would not go away. On the sixth
day, off to the west, he could see the land rise slightly and
he knew where he was. He came to a wide rushing creek
and waded out into the center. This was Beaver Creek, and
it marked the southern boundary of his people's territory.
Crossing, he made a sleeping shelter for the night just up
from the bank. He awoke refreshed before dawn and began walking immediately, anxious to get home. He won-

dered if the village would be changed. A bad thought
chilled him. Would it even be there? As the sun appeared
above the trees, he suddenly caught the faint scent of
wood smoke. Yes, it would be there. He increased his pace
and his heart beat faster as he passed the secret hiding
place he and Tiamai used to use. Who had she married?
The thought plagued him. And how did she look? He
walked on and came to one of his people's fields. It was
planted with new corn that barely came up to his knees.

He knelt to touch it and breathed in the smells of the recently wet earth. An arrow landed in the mud just a few
feet from him and three braves ran toward him. He got
slowly to his feet. They were young and vaguely familiar
to him, but he did not know their names.

The biggest of the three stood before him. Thickly muscled, with a deep scar high on his cheek, the young man
said in a demanding tone, "What are you doing here?"

"I have come home," said Calling Crow.

The men laughed as they inspected Calling Crow's
strange breeches and tunic.

"Home?" said the scarred man. "I think you must be
lost or else you are crazy. This is not your home."

"Is that not the village of Tumaqua up ahead?" said
Calling Crow. "Is it not home to the Turtle Clan? Does it
not harbor the bones of the great Chief Caldo? Is it not
home to the men called Sun Watcher, Birdfoot, and Runs
Like Deer?"

The men looked at him as if he were a ghost. "Who are
you?" demanded the scarred man.

Calling Crow suddenly realized who the young man
was. "Could it really be you, Slim Boy?" he said. "There
must have been many good harvests and much game, eh?"

The other men laughed as the scarred man's face darkened. "My name is no longer Slim Boy. It is Battle Face.
Now I shall not ask you a third time. Who are you?"

Calling Crow smiled. "I am Calling Crow. I left here almost four turnings of the skies ago to find the secret of the
cloudboats."

"*Aieyah!*" said the smaller of the other two. "Now I remember. It is indeed him." He stepped closer to Calling Crow. "Do you remember me? I am Big Feet."

Calling Crow smiled. "Yes," he said, "I remember." He looked down briefly at the man's feet. "And now the rest of you has caught up."

Big Feet and the other man laughed.

Battle Face's eyes narrowed as he looked closely at Calling Crow. "Are you sure it is him?" he said to the other two suspiciously.

"Yes, it is him," said Big Feet. "Older, and very strange-looking, but him just the same."

Chapter 50

Calling Crow was happy to see Tumaqua again. It had not changed except for the addition of ten or so new huts. As he walked through the gate, people crowded around him. Old people and children pointed and laughed at his woolen tunic, reaching out to touch it. "It *is* Calling Crow," someone shouted happily and the crowd grew even larger.

When Calling Crow got to the chunkey yard, he saw a familiar figure walking up to him. It was Birdfoot, dressed in the black and white feathers of the shaman.

Birdfoot warmly embraced him. "It is wonderful to see you again, my friend," he said.

"Yes," said Calling Crow, "my heart sings. I see that our old shaman has died."

Birdfoot nodded. "He chose me as his apprentice just after you left, and he was gone the following winter."

"Did he have a good death?" said Calling Crow, remembering old Mennewah fondly.

Birdfoot smiled. "Yes, with everyone we could fit into the chokafa singing for him."

Sun Watcher and five other braves ran onto the chunkey yard. As they approached, Calling Crow saw that Sun Watcher was wearing the mantle of the Chief. He was taken aback by the sight, but he'd suspected that the mantle would go to Sun Watcher.

Birdfoot saw his surprise. "Sun Watcher became our Chief when we thought you had died. He has ruled well all this time."

Calling Crow bowed to Sun Watcher. "It is good to see you again, my friend. The Old Men have chosen wisely."

Sun Watcher seemed to grow taller at the compliment. "Thank you, Calling Crow. Much has happened since we were young men in this village. Tiamai is now my wife. She has given me two sons, the last one born only two moons ago."

Calling Crow felt a little tug at his heart. He was glad she was not here now. It would have hurt him to see her when he heard this. "It is good," he said. "Tell me, Sun Watcher, how is Runs Like Deer?"

"What do you mean?"

The crowd of people grew, pushing around Calling Crow, Sun Watcher, and the other braves.

"Did he not come back?" said Calling Crow.

"No, no one came back till you. What happened?"

Calling Crow felt a stab of sadness in his heart. Perhaps Runs Like Deer had been captured by the Flatheads as he tried to make his way back to Tumaqua. "Big Nose and I sent him back to bring all of you to help us."

Sun Watcher shook his head. "When no one came back, I and some other braves tried to track you, but we could find no trace. We had all thought you dead, drowned and lying on the bottom of the sea. Even Birdfoot, who held out hope the longest, finally dreamed that you were down in the land of the dead."

The crowd laughed and Birdfoot shook his head in embarrassment.

Calling Crow spoke. "I was taken far away by the Spanish and I despaired of ever getting back."

"Who are the Spanish?" shouted a man from the back.

"They are the people who sail the cloudboats out on the big water. They live very far away, on the other side of the big water."

The crowd began chattering, wondering aloud about these things. Sun Watcher held his arms up for quiet.

"How could they catch you," one woman shouted out, "for you and Sun Watcher were the fastest runners in the village?"

"Yes," someone else wondered, and again the crowd began talking all at once.

Calling Crow looked round at the group. "The Spanish were riding on horses when they captured Big Nose and me on the beach."

"Where is Big Nose?" asked Birdfoot.

"Dead," said Calling Crow.

"Horses?" shouted an old man. "What are horses?"

Before Calling Crow could answer, Sun Watcher pushed in next to him and turned to the crowd. "Let us give Calling Crow time to rest. He must be purified now that he has come back to us, and I am sure that he wants to see his Aunt Three Pearls."

As they withdrew, the men and women smiled and called out their gratitude that Calling Crow was home safe.

As Birdfoot and Calling Crow walked in the direction of the chokafa, an old woman grabbed at the woolen tunic Calling Crow wore, wondering aloud about it. "It is not a skin," he explained to her, "it is cloth, woven in the same way you weave your bark blankets."

"Oh," she said in wonder. "What is it woven of?"

"The hair of a sheep."

"Sheep?" she said, her face screwing up at the word.

"You will need many days and nights to tell us of all the things you have seen," said Birdfoot, laughing.

They walked on.

Another small crowd had gathered around them by the

time they reached the chokafa. Birdfoot dispersed the people before they entered.

Two women sat around a small fire inside. Birdfoot sent one of them off to get him some things. The other moved away to the rear of the hut.

Birdfoot took down the ceremonial calumet. As he was about to light it with a stick from the fire, he stopped and looked at Calling Crow, concern etching into his brow. "Calling Crow, you must take those garments off now that you are back."

As Calling Crow began removing the tunic and breeches, he wondered if he would miss the warmth they had provided him on cold mornings. The thought surprised him.

Birdfoot called out to the woman at the far end of the hut. "Go get him some proper garments."

The woman returned with a skin girdle, breechclout, and mantle, all of which she handed to Calling Crow while averting her eyes.

After Calling Crow dressed, Birdfoot said a prayer of thanks while he shook his prayer rattle. He blew the sacred smoke over Calling Crow while singing the song of purification. When he finished, light flashed into the hut as someone opened the skin covering. Three Pearls, still fat and pretty, with just a few more lines about her eyes, knelt beside Calling Crow.

"They told me and I could not wait for you to come to me," she said, smiling.

Calling Crow embraced her. "I am sorry about Runs Like Deer," he said.

A shadow darkened Three Pearls' smile momentarily. "I missed you both very much. Now at least I have one of you back."

A young brave quickly entered the hut and whispered in Birdfoot's ear.

Birdfoot looked at Calling Crow. "Sun Watcher has called a meeting of the Council of Old Men for tonight. He wants you to tell them all about the strange things you saw before you tell the people. He is afraid you will frighten them."

Calling Crow nodded and turned back to Three Pearls. "I will come to your hut soon," he said.

Three Pearls smiled. "I will have a feast waiting."

Calling Crow frowned as he and Birdfoot walked back from Three Pearls's hut to the chokafa. "You know, Birdfoot, Sun Watcher is right in not wanting me to frighten the people, but there is much to be concerned about. And I think that this concern is a good thing if it leads to the proper actions."

"What actions are you talking about, Calling Crow?"

"Preparations for war. We must prepare for the possibility of the Spanish coming here." Calling Crow stopped and grabbed Birdfoot by the shoulder. "You see, the Destroyer of my dream is a Spanish. I am convinced of this."

Birdfoot looked at him gravely and then led him into the chokafa.

Sun Watcher sat with the Chief's mantle over his wide shoulders, cradling the sacred calumet in his arms. The Old Men sat behind and beside him, and selected braves sat behind them. Birdfoot indicated that Calling Crow should sit facing the others.

Sun Watcher took a puff of the sacred tobacco smoke and offered the calumet to Calling Crow.

Calling Crow took smoke deep into his lungs, held it, and exhaled a thin stream heavenward like a geyser. He smiled. "Every night I dreamed of this day. My heart beats faster than the wings of a sparrow."

The Old Men nodded and smiled at his words.

Old Black Bear rose to speak. He nodded respectfully to Sun Watcher, then turned to Calling Crow. "You used to be our Chief and then you went away. And we picked a new Chief, a good Chief. Sun Watcher will continue to be our Chief. He has led us well. Still, you are a brave and good man. We have decided that you should be on our Council." Black Bear turned to look at the others and they all nodded. He looked at Sun Watcher.

"It is so," said Sun Watcher.

Black Bear smiled and sat down.

As Calling Crow looked around at the men assembled before him, he was suddenly saddened by their vulnerability. Eight or ten Spanish on horses and a company of Spanish on foot, all protected by their iron armor and armed with arquebuses and crossbows, could easily slaughter this entire village. Their stone clubs and arrows would be no defense. If he was Chief he could lead them in the right direction, make them take the right precautions against what could come. Now his task was more difficult. Without the mantle of Chief and the power that came with it, he would have a difficult time convincing them of what was out there, and what they must do. It would not be easy.

Sun Watcher spoke. "Calling Crow, you talked of many things out in the chunkey yard that I wanted to know more about. Tell us about Big Nose. How did he die?"

"He died after he was captured of the Spanish disease."

The others looked at him strangely, and he went on.

"This is a disease that the Spanish give to others. It is like a spell or a curse." Calling Crow noticed a few strained looks on the faces before him.

"Tell us about these horses," said Sun Watcher, "the creatures that the Spanish ride upon."

Calling Crow smiled at his old friend. "They are fine beasts. They are like dogs, only very large, and the Spanish ride upon their backs. When they are seated on their horses they can see very far and ride very fast, easily outrunning a man."

Calling Crow thought Sun Watcher looked troubled by his answer, but he went on anyway. "Big Nose was knocked down by one of the Spanish on a horse. I was run down by one of them and then attacked by many Spanish on foot. They then took us on their cloudboats where Big Nose died from the Spanish disease. Then we went south and the Spanish captured many other people, an entire village."

Old Black Bear raised his hand patiently. "Calling

Crow, how can they capture an entire village? How many of the Spanish were there?"

"They were not that many in number, but they used their arquebuses." Calling Crow saw the questioning looks on their faces and went on. "These are sticks which, when they point them at people from a distance, discharge thunder and fire, striking people dead in their tracks."

Calling Crow waited for a response or a question, and when none came he realized that, although they had all listened politely and nodded their heads, they had stopped believing what he was telling them. It was too crazy for their ears. He thought that if he had never left Tumaqua, and someone else was now telling him these things, he would not believe them either.

"All that I have told you is true," he said. "You must get the village ready in case the Spanish come here."

"We are not afraid of them," said Sun Watcher.

The others voiced their agreement.

"Of course," said Calling Crow, "I know you are very brave, but the Spanish have very powerful medicine. Every Spanish carries what they call a sword. It is a weapon like our own knives, but much longer and sharper, and very hard."

"That is of no consequence," said one brave, "for we are allied with the Wolf Clan now. It was on their behalf that we fought the Flatheads. The Wolf Clan would help us if we asked them."

"Their help and even the help of the Flatheads would make no difference," said Calling Crow, "because the swords of the Spanish are made of iron. Stone knives and clubs would be useless and we and the Wolf People and the Flatheads would all end up Spanish slaves."

The Old Men began murmuring among themselves worriedly. Sun Watcher looked around at them angrily. He turned back to Calling Crow. "What is this iron? I have never heard of it before."

"They dig it up from the earth," said Calling Crow, "and then they heat it up in a fire and beat it to shape it. I have seen this with my own eyes and I think that we

could do the same. I have seen what this iron looks like
when they dig it up from the ground and I think there may
be some of it in the bogs at the source of the creek. I will
go there tomorrow and see."

"We do not need iron to fight these Spanish if they
come here," said Sun Watcher angrily. "I will hear no
more talk of it."

Calling Crow felt his own anger growing. "Would you
hear no more talk if there was a hungry bear in the next
bush I was trying to warn you about?"

Sun Watcher and the younger braves said nothing, instead fixing angry looks on Calling Crow.

Birdfoot raised his arm. "Let us talk no more of this
now," he said. "I will seek a dream to see if these Spanish
are a danger to us. But now we should let Calling Crow
roam the village freely and renew old friendships."

Sun Watcher raised his hand. "Yes, our shaman speaks
well. Let us do as he says."

The young braves clustered tightly around Sun Watcher
as they left the chokafa. Birdfoot and Black Bear walked
off with Calling Crow. Birdfoot looked back at Sun
Watcher and his young coterie of braves as they headed
for the chunkey yard. "You are not back one day and your
old rivalry with Sun Watcher is renewed," he said.

Calling Crow laughed. "Yes. It is so."

Black Bear smiled. "It is as natural as rain. I have seen
it now for many years."

As Calling Crow stopped to talk to the people, he was
struck by the fact that with their skin garments and simple
tools, they were not much different from the Saturiba People. They were a prouder, harder working people, though,
he thought. They grew their own crops, storing them for
the cold winter. Still, all their work and pride would prove
useless against Spanish iron and horses. He decided to go
off in the morning to the bogs and look for iron.

Black Bear grew tired from the walking and left Calling
Crow and Birdfoot at the village edge. Calling Crow and
Birdfoot left the village, walking alone on a path through
two fields of young, green corn shoots. The sky was deep

blue and a solitary hawk could be seen flying high and off
in the distance, hunting for field mice. Some women
worked in the field on their right, pouring water on the
young corn plants. Calling Crow looked at his friend and
was pleased at how well he had grown. Although still thin,
Birdfoot had a determined strength about him now and his
eyes burned with a fiery intensity. Calling Crow was not
surprised that old Mennewah the Shaman had chosen him
as his replacement before he died.

"How have things been here in Tumaqua, Birdfoot?"
said Calling Crow.

Birdfoot looked skyward. "The Great Spirit has been
good to us. We had war with the Flatheads, but that did
not last long. Two of our braves were killed, and three of
theirs. We had a bad storm three turnings of the seasons
ago and it washed out two of our best cornfields, but at
that time the fishing was very good and that made up for
it."

Birdfoot stopped and turned to him. "How good it is
that you have returned, Calling Crow. Forget about this
iron business for a while and let's go hunting tomorrow."

Calling Crow shook his head. "No, Birdfoot, the Destroyer exists. I have already met two Spanish who could
well be this Destroyer, and there are many others who
have the power and the will. I must work to protect
Tumaqua. Why don't you come with me to the bogs and
we shall also do some hunting there."

"Very well, Calling Crow. We will go there tomorrow."

As Birdfoot spoke, they noticed someone coming along
the trail from the village. It was Tiamai. Calling Crow saw
that she was still beautiful, although she was bigger now,
no longer a shapely girl of fifteen. A small naked boy who
did not reach her hip walked by her side, and she carried
a baby in a sling over her back. Calling Crow turned to
speak to Birdfoot, but he had walked off, going in the direction of the forest.

Tiamai said nothing when she walked up to Calling
Crow, instead looking at him closely. "It *is* you," she said
finally. "I could not believe when I heard."

"Yes," he said. Although he looked at her and the boy and smiled, inside his heart was heavy as he saw what could have been if he had never gone away.

"That is my boy," she said.

Calling Crow looked down at the boy and smiled.

"My father is the Chief!" he said.

"Ah!" said Calling Crow. "That is good."

"And this," said Tiamai, indicating the baby over her shoulder, "is my baby boy, now only two moons in this world."

Calling Crow looked at the sleeping baby closely and smiled. "It is good, Tiamai. It is good."

Tears formed in Tiamai's eyes. "Yes. It is good." She grabbed the boy's hand and ran back toward the village.

Calling Crow felt the emptiness in his heart. He turned to look for Birdfoot and saw him almost to the trees of the forest. He began running after him, his sadness leaving him only when he began to sweat from the exertion.

Chapter 51

Calling Crow walked along the main dirt street of Tumaqua on his way to the chokafa to meet Birdfoot. He carried some fine skins and some bone needles with him to make the bellows for the forge. Birdfoot would have several fine clay bowls they could try as crucibles. Father Sun still had not risen from the big water and the light was subdued, the air cool. He saw one of the braves who had challenged him when he'd first entered the village's territory, the one called Big Feet. He was lying on a skin outside one of the huts, and an old woman was leaning over him, dipping water from a calabash onto his head. Ignor-

ing Big Feet's groans, she smiled and nodded to Calling
Crow as he went by. He walked on, the people greeting
him happily as he passed. He almost collided with a pretty
maid as she exited her hut. She laughed shyly as she
backed off, averting her eyes. Calling Crow felt his heart
lighten. There were many things he must do to protect the
people, but now the task seemed not so impossible.

Calling Crow went into the chokafa. Birdfoot sat around
the fire with old Red Dog and Flathead Killer. They nodded as he sat down beside them.

"Birdfoot tells me you go to the bogs to make iron,"
said Red Dog.

"Yes, Grandfather," said Calling Crow.

Red Dog smiled. "Make sure you show me it first when
you return."

"Yes."

Birdfoot looked over at him. "Battle Face and Sings At
War are against you now. They don't trust you. But Sun
Watcher is still undecided."

"And the other strong braves?" said Calling Crow.

"Big Feet and Laughing Man are for you, but they don't
have as much influence."

"The other old men think you are crazy," said Red Dog.
He turned to Flathead Killer. "Tell him what they told
you."

Flathead Killer smiled. "They say that you must have
fallen off a rock and landed on your head. That is how
they account for your stories."

Calling Crow looked at him sharply. "I have my garments made from Spanish wool. How can they explain
that away?"

Red Dog said softly, "Dull Lance said that it is merely
the skins of some strange animal."

"Ah!" said Calling Crow in exasperation. "Any woman
in the village could tell him my garments are not made of
skins." He was amazed by their stubborn refusal to see
what was. He remembered Juana arguing with him, cajol-
ing, while he stubbornly refused to see what she was trying to show him.

Red Dog's woman brought a calabash full of steaming soup over to him. He shook his head, and she said to him sharply, "You must eat! You did not eat last night."

Red Dog looked at her tiredly. "I have no hunger."

She turned angrily and moved off, dumping the contents of the calabash into a stone pot.

Birdfoot looked at the old man as he got to his feet. "Are you well, Grandfather?"

Red Dog smiled at Flathead Killer. "To *be* old is to *feel* old. These young men will know what it is someday."

Flathead Killer's thick lips turned up slightly in a smile.

Red Dog looked up at Birdfoot. "I am very tired lately and I want to go to sleep a lot. I will be well by the time you and Calling Crow return."

Calling Crow and Birdfoot said good-bye and left the hut.

Chapter 52

On the sandy bank of the bogs, Calling Crow smiled over at Birdfoot as he carried the dried mud bricks under the hot sun. Birdfoot's body was dripping sweat as he put them down where Calling Crow was building the oven.

Birdfoot paused a moment before going back to his carrying. "What crazy people these Spanish must be to do so much work as this."

Calling Crow fitted a brick into its niche and reached for another. "They were not crazy; they made us slaves do the work."

"*Aieyah.* I see." Birdfoot went back to his carrying.

Two days later Birdfoot was working the wooden lever

of the crude bellows Calling Crow had constructed while Calling Crow knelt before the forge, pushing in wood.

"Pump it harder," said Calling Crow. "This is how they did it at the mission school and I think it is almost ready."

Birdfoot worked the lever furiously, finally breaking it off with a loud snap. He sat down immediately as Calling Crow looked up to see what happened. Realizing that the fire would begin cooling, Calling Crow pushed the wooden rake he had made into the front of the forge. He pulled the clay crucible out and it tipped over, spilling its contents onto the sand. He poured water on it and it hissed loudly, sending up a sulphurous plume of steam. When it had cooled, he poked through the mess with a stick and pulled out a black mottled piece the size of his hand. It was flat like a stone from the stream and one end was grooved and tapered down like the tail fin of a fish. Touching it quickly, he found it cool enough to be handled. Birdfoot came over to see.

Calling Crow handed it to him. Birdfoot was amazed at the weight of it.

"So this is iron." He handed it back to Calling Crow.

Calling Crow fingered it as he looked at the destroyed forge in disgust. He threw the iron into the bog.

Birdfoot ran after it and fished it out. "Why did you do that?" he said as he walked back.

Calling Crow sat down in the sand tiredly. "What good is one piece?" He looked back at the forge. "We can never make enough to do us any good."

Birdfoot looked out over the bog as he fingered the strange piece of iron. "We could send a trading party to see the People Who Live by the Great River. They trade with the People of the Seven Cities and they make things out of metal."

Calling Crow scowled contemptuously. "No, they make little pretty things out of gold; they make nothing of iron."

Birdfoot said nothing. He put the iron in his shaman's bag.

Somewhere out in the trees of the bog a woodpecker rapped against a tree as it looked for insects to eat.

Finally Calling Crow said, "I have been thinking about the Spanish a lot lately. They have many powerful things, but they rely on them too much. When they attacked the Saturibas, they had horses, but their horses were not much good in the great forests. And they were so convinced of their power and eventual success that they did not bring enough food stores and they almost starved."

Calling Crow got to his feet. "There is only one thing to do. We must convince the Council to move the village far inland. It is the only way to safeguard the people. Come, let us go back to the village."

As soon as Calling Crow and Birdfoot reached the village they heard some people wailing, mourning a death. As they walked through the village they passed the hut where the mourners had congregated. Calling Crow looked down at the body on the pole litter and saw that it was the young brave who had appeared sick the day he left with Birdfoot, the one called Big Feet. They walked into the chokafa and saw Red Dog's woman crying while two others attempted unsuccessfully to console her.

One of the women looked up at them as they entered. "Old Red Dog died just two days after you left," she said. "He grew feverish the first night and then lay down to sleep. For a whole day he never opened his eyes and last night he stopped breathing."

"*Aieyah,*" said Birdfoot.

Calling Crow felt a sadness fill him, but he was also conscious of another feeling—a vague foreboding. It would not come into his heart where he could understand it, but instead remained hidden, like a wildcat prowling the darkness at the edge of a camp fire. "Where is he?" said Calling Crow. "I would like to pray for him."

The woman nodded toward the beach. "He is down there."

One moon passed and many more villagers grew sick. Five died and the wailing of the women went on day and night continuously. Calling Crow thought it was like the Spanish disease, but there were no Spanish here and therefore it could not be so. Like many others, he thought it must be a spell. Despite the deaths, he tried to prepare the villagers for what might come. He had fashioned some armor out of wooden slats, but Sun Watcher and the other braves refused to consider doing the same, saying it would be cowardly to wear such things. Calling Crow continued to attempt to persuade the Council to move the village further inland to no avail. One day a runner came to his hut and told him the Council was meeting. He hurried off to the chokafa.

Battle Face was the first one recognized to speak. He stood solemnly and looked at the assembled men. "Today Jesting Woman and Two Clubs died. That makes thirteen. Many more are sick. I believe that Calling Crow has cast a spell on us."

Some of those assembled gasped at the accusation. Others shouted in agreement.

Calling Crow leapt to his feet. "This is not true," he said angrily. "Battle Face says this because he is frightened. I would never harm my own people. All of you who know me know this is so!"

Battle Face shook with anger as he shouted, "It started after you came back to us, and it will end when you are gone."

Some of the braves echoed Battle Face's words.

Black Bear raised his bony arm. "No, it cannot be, for I held Calling Crow on my lap when he was a child. I also helped his father train him to hunt. It is not so. It cannot be."

The voices for and against Calling Crow seemed to be evenly divided. Everyone waited for Sun Watcher to speak. He got slowly to his feet and looked round at the group. He looked at Calling Crow. "We need more time to think about this," he said. "I have played with Calling Crow as a child, fought with him as a young man, ran races against him, hunted with him; because of that I cannot believe he would do these things to us. We will wait awhile longer."

The men were silent as Sun Watcher sat back down. Many of them were against Calling Crow, but they would never contradict their Chief.

Birdfoot got to his feet. The club he had fashioned out of Calling Crow's piece of iron hung proudly around his neck. His eyes burned with a fiery passion. "I, too, say that Calling Crow is not responsible for these bad things. If there is a spell, then it must have been cast by our enemies, perhaps someone in the Wolf Clan."

This started new murmurs and discussions in the hut.

Chapter 53

Calling Crow and Birdfoot walked out of the chokafa into the cool afternoon air. Calling Crow looked at his friend, concern etched deep into his face. "We must get them to move the village. It is too close to the sea. If the Spanish come, they would surely spot someone and land. We must move!"

Birdfoot nodded. "I will do what I can."

Calling Crow embraced his friend and began walking off.

Birdfoot called out to him. "Calling Crow, I would like to have the Spanish garments you brought back with you."

Calling Crow looked at him inquisitively.

"I am going to seek a vision and they will help me."

"Very well," said Calling Crow. "I will bring them."

After Calling Crow dropped the tunic and breeches off, he walked alone out of the village. He headed for the big dune where he had first seen the cloudboats so long ago. When he arrived, there were a good many people there already, the dune being a popular place to sit in the early evening and catch the breeze blowing off the land.

Calling Crow climbed past two old men who smiled and nodded at him. He picked a place almost at the very top of the dune and sat down, looking out at the clear blue sea. Father Sun had already begun his descent over the forest behind him and the air was cool. He should have enjoyed the beautiful day, yet he could not shake a feeling that had been haunting him. It skulked about at the edge of his understanding. It was something bad, and it had to do with him, but it refused to show itself. He was diverted from his dark thoughts as some boys came near him and began playing roughly in the sand as he and Sun Watcher and Birdfoot used to do as boys. An older boy named Hairy Chin walked up and sat next to him. Calling Crow turned round and noticed that the old men had left, but someone else was climbing the dune. He was surprised to see that it was Tiamai. Her little boy was not with her, but she carried her baby at her breast.

She sat not far from him, and he and Hairy Chin looked her way, but she did not acknowledge them. Calling Crow watched her put the baby's tiny head to her breast, a breast that he had once longed to suckle at himself. The nipple was poutingly pointed and purple, fairly bursting with milk, but the baby's eyes remained shut, its hands curled closed at the end of its little arms. The mouth no longer suckled, but remained open, the lips parted slightly. A shadow of fear darkened Tiamai's face and she bounced the baby gently as she mouthed soothing sounds. Again she placed its unmoving lips against her breast. Calling Crow and Hairy Chin looked away. A moment later her scream shattered the stillness of the evening, followed by her heavy sobbing.

"Take her back to the village," Calling Crow said to Hairy Chin. As the boy ran to her, Calling Crow got to his feet and climbed to the very top of the dune.

* * *

The shadow the chokafa cast was almost as long as the chunkey yard itself. Inside the chokafa, several torches set into the walls were already lit, providing dim pools of quivering light. Birdfoot leaned up against the wall in one of them, too weak from his fast to sit upright. Beside him Calling Crow's strange garments were wrapped in a bundle. Birdfoot ran his hand over the bundle to make sure it was still there. Outside, the sun had sunk low, casting long shadows across the chunkey yard. In his stupor he heard a sound and saw the large round form of Owl Woman as she carried another calabash of the black drink over to him. As she handed it to him, someone entered the chokafa.

Sun Watcher knelt before him. "You are going soon to the spirit world, I see."

Birdfoot nodded weakly.

Sun Watcher put his large hand on Birdfoot's small shoulder. "Help us, brother. This spell must be broken. You must find out what we are to do. The people must be saved."

"Yes," Birdfoot managed to say weakly as Sun Watcher's image split into two. Blinking rapidly, he managed to move the two images back into one. Birdfoot lifted the black drink and saw his own face reflected on the steaming surface. *"Hai ha!"* he sang weakly and then he drank the bitter liquid quickly, almost choking from the taste. He smiled at Sun Watcher and Owl Woman as he put the calabash down. He wanted to tell them something, and then they were gone and he was running through the forest. He knew something was wrong, dreadfully wrong, as he crashed through bushes, stumbling then rushing forward again wildly. Panting hoarsely, he came out onto the sandy ground of the dunes.

He picked up the beach trail and ran in the direction of the village. His heart sank when he got there. Tumaqua was in ruins! All the huts had been knocked flat and all that remained of them was a few upright sticks of rotted wood. A strong gust of wind suddenly pushed through the square, whipping up sand stingingly as he searched in vain for any sign of life. He saw the vague outline of something

ahead and walked toward it. It stood waist-high and when
he drew near he saw it was the stone structure of the
firewell. He looked inside and saw that the village's sacred
ashes had long ago been swept clean by the winds, leaving
nothing behind but earth. He sat down on the firewell as
a great sadness filled him. Then he thought he heard a
voice above the wailing of the wind. He turned and saw a
man walking away from him toward the south. He ran toward him, feeling repulsion as he saw the familiar garments. "You!" he yelled. "Stop!" The figure continued to
walk away from him. Birdfoot ran, catching up to him,
and the man stopped. Birdfoot felt afraid and stepped back
a bit. Slowly the figure turned round and he saw that it
was Calling Crow. Calling Crow smiled and put out his
arms as if to embrace him. Birdfoot held up his hands and
screamed.

Sun Watcher and Battle Face looked down at him in the
torchlight. "What is it?" said Sun Watcher.

"I saw the one who has done this to us," said Birdfoot.

"Yes . . ." said Sun Watcher as Battle Face looked on,
his eyes wide with incredulous anger, "who is it?"

"It is the Destroyer."

"*Aieyah,*" said Sun Watcher. "But who? Who is this
Destroyer?"

Birdfoot said nothing; he continued to stare blankly into
space.

Sun Watcher shook his shoulder violently. "Who is it?"

"It is Calling Crow." Birdfoot began sobbing, holding
his head in his hands.

Birdfoot hurriedly ate the porridge Owl Woman had
made for him to give him strength. Outside in the blackness he could hear the drumming and singing growing in
intensity as Sun Watcher and the braves prepared to hunt
down and kill Calling Crow. He would have to find him
before they did. But where? Still dressed in his ceremonial
feathers and paints, Birdfoot got to his feet and staggered
toward the entryway.

A crowd of boys ran, shouting and fighting as they

kicked a ball in the chunkey yard. Birdfoot grabbed one of
them by the shoulder.

The boy looked at him, trembling slightly in fear.

"Have you seen Calling Crow?" said Birdfoot.

"No. I have not."

Birdfoot ran down the trail toward the sea. Behind him
the drumming filled the night air like the pounding of an
angry heart. He saw some people ahead coming up from
Big Dune and he ran toward them. Tiamai was among
them. She looked right through him as she carried her
baby at her breast. Birdfoot saw that the baby was dead,
but she seemed in a daze and unaware of it.

"Have you seen Calling Crow?" he asked her.

She said nothing, continuing to walk.

He shook her. "Tiamai! Calling Crow, where is he?"

She smiled as if seeing him for the first time. "Ah,
Birdfoot. He is down at Big Dune."

He cast one last worried look at her and ran off down
the beach.

Birdfoot saw Calling Crow sitting alone at the top of
Big Dune. The sun had set but still lit the sky, painting
the clouds in the west with a rosy glow. Birdfoot ran up
the dune as quickly as he could. Breathing hoarsely, he
stopped thirty feet from Calling Crow.

Calling Crow turned and smiled at him. "Birdfoot, why
don't you come closer?"

Birdfoot almost choked on his sobs. "Why? So you can
kill me, too?"

"What madness possesses you, Birdfoot?"

"Calling Crow, they are coming now to kill you!"

"What are you saying, Birdfoot?"

"Sun Watcher and the other braves are coming to kill
you!"

Calling Crow's face darkened. "Why, Birdfoot?"

"Because it is you, Calling Crow. You are the Destroyer!"

Before Calling Crow could answer he heard shouts and
cries of rage. He and Birdfoot turned as the braves
emerged from the forest at the edge of the beach. In their

red war paint, they seemed as brilliant as the sun-tinged clouds overhead as they raced for the dune.

Birdfoot turned back to Calling Crow. "Go! You must run away now!" Before Birdfoot could say any more, an arrow struck him in the back and he fell onto the sand. Calling Crow ran to him, kneeling beside him. Birdfoot took the iron club from around his neck and handed it to him. "Take this and run."

Calling Crow looked back at the war party. Sun Watcher was in the lead as the braves approached the base of the dune. Calling Crow ran back to the top of the dune and down the sea side, kicking up waves of sand as he pumped his legs furiously. He looked back and saw that he had a good distance on the others, but he knew he wouldn't be able to keep it. Many of them were much younger than he.

Calling Crow crossed a tiny stream which ran into the sea, his feet splattering the water into the night air. Up ahead, the forest came down close to the sea and he came to a creek where there were three small dugouts pulled up onto the sand. With the screams of the others growing louder, he quickly knelt in one of the canoes and began attacking the bottom of it with Birdfoot's iron club. Soon water bubbled up through the hole he had made, and he jumped into the second. As he chopped, he knew they were very close for they had stopped their shouting and were now listening to him as he chopped. Finally his club cracked through the bottom of the canoe, and he almost dropped it. He jumped for the third dugout and pushed it out into the surf.

There was now hardly any light left. The water was black with patches of white foam. Calling Crow had barely made it to the breakers when his pursuers reached the two sabotaged canoes. He heard their surprised voices and then a scream of rage as someone saw him.

Calling Crow dug the paddle deep into the dark water. He turned and saw a few heads sticking out of the black water behind him. They were swimming after him! As he listened to their angry shouts, he still could not believe what Birdfoot had said and what had happened. The entire village must be mad or else under some kind of spell. Why else would they say that he was the Destroyer? He looked quickly over his shoulder and was startled to see that one of the swimmers was gaining on him. Digging his paddle deep, he pulled as hard as he could, but the brave continued to gain. Again and again Calling Crow dug the paddle in, putting all his strength behind it. Finally the faceless swimmer gave up and headed back to the shore.

After his pursuers had gone, Calling Crow began to feel afraid of the vast rolling black sea. There was a creature beneath the canoe. It was large as a hut, a demon that would rise up and take his tiny dugout in its teeth, swallowing him up forever. He paddled as hard as he could, the tiring, painful effort blotting out the horror of the thought. After a while the dark shadow of the land melded with the blackness of night, and he was unsure of the direction he was going in. Still he continued paddling as hard as he could, thankful that the sea, at least, was still calm. All night he paddled, sometimes falling asleep, but always paddling. Sometimes he would jerk awake when the large sea creature came close. Calling Crow could feel it scrape the hull of the dugout as it scratched its back. The vibrations passed sickeningly through the wood of the dugout and into Calling Crow's own damp skin and bones. Finally the blackness of night began to lift, revealing a mass of gray clouds overhead and the dark shadow of the land behind.

Calling Crow turned the dugout round and began paddling for the land. Now that the surface of the sea was visible, his terror of it grew. He prayed wildly that there would be no storms, and he was grateful when the day brought no roughness to the watery surface. As he drew closer to the land, he did not recognize it. He must have been caught in a powerful current during the night. At least he was safe from his pursuers for the moment. He reached the breakers after a long arduous morning of paddling and dragged the dugout up into the trees to hide it. This done, he made a sleeping shelter inside a copse of myrtle trees, filled it with leafy litter, and fell asleep.

* * *

Calling Crow awoke in the afternoon. The day was cold
and gray, and he sat up in the copse and stared out between the leaves at the clouds, unable to move. He
thought, I lost my woman, Juana, and now I have lost all
of my people. I must have truly died and must now be a
ghost. All that remains is for my body to die.

He decided to stay where he was, allowing Sun Watcher
and the other braves to find him and kill him.

His decision made him feel a little better, and he walked
down to the beach. Staring at the sea, he sensed the presence of the creature that had followed his canoe. It was
still out there beneath the water. He peered at the waves,
but could not see beneath them. He went back up to the
shelter and slept again, dreaming of Juana.

Calling Crow's hunger awoke him. He could smell the
clams buried in the sands not far from him; he could hear
the rabbits and rodents scurrying around in the leafy dead-
fall behind him, but he made no move to dig for food or
to make snares. Instead he must quiet his hunger. Dead
men did not need food.

The next day a light rain fell. Vigorously twirling a
piece of maple between his palms, he made a small fire
and sat unmoving in front of it. Then he slept. After several days of this he grew so weak he could hardly stand.
One day the skies cleared and it grew very hot. When he
felt the presence of the sea creature again, he got shakily
to his feet and walked down to the beach to shout at it.
When it moved on, he walked the beach under the hot sun.
At some point he fell in a faint and lay on the sand with
the sun baking down on him. He heard voices. Hoping it
was Sun Watcher and the others, he opened his eyes, but
there was no one that he could see. Then the voices came
again; he knew they were discussing him as he lay there,
but he didn't understand what they were saying.

"Why has this come to pass?" he shouted at them and
for a moment there was silence. Then one voice began
laughing, then another, then several more until the sound
of the laughter was deafening.

"Why?" Calling Crow screamed at them, and they only laughed louder. He shouted at them for a long time and then his anger broke and he, too, began laughing. He laughed until his voice was gone and then a thought came into his head. It was a thought which had long eluded him. He was tainted with Spanishness! *It* was in him.

The more he thought of it, sadly, the more he knew it was true. There was Spanish in him and that was why he brought the Spanish disease to his people. There was Spanish in Juana also. She had taken Spanish things to survive, but she had remained noble. So had he! It was part of what brought them together and perhaps that was why they were such a good match. His heart grew very warm at the thought of her.

He got slowly to his feet. He went up into the forest away from the noise of the sea, into the soft light. He sat down on the long corpse of a fallen tree overrun with ferns and moss.

The air was subdued, but bright shafts of sunlight broke through the overhead canopy of leaves. Dust motes floated through the nearest one and it was very quiet. He remembered Juana laying her head on his chest. She said to him, "I go with you always and anywhere, my love." He shed a few tears and then clamped his eyes shut.

Calling Crow ran his hand across the thick coat of moss the log wore. It had a texture like the velvet the Spanish wore. Something flashed by overhead and he looked up. A large black crow jumped from one branch to another, angling its head down to get a better look at him. As he met its scrutinizing gaze, it cawed loudly then took flight, flapping its black wings powerfully. It circled him once and then headed south, calling him as it went. Juana was that way, he thought. He got to his feet and followed it.